ÆTHER/AKASHA
DREADLOCKED: Catalyst Black

For all the friends and family who never let us forget
that we had a world to create.

TABLE OF CONTENTS

ÆTHER/AKASHA
DREADLOCKED: Catalyst Black

00– THE COUNCIL

-The fate of millions is always dictated by the decisions of a select few.-

The time had once again arrived for Damien to deal with his business-district rival, Mr. Bradley. The meetings were always organized by Magnamus City's (more commonly reffered to as Mag City) Council of Governance: who claim neutrality in the distribution of finances between the districts for the greater good of the city, yet seem to regularly place the needs of Revco district's above that of Eratech's. All economic numbers from both districts had been previously submitted to be reviewed by the council; the meeting served only to officially announce the results. Damien was the last to join the teleconference, displaying nothing more than his name. Mr. Bradley and all four members of the council were already doing the same.

Mr. Bradley: "Damien, you're late. I'm always waiting on you."

He said snidely.

Damien: "If only to tell me what you've already done. I'm just here because I have to be."

Damien responded with a tone of indifference. His hands clasped in front of his face as he stared at the names on the screen.

Mr. Bradley: "Of course you are. I know *I* wouldn't want to listen to the council snub me again either."

Not one to hurl jabs back and forth, Damien let the insult go.

Damien: "Council of Governance: I'm here as requested. I'd apologize for being late but I don't care."

Council of Governance Speaker: "The offence will once again be overlooked. As told to Mr. Bradley, there will be no changes to fiscal obligations this year. Revco will pay their usual military license fee of 500 million Dregs. Eratech's military fee of 750 million Dregs will be paid as usual in addition to their outstanding debt of 6.3 Billion Dregs. Once the debt has been cleared, council support will resume. Damien, we would ask if you had any questions but we don't care. Meeting is adjourned."

The Council members simultaneously disconnected from the teleconference, leaving Damien with Mr. Bradley. Before he had a chance to disconnect himself, Mr. Bradley caught Damien's attention.

Mr. Bradley: "Nothing like having your own attitude thrown back at you. Even the council has a better sense of humor than you do Damien."

Mr. Bradley said through a laugh. He was more antagonistic than usual this meeting.

Damien: "Someone has to be the adult in the conversation."

Mr. Bradley had ensnared him.

Mr. Bradley: "Humorlessness is not maturity. Which is why I was so surprised to hear that you opened up a new club in your district. It's good to see that you at least like to see other people enjoy themselves."

Damien's eyebrow rose just above his shades.

Damien: "I don't deal with that kind of business. What're you talking about?"

Mr. Bradley: "You don't? Well someone in your district does. I'd look into that if I were you."

Damien disconnected. He could only stand so much of Mr. Bradley's condescendence, but if there was any truth to his words it was worth investigating.

01– THE CYCLE BREAKS

-As the passing of a day grew longer and longer, it grew to resemble the four seasons as much as it did the rising and setting of the sun. Thus the ætherlings formed their own clock; a thirty-hour "cycle"to organize their lives.-

Cyclebreak was a new dance-club in west Eratech's district town of Old Light that seemed to have appeared from nowhere; its popularity equally spontaneous. Word spread quickly throughout the surrounding ghetto until the hidden gem could no longer be kept a secret. Its original patrons were exclusively members of the veast gang "Black Soulz" but word eventually spread to non-gang members; some questionably young. However, as long as the money continued to flow, the proprietors were willing to overlook almost anything.

Inside, *Cyclebreak* housed a hedonistic atmosphere. The dancefloor was near the entrance; its first impression was loud, pulsing, and energetic: It made a bold statement. Strobe and laser lights flashed all colors and danced with the music. Each note beat upon the chest, immersing the crowd further into the scene. As any good club would have, there was a well-stocked bar and a busy staff competing to make tips. Across from the bar was a room that led to the VIP section where one could engage in private dances among other indulgent activities. If anything unsavory occurred at *Cyclebreak,* it did so beyond those doors.

Jin was an outsider in his late twenties who hailed from beyond the barrens that lay outside of Mag city. Although so much time had passed since he had thought about it, he couldn't recall from which direction. His hair was a dark-auburn that was contrasted by his fair skin and green eyes; above which had three small ore stones that pierced into his left brow. In addition to his origins, Jin was unusual in that no matter where he traveled he always carried with him a machete given to him by his former mentor sheathed at his side: a blade named Hermes. Hermes was a slightly curved machete with a ring pommel.

Jin had gotten word of *Cyclebreak* from someone he had delivered a package to and decided that he would check it out as he hadn't taken time to enjoy himself in seasons. Not for lack of effort, but for lack of funds. The bouncer frisked Jin and made him check Hermes before letting him inside, who after giving it a curious look, tossed the blade into a heavy wooden crate near the door. Jin strode his way through the patrons of the club, past the dancefloor and to the bar. He wasn't a veast, a Black Soulz gang member, or a regular and most people could tell but he carried himself confidently enough to not draw too much attention. After a few suspicious looks, no one cared about him anymore. He shouldered his way to the front and ordered a drink. The bartender rolled his eyes in annoyance, ignoring Jin and continued making drinks for other customers. While the bartender didn't have the racial patience for Jin, others took interest. A pair of girls next to him made drunken advances. They were too far gone for his liking, but he flirted lightly anyway.

From the corner of his eyes, Jin noticed a man approaching the bar. Everyone tried to stay out of his way as if being too close to him would cause them harm. He was a tall, bearded man with dark skin and dreadlocks tied into a ponytail. The tall man had an athletic build but wasn't large by any means. He walked with determination and urgency that carried more weight than his frame. What stood out the most about him was that he was wearing shades, which had a purpose outside during the tail end of the noon season, but had no place inside a dance club. Jin found it impressive that he was able to navigate in this level of darkness. He stepped behind the bar and exchanged words with the bartender who looked terrified to be dealing with him. They conversed for a moment, but Jin was only able to make out the word "Vangard". The bartender pointed to the door behind him and the tall man stormed through. The bartender composed himself before returning to serving drinks, all of which were shaken.

Not long after, there was a commotion in the back room. Even among the booming bass of the music crashing sounds could still be heard from behind the door. The tall man reemerged from the backroom and gave the bartender a murderous glare. The bartender looked uneasy as if he knew he was being watched but attempted to ignore it by tending to customers. The tall man headed toward the exit as swiftly as he had entered. Jin wondered if that was the club owner, unsatisfied with the way his men were running the club. This wasn't the best neighborhood and to see things being run in this manner fit the establishment. Another commotion started, this time near the exit of the club; a fight had broken out with the tall man.

The club quickly circles the fight and Jin muscles his way into view. One of the bouncers was already on the ground, crawling out of the circle. Another bouncer charges the tall man with a straight punch and promptly receives a broken arm. The remaining bouncer weighs his options after looking at his friends. The tall man watched the remaining bouncer. The bouncer reaches behind his back and pulls out a gun. Faster than the crowd could react and faster than the bouncer could brandish and aim, the tall man steps in close and points his own gun at the bouncer's face; he fires. The gunfire panics the crowd and they disperse in search of exits. The tall man puts his gun away in his jacket as he looks around at the surrounding chaos and sees Jin's calm composure among the madness. Jin notices the exiting crowd split around a group of people fighting their way into the club. Jin looks back at the tall man who was already marching toward the approaching threats. After breaking through the crowd, they reveal themselves to be armed with sub-machine guns and open fire. Jin dives over the bar for cover. The tall man returns fire; his gunfire had a distinct "crack" about it that stood out from the rest. After each one of his shots, there were less gunfire from the others.

The door behind the bar flies open and four thugs rush out. Jin tries to get their attention to figure out what was going on. The thug shakes Jin off and attempts to strike him with the butt of his gun. Jin instinctively separates the thug from his weapon and shoves him into the others, who now shift their attention toward him. The thugs conclude that Jin is with the tall man as they divide their hostilities between the two offenders. Two of them return their focus to the tall man; the remaining two raise their guns against Jin. Naturally, Jin reaches for Hermes and curses having checked it at the front. Instead, he hurls the stolen gun at one of the thugs and kicks a stool at another before charging both thugs. As the gun falls to the floor, Jin catches it, bringing it upward to strike the chin of a thug; followed by a hard spin kick to the face of the other, taking them both down. To make sure they don't get back up, he follows up with another kick to the face of one of the thugs while he's down and gun-butts the other, smashing his head hard against the floor. The remaining two thugs glance back to see Jin's work. As one of the thugs is distracted with Jin, his body is rocked by a hail of shots from the tall man. The last thug frantically looks at both Jin and the tall man. He wisely drops his gun and slides it away as he raises his hands in surrender before making his way toward the exit.

The tall man looks Jin over, gun in hand. The barrel was still smoking and the slits on the side were venting to cool itself. It was an unusual design for a gun to vent in that manner; most weapons require the user to manually expose the AP crystal to air for it to vent properly. The tall man's guns took longer to vent than other weapons Jin had seen. Then again Jin didn't have a lot of experience with guns. The tall man nods to Jin, who returns the gesture. As the slits snap shut another group of thugs arrive, looking down from an elevated floor across the club and open fire. Jin and the tall man disperse in opposite directions; Jin back toward the now familiar bar around the corner, and the tall man fires a few shots as he ducks into the VIP rooms. Jin and the tall man hold their positions before realizing that the thugs had no reason to risk getting closer. The tall man gets Jin's attention by throwing a bottle near him. He signals for Jin to go through the door behind the bar and head toward the thugs. The tall man begins blind-firing shots to keep the thugs attention as Jin slips away. The door led to the kitchen area. In the wrong direction were a few rooms that led to the offices, while the other was to a hallway leading toward the front of the club. He hurries to catch up and do his part. Jin opens the door and finds himself back at the entrance. Through the other doorway, he can see the backs of the armed thugs. Jin had no attachments to the tall man; if anything, Jin had a problem with him for ruining his night out. On the other hand, the tall man hasn't tried to shoot him yet and at least gave him the opportunity to sneak out. It was a favor worth repaying. Jin rushes in and grabs a thug and throws him into another which split their attention between Jin and the tall man. Jin continues his assault on the two closest thugs, delivering a hook kick to one of them, stumbling him away. The other thug begins firing but Jin slaps the gun away, redirecting the gunfire. As the thug corrects his aim, Jin yanks the gun, pulling the thug to the floor. A series of strikes with the butt of the gun rendered him unconscious. After regaining his footing from the kick, the thug steps away to widen the distance to shoot but is fired upon by the tall man.

Jin looked at the aftermath of the fight. He could hardly believe that less than five minutes ago he was ordering a drink. Now the club was littered with broken glass, gunshot holes, and corpses. Jin decided a drink would calm him down. The tall man had already made his way behind the bar and was making himself a drink.

Jin: "I'm guessing you don't work here. Or maybe you use to and you're doing the whole disgruntled ex-employee thing."

Tall man: "No, I just own the place."

The tall man had a raspy voice from years of chain-smoking.

Jin: "That's one way to treat your employees. You may want to work on your managing skills."

Tall man: "They weren't my employees."

The tall man poured himself a glass of whiskey and Jin a beer. He then lit a cigarette and offered one to Jin who declined. Without as much going on, Jin was able get a detailed look at the tall man. He wasn't unusually tall, but the way he carried himself made him seem larger. Perhaps he made everyone else seem smaller, Jin couldn't decide. Throughout the entire fight, the tall man managed to keep his shades on. It both bothered and impressed Jin and he wanted to address it, but the tall man spoke first.

Tall man: "I don't think I know you. I'm curious as to why a complete stranger would come back to help me out in a fight. I appreciate it."

Jin: "I was planning on sitting it out but they thought I was with you."

Tall man: "That makes sense, I hardly ever work alone. Sorry about that."

Jin: "I didn't get shot so I guess its okay. Name's Jin by the way."

Tall man: "Damien."

They raised their glasses.

Damien: "I'm surprised to see another æthean in here. Especially with so many Black Soulz around."

Jin hadn't noticed. He was barely able to tell the difference between veast and ætheans other than the most obvious sign: veast eyes were more animalistic in darkness, reflecting different bands of light depending on the angle. But in the vibrant lighting of the club, it was difficult to use that method. Jin was aware of the establishment's gang association however.

Jin: "I've heard of them but I didn't know they were running legit businesses now. Good for them I guess."

Jin said with a shrug. He finished his beer and Damien slid another one to him before Jin had a chance to ask.

Damien: "Business: yes. Legitimate: no. This is my property and they're squatting."

Jin: "If you own the place, why is it filled with people that want you dead?"

Damien: "That's the question. I just found out that this club was here a few hours ago. The only person who could do anything this fast under my nose would be Vangard but if these guys worked for him, they would know better than to attack me."

Jin: "Maybe he hired outside of his normal circle; brought in people who don't know any better. I know if I were hired as a bouncer for this club a few cycles ago, I wouldn't have known to not attack you."

Damien finished his cigarette with long drag before flicking it across the room and exhaled a plume of smoke that masked his face.

Damien: "I hadn't thought of that. Looks like I've still got a lot of work to do. Thanks for the tip. Help yourself to anything you want. Drinks are on me."

Damien exited the club without showing any concern for its dilapidated state despite being the owner. Jin finished his beer before searching for a container for the alcohol. Jin grabbed the biggest container he could find and loaded it with all the bottles of alcohol he could fit: a large suitcase with a long handle and wheels. He couldn't figure out why anyone would need it at a club, but wasn't going to complain about the convenience. He reacquired Hermes from the crate on the way out.

Jin: "At least I won't need to buy alcohol for a while."

After being in the darkness of the club, the light of the surface slammed Jin's eyes. The sun was still as it was when he entered, illuminating the massive planet Akasha and its violet haze. And why wouldn't it be? It was the back half of the noon season; or summer season as some of the city's population called it. In a few weeks the sun would begin to set marking the slightly shorter (and colder) dusk season which Jin hated almost as much as the frigid night season.

Following the commotion at the club, there was still a crowd outside. Damien was nowhere to be seen but the sound of a heavy engine blazing down the streets echoed through the air.

Jin drew the curiosity of the crowd as he emerged. He was assaulted with an array of questions: "Yo what happened in there?", "The D-man ain't kill you?", and "The dude with the shades left you alive? Aye, don't mess wit this man!" The crowd cleared around him and let him pass. Jin played the part and kept quiet, letting them live in the illusion. They weren't wrong.

Old Light was the former capital of the district and had fallen from the grace of its peak decades ago. The district was unable to (although not without effort) erect a new capital to replace it. Old Light, beyond its first impression of a rundown neighborhood, had a charm to it. It's still known throughout the rest of the district as having some of the best street food, a theatre, and an old library, which has been closed for decades. The owner mentioned going on an extended hiatus but never explained why or for how long.

Jin had lived here for as long as he had been in the city. It's the only place he had known. He had always been curious about the neighboring district Revco; with its superstructures towering over the rest of the city. The shadow it cast on Eratech seemed to put the district down. Despite the grime and cast shadows, Jin couldn't picture city-life being any other way.

Jin had completely lost track of time and had no idea what hour it was as there were still plenty of people in the streets. Aside from the dispersing crowd of people from the club, there were groups of people, likely Black Soulz, still loitering about. It *was* their territory after all. Jin displayed Hermes by carrying it over his shoulder. They watched him as he walked but no one was interested in starting trouble with him. After about a half-hour of walking, he arrived at his apartment. It was a single room apartment. The only thing separating it from a jail-cell was that the bathroom had a folding wall (which he had put up himself). He flipped the switch on his generator to power up his home. The poor machine coughed and sputtered weakly before giving up; its AP crystal had given its last breath. Jin was short a few hundred dregs for buying a new AP crystal and considered selling the alcohol to make ends meet. Exhausted, and annoyed, Jin decided to sleep. He would sort it all out when he awoke.

02– THE KEEPERS OF OLD LIGHT

-By the time the light of a star reaches your planet, it has traveled for millions of years. For all you know that source could have died a million years ago and you would have no idea.-

Damien stepped inside of a dark windowless building. It stood out, being kept in better shape than the other buildings in the surrounding area. He navigated his way through the darkness effortlessly. He had long since forgotten what was in the building but had every step memorized. Hidden away in a room just out of view from the front door was a gentle green glow. It was the light of a button for a metallic elevator door. Damien pressed it and a lighted panel flipped open. After scanning his hand, an artificial voice greeted him: "Colonel Masters arriving." The hum of the elevator motor pulling the lift from the depths filled the silence of the darkness.

After a short descent, the doors opened to a vast underground hangar: groups of technicians and engineers directing workers building heavy machinery, bright lights glaring from an untouchable ceiling, the clicks of keyboards and panels, vehicle engines, shouting, and an array of tools clanking rushed the senses. The same artificial voice repeated the announcement of Damien's arrival over a loudspeaker and all workers on that level stopped their work to salut Damien as he passed. Damien returned the gesture. This was Damien's home, his fortress; the hidden base of Eratech: Dread Locked Citadel (DLC).

Damien's first order of business was to check how the Citadel has been operating. Not that he didn't trust how things were run without him, but to stay informed. From his office overlooking the hangar floor, he called for Eratech's overseers and two people enter shortly after; a teenaged girl and an elderly man.

The girl's name was Oska Haruki; a girl in her late teens with shoulder length hair dyed pinkish-auburn and rounded glasses. Oska had a bookish frame that suited her interest. She was seldom without an earpiece and a forearm mounted computer she called her "sidearm" that projected holograms of interactive light rather than a traditional glass screen. Oska was upbeat and effervescent, which was in stark contrast to Damien who was always dry and stern. She brought an energy that the upper ranks of Eratech lacked. Oska was more to the company than just an uplifting spirit however; she was in charge of the company's networks, computers, and information gathering. Damien hired her for her technical knowledge in hopes of protecting his own network, but later discovered her to be an information gathering genius as well. This quickly earned her a senior position at DLC.

The elderly man was Everett Styner. Styner had looked over Damien since he was a child. Originally a caretaker and bodyguard, he eventually became a mentor once Damien was capable of operating on his own. Styner was a burly, mustached man who was only slightly taller than Damien, but considerably stockier. His body was scared from years of military conflict. Every scar and bruise was waiting to tell a story to anyone who saw it. But despite the wear-and-tear, none of it seemed to slow him down. He had as much energy as someone half his age.

Oska: "Welcome back. What're you doing' here so early?"

Damien: "Early? It's..."

Damien looked at his watch. He hadn't noticed that the work-cycle had only just begun.

Damien: "That explains why everyone's busy. I guess I lost track of time."

Oska: "Doing what?"

Damien: "Looking into a tip. Turns out that the Black Soulz set up a dance club right under our noses in Old Light."

Oska: "When did they get into running clubs?"

Oska barely looked up from her sidearm, working nonchalantly yet still too quick for anyone to follow her movements.

Damien: "A few cycles ago apparently. But they didn't get started on their own. I went in and asked around and the name Vangard came up."

Styner: "I'm not surprised."

Oska: "Did they tell you where to find him?"

Damien: "No. Things got out of hand fast and we had to fight our way out. I don't think the goons knew who I was."

Oska: "I'm sure there was a better way of handling the situation that didn't involve killing people. Wait, who's we?"

Oska stopped her rapid computing to ask her question.

Damien: "Some guy in the club decided to help. He was pretty good."

Oska: "Oh cool. Where is he?"

Damien: "I don't know."

Oska: "Did you scare him off?"

Damien: "Not this time."

Styner: "If he's any good in a fight you might want to scoop him up before any of the gangs do, or even worse Vangard."

Damien: "Vangard only had one person of note left and I think Scratch knows better than to cross me."

Styner: "That may be true but Vangard's notorious for his subtle hand; he can accomplish a lot with very little. It'd be best to keep him from getting his hands on more than he needs."

Styner lectured. Slightly annoyed Damien hadn't realized what he thought to be obvious.

Oska: "And who knows maybe he turns out to be a specialist."

Damien: "True enough. I'll head back out next cycle and see what I can turn up. In the meantime, what's been going on while I was gone?"

Oska returned to scrolling through her sidearm. Light emitted from the device as she swiped and cycled through its three-dimensional interface.

Oska: "As far as veast gang activities go: Black Soulz have been quiet, now I know why. I'll see what pops up with them this cycle. Hallowed eyes have taken some losses from their skirmishes with the Gnashing teeth and are probably going to continue getting wiped out over the next season. Near Grave Town outskirts, there's been a lot of talk of the Black Tempest cult again. Not sure what that's about, but I'll keep looking into it. And… that's all I picked up while you were gone. This cycle's been pretty mundane."

Damien: "Styner, you got anything for me?"

Styner: "Nah. I'm going to help Oska with rounding up all this gang Intel and I'll come up with a solution. Go get some sleep."

Damien: "Yeah, I'll do that. Sounds like you guys got everything covered. Keep up the good work."

Damien departed the office and made his way toward his room which was a studio loft in the dormitories. Damien wasted no time getting settled and lying down, nor did sleep waste its time as it took him.

*   *   *

Jin awoke to the sound of his phone chirping. It was his postmaster. He answered with the grog of sleep still in his voice.

Jin: "Hello?"

Postmaster: "Wow, you *never* pick up on the first call."

Jin: "Got any work for me?"

Postmaster: "I wouldn't be calling you if I didn't. Two deliveries this time. Pay's not bad either."

Jin: "I'll be there in about an hour."

Postmaster: "Sounds good."

Jin rolled out of bed and began his wakeup routine. He was feeling sore from the club, but it was a good sort of sore that followed a satisfying workout. Thinking back, he was amazed at his drunken luck; his not getting shot was nothing short of a miracle he thought. He grabbed the last fistful of hornberries and popped them in his mouth on his way out the door. In the small alley beside his apartment, Jin removed the tarp from his motorcycle. Once upon a time, it could have been considered a nice bike but that was long before Jin had owned it. At least two decades, an unknown number of owners, and countless backyard repairs later, it had made its way into Jin's life. After a few cranks it fired up, whirring and popping as it sputtered to life. Every time Jin turned it off, he wondered if it would ever start back up. If it *did* break, he couldn't afford to have it fixed.

Jin arrived at the post office and went directly to his boss. The small office consisted only of an open reception area with a single door that led to two back offices and package-processing.

Postmaster: "Damn you got here fast."

Jin: "I'll finish the jobs fast too. Where're they going?"

Postmaster: "Yeah, about that."

The postmaster's voice trailed off and his eyes drifted away from Jin's.

Jin: "Yes…?"

Postmaster: "Those jobs are gone. I gave them to Pellus."

Jin: "Why the hell would you call me to take the jobs, give them to Pellus, and then not tell me before I got up here?"

Postmaster: "If it makes you feel any better, I *do* have a new one for you."

Jin paced back and forward in the room while trying to decide if he wanted the job. It was merely a show of protest; what he wanted was irrelevant to what he needed and he needed money.

Jin: "(sigh) What is it?"

Postmaster: "I need you to take this one to an apartment on the west side of town. The address is in veast gang territory. I heard there was a shoot-out late last cycle. Be careful out there."

The postmaster handed Jin a paper with the details. Jin scowled as he read it.

Jin: "Are you kidding me? You called me out here for this?"

Postmaster: "I called you for the other jobs, but time became an issue and…"

Jin: "No. You had this job lying around and no one else would do it, so you told me about some shit Pellus was already doing just to get me up here."

The postmaster didn't have anything to say. Jin had seen through him. Unfortunately for Jin, he wasn't in any position to turn down any work; Even petty deliveries.

Jin: "Just give me the damn package."

Postmaster: "Thank you. I owe you another one."

Jin: "Your tabs really starting to add up."

Jin exited the office to earn his pittance.

03– NEW LIFE

-Seeking a fresh start, the former citizens of other cities set out to make a new home: One built for this now changed world. Magnamus was born and a city raised around him.-

Early in the cycle, Damien approached Oska at her operations computer. When she was hired, she convinced Damien that she needed something more powerful for what he wanted her to do. He funded it but she had to build it herself. And while he wasn't happy about the money spent, the work she was able to do proved to be worth the expense. From her ability to scour the depths of Eranet (Eratech's district based internet) to acquire information, to being able to manage nearly every aspect of the company from one station. It was a beast of a computer. At the moment, she was working on a detailed map of the city.

Damien: "Is that the area near Grave town?"

Damien took a sip of coffee. Too close to Oska's computer for her liking.

Oska: "Please keep that away from the console."

Damien took a step back and Oska continued.

Oska: "Yeah. There's something going on in the area but all sensor data says unknown."

Damien: "Where exactly is it?"

Oska: "It's right at the outskirts just before the Barrens. That part of the sector is mostly abandoned save for the occasional bumpkin."

Damien: "I take it we don't have any assets out there?"

Oska: "Nope. Pretty much everything's been scrapped, moved into the city, or just abandoned if it wasn't worth the effort. People mostly just stay away from the area because of lawlessness."

Damien: "If no one's out there, what do you think it is?"

Oska: "I don't know. Adaptation Particle interference, Solar flares, Akashean Adaptation Particle storms, demons ripping through space; It could be anything."

Damien: "Any chance it's the computer?"

Oska laughed. Damien didn't find the question as funny as she did and Oska stifled her laughter. Damien continued.

Damien: "How long has it been there?"

Oska: "About two cycles. I have nothing to work with but I'll keep at it."

Damien: "Take a break. Come back to it with a fresh mind. C'mon, it's training time."

Oska reluctantly locked the computer and joined Damien. They departed Oska's office and made their way to the hangar floor. The hangar was where a majority of the activity was done. The hangar stretched far enough that it was difficult to make out what was happening on the other end and was much longer than it was wide. As Damien and Oska passed, mechanics stopped working and paused idle chatter to salute Damien, who always returned the gesture. It made the walk to the training area longer.

There were about fifteen people who were awaiting Damien's arrival. They were all new recruits to DLC. Damien liked to personally do the introduction training for recruits. It allowed him to meet all of the soldiers working for him and build a base relationship. Recruits came from all over the district; some even from the outskirts. DLC rarely turned people down outright and could find at least one use for everyone willing to work for them. Some recruits find their way directly to the military branch; often youthful, homeless, dejected, people. DLC gave them a home, friends, and focus. For that alone, many people were loyal to Damien and DLC.

As Damien approached the front of the group of recruits they fell into formation. Oska joined in at the back of the ranks. The recruits were a broad mix; ranging from young adults to middle aged, male and female, veast and æthean.

Damien: "Thank you everyone for your patience. Sorry I'm a little late. Because of that, we're just going to jump right into it. This cycle's focus is knife basics. In battle, when all your weapons are burned out or your opponent is too close, your next best option is your knife. They're always ready and don't need to be vented. Knowing how to use one can *only* help save your life. With that being said, I want everyone to grab a training knife and pair up."

Everyone walked down the line and grabbed a training weapon. A few of the younger recruits made stabbing jokes, but a cold stare from Damien stopped them. Damien paired up with Oska. Once everyone else was paired up, he began running through fundamental techniques. They ran through a series of drills going back and forth with the weapons, covering quick flurries, disarming, and ways to prevent from being disarmed themselves. It wasn't long before Oska grew impatient with the training.

Oska: "Why do I have to do this? I'm never going to be anywhere close to combat."

She and Damien exchanged strikes and traded blocks. Oska had received some training before from Damien and had become comfortable with the movements, but not proficient.

Damien: "You never know when you're going to be in a dangerous situation; especially outside of battle. My point being, there's no reason you shouldn't learn self-defense."

Oska: "All you got to do is stab and not get stabbed."

Oska lunged at Damien, who dodged with only the slightest of gestures. She stumbled past Damien falling on all fours. She scanned the area for her weapon. Oska looked up at Damien to see him holding two weapons in hand, staring down at her. Damien returned her weapon and the two of them continue training. Oska now more open to instruction.

Damien: "I want you to carry a knife with you at all times. I don't think you're the type who can handle having a gun on you but a knife is a nice second option."

Oska: "Have you seen the way I dress? I'm not going to add a sheath to my wardrobe."

Oska's attire was simple: she often wore skirts and form-fitting shirts (during the noon season) with the exception being the athletic clothing she wore for training.

Damien: "Just find a way to keep safe. That's all I'm asking."

Oska nodded in agreement.

Once they finished the last drill, everyone fell back into formation as Damien stood out in front. He told them how well they did, and what they'd be doing next time before dismissing them. Oska made her way back to Damien, who was having a drink of water.

Oska: "Are you still going on your search for our mysterious fighter this cycle?"

Damien: "Once I get cleaned up. I had Styner do some research for me while I was down."

Oska: "He didn't use my computer did he?"

Damien: "No. He wouldn't know what to do with that thing anyway. He did it the old fashioned way; phone calls and footwork."

Oska: "Just COMMs me when you leave. I'll support anyway I can."

Damien: "I don't think this'll be that kind of mission. Just keep working on the Grave town anomaly."

Oska: "Got it. Good luck out there."

*   *   *

Jin stored the package in his motorcycle compartment and began the arduous task of starting it up. He has less luck than he had earlier. All of his usual tricks failed to fire up the now expired machine. Scraping it for parts would be the only way to get anything out of it at this point, but he didn't have time for that. Jin kicked the motorcycle in frustration, and it coughed to life; barely. Unsure of how long it'll last, he wasted no time setting off. He took the fastest route to the delivery location which led him down many side streets and alleys. The side streets were littered with graffiti tags of the various gangs in the area. As Jin got closer to his destination, he realized how obvious the territorial markings were and was embarrassed that he missed them all last cycle.

During the ride, the motorcycle died and revived itself several times, but never long enough to come to a complete stop. This was certain to be its last ride. It coughed its final breath a few blocks away from Jin's destination as it sputtered to a stop. Dead. Not even an attempt to spark to life. A dead AP crystal was likely the culprit. Although a number of heavily corroded or cracked parts could also be the problem. The motorcycle was nothing more than an assembly of scrap parts waiting to be repurposed. Jin grabbed the package and set out on foot.

In the distance, Jin could see *Cyclebreak*. There was a group of people loitering near the entrance. They took notice of Jin from across the street. A woman's voice politely called out from behind.

Woman's voice: "Excuse me, can you help me?"

Jin turned around to a girl dressed in gothic attire. Clad in an all-black hooded-trench coat that was studded with buckles, zippers, and oversized sleeves. She pulled her hood back just enough to reveal her face and features. She also had several piercings in her unusually pale face along her brow, nose, and lip. Her voice was sweet and didn't meet expectation. Jin couldn't help but feel as if she was trying to compensate for her soft voice.

Jin: "I probably can't help you. I don't live around here."

This was somewhat of an untruth. He was at least familiar with the area, but didn't want to delay any longer. As he tried to walk away, the Goth girl grabbed his wrist.

Goth girl: "Well you never know. We're looking for a guy who trashed the club last cycle. He had red hair, a studded brow, biker jacket, and a sword. Ring any bells?"

It was obvious she was describing Jin. He was certain the situation could become hostile, but continued to play the fool. It was strange that she didn't mention Damien.

Jin: "Was the club called… break something? I heard the name somewhere."

The Goth girl's expression and tone changed from soft to aggressive as she rolled her red eyes in irritation.

Goth girl: "(Sigh) Are we really going to do this? Cut the shit."

Jin: "You started it. We both know you're looking for me. What do you want?"

Goth girl: "My boss wants to meet you. Come with me."

Jin: "Who's your boss?"

Goth girl: "You'll find out when we get there."

The Goth girl turned to start walking away but stopped when she realized Jin wasn't following.

Jin: "Not happening. If your boss wants to meet me, he should be out here. I'm not seeing anyone who sends flunkies out to go fetch people. Piss off."

Goth girl: "Look, you have two options: Either you come with me willingly or things get ugly for you fast."

Jin: "Are you serious? I just murdered a club full of armed gunmen by myself. Do you really think that you can make me do anything?"

Another untruth; Jin didn't kill anyone but he fought off gunman while unarmed which is a feat in itself. He set the package down and clutched Hermes. To his surprise, the Goth girl stood her ground. Jin considered that she may not be all bluster.

Goth girl: "Fine. You're no good to our boss if you've been ripped to shreds. Please just reconsider…"

She cuts her words short as she hurls two hooked knives from her sleeves at Jin. Only one hook was accurate, the other sails harmlessly past him. Jin draws Hermes and quickly spins toward the Goth girl. As he comes around, he sees the glimmer of light reflecting off of razor thin wire tied around the handles of each hook leading back into her sleeves. Jin intended to make short work of it. He slices upward at the wire. It holds against Hermes' edge. The Goth girl yanks both wires hard, wrapping one wire and hook around Hermes and pulling it in. Jin lets her have it for now as he focuses on dodging the other hook. The Goth girl expected a fight for Hermes and his awkward decision threw her off balance.

Jin closes the distance to Goth girl, who was fumbling with Hermes. She had her free hook wire spinning rapidly, but could only make large slow swings with the hook wire that held Hermes. Her rhythm and coordination were impressive. She whips the hook holding Hermes at Jin and pulls it back as he reaches to catch it. As she pulls Hermes away, she hurls the free hook wire out at Jin. Jin uses his sheath to wrap the wire and lets her pull it back, leaving her with two blunted hook wires.

The Goth girl realized Jin had the advantage at this distance. He could easily move in close as soon as she attacked or if she tried to release Jin's weapons. She slows the whirling wires and lets them drop.

Jin: "Smart move."

The Goth girl detaches the wires and they coil to the ground. She kicks Jin's sheath and Hermes to him. As Jin reaches down to pick them up, the Goth girl launches another pair of wired hooks. A risky move considering Jin was even closer than he was before. Jin hops back as the Goth girl yanks her wires. He lets the hooks catch Hermes. He tightens his grip and yanks, sending her stumbling toward him. He grabs her and presses the blade against her neck.

Jin: "Are you done?"

Goth girl: "Yes. Now get your goddamn sword off my neck."

Jin: "Nuh uh. Lose the coat."

Goth girl: "Are you serious? Do you know how many buckles are on here?"

Jin: "Nine. Get to it. No more tricks up your literal sleeve."

Goth girl: "I'm not doing that."

Jin: "Lose the coat or lose your life. Hurry up, because I'm losing my patience."

She sighed and began unbuckling the coat. It took less time than she made it sound like it would; which was fortunate as the situation was awkward for both of them. Jin separated her from the coat and made her take a few steps away before turning around. She was wearing a black vest which also had a lot of buckles and zippers. On both her arms, she had gloved bracers. Each of which had two more hook blades on them. Jin couldn't figure out where the wire was coming from however.

Goth girl: "There, secrets out. Can I have my coat back now?"

If she still wanted to fight, she didn't need the coat to do it. In fact, she could have surprised him by launching more hook blades when he was holding her. Jin threw it back to her.

Jin: "You're going to have a heat stroke wearing all of that at noon."

Goth girl: "Do you see how pale I am? I'm not a fan of the sun."

Jin thought it was makeup, but her ghost-white skin and platinum hair was her own. Her bright red eyes were not just of her veast ethnicity, but albinism.

Jin: "But seriously, who's your boss?"

Smokey voice: "A veast named Vangard.

The Goth girl was visibly startled at the sound of the voice. Jin recognized it as well: it was Damien. He was wearing a travel vest that swung with each step, giving a glimpse of his guns strapped to his sides underneath. He still carried himself in that intrepid, sure-footed manner he had in the club. He stopped close enough to the Goth girl to have to look down on her.

Damien: "And Scratch, why is Vangard harassing people in Old Light?"

Jin: "Scratch? Really?"

Scratch: "Shut up. Vangard is only using assets that you've abandoned or ignored. *Cyclebreak* was long since abandoned and Jin here was also disregarded."

Scratch's tone had become gentle and dulcet again.

Damien: "That's the second time Vangard's come up in all this. What's he doing with the Black Soulz?"

Scratch: "That's something you'll have to ask him yourself. I have no idea."

Damien: "Then where is he?"

Scratch: "He mentioned setting up a meeting with you soon. When would be a good time for you?"

Damien: "Now."

Scratch: "Umm… *after* this cycle."

For the first time since he had arrived, Damien glanced at Jin out of the corner of his shades. There was a long pause before Damien turned fully to face Scratch.

Damien: "Sixteen cycles."

Scratch: "I'll let him know. If there's nothing else…"

Damien: "Be sure to tell Vangard to keep his business out of Old Light if he's not going to do it through me."

Scratch nodded as she departed. She hopped into a red compact sports car on the far side of the street and jetted off. Damien watched her disappear as he lit a cigarette and greeted Jin.

Damien: "That's two fights in two cycles. You don't come off as the type who looks for trouble. But then again carrying a sword in plain sight tends to draw challengers."

Jin: "Maybe one of these days I'll bump into one who's an actual challenge. So what was her deal?"

Damien: "I'm sure you've figured out that she works for Vangard. She was here to recruit you."

Jin: "Then what brings *you* back here?"

Damien: "With your involvement at the club, you've grabbed Vangard's attention and not even I know where that could go. But after seeing you at work twice now I can see why. I figured it'd be better to have you on my payroll than have to worry about you slicing up my guys later."

Jin was sold at the word "payroll".

Jin: "Say no more, I'm in."

Damien: "Just like that? You're not even going to try to negotiate?"

Jin: "I don't think I need to. The pay can't possibly any worse than my last job. "

Damien: "Luckily for you, I'm not in the business of cheating people."

Jin: "That sounds like something someone in the business of cheating people would say."

Damien: "Heh. Yeah, you'll get along with Grihm just fine."

Jin: "I got a question for you: How the hell does everyone keep finding me?"

Damien: "You can find almost anyone if you know who you're looking for. Vangard specializes in that and I have solid resources. So what made you move out into Old Light?"

Jin: "Work. I work for… or I use to work for the postmaster here. Speaking of which…"

Jin looked around for the package he dropped before his fight with Scratch. He headed over to retrieve it, but thought better of it. If there was ever an opportunity to leave his past behind, this was it. The package was no longer any of his concern.

Damien led Jin down the streets where a pristine gunmetal gray muscle-car was parked on the road. What was odd about it was that the front of the car was angled almost to a point as it were used to plow into (or through) other vehicles. Damien revved up the loud engine and Jin recognized it as the vehicle he heard speeding away from *Cyclebreak* as he stepped outside. After the doors were closed, the sound of the engine was almost non-existent.

Jin: "I know I said that I was in already but what kind of work am I going to be doing?"

Damien: "We need someone to make deliveries."

Damien said tersely. Jin hoped that he wasn't serious but Damien didn't present himself as the type of person to joke.

Jin: "That's not even close to funny."

Damien: "For now, odd jobs."

Jin had called Damien's bluff. Damien didn't crack even the slightest smile. Jin relaxed in his seat.

Jin: "So I'm a goon?"

Damien: "Just until I figure out what you're best at."

It was only a few minutes before they reached their destination. Jin had no shortage of questions along the ride, but didn't want to come off as annoying. Damien had no problem with long silences. Jin followed Damien to a windowless single-level building. It was pitch black inside. Only a tiny bit of light from what was able to make it in the doorway before Damien closed the door.

Jin: "This is probably where I get jumped."

Damien: "I wouldn't need to bring you here for that. Just watch your step."

Jin struggled to listen to Damien's steps through the room but he strode silently across the darkness. From the opposite end of the darkness, Jin heard a door open and a small light emanated from it. Jin moved to follow. After kicking over a number of unknown objects, Jin stumbled into the back room with the elevator.

Jin: "Why aren't there any lights in here?"

Damien: "I don't need them."

Damien closed the doors and the elevator began a long descent. As the doors opened Jin was assaulted with military-industrial sounds of the hangar. He eagerly stepped ahead of Damien and leaned over a rail to take in the sights of the hangar below.

Jin: "What the hell is this?"

Damien: "This is Eratech's military command: Dread-Locked Citadel."

Jin: "I didn't know Eratech still had this much of a military left"

Damien: "And it's damn good too."

Damien stood with his arms crossed looking over the hangar as well. He was beaming with pride.

Jin: "I've been recruited by the military?"

Oska was alerted to Damien's arrival as soon as he had accessed the elevator. She left her battle station to meet him at the entrance.

Oska: "You make it sound like you've sold out. You haven't done anything yet, relax. Welcome to the team Mr. Jin. I'm Oska."

Oska extended her hand for a handshake and Jin accepted the offer.

Jin: "Nice to meet you. Seems like everyone knows who I am."

Oska: "That's *all* we know. That and what Damien's seen."

Jin: "So *you're* the one doing research on me?"

Oska: "I was one of them."

Damien: "Oska will begin your admin process and give you a tour. Welcome to the team Jin. I'm looking forward to working with you. Oska if you need me, I'll be in the war-room with Styner finishing the plan for the fiscal year."

Damien nodded to them both before leaving.

Oska: "Okay, first things first. Would you mind laying your hand on this?"

She presented a tablet to Jin. The screen had an outline of a hand. Jin placed his hand on the screen and after a few seconds it beeped.

Oska: "Cool. Now you have access to the main elevator at least. Now let's begin our tour."

Oska led Jin to the other side of the main hangar via the overhead platforms. Jin lagged behind for a moment, still attempting to keep up with his rapidly changing life.

Jin: "Uh… right… I'm coming."

Oska: "This is the main hangar. From this balcony is where you can get the best view of the Citadel. This is where forces are organized and deployed."

Oska hit a button on the wall which opened an elevator. This elevator was considerably nicer than the one he used to enter the citadel. There was even music.

Jin: "This is going to seem weird, but how old are you? You seem a little young to be running all of admin here."

Oska: "No that would be insane. I only do the admin for certain individuals. To answer your question: I'll be eighteen come dawn season."

Jin: "Damn. Good on you for landing this job."

Oska: "Thanks. He originally paid me just to improve and secure his network. But I ended up doing all sorts of other stuff like mission dispatch and Intelligence collection."

Jin: "If you can do all of that, I can see why he'd hire you."

The doors opened.

Oska: "This floor is the third level: Research & Development (R&D). Pretty much explains itself. You probably won't be down here unless you're with someone who has access. It's kind of a "need-to-know" area."

The doors closed and the elevator descended to the next level.

Oska: "The fourth level is the barracks/dormitories. With a few exceptions, this is where everyone lives."

Jin: "Some people live out in town? Why?"

Oska: "Not everyone wants to deal with the small rooms and military life. Sure you have everything you need here, but some people just need their own space."

Jin: "Do you live here?"

Oska: "Only during the summer and winter seasons."

Jin: "Why're we walking through the barracks?"

Oska: "Taking you to your room."

Jin: "I have a room already?"

Oska: "Yep. It's not fully furnished for you because we didn't know what you'd like."

Oska pointed out a large office to the left. The sign above the door read *Clinic*. The sign was dim, and the lights were off inside the windows. She continued.

Oska: "And this is the office of Dr. Malerius Jackson, the psychologist. With the increased workload lately, we figured it'd be a good idea to have someone who knows about helping people deal with the stress of military life. Malerius is hardly ever in his office though."

Jin: "I'll pass on meeting the head doctor. I don't have any emotional baggage to unload."

Oska: "Between me and you, I don't like being around him. I can feel him leering at me when I walk past him. Freaking creepy."

Oska swiped a card in front of a panel on the wall and a door opened. They stepped inside and lights turned on. It was a simple room with plenty of space for options.

Jin: "Yeah, this kicks the shit out of my apartment. I thought you said it wasn't furnished?"

Oska: "Well it is, but I'm sure you have some preferences. Anyway, get settled in for now. There's a lot of administrative work we have to do next cycle."

She closed the door behind her. Jin stood in his new quarters trying to take it all in.

04– THE MAD GROVE

-Such a bizarre land this Grove. With plant life even stranger than that of Akasha, it has given birth to its own ecosystem of creatures as well. As resilient as it is alien. I look forward to watching it grow and once again bring life to the surrounding Barrens.-

-Excerpt from the Celestilium

Being from beyond the barrens, the rigid military lifestyle was even more foreign to Jin than it was to the average citizen of the city. He had difficulty adjusting to the many deadlines and hated the "Hurry up and wait" mentality most of all. Luckily for Jin, he wasn't subject to the same orders as the rest of the military soldiers; at least not after a week of basic training which mostly consisted of teaching him how things are run at the base and where things were. Following his indoctrination, Jin was as comfortable around the citadel as anyone else. Jin furthered his understanding of operations by lending a helping hand whenever he felt he could. He volunteered for various jobs such as basic manual labor and standing watch. If he couldn't stand a watch, he would drop by and spend time with those who did. In a short time, Jin had built a foundation of trust with DLC; he proved that he was happy to be there.

Jin didn't work with Damien after his recruitment and training, although he would see him training others and working with Oska often. Jin also noticed him returning from the surface with a group of individuals but was never introduced to any of them. Jin occasionally worked with Oska however. Early in the work hours one cycle, Jin entered Oska's office. She was at her battle station having conversation with someone over a headset. He waited at the entrance.

Oska: "Considering where it is, I don't think they know about it yet. We can get to it first, but we have to hurry… Shina's team is available. I can have them en route in thirty… Can I make another suggestion? I think Jin should go with them."

There was a long pause.

Oska: "Got it. I'll have an update for you by the time you get back."

Jin knocked on the door as he entered.

Jin: "What was that about?"

Oska blurred through several screens of maps and spreadsheets before swiping them all clear with a wave of her sidearm.

Oska: "Just the man I needed to see. You're going on a mission."

Jin: "What is it?"

She began walking out of the office as she worked on her sidearm knowing Jin would follow close behind.

Oska: "You're going to join a team of four to acquire something of considerable value. I'll tell you more when we meet the rest of the team. You'll get more details throughout the mission. C'mon, we're meeting in the hangar."

Oska didn't give Jin a chance to get a word in. They hurried to the hangar to await the arrival of the others. She impressively coordinated the efforts of personnel in the gathering of equipment. Despite her youth she showed an aptitude for managing others better than anyone Jin had ever seen.

Oska: "… C'mon! This is why we spend all that time training. Let's go! We got to be done in fifteen minutes or this launch is a failure. There're only four motorcycles here, we need one more. Move!"

The hustle increased at Oska's urging. A weapon rack was wheeled over, and personnel checked and loaded the weapons on them. They prepared extra AP crystals for the weapons, COMMs equipment, and breathing apparatus equipment.

With so much noise and commotion in the area, no one heard the approach of a woman and three robots standing behind Oska.

Female Soldier: "Ma'am, Support team reporting."

The woman was built like a soldier and carried herself in a surefooted manner that only a soldier could. In stark contrast to her frame, her face carried soft, friendly features. Her hair was buzzed on the left side but the rest of her hair hung down over the right side stopping just below her chin. What was most striking about her was that her hair color was a vibrant rainbow that seemed to change colors before your eyes. She also had small cybernetic implants just behind her left ear and another that went down her spine.

The robots were a model created decades ago during Eratech's time as an engineering company; before the DLC was formed. Their model was originally designed to work with shipping and freighting but the AI was too underdeveloped to operate on its own. More time was spent walking them through the task than was spent on actual work and the product line was eventually discontinued. These robots were beyond the functional capabilities of their siblings as they were capable of following the female soldier's every whim with only simple gestures and even imitated the same mannerisms.

Oska wasn't startled by their silent arrival. She continued overseeing mission preparation.

Oska: "Good, I thought I was going to have to call you again. I'll get right into it while we're waiting on the last bike so you can depart as soon as it gets here. Introduce yourselves on your own time."

Jin took notice of the female soldier's militaristic posture and realized how sloppy and unrefined he looked in comparison. He tightened up and stood at ease.

Female soldier: "Got it. Mission?"

Oska: "We've detected a hazard spout in the vicinity of the Mad Grove. You are to infiltrate and harvest as much hazard as you can. For mission purposes, the Mad Grove is considered hostile territory and every reasonable precaution is to be taken in accordance to the operation parameters."

The element known as hazard is a mysterious substance that "spouts" through the ground in random locations throughout the world. It flows like a thick gel and is colorless save for its static shimmer. The defining property of this element is that it breaks down whatever it touches into base Adaptation Particles (AP) and the only known way to contain it is with specialized AP energy containers. Once this was discovered, it was not long before it was weaponized to horrific affect.

A worker arrived on the last motorcycle and dismounted. The Jin, the female soldiers, and the four robots quickly donned their mission equipment and were mounted on the bikes in moments. Jin wasn't a fan of being weighed down with extra equipment; He grabbed everything required, but only intended on carrying the breathing apparatus once they reached the destination.

Oska: "4A Squad, you are clear for departure."

Oska gave 4A Squad and Jin a thumbs-up and they jetted away. Oska looked at a timer she had set on her sidearm.

Oska: "18 minutes and 32 seconds. I think that's a new record."

*   *   *

The squad blazed through the streets. The motorcycle was brand new and had not yet been broken in. Jin wanted to test the limits of a working machine being that he had never rode on one that wasn't falling apart. Jin felt he could easily outride the others, and would have had he known the route. The squad cut through traffic recklessly, both coming and going. Not even the sidewalks were off limits. The team rode single file with Jin in the rear. Shina's robots moved in perfect synchronization; almost as if they were controlled by a single mind. Jin's movements seemed out of place by comparison.

It wasn't long before they reached the outskirts of the district. There was less traffic and the roads were wider. They shifted into a two-by-two formation, with Jin riding rear-center. Once the route became easier to follow, Jin opened COMMs with the squad leader.

Jin: "Nice riding back there. How'd you teach those bots to ride like that?"

Female soldier: "Hold that thought; mission details incoming."

Oska: "I'm sending you the location of the objective now."

Female soldier: "Got it. Standing by."

Oska: "The hazard spout is on the eastern side of the river, far north of the God tree."

Female soldier: "That's lucky."

Oska: "Not lucky enough. We're not sure where the concentration of madness pheromones is dense enough to have noticeable effects. So turn your equipment on as soon as you notice strange vegetation or feel anything."

Jin: "Actually, the madness pheromones won't have any effect until you inhale a large amount. So if you feel anything, it's already too late. The amount needed depends on the person."

Oska: "You know about Grove Madness?"

Jin: "Only a little bit. Those effects will still be minor unless we run into any Tchrnn. If that's the case, there're a lot of variables. None of which are good. Our best bet is to avoid any sentient Tchrnn we see."

Female soldier: "Good to know."

Oska: "As far as getting the hazard spout, you're going to have to ditch the motorcycles and climb through some dense vegetation. Unfortunately, the Grove is largely unexplored territory, so we don't have a lot of terrain info on it. Hopefully you guys can bring us something back."

Female soldier: "Will do. 4A Squad out. And thanks for the added info Jin. Nice job keeping up."

The team, now with more direction, sped ahead. Jin was curious about the robots. Their movements intrigued him.

Jin: "Do they have names or should I just refer to them as robots?"

Female soldier: "I've never thought of that. No one's ever worked with me before. I'm Shina by the way. Don't worry about the bots, just direct everything toward me."

As they traveled to the fringes of Eratech territory, the paved and painted city streets became stony, unkempt, rural dirt roads. The familiar urban scenery had transitioned to flat, open countryside. Fields rolled as far as they could see in nearly all directions and the clean country air was well appreciated. Sparsely peppered throughout the countryside were small simple houses, barns, and windmills. Further on, even the farmland stopped. The people who lived this far out certainly didn't belong to the city. In the distance, the mad grove began to roll into view: An enormous tree rivaling many of the superstructures in Revco district flourished into the sky far above the lush forest. The plants seemed almost alien to what grew in and near the city. Toadstools grew as tall as normal trees, and trees stood taller than that; all of which displayed their own dizzying palette of colors.

The terrain eventually became too forested for the motorcycles to be useful. The ground was uneven with root growth and shrubbery, divided further by stony hills and tiny cliffs. The team dismounted to continue their journey on foot. As they walked, Shina gave her full attention to Jin. The robots walked in front of and both sides of Jin and Shina, acting as lookouts for them. If there was an unusual sound or sight, Shina reacted with the robot that spotted it while the others continued to watch their respective areas.

Shina: "Do you know anything else about Grove Madness? What's this about staying away from Tchrnn?"

Jin: "From what my mentor taught me, the Grove is one collective entity; complete harmony in nature. Many of the plants here emit the same type of pheromones but the Tchrnn are a little different because they emit their own type of pheromones. On top of that each Tchrnn has a different way of spreading those pheromones. I was just told to keep away from them if I could."

Shina: "Do you know what they look like?"

Jin: "Nope. But I imagine we'd know it if we saw one. To be honest, they're all probably near the great tree anyway."

Shina: "Or there are plenty of them scouting the perimeter since they probably know we're here already.

Jin: "I don't think so. Lots of things and people come to the fringe. There are plenty of hallucinogenic and medicinal plants to be found here."

Shina: "What do you know about medicine?"

Jin: "Not much but I *do* know which plants to eat to help build a resistance to Grove Madness."

All three of Shina's robots turned inquisitively toward Jin.

Shina: "That sounds pretty damn useful. You wanna share?"

Jin: "First: You'd have to take your mask off to eat it. And second: it takes a few weeks to build up your immunity. Not to mention all the side effects. It's not useful right now."

Shina: "I guess you've built up a resistance to the pheromones then?"

Jin: "I Hope so. I haven't had a chance to try it."

After seeing Shina's robots in motion and the conversation about the pheromones, Jin wondered why they should even risk going into the Grove.

Jin: "I have a question for you: why are we going in on foot exposing ourselves to pheromones, when we have these bots for that?"

Shina: "I can only control them from so far away. After about a hundred yards, they revert back to their base AI which isn't any good."

Jin: "Is that what the implants are for?"

Shina: "Yeah. A guy back at the Citadel, Heiretsu, got the idea that the shipping bots might work better if they had another input source and assistant processor since transmissions from the Citadel weren't fast enough for rapidly changing situations like combat. Waypoints would be too expensive and ultimately unreliable. Eventually he concluded a person would be the best option."

Jin: "How'd you get roped into that?"

Shina: "I volunteered. The practical applications for this could be amazing if not just for para and quadriplegics. Unfortunately, the surgery is pretty risky. I actually died for a few minutes during the operation. And there are still other side effects."

Jin: "Like what?"

Shina: "That's what we're trying to figure out."

They arrived at what is considered Greater Grove territory; it felt like stepping into another world. The unfamiliar foliage and shifting ambient noises made them feel unwelcome; as if the forest was watching. The sounds of animal chirps and howls echoed into their ears; but all from a distance. As they approached, the sounds fell silent. Curiosity got the better of some creatures: a large magnus stag strode prominently across their path, letting them know that they were in his territory and that he was watching them before leaping across the glade into the brush. Male magnus stags are known for their sharp horns and violent displays to impress potential mates. This one had a great number of scars and was announcing his presence to the intruders. Shortly after, several other magnus stags trotted across their path behind the leader. The team waited for the last of the stragglers to pass and get a good distance before continuing on.

The warmth of the summer sun began to fade as the grove canopy grew denser. In the forest gloom, Shina began to stand out more. Her hair was more radiant than before, almost like it was emitting a soft light. Jin was certain that her hair did change color and it wasn't just him.

This deep within the Grove, the plants barely seemed to be from the same planet. Trees spiraled outward in wide helixes before reaching to the sky. Ferns and brush plants shied away from them as they passed, stretching their leaves out again if they stood still or moved away. Inversely, a different tree seemed to reach out to brush against them. They realized that the grove was more alive than they thought a forest could be. Each plant and tree was an individual; a citizen, not unlike themselves being citizens in the city. In that sense, the forest felt less alien and they themselves tourist in a foreign land.

The feeling of bewildered visitor eroded and became that of intrusion; as if they were unwelcome. Shina felt a sound in her ear just loud enough to be heard, but too soft to make out the words.

Shina: "What?"

Jin: "What do you mean *what*?"

Shina: "What did you just say?"

Jin: "I didn't say anything. Maybe it was one of the bots."

Shina looked back at the robots. Two of them shrugged their shoulders while the third was trying to eat a kaleido pear, rubbing it against its faceplate. Kaleido pears were the only familiar plant they'd seen since they arrived in the grove. A fruit that comes from a tree that is tricky to grow outside of the Grove. Named after its dazzling skin patterns.

Shina: "What the hell are you doing? You don't eat."

Shina felt the sound in her ear again. This time the words were clear.

Soothing voice: "Relax. It's just having a snack."

Shina: "But robots don't eat. He knows that. *I* know that. Why would I make it do that?"

Soothing voice: "Robot? These creatures of metal? Is that why they feel different from you two? As long as they're docile I suppose there's no harm. You should relax and have a pear yourself. You'll probably never have them this fresh again in your life."

Shina: "You're right. We've earned a break. Pass one of those over here."

Jin watched as a sixth person tossed a pear to Shina and himself. Even though he wanted to, Jin couldn't focus on the new person among them. Even as he looked directly at his grayish-green, leafy skin, petal shaped ears, and bushy hair; they all seemed mundane and the moment Jin looked away he would instantly forget all details. Shina removed her mask and began eating. Although Jin was stricken with confusion, he kept his mask on.

Shina: "I don't think I've ever enjoyed something this much before. These *are* really good!"

Soothing voice: "Please, call me Chrys."

Jin had a moment of clarity; albeit a brief one. He belted out his thought before that too fluttered away.

Jin: "Who the hell is this guy?"

Shina: "He just told you. His name is Chrys."

Jin: "No, where did he come from? He didn't ride in with us."

Chrys: "No I just live here."

Shina was enthralled by Chrys, yet she seemed genuinely interested in what he had to say.

Shina: "That's so cool. It's so tranquil; seeing all of the natural creatures in their homes. Oh! We saw a herd of magnus stags on our way here. They were so majestic and graceful."

Chrys: "They are some of my favorite denizens. It's good to see there are people from the metal forest who appreciate true nature. You don't seem out of place here. In fact, the grove is comfortable with you."

Shina: "Appreciate? I wish I could just live out here. Or at least close enough to go on strolls through the forests. I'm not a big fan of city life. My girlfriend and I want to move out of the city but my job keeps us there."

Jin had become interested in what Chrys had to say as well. He shook his head to regain his own thoughts.

Jin: "Hey! Can we stay focused? And stop eating."

Chrys: "Maybe you should *start* eating. They're really good."

Jin: "I will as soon as you tell me who you are."

Chrys: "Fine, since you couldn't keep the conversation pleasant. I'm here to figure out why *you're* here. Why the five of you are marching this far into my home."

Shina: "We're actually here to help you. Well… help ourselves. This will in turn help you."

Jin: "I guess it's not a secret then?"

Shina: "That's because we're in his home. I don't want him to think we're the enemy."

Chrys: "Thank you. You've been really helpful. What's your name?"

Shina: "It's Shina."

Chrys: "It is a pleasure to meet you Shina. What's this thing you're helping yourself to?"

Shina: "It's a hazard spout. One's surfaced in the grove and we've come to extract it before anyone else does, or before it does any damage."

Chrys: "Then it's a good thing I caught you before you journeyed all that way. The Grove is already dealing with it."

Shina: "How? It's caustic and you don't have any machines to contain or extract it."

Chrys: "There's a reason the Grove has flourished here. We're able to adapt quickly to survive. This was only a tiny threat. Hazard is more of a threat to things constructed. In nature, it's simply another element. Just because you don't know how it can be done without machines, doesn't mean that it can't be done. There was a time when there weren't any machines to do everything and the world got along just fine."

Chrys gave Jin a look that left him with an impression that he was smiling. The most relatable facial feature Chrys shared were his eyes, but only just.

Chrys: "How was the fruit?"

Jin was holding an eaten keleidopear core. He didn't remember eating the fruit, or taking off his mask for that matter.

Jin: "I think it was delicious. I don't remember."

Chrys: "I'll let you take a few more for the road. But your work here is done."

Shina: "Sorry we couldn't help you."

Chrys: "It's fine. We appreciate the thought. It's good to have neighbors who look out for one another. We'll try to keep communication between our people so this little mishap doesn't happen again. Next time, just ask. Otherwise, things may not be so… cordial."

Chrys handed Shina a bushel of pears wrapped in a large leaf before sending the squad on their way. They didn't bother putting their masks back on since they had already breathed the spores and eaten the fruit.

The feelings of being an alien were no longer with them. They felt welcome as they traveled outward. The team had learned a lot about the Mad Grove; more than anyone else at DLC for sure. They also learned that they still didn't know much at all. They arrived back at the motorcycles. The sight of technology reminded them of their mission. All of the strange emotions and collective feelings shared between them had faded. They felt like themselves again; in control.

Shina: "Jin, how're you feeling right now?"

Jin: "Kind of like I let someone else drive my car and now everything's out of place."

Shina: "That's a weird way to put it, but I think I know what you mean. I'll let Oska know."

It suddenly dawned on Shina that she had not received any COMMs from Oska since they had arrived at the fringes of the Grove.

Shina: "Have you heard from Oska since we got here?"

Jin: "Now that you mention it, no."

Shina made several attempts to contact Oska; trying every possible setting. She then realized that her COMMs device was disabled. Jin's was the same. After turning it back on, Shina immediately COMMed Oska.

Shina: "Oska come in. This is 4A Squad reporting."

Oska: "What the hell happened out there? Are you two okay?"

Shina: "Affirmative. We're fine and there was no threat or danger. The asset *was* compromised, but is not in danger of falling into enemy hands. We're en route DLC."

Oska: "Copy. I got readings here saying that you manually turned off their COMMs equipment. Any reason?"

Shina: "We're not sure. Looking back, a lot of strange things occurred after we last contacted you. We'll debrief you when we get back. 4A Squad out."

They took their time driving back to the citadel. Shina and Jin still felt sluggish, but improved as time passed. Returning to the city felt almost as strange as arriving at the grove. Now *this* environment made them feel uncomfortable. The grove was nature thriving undisturbed. The city had become unnatural to them, yet awe inspiring. It was noisy, fast, and alive. Their minds fought to adjust to this environment again. By the time they returned to the Citadel, they felt completely like themselves again. Their minds were clear enough to recall the events of the mission in detail. Shina lead the way to the war room: A room specifically for special mission briefs. Nearly every mission brief and debrief that took place in this room and was attended by Damien, Oska, or Styner. The walls were laden with monitors depicting maps of areas all over the city and elsewhere. The screens gave the room a warm-blue hum. In the center of the room was a large round table with seven chairs spaced evenly apart. The table was large enough to comfortably seat another three chairs. Damien and Oska were already seated and awaiting for Shina and Jin to take theirs.

Damien: "First of all, welcome back. Glad to see you both back in one piece."

Shina: "Thank you. The mission was concluded without major incident."

Damien: "So I'm told. You mentioned that the asset was compromised."

Shina: "We never actually saw it. But we met someone from the Grove who said that they already had taken care of the hazard spout and that our help wasn't needed."

Damien: "I didn't know people lived there"

Jin: "He was a Tchrnn. And now that I think about it, would explain a lot of things."

Damien: "A Tchrnn? You mean those stories people tell kids to keep them from wandering into the Grove? Just start from before you lost contact with Oska. We'll get back to this Tchrnn."

Damien wasn't thrown off by the mention of something seemingly fantastic. He was more intrigued to get to the bottom of the story.

Shina: "The last COMMs I remember hearing from Oska was a few minutes before we parked the motorcycles, telling us the approximate location of the spout. At some point after that, we all switched our COMMs equipment off."

Oska: "You switched off about forty minutes after we spoke. I didn't know if it was mission related, so I waited before trying to request alert messages. I didn't hear anything from you until you switched all of your equipment back on."

Shina: "Before you ask why, we think the Grove pheromones altered our judgement. The equipment provided didn't do much once we were deep inside."

Jin: "The equipment was fine. But I think you were right about the Tchrnn patrolling the edges of the Grove. He was probably following us ever since we started walking, infecting us with his Pheromones, and then started messing with us once we were further in. I noticed you started acting a little strange."

Shina: "Why didn't you say anything?"

Jin: "I was freaking out too. I could tell something was wrong, I just couldn't do anything about it."

Damien: "So the Tchrnn pheromones are more potent than regular grove spores?"

Shina: "Yes, Jin knows more about the Grove."

Damien: "What exactly is a Tchrnn? I didn't know they were real."

Jin: "Tchrnn are a species of people that live in the Grove. They're sentient plants that defend the grove. They're really secretive and don't trust outsiders. We got lucky though; this one seemed to like us. At least he liked Shina."

Shina: "Very lucky. If he wanted to kill us, he wouldn't have had any trouble. The pheromones made us completely docile. It never occurred to me that he was an enemy. He talked us into taking off our masks and eating pears."

Jin: "Speaking of which…"

Jin set the wrapped leaf bag on the table and opened it, revealing a pile of kaleido pears.

Jin: "He was nice enough to give a few of these if anybody wants some."

Oska looked at the fruit with a hunger in her eyes but resisted. She glanced over at Damien to see his reaction. He remained stoic as always. Then slowly, reached a hand out and grabbed one and set it in front of him. Oska followed suit, but with more enthusiasm.

Damien: "Let me get this straight: Instead of extracting the hazard spout, you were manipulated by a Tchrnn and sent home with a bunch of fruit without even so much as asking how they contained it or what they were planning to do with it?"

Shina: "That is correct."

Jin: "Well, we *did* ask why; he just didn't tell us."

Damien sat silently for a moment as he mulled over the information. His posture didn't change, nor did his face and his eyes ever-hidden behind his shades.

Damien: "I suppose if the enemy didn't get it, then it's not a loss. And now we have some information about the Grove. Good work rolling out this mission Oska. Same for you two. Good work."

Damien nodded at Shina, dismissing her from the meeting.

Damien: "Jin, we need to talk."

Jin: "Sure, what's up?"

Damien: "You seem to know a decent amount about the Grove. I want you and Shina to get with Oska and expand on our files. It's not urgent, but I'm putting you in charge of that project."

Jin: "No problem. Anything else?"

Damien: "I hear you've been working pretty hard getting settled in and that you've made a decent name for yourself down here. You've gotten to see our little home and how we do things. It takes a lot of trust to let a stranger into your home. Trust I don't normally share but thanks to Oska, I gave it a shot. I gave *you* a shot. And so far, I think it was a good call."

Jin: "Thank you…There's another "but" isn't there?"

Damien: "But we've come to a bit of a snag with your background check."

Jin: "Are you checking on my credit history? I know it's bad, but I plan on fixing it soon. I promise."

Damien: "Actually, you don't have any credit. While unusual, isn't a problem. The problem is that there isn't much of anything on you. There's only mention of your last job and a few apartments which is pretty suspicious."

Jin: "I can see how that's a problem. Look, if you're thinking that I'm some kind of corporate spy or something, they would have made up a background that would be at least somewhat believable."

Oska: "We considered that. It's *too* weird to be falsified."

Jin: "You don't have to be worried about me. I'm just a nobody from nowhere."

Damien: "I'm sure. Why don't you give us the full story?"

Jin: "Okay. My background is borderline blank because I don't have one. I wasn't born in the city. And I didn't legally become a citizen either. No birth certificate, no diplomas, no medical or police records, no license even though I've been here for almost twelve years. I worked off the record and got paid under the table doing odd jobs until I finally managed to join the legal world with my courier job. I'm just a guy trying to make a living."

Damien: "The city life usually draws in teens one way or another."

Jin: "Not quite. I didn't know anything about the city. I didn't even know what a city was. My mentor brought me here. He showed me a path into the city and when I came out on the other side he was nowhere to be seen. Just up and left me. Ever since then, it's just been me, my wit, and my sword."

Damien: "That explains a lot then. You were just a stray. In that case, you're doing well for yourself. Not a lot of strays can keep their noses clean and integrate into society. It can get pretty rough out there."

Jin: "It wasn't so bad. You learn a lot of things growing up on your own."

Oska: "That's one of the most depressing things I've ever heard."

Damien: "What happened to your mentor?"

Jin: "No idea. I haven't heard a thing from him since. I'm pretty pissed at him but at least he set me up for success. If you're wondering, yeah, he did teach me what I know about the Grove."

Damien: "Noted. That's all for now. We'll pry more another time. Good job on your first mission. There will be others. Dismissed."

Jin made his exit.

Oska: "So he can fight, has no connections, *and* he has knowledge about things we don't. And you almost walked away from him."

Damien: "I still have to feel him out. I'll take him with me to see Vangard. It'll be good for him to be seen with me."

05– MOTHERBOARD

-The heart, soul, and foundation of any good computer.-

Oska's sidearm chirped for her attention; it was never
silent for long. As DLC's mission and systems overseer, there
was never a shortage of work for her; work that often
overflowed into her personal time as well. But as exhausting as it
was, she loved being a pivotal part of DLC. She knew that if she
decided to take a personal day without proper planning, the
flow of the Citadel would be disrupted to say the least. Her
parents would undoubtedly be proud of her job but the nature of
her work was nearly exclusively classified so she must settle
with the public title of "Secretary". Her parents are proud of her
nonetheless, and her peers are impressed as well although more
so with the money she made.

Oska's constant workflow through the noon season
wore heavily on her the closer the dusk season drew near. Even
the basic task of dragging herself out of bed had become a
challenge. She attempted to hold on for a few more minutes
before beginning her long cycle of sitting in front of her
computer. It chirped again, and again, and again until it became
an endless choir of beeps and chirps. Accepting that her peace

had been ruined, she grabbed her sidearm to gauge her duties for the cycle. The alerts were from all over DLC: Inquiries, mission updates, and check-ins. Her sidearm was ideal for keeping her abreast of the happenings around the citadel, but not for handling them. She would need her battle station for that. She headed there post-haste.

Exiting the dormitories, she had to pass the clinic; an area that she always attempted to scurry past as quickly as possible. She swore that she could feel the doctor watching her as she passed his office. As usual, his light was off. A wave of relief washed over her. Turning the corner, she saw the object of her angst: Dr. Malerius Jackson. A chill surged up Oska's spine. Malerius was one of the non-æthean races who worked in the citadel. The term "æthean" defines the most common sentient humanoid beings of the moon (Veast are a slight evolutionary offshoot of ætheans). Ætheans are not to be confused with ætherlings; which describes all inhabitants of planet Æther. He was an akashean; a being born of the planet Akasha. Malerius had long ears, budding tusks from either side of his chin, and a mane of curly brown hair but otherwise greatly resembled an æthean. He was usually seen wearing the standard DLC working uniform and an easy-going smile.

Malerius: "Oska, I haven't seen you lately. Where are you skittering off to now?"

His voice was calm and relaxing, so much so that it felt unnatural. No one would seriously talk the way he did Oska thought.

Oska: "Work. I have a lot of it to catch up on. So if you'll excuse me…"

Malerius took a step to block Oska's path. His hands clasped behind his back. Oska took a step away to meet his eyes, and to be out of his proximity.

Malerius: "I'm sure there's plenty to be done. There always is. You look stressed. Is there anything I should be concerned about?"

Oska: "No, I just want to do my job. That's all."

Malerius: "Don't we all. But we can't let ourselves get so into our jobs that it takes away from us personally. Your job is very demanding Oska. I can't imagine you doing any more than you already do."

Oska: "It's fine. I just keep busy working and I don't notice it."

Malerius: "I'm afraid that you don't let yourself relax. And one day you're going to put too much on yourself and have a break down. I would like to have a day with you to help you relax so that doesn't happen."

Oska: "You know I can't take a day off. We've been through this."

Malerius: "I know. I can't make you come to my office. But when you push yourself too hard, everyone is going to look to me and ask "How did you let this happen." I want them to know that I did everything I could. I'll speak to Damien about getting you some time off. I'm sure there are some child labor laws being violated with the hours you work. We *will* talk Oska. One way or another."

Oska: "Thanks for the concern Doc."

Oska slithered past Malerius, who didn't move an inch to let her pass. The conversation would have felt sincere if it weren't for the last thing he said. It only reasserted the thoughts that Oska already had. She made a mental note to talk to Damien before Malerius did.

Cutting across the hangar was the fastest way to get to the upper offices where she and Damien did all of their computer and administrative work, although the hangar was full of people who would no doubt need her for something. It was a calculated risk that she was willing to take. The worst that could come of it was that she'd address another pending issue. Work continued and bustled as always: engineers and technicians tested and repaired vehicles and military materiel; new recruits were being pushed and hazed through their basic training. Oska was especially grateful that she didn't have to go through basic training being that she could barely tolerate her training with Damien.

One of the engineers perked up when he noticed Oska passing through.

Abrasive Engineer: "Hey! Don't run. C'mere."

It was Heiretsu, the head engineer at DLC. He spoke on behalf of the engineers and conducted business with Damien, Styner, and Oska to acquire the parts required to build and repair the equipment. A true genius at his job; he helped develop many of Eratech's experimental weaponry. This more than made up for the fact that he seemed to enjoy antagonizing non-engineers. Unlike Malerius, Heiretsu always seemed to be at work (to be exact; he was only ever seen in the hangar). Heiretsu calls himself an Illuminaught: A being whose body consists entirely of light. For the sake of other creatures, he wears a dark body suit with a black tinted helmet and describes his body as a twinkling star in the night sky, only close enough to touch. He claims that he came to Æther from beyond but is always fuzzy on the details of how. DLC was more than happy to have him around, whatever his reasons for being here are.

Oska: "What do you need? Keep in mind I'm in a hurry."

Heiretsu: "I'm in a hurry too. But I can't hurry when my people gotta wait around for parts."

Oska: "Are you still waiting on parts? I put the order in a week ago."

Heiretsu: "Yeah, I know. They do this every time. We order the parts and they take a week before they realize they ain't even started putting our order together. Then we gotta wait another week. They deliver half the damn parts, and we *still* gotta drive down there and pick up the rest ourselves. Why do we keep giving them money? Doesn't Damien own the district? Can't he make them…? I don't know, better?"

Oska: "We can't just make people *do* anything. That would defeat the purpose of free enterprise. But I think you're right…"

Heiretsu: "I know I'm right."

Oska: "The only reason we haven't moved on to a new provider is because no one else makes those parts."

Heiretsu: "How 'bout this? We get this last order, and then the money we used to pay them we invest in house so I can set up something to where we manufacture our own parts."

Oska: "That's not a bad idea if you feel like putting in the work to make it happen. And I think Damien would like the idea of being even more self-sufficient. I'll pitch it to him, but it's not something that'll happen any time soon."

Heiretsu: "Why do I have to wait so long for everything? Nah, I'm playin'. That sounds good. Thanks."

Heiretsu returned to his team and Oska wasted no time getting back on her way. The rest of her path to the upper offices was uninterrupted. She plopped down at the battle station, already feeling the weight of the cycle. She then realized that she hadn't eatin yet. Luckily she had convinced Damien to put a refrigerator in the office. He hated the æsthetic of it and almost never used it himself, but Oska took advantage of it. It needed to be restocked. She had already eaten her favorite flash cooker snacks and now there was only a sad pair of boiled coiler eggs wrapped in a small plastic bag. Oska made do.

The computer fired up. It responded to her presence as she sat in front of it and it read her hand and eye movements. It was designed to be as intuitive to her needs as possible. Oska needed a computer that could keep up with her. Here at her station, Oska truly was the heart and soul of the Citadel.

Oska: "Greetings Citadel. I hear your prayers and bestow upon you my blessing."

She said jokingly to herself as she always did starting her shift. The monitors lit up and Oska immediately began reading through the alerts. Two of them were addressed on her way up: Dr. Malerius and Heiretsu no longer needed to see her. The next alert that caught her attention was the anomaly from Grave Town. The map alerted her with the message "anomaly unknown". Whenever she tried to delve further into the issue, it would only repeat the message. Oska decided that she'd come back to it as more timely alerts were pending.

The urgent alerts were from DLC specialist team known simply as DL: A team consisting of unique and singular individuals that operated in tandem to satisfy the most urgent and paramount of DLC missions. The team was barely spoken of among most of the company personnel. The only people who knew any details about the team were: Medical staff for tending injuries, Oska (who is an honorary member herself) for mission dispatch, and intelligence, Malerius for performing psych evaluations of team members after traumatic missions, Heiretsu, who helped develop weapons and equipment, and Shina who could be called on at any time to provide support.

DL was conducting a mission in Old Light. The alert was from standing team leader: Bianca Calenite; AKA Grihm. Grihm's strong-will and honest heart had earned her the right to lead the team in Damien's absence. Everyone knew they could count on her to make sure everyone made it home. Her specialty was an almost paradoxical combination of explosives and covert operations. Oska COMMed Grihm.

Oska: "Come in Grihm. I received your alert and am requesting a status update."

Grihm answered back immediately as if she were waiting.

Grihm: "Have you read the data-burst I sent you?"

Oska had not in her haste. She saw that one had been sent but hadn't had the chance to read it.

Oska: "Requesting up-to-date details."

Grihm: "Hallowed eyes, Black Soulz, and Gnashing Teeth are deep into it right now. Black Soulz has almost been killed off by both gangs. It looks like the other two didn't like them moving up in the world."

Oska: "And how're the other two?"

Grihm: "Hallowed Eyes seems to be doing the best, but barely."

Oska: "What's your position? How're you watching all of this?"

Grihm: "We *were* watching from inside of an apartment but someone spotted us and we got dragged into the fight. At least Saber did. She's down there now working both sides."

Oska: "Got it, I'll check in with Saber. Oska out."

Oska switched channels to reach Saber. Saber's real name is Salena Bellard. Saber was largely indifferent to team work. Her largest contribution was being skilled at covert operations, intelligence gathering, stealth, and assassination. She was usually on the field first. Missions often began with her.

Oska: "Come in Saber. Status update."

Saber: "Wait one."

There was the sound of a scuffle coming from Saber's microphone followed by pleading.

Frightened voice: "Please no, I give up. What do you want from me?"

Saber: "Smart choice."

There were sounds of shuffling followed by a long silence. Saber returned to COMMs.

Saber: "I forgot to turn the mic off. I'm sorry you had to hear that."

Oska: "It's fine. I'm glad you let that one go."

Saber: "So is he."

Oska: "Grihm made it sound like there wasn't much for you to do out there."

Saber: "Not anymore. Everyone's starting to disperse. Grihm's keeping over-watch and Sev and Trigger are standing by for stragglers but I don't think it'll come to that.

Oska: "Got it. Thanks for the update."

Oska switched again, this time to reach Trigger. His real name is Amon-Ræ. Trigger was extremely friendly and seen as the big brother of the team and the only person whose moral compass may be straighter than Grihm's. Despite this however, he tended to keep a lot to himself. Originally hired as an extra gunner for the team, he had proven to be an excellent sniper as well. Oska contacted him over Sev because Sev was the newest and youngest member of DL. His birth name was Sayaires Rasa but he's Sev to DL. Sev was Oska's age and one of her school-mates during the dawn and dusk seasons. And while he was Oska's age, he had an entirely different set of skills. As Oska spent countless hours alone learning computers and technology, taking in everything she could on the subject, Sev grew up in a different environment. His parents were former DLC personnel and he was surrounded by the structured military lifestyle. His military knowledge is only hindered by his lack of experience, which is why he is always paired with a senior member during missions. Until he found his niche, he was primarily tasked with support and cover fire.

Oska: "Trigger come in. Requesting status update."

Trigger: "Yes ma'am. Status is awesome."

A laugh slipped out of Oska.

Oska: "Confirmed. How's Sev?"

Sev: "Good I guess. The gangs are falling back. "

Trigger: "Between all of the fighting and Saber's interference, all three gangs are done for. They'd have to ban together if they want to survive at this point."

Oska: "Got it. If you're finished there, rendezvous with the others and return home. You know the routine; debrief with Damien and dismiss."

Trigger: "The ol' three-D. Best part of a mission. We'll see you soon lady."

Sev: "Bye Oska."

Oska: "Bye Sev. Oska out."

Oska leaned back in her chair and took a deep breath. She swirled around all the pending tasks ahead of her, setting her priorities. Anything involving Damien came first. Not because of urgency, but because when he was involved, he would take a lot of the workload. She reached forward to contact Damien on her computer.

Oska: "Come in Damien. I have an update on DL."

Damien: "Hit me."

The voice came from behind, startling Oska. Damien was already in the room.

Oska: "Update: The team's finishing up and they're heading home soon. The gangs took each other out."

Damien: "That's good. I'm not going to be around for debrief so Styner's going to take this one."

Oska: "Got it. So… where're you going?"

Damien: "Jin and I are going to meet with Vangard."

Oska: "I almost forgot about that. Do you have any idea of what Vangard wants? It's weird that *he* set up a meeting with you this time."

Damien: "No idea, but at least we now have a set location for him."

Oska: "Good luck out there."

Damien: "Anything else for me?"

Oska turned back to her computer to bring up the unknown anomaly. Nothing had changed.

Oska: "Yeah. I'm still trying to figure out the Grave town anomaly. I want to get some eyes on it. I can't do anything from here."

Damien: "Finally, something that computer *can't* do."

Oska: "That's not a good thing."

Damien: "Talk to Saber about it after debrief."

06– A NEW CHALLENGER APPROACHES

-…And what makes you think this is all that I'm capable of?-

One of the many perks of being an employee of DLC was that everyone was given everything they needed. If you didn't have a home you could stay at the base; family included. Medical and pharmaceutical needs were met and you were part of a community. Jin found he enjoyed this aspect the most. More people had begun to recognize him as a familiar face. Something he had never been before.

Jin's phone rang in his pocket. There weren't many numbers saved in it but it came with Damien's, who was calling him. Jin answered.

Jin: "What's up boss?"

Damien: "Grab your shit and meet me in the hangar."

Jin: "Got it. Something wrong?"

Damien: "There will be if you don't hurry up."

Damien disconnected. Jin wasn't sure if the phone call was a good or bad one. He returned to his room to grab Hermes and left immediately. Damien was waiting in the hangar next to the elevator Jin rode on his first day coming into the base. Damien was wearing a light tactical vest; Jin could still tell that there were guns tucked underneath.

Jin: "Ready when you are boss."

They rode the elevator to the dark room again. Jin didn't remember the path to avoid tripping on things and once again plowed his way across.

Jin: "Are you ever gonna clean this place up?"

Damien: "It's not high on my list."

They walked outside briefly only to reenter the garage annex. The door opened revealing Damien's muscle car. Jin enthusiastically jumped in. Damien fired up the beast and they blazed off. Jin killed the silence with a question.

Jin: "Where are we headed?"

Damien: "Do you remember your run-in with Scratch?"

Jin: "Yeah. Has it been sixteen cycles already?"

Damien: "It's been busy."

Jin: "If it's just a meeting, why'd you want to bring me along? I'm sure Oska or Styner would've been more useful."

Damien: "True. But this isn't supposed to be anything major. We're just meeting to catch up. It shouldn't take too long."

Jin: "I didn't think you were friends."

Damien: "We aren't. Vangard's been quiet for a little longer than I like. I want to keep a close eye on him to make sure he's not up to anything sneaky."

Jin: "That makes more sense. But it sounds like he's been up to no good anyway. He's at least had *something* to do with *Cyclebreak*."

Damien: "That's on the list of things to catch up on."

Jin caught onto what Damien meant by "catch up".

Jin: "What does Vangard do? How does he make money?"

Damien: "He has his hands all over the place; but primarily information broking. So he actually makes some money from the Citadel. But he's also known to conduct other businesses as well. He used to operate in Revco selling mind blank on the streets. But when they cleaned up the district his business was one of the first things that had to go. He tried it here but we put a stop to it again."

Jin: "Blank, as in Mind Blank? I hear that's pretty nasty stuff. Never seen anyone strung out on it though; no one in my circle had that kind of money. Why'd you let him continue working here?"

Damien: "He talked his way out. So far he's kept his word but he stretches the meaning behind his promises. His info broking is the main reason though."

Jin: "Aren't you worried he's selling info to Revco or something?"

Damien: "There's nothing to sell. At least not that he knows of. No one at the citadel has any connections to Vangard."

Damien parked the car on a sidewalk in front of an alley. It led to an old warehouse covered in graffiti that was tucked away from the eyes of the street. There was a front door which they ignored as they walked to an alcove in the wall with two veasts standing inside. Once they laid eyes on Damien, stirred to life and kept their hands near their weapons.

Damien: "Easy fellas. I'm just here to talk to Vangard."

Veast guard: "I should drop you for what you did to our boys at *Cyclebreak*."

Damien: "I wasn't looking for a fight then either but I found myself in a similar situation."

The veast guard sneered in Damien's face.

Veast guard: "You don't scare me. Vangard can make me work with the other gangs for now but I draw the line with you. Best step off."

Damien looked at the other guard who didn't share the same animosity toward Damien as his counterpart; he shook his head and stepped back. Damien palmed the offensive guards face and slammed it into the wall as he brandished his gun and rammed the barrel into his chest. Damien's finger leaned on the trigger. He stopped just before it fired. He thought better of it; not wanting to introduce Jin to brute force diplomacy. Even though Jin had already seen Damien use it to solve his problem at *Cyclebreak*, he wasn't the first to strike then. Killing this man here would certainly make Damien the aggressor. He threw the guard to the ground, sparing his life.

Damien: "If you so much as make eye contact with me on my way out, you're dead."

Damien lit up a cigarette and took a hard drag. Jin remained quiet throughout the altercation but kept a casual hand on his hilt. Damien and Jin powered through a second set of doors into Vangard's warehouse. They were hit with a wall of sounds reminiscent of the DLC hangar but on a smaller scale: machinery moving, voices directing movements of crates, boxes, and supplies. It was too busy for anyone to have noticed that the two of them had entered. Damien stepped prominently through the warehouse, daring someone to stop him. They exited the warehouse floor by ascending a set of stairs that led to an overhead office. The office was lavishly decorated and somewhat out of place in the warehouse. The floor had black and white checkered tiles with a red rug accented with gold embroidery that led directly ahead to a large polished wooden desk. The entire back wall was adorned with a book shelf of the same finish as the desk. The shelves were decorated with a variety of items ranging from books, an unidentifiable animal skull, telescope, and tiny chests. In either corner of the office stood abstract golden statues of what may be considered art to some, but wasn't attractive in its own right. In the center of it all sat Vangard: A veast with pale skin, piercing gold eyes, and striking crimson hair that stood on end like fire. His face was effeminate, but it didn't take away from his overall intensity. He wore a black suit, red dress shirt, with golden cufflinks and a matching tie clip. Standing beside the desk was Scratch; wearing a black strapless gothic dress that showed off her fair-skin. She had removed all of her face piercings and Jin found her more attractive than he had before. She had a unique beauty about her and a style that accentuated her distinct traits.

Vangard stood up to greet Damien and Jin as they entered, making his way around his large desk. His tone and gestures are open and inviting but felt forced; as if he were an actor on a stage.

Vangard: "I was just getting ready to call you. I was beginning to wonder if something happened."

Damien: "One of your door guards wasn't a fan. I had to him straight."

Vangard: "You killed Benny? He was stupid but his grandmother is such a nice lady. I'll send her flowers."

Damien: "Relax. I didn't kill anyone. At least not on the way in."

Vangard: "Amazing bit of restraint on your part. Benny's a good worker. He's loyal if not uninformed; as you are aware now."

Vangard cut his sharp eyes toward Jin.

Vangard: "So *you're* Jin. Scratch told me all about your little scuffle. I'm impressed, she's a skilled fighter. Hands down my best."

Jin: "If you say so."

Scratch rolled her eyes, letting the jab pass over her.

Vangard: "And to think, I was so close to employing you."

Damien: "I could say the same about Scratch."

Scratch tilted her head in curiosity, but remained silent. Vangard offered Damien and Jin seats which Damien initially declined. Jin quickly took his seat, reminding Damien that not every situation required him to be at the ready and standing for intimidation; he took his seat as well. The chairs were hedonistically comfortable. Vangard watched the tension ease out of Damien as he sank into the seat.

Vangard: "I'm sure you're a busy man Damien so I won't waste your time. I wanted to meet with you to clear the air. I want to put the fear of you kicking down my doors and killing all of my people behind me. I want to come clean."

Damien: "You have my attention. But it's going to take more than empty promises to make that happen."

Vangard: "I agree. On both our parts."

Damien's eyebrow rose above his shades in curious annoyance.

Vangard: "Not that I expect any initial effort from you. I need to keep you informed of my actions. Of my movements. I can be very busy when I set my eyes on a goal. And that in turn will require you to be just as busy trying to keep up."

Damien: "Then let's start from the top. The last I heard from you, you were going to clean up the last of the blank you were trying to deal in the district. That was almost a year ago."

Vangard: "I *have* kept that promise. In fact I've gone above and beyond the call. When I first came here, I almost immediately began teaching individuals how to cook up mind blank to make new product for me. Individuals who would use their new found skills and money to startup their own gangs. You might know them as: Hallowed Eyes, Black Soulz, and Gnashing Teeth."

Damien: "You're not making a good case for yourself."

Vangard: "Not yet. I sought to fix this mistake but I couldn't go in guns blazing like you. So I had to fix the problem the only way I know how: manipulation. I convinced the various gangs one by one that Black Soulz was being sponsored and needed to be dealt with before they became too powerful as evident by their new spot *Cyclebreak*."

Damien: "I was there and they said that you were their sponsor."

Vangard: "I was. A lie is easier to sell but the truth brings customers back. The other two gangs came together to fight the threat but they each thought that the other was receiving support from the district. And the alliance broke mid-fight."

Damien "You instigated a gang war and used DL to turn them against each other."

Vangard: "I told you I'd undo my mess. The gangs are gone and so is the blank."

Damien: "Gangs don't just disappear."

Vangard: "Well no. They just find other gangs. I've taken the remnants of each and hired them to work for me. Now I have a work force and the streets are clean. Everybody wins."

Damien wasn't pleased with the idea of being manipulated, but was satisfied with the results. Vangard *did* keep to his promise in his own twisted way.

Damien: "Congratulations, you broke even."

Vangard: "Good. I'm glad that you agree. As I recall, you were also looking for me. Did I answer your questions already or did you need something else?"

Damien: "You and I haven't had the best communication in the past. We need to fix that. I'm glad to see you working to be more legitimate, but that can only work if we stay in touch. What're your plans for the future? I know you're not going to just settle where you are now."

Vangard: "I haven't decided yet. So much was resting on you. For now I can keep up with info broking. But I'll have to sell to anyone looking for information to make ends meet."

Damien: "You could stop blowing so much money on all of this crap for starters."

Damien gestured to the wall of oddities behind Vangard. Vangard seemed disappointed at Damien's lack of appreciation for his decorations.

Vangard: "Some of these are relics and treasures from when this city was just a settlement. They are actually worth quite a lot of money. In a sense, I'm a curator and this office is a small exhibit of antiquity. Certainly worth more than I paid out. "Investments" is the word you're looking for."

Damien: "Unless you open up a museum to the public and charge for admission, they're expenses."

Vangard: "Maybe I plan to do that in the future. I have a *lot* of freight downstairs being moved."

Damien: "And what would that be?"

Vangard: "Just leftovers from gang bosses. Nothing you'd be interested in. But now that we've established that the slate is clean, what are you offering for information. If you want to know something, you'll have to give me something useful in return."

Damien realized his folly by forgiving Vangard's debt before making his own proposition. Not one to go back on his word, Damien took it as a lesson to pay more attention when dealing with Vangard.

Damien: "I don't care about your business unless it's shady. And if it is, it'd be best if you come clean now."

Vangard: "You might care if I know something about Grave town."

Damien's eyebrow rose again. This time from genuine curiosity.

Vangard: "I'm glad I have your interest but *that* information is premium. I can't give it away for free."

Damien: "Fine. You don't have to bother with the cleanup effort for the mess you made with the gangs."

Vangard: "I've already started on that."

Damien: "I'll personally approve your next business investment."

Vangard: "Meh…"

Damien sat back in his seat and stroked his beard. There was a long silence of anticipation of his next words.

Damien: "This better be good information. *Cyclebreak*: I'll cover all expenses to rebuild and overhaul it as long as it's not anything ridiculous. But in the future, I'll grant you freedom to create and run businesses within my district but all propositions *will* be made by you in person."

Vangard: "Wow, a brute *and* a businessman. I'll take that deal. You must really need this information."

Damien and Vangard hardily shook hands. Jin had almost no idea of what had just occurred. The business world was alien to him. He wasn't sure but seemed to him like Vangard was the winner of this transaction.

Vangard: "I say this is cause for a celebration. Scratch, four glasses of the Mirage whiskey."

Scratch poured four glasses and dropped a few whiskey stones in each. She looked at her glass pensively as Vangard raised his.

Vangard: "To renewed business friendship. May it forever prosper."

Everyone downed the drink. It was smooth, with a distinct after taste that no one was able to identify. It's always described differently by everyone each time they drink it. And after exhaling, the taste shifted one last time. Damien considered finding a bottle of his own.

Vangard: "Now back to business. I'm going to go out on a limb here and guess you're also aware that something is happening in Grave town."

Damien: "We've been tracking something for a few cycles now.

Vangard: "I Thought so. And you'd be right to be concerned. A cult has recently taken residence in the cathedral. They call themselves *The Black Tempest Cult*. Normally that wouldn't be anything worth mentioning, but this cult is modern, militarized and lead by a scientist of sorts. He's discovered something recently and whatever it is has inspired a following and brought in enough money to continue his experiments. I'll give you this last little bit: What he's doing is big enough to grab *other* people's attention. I'd tread carefully if I were you."

Damien: "Other people? Who else knows about it?"

Vangard responded with an insidious smile; a smile that spoke the answer to Damien.

Damien: "Vangard, Scratch."

Damien stormed out of the office without another word. Jin looked about confused. Attempting to put together the missing pieces but to no avail. Damien immediately called Oska when he got in the car.

Oska: "How'd everything go?"

Damien: "Good. Too good. Did you find out anything about Grave Town?"

Oska: "Still getting weird readings, but Saber's on her way there."

Damien: "Tell her to keep her head down and be on the lookout for other scouts."

Oska: "Other scouts? Oh shit. Got it."

Jin: "Question. *Questions* actually."

Damien realized how quickly everything most have moved for Jin. He was used to working with people who were as well informed as he.

Damien: "The Black Tempest Cult is a group of crazies living on the fringes and underbelly of the city who mostly get together to worship some bogus-ass ancient god. But it looks like they've actually gotten into something heavy and it's gotten Revco's attention."

Jin: "Revco? *Those* are the other guys you keep mentioning?"

Damien: "Is that a problem?"

Jin: "You're asking if competing against Revco is a problem? The city of cities? Yeah, that's a problem. Why do they care about anything that happens over here? Don't they just do city development, marketing, mass media, and all that other shit?"

Damien: "That's the big question. But if what's going on is big enough to grab their attention and send people skulking around our district, then we need to address the issue before they have a chance. When we get back, meet with Styner and gear up. It's time for your first DL mission."

*   *   *

Vangard sat at his desk, contemplating the reasoning behind Damien's uncharacteristically generous offer. Scratch sat on the edge of the desk, twirling a knife by the wire.

Vangard: "I don't get it. He didn't get violent, he didn't threaten me. He just came to talk."

Scratch: "He must've *really* wanted that information. Actually, I'm surprised you told him that one."

Vangard: "It was fresh on my mind. Like I said, the truth brings customers back. And Damien is a valuable customer."

Scratch: "I have a question: Was Damien actually scouting me before you hired me?"

Vangard: "Yeah. That's what he does. But working for him wouldn't have given you the same opportunities as I've given you. You'd just be one of his little *specialists*, doing whatever he bid. Here, you help me run things. You're my left *and* right hand. My eyes and ears on the street. I wouldn't be able to work as well without you. You are half of my best assets."

Scratch: "Whatever. You just had me pour drinks."

Vangard: "Because you're my left and right hands. I could sit all day and remind you of all the things you do here, but you already know that. Honestly, I trust you to run everything without me."

Scratch: "Now there's a thought."

07– THE BLACK TEMPEST CULT

*- Gnarled ebon spire atop a crown of scale. Lightning strikes the
mountain peak and the planet shudders.-*

Jin wasn't keen on the idea of wearing a uniform of any
kind but understood the practicality of combat attire. He donned
the uniform. It was a perfect fit; the boots were light and flexible
to allow Jin to freely move around without feeling restricted. The
pants and jacket were thin and also didn't feel cumbersome. The
belt even had a slot to sheath Hermes. Jin's fighting style had
been taken into consideration when this was being prepared.

Styner: "How's it feel?"

Jin: "Like a second skin."

Styner: "Good. Now head to the war room."

Jin: "Do you know anything about this mission?"

Styner: "They'll tell you at the brief in the war room. I'll see you
at dispatch."

Jin set out to attend the brief. Sitting at the war room
table was Damien, Oska, and three other people Jin didn't

recognize; a woman, and two men. Upon closer inspection, one of the men was actually a teen. He looked to be about Oska's age, but was built like a weight lifter. His size threw off Jin's initial guess. Jin counted eight chairs at the table this time.

Damien: "Alright, let's get started. I'm just going to assume that most of you haven't met yet. This is Jin, our most recent specialist. He's proving to be an increasingly capable fighter although he hasn't been tested yet. I'm giving him the benefit of the doubt because I think he can handle himself for this mission and it'll be a great chance for him to meet the team. Jin, this is Grihm, Trigger, and Sev. You've already met Oska and Styner. And you'll meet Saber in the field. Welcome to DL."

Jin: "Wow, thank you."

Grihm: "That's pretty high praise coming from Damien. Actually, any praise is high coming from Damien. Don't expect a lot of it."

Grihm was a woman with short, spikey blonde hair. She had green eyes. She was slightly taller than most women, but not so much as to stand out. When she spoke she flashed a smile at Jin. It was a gorgeous smile.

Grihm: "Joking aside; if Damien thinks you can handle yourself on a mission already, you must've really impressed him."

Trigger: "You look like a pretty laid back guy, which is good because Damien brings the mood down. He doesn't like jokes."

Trigger spoke with an outskirts drawl that had faded some no doubt from living in the city. He had brown hair tied in a ponytail that draped over his shoulder and a stubbly beard. He was a stern man with a steadfast gaze and cool blue eyes.

Sev: "Hey… That's all I got."

Now that Jin had a moment to look at him, Jin was certain Sev was about Oska's age. There was no facial hair on his exuberant face. His fine black hair was held back by a red bandana. He was large for his age.

Damien: "Right. You can talk more on your own time. The mission at hand is as follows: Several cycles ago Oska detected an anomaly in Grave Town but our systems couldn't make any sense of it."

Sev: "Is it a Hazard spout?"

Oska: "We have no problems getting Hazard readings. These readings were something different. Saber went ahead to see if she could get something more substantial from up close. The readings she sent us were closest to astral AP readings: a type of AP even rarer than Hazard. Other than that, the high levels of energy given off were sporadic and inconsistent."

Damien: "We're not sure what so much astral AP is used for, but it's definitely worth investigating."

Jin: "Astral AP is the use of space and distance: Instantly moving objects or energy from one location to another."

Grihm: "There are AP crystals that can teleport things?"

Jin: "AP crystals can consist of any element; even celestial ones."

Damien: "Meaning something's coming here, or something's leaving. If it's leaving, I want to know where it's going. If it's coming here, I want to make sure it's not going to be a problem."

Trigger: "Okay, so we got this astral thing goin' on, whatever. My question is: whose doin' it?"

Damien: "A cult called *The Black Tempest*. They've been around for a while but have never been anyone of note."

Sev: "If it's just a cult, can't we just go rough 'em up?"

Damien: "We won't if we don't have to. But cults aren't known for being reasonable."

Grihm: "So we got a cult doing dark stuff; what's our goal then?"

Damien: "As of right now, we're going to observe. If it's nothing we'll walk away. But if it ends up being something more, we're going to put a stop to it. Grihm, bring your demolition kit. If we see things get out of hand early enough, we'll solve the problem before it does. Even though this is currently a recon mission, we want to be prepared for a worst-case-scenario. Any other questions before we head out?"

There were none.

Damien: "Alright DL, let's move out."

All but Oska headed to the hangar for departure. Oska went to her battle station to oversee the mission. Styner was waiting in a covered troop transport truck for DL to arrive. After DL hopped into the back of the truck, Styner drove off. The ride was quiet save for the running of the engine and the sounds of the street passing them by. Not being a fan of silences, Grihm sparked up a conversation with Jin.

Grihm: "I think it's pretty cool to have another blade user around. Mind if I see?"

Jin unsheathed Hermes to show Grihm. It cast a glare across her face, highlighting her amid the dimness.

Jin: "Who's the other blade user?"

Grihm: "Saber. But she uses a tanto. I'm sure she'd love to talk blades with you sometime."

Trigger: "I'll give it to you; that's a fancy knife but I'll take a shooter any day."

Jin: "What happens if the enemy gets close?"

Trigger: "First: There're side arms for that. Second: If the enemy gets close, that means you all failed your jobs."

Jin: "Not a fan of the up-close fighting?"

Trigger: "Now I'ma stop you right there. I ain't afraid of being in the fight, but if I can finish something before that then I will. I ain't got nothin' to prove."

Jin: "I ain't… didn't mean it that way. It's good to have a sniper watching your back I guess. I've never worked with one. It sounds cool."

Grihm: "Does she have a name?"

Jin: "His name is Hermes."

Jin corrected politely. Sev wasn't part of the conversation. Jin noticed he had a pair of ear buds in and was listening to music. Grihm saw Jin's curiosity about Sev.

Grihm: "It helps him get into the right mind set. Don't worry, he'll be fine."

Jin didn't like the idea of such a young soldier, but felt it wasn't his place or the time to argue. He then thought about how he grew up. And while he wasn't a soldier, he had periods in his youth that exposed him to things that made him grow up faster than he should have; but always as fast as he needed to.

Jin glanced out of the truck to see they were entering the fringes of Eratech district. This route was different than the one he traveled on the way to the Mad Grove. The roads were still managed, although barely. There were hundreds of plots of land with rounded signs sticking out of them that resembled headstones.

Jin: "Grave Town. Now I get it. So what happened here?"

Damien: "All those signs you see are… were plots of land aimed at the massive amounts of people living in Superstructures over at Revco. The plan was to coerce them into moving here and raising the population. You know, so the district could get more Council support."

Jin: "I don't know, but go on."

Damien: "Shortly after Eratech began advertising to the Superstructure citizens, Revco began rush construction on that massive wall between our districts then implemented new laws targeted at the people living in the Superstructures which made it difficult and expensive for citizens to transfer districts. Once it became apparent the primary demographic was blockaded, the project was scrapped. Each headstone represents a dead dream."

Jin: "I guess Revco continued to get that extra council support?"

Damien: "Yep."

There was a bang from the front cabin.

Styner: "Five minutes!"

Damien knocked back. He leaned forward and held out his palm. A small device in his hand lit up, displaying a holographic map of a cathedral and surrounding area.

Damien: "Listen up. Saber and Oska could only get us so much information. Oska got us a layout of the inside based on historic records, which is pretty basic. It's essentially an open area broken up by rows of pillars. It looks like there's a second floor to one side that overlooks the main area, but that's all we could gather from these few pictures. The outside is also an open area; it sits on top of a hill that overlooks Grave Town."

Grihm: "Anything new about what's going on?"

Damien: "Negative. But we're about to meet up with Saber right now. Let's move."

The truck stopped and DL jumped out. The cathedral could be seen in the distance with the sun beaming just over its spires. The noon season sun was beginning its retreat toward the horizon, bringing the first changes of color in the skies and the misty amethyst glow of planet Akasha now more visible than it had been since dawn season. It was a refreshing sight among the eerie lot in which it was nestled. The cathedral grounds were expansive and as they approached, it began to look more like a defensive fort.

Grihm: "Damien, I thought you said cathedral, not a fortress. I don't know if I have enough explosives for this."

A new voice spoke that Jin hadn't heard yet.

Female voice: "Maybe I should've emphasized the scale more."

Jin looked around and saw a new woman standing between Damien and Grihm. It was Saber, the final member of DL. Her hair was a dark shade that carried a glimmer of violet in the light. She had olive skin that was speckled with unusual spots around the left side of her face, and intensity in her red eyes that oddly reminded him of Vangard. Saber was gorgeous but also short statured which also made her cute as well. Everything about her was exotic which only added to her appeal.

Damien: "No kidding. Notice any other scouts?"

Saber: "No. I don't think they've made it here yet. Unless they're hiding under patches of dirt, I would've seen them."

Her attention shifted to Jin and stepped to greet him.

Damien: "Jin, this is Saber: Our covert specialist."

Saber: "Is that all I am? Either way; it's nice to finally meet you Jin. Damien's told me a lot about you. I think you'll be a good addition."

As they approached the cathedral, they felt uncomfortable at the lack of life. No one was outside standing guard, no flapping or avian chirping, no insect calls; the silence was haunting. Entering the cathedral courtyard, they finally saw another person; an elderly man who was staring up at the sky motionless. He appeared to be looking at a tiny light glimmering on the surface of Akasha. The light flickered and the elderly man's enthrallment was broken. His glasses glared gently as he turned to face DL. He had a full beard speckled with strands of red and gray like a smoky fire. The hair on his head had the same coloration and spiked forward over his forehead.

Damien: "You with the guys inside?"

Saber elbowed Damien.

Saber: "Don't mind him. So what's going on up there?"

The old man cackled.

Old man: "I'm just talking with my friend. Go 'head, say "Hi" everybody."

Only Grihm and Saber waved awkwardly to the sky to humor the old man. If the others could see through his shades, they would've have seen Damien violently roll his eyes. Trigger and Jin weren't sure whether or not to take the situation seriously. Sev missed the entire conversation and only just removed his earbuds. The light flickered again as if in response to their greeting.

Old man: "He said hi… in his own way. But to answer your question shades: I'm not with those guys. I'm here for the same reason you are."

Damien: "I doubt that."

Old man: "You're not here to see the sites?"

Damien: "See the sites?"

Old man: "You're not tourists? You came here on a bus."

Damien: "I think you're a little late for cathedral tours. I don't know if you've noticed, but this areas been abandoned for decades."

Old man: "So it has. I figured I'd get one good look at the place before hoodlums tear it up. It's funny: I can't remember the last time I've been here. It must've been ages."

The old man took a sudden interest in Jin and put his arm around his shoulder; with his other hand pointed to Akasha. The light was flickering again, but this time the flickering was rapid and bright.

Jin: "What the hell is that?"

Old man: "I think I've held you kids up long enough. Have fun on your tour."

Oska COMMed in, speaking to the entire team. The message was urgent.

Oska: "I don't know if you guys can see it down there, but here the readings are off the charts. There's a massive astral spike in the center of the cathedral. I've never seen any AP readings like this before. Get in there!"

Damien: "Got it. Change of plans DL: Grihm, I want you to set up your demo charges outside first. The walls are too sturdy for the original plan. Get to the roof and set up to make the ceiling collapse. Sev, you stick with her. When she's done, both of you swing back inside. The rest of us'll have to stay creative. We don't know what's happening inside, but remember: stay flexible, stay focused, and stay frosty. Let's move!"

Grihm and Sev broke off to complete their objective. The rest of DL charged toward the grand doors. Jin took a brief moment to look for the old man, who was nowhere to be seen. As strange as he was, Jin wished he had more time to speak with him.

With a single massive thrust, Damien kicked the cathedral common door open, guns drawn. Inside, the cathedral split into three directions: The main corridor, leading directly ahead to the cathedral's main chamber, and a corridor to either side; both of which appeared to wrap around and ran parallel to the main corridor. The cathedral was no longer in its finest day. Decades, perhaps a century of neglect had left it in a state of dejection. Its current occupiers, not interested in its former grandeur, repurposed the inner halls and pillars for their own specific needs. The cathedral was still and dusty, save for the sparking of lights flashing from the main chamber. The echo of the doors rang throughout its halls. When it subsided, DL could hear the sounds of chanting and sinister science. Damien signaled a series of commands through hand gestures to Trigger and Saber. They broke off toward the left corridor. Jin didn't learn any silent commands or at least didn't remember any. He stood in place, hoping they weren't for him.

Damien: "Jin, you're with me."

Damien and Jin began marching down the central corridor into the thick of what could have easily been madness. The lack of resistance, even inside the cathedral, gave Damien the impression that whatever was occurring in the main chamber demanded the complete attention of everyone involved. Once they stepped out from the foyer, the true eminence of the cathedral took hold. The central opening was lined with massive pillars, each wider and taller than any tree that stood in the city. Dusty tapestries draped from the ceiling to only a few meters above the floor and fluttered gallantly. There were stained glass windows with a few broken frames that spanned ten feet across. The opposite wall had paintings just as large. The central altar sat above the rest of the floor, looking down on all who entered. Over a hundred robed individuals were participating in a chanting ritual centered on a strange device that Damien and Jin could only see the tip of over the crowd. The device breathed a ghastly cloud of putrid smog. Standing at the altar above the others was yet another robed individual who led the chants. His voice boomed over the others. Damien touched the frame of his shades, sending images and information directly to Oska. Jin continued listening to the oms of the crowd. The chant leader began to speak out.

Chant leader: "Curiously, unsurely, and bewildered. The horrors that undoubtedly awaited them did not balk their advance. No! It only fueled their intrepidness. Meandering into the sanctuary of *The Black Tempest* uninvited and unwanted has only marked them for our lord to be willing sacrifices to complete the pact that oh so many are unable to fulfil. Another gift to our lord."

Jin: "Uh, D. I think he's talking about us."

Damien: "Good. Then this won't take long."

Damien approached the lead chanter and took aim with his gun.

Damien: "You're done here. Shut down the device, or we'll do it for you. And if we have to do it, we're killing everybody in here first."

Damien decided that brute force diplomacy was inevitable here. The lead chanter laughed at Damien's proposal.

Chant leader: "I don't believe you can fire fast enough to stop all of us. I am Turchess, and *The Black Tempest Cult* is no longer some rag tag band of scum you can intimidate. We have knowledge of a world long forgotten, yet looms over us constantly. The time for stopping the ritual has long since passed. Listen to his laughter as he approaches Æther. Welcome your new master: The Black Tempest, The Mountain Storm. Behold!"

Damien and Jin looked through the crowd of cultists. There were noticeably fewer then there had been moments ago.

The cultists in the inner circle were inhaled into the abyss faster than they could make a sound; the screams that followed indicated that the end of their journey was unpleasant. Chants became praises as the abyss spewed an otherworldly cloud. The abyss bellowed an abomination that barreled into the crowd, still draped in the corpses of cultists. As it flopped to its feet, the cultists staggered away from it, giving Damien and Jin a clear view. Everyone could do nothing but gawk in horror. Bodies rolled off the shoulders of the tall, sinewy, emaciated abomination as it rose to its full height. Its arms hung lower than its spindly knees. Its hands were larger than a man's torso; each finger a scythe, every bone a sword. Its glaucous skin glinted against the flickering light of the cathedral. The head was skin stretched over skull with a toothy grin that wrapped around behind its temples.

Turchess: "What blasphemy is this? You are not our lord."

The abomination twitched unnaturally; its bones cracked with every convulsion.

Abomination: "Can't summon the summoned, so Hellcrow answered."

Hellcrow failed to hold still even as he spoke. It picked up a corpse and it with a simple stroke of its finger, disemboweled it. It studied the effects and the reactions it invoked, laughing at the horror it wrought.

Turchess: "*Black Tempest*! Heresy has been committed by this "Hellcrow". End its miserable existence and that of our other guest as well. May the Flames of Sacrifice guarantee your success."

Turchess makes a number of hand gestures and red runes encircle him. He raises his fist to the sky and jets of flame explode throughout the cathedral setting it ablaze. When Damien and Jin look back at Turchess, he was nowhere to be found. Jin recognizes Turchess as an AP caster: A being that can bend elemental forces to their will. Jin has only known himself and his former mentor to know how to cast AP but always expected there to be others. His mentor taught him that it was a lost art in this age. It would seem not entirely.

Jin: "Damien, I'm thinking this should've been the time we went in guns blazing."

Jin takes a combative stance.

Damien: "You don't get paid extra for retrospect."

Damien grabs two large gray shells from his bullet belt and loads one into each gun. The casing was a metallic gray with a window that showed it was filled with a fine AP powder. Damien scans the area, assessing the situation. The cultists reach into their burlap robes, brandishing an array of weapons from makeshift guns to blades. A few of the blades had been augmented with fire AP crystals to give them an elemental advantage. The blades glowed red as if pulled from a furnace. Without leadership to guide them, the cultists were slow to act. Unable to determine the more significant threat: The erratic Hellcrow, or the armed individuals readying their weapons. The moment of indecisiveness is broken by a horrid wail. Hellcrow had decided for everyone and began his assault; violently whipping its arms about at everyone in range; savage in its effectiveness.

A few of the cultist closest to Damien and Jin turn their attention toward the duo. Damien fires the first shot, killing the closest of the cultists. Jin charges into the battle, swinging wide to give Damien room to shoot freely. Damien's shots eliminated the cultists armed with the guns before they had a chance to shoot, leaving Jin to deal with the flame blade wielders. Jin could see the uncertainty in their stances; how tightly they gripped their weapons. They knew little to nothing about sword combat, relying solely on their weapons to bridge the gap between their lack of experience and skill. Jin leaps at his opponent, feigning an aerial attack. The cultist in front guards high. As Jin lands, he spins backwards and chops into the ribs of the cultist. He follows through with the blade quickly enough to block an overhead strike from the next attacker, locking blades. As the third approached, Jin kicks the cut guard into him, sending them both to the ground. Switching his focus back to the cultists in sword lock, Jin parries, pushing him backwards. He slashes down across his chest. The remaining cultists had returned to his feet and rushes toward Jin. This cultist at least knew to use the advantage of his sword length over Jin's. His own strikes were predictable and he wasn't fast enough to cover the added range of his weapon. He only succeeded in drawing out the fight. The situation was too urgent for Jin to duel with a petty cultist. Jin cocks his sword arm back and hurls Hermes at his opponent, impaling him. Jin retrieves his blade before the body hit the ground.

Jin's attention broadens to the overall environment again. The cathedral is filled with the sound of combat: gunfire, metal clashing, and battle cries. Damien and Jin take cover behind a set of pillars across from the cultist battling Hellcrow.

Damien: "DL, engage the enemy. Grihm, Sev, get in here!"

Seconds later, Heavy gun fire is heard from an overlook on the second level. Trigger had moved into a sniper position and was sniping targets based on their weaponry. He spent the first few moments setting up his rifle and mentally making a priority list. His rifle wasn't able to fire rapidly because each shot required a brief charge. The purpose of this design is to prevent the weapon from ever overheating and maximize accuracy. He missed his opportunity to take out Turchess, but sought to make up for it. He considered shooting Hellcrow, but as long as it was battling cultists, he decided it could wait as a target.

Saber kept close to Trigger, covering him from any would-be-attackers. A pair of cultists takes notice of Trigger and wastes no time addressing the threat. Saber rushes the first as he cleared the final step onto the overlook, tackling him to the ground. She brandishes her tanto, a blade she calls Beyonder, and slides it across his throat before flipping off the corpse and over the shoulders of the next cultist. Before he has a chance to react she bites into his neck with her veastial jaw strength, pulling back a mouthful of meat and spits it to the floor. She kicks off of the collapsing body, sending it tumbling down the stairs. She hears another set of cultists approaching from a set of stairs on the other side of the overlook. She smiles softly to herself.

In the main chamber, the stained glass window high behind the altar shatters as Grihm and Sev repel into the cathedral. Grihm drops two small bombs into the crowd near Hellcrow before landing, rolling and throwing three more at Hellcrow. She takes cover behind the pillars near Damien and detonates the salvo.

Grihm: "What the hell was that thing I just blew up?"

Damien peeks around the pillar. Hellcrow was still fighting the cultist, un-phased and splattered with blood. The cultists had lost all of the blade wielders but kept Hellcrow surrounded, unleashing an endless barrage of gunfire. Hellcrow however, only seemed to revel in the damage it received. It flinched and spasmed periodically; sometimes from the pain and sometimes for what seemed like no reason at all. Hellcrow proved to be too much for the cultist to handle even though it was no longer paying attention to them. It was now looking directly at the pillar Grihm was hiding behind.

Damien: "That's a Hellcrow and I think it saw you."

Grihm: "What's it want with me?"

Damien: "Let's not find out. Do you have any explosives left?"

Grihm: "A few."

Damien: "Good. I'll get Hellcrow's attention. You finish setting the explosives."

As Damien steps out from the pillar Hellcrow immediately disengages the cultist. It screeches and lunges at Damien. Hellcrow was impossibly fast. Damien dodges its first attack, but Hellcrow doubles back and follows up with another leaping strike. Hellcrow was too close and much too quick for guns. Damien switches to his combat knives. He unsheathes them, narrowly blocking another wild strike from Hellcrow. This time it locks blades with Damien, leering directly into his eyes with its hollowed sockets.

Hellcrow: "Locked gaze, locked in battle, locked lives."

Damien feels Hellcrow's stare caress him like a predator leering at its prey. He kicks away from Hellcrow, who found amusement in the chase. It continues to pursue Damien. With Hellcrow after Damien, the cultists divide their attention to the pairs of DL members. What the cultists lacked in training, they made up for with their fearless battle valor. Not a single one of them showed any signs of retreat. It made combating them unusual as opponents.

Trigger now took aim at Hellcrow on the heels of Damien. It's lanky, jagged frame, unnatural speed, and psychotic movements made it a difficult target to snipe. He tries to predict Hellcrow's movements by watching Damien; he was able to make sense of Damien's movements. The tactic worked. Trigger's first shot on Hellcrow struck under its arm as it prepared to attack. The impact was enough to make it flinch, giving Damien a clear shot to follow. Damien brandishes a gun and presses the secondary trigger, firing one of his gray shells. A massive crack rings throughout the cathedral. The shell explodes on Hellcrow's chest, sending a shockwave that blows the tapestries to the walls. Damien's gun vents a plume of AP smoke to both sides of Damien. The shot bends Hellcrow over backwards. If it had a working spine, it would have been broken. Its feet remained standing in place, its arms dangle listlessly to its side. It twitches; first the legs, then the arms. Slowly, it flips its legs over its head, landing on all fours and facing Damien, with an even wider smile. Hellcrow screeches as it leaps at Damien with its arms outstretched. Damien focuses again on evasion, looking for a chance to pawn Hellcrow back off onto the cultists. Hellcrow chases Damien into a direction where Trigger couldn't cover without relocating. Trigger turns around to find Saber fighting off a horde of cultists single-handedly.

Trigger: "What the hell Saber? Why didn't you say anything?"

She was too focused on fighting to respond. She was a small target using the crowd to her advantage. She moved from one attacker to the next, never striking anyone more than twice at a time; she was a bladed whirlwind. Trigger fires at the cultists furthest from Saber and works his way closer.

The cathedral had too many support structures to simply place explosives around; at least with the explosives Grihm had on hand. She spots a few corners and hopes that the fire would eventually do the rest of the work. Sev stays by her, attempting to keep the cultists at bay. His efforts proved to only delay them since they cared little about dying. When one would fall, another would pick up his weapon, firing two guns as he marched forward. The gunfire quickly became too much for Sev to continue to suppress them. Sev takes cover and COMMs Trigger.

Sev: "Trigger we're pinned down. Can you cover us?"

Trigger: "No can do. Our hands are full up here. Where the hell are these guys coming from?"

Trigger closes COMMs. The fighting sounded urgent. Sev didn't want to distract anyone from their own problems.

Sev: "Grihm, we gotta move. They're surrounding us."

Grihm: "Just a little longer."

Sev: "I already gave you little longer. We gotta move now!"

Grihm reassesses the situation. Accepting that she doesn't have nearly enough explosives to do what Damien asked anyway, she decides to repurpose what she had remaining. She hurls one to either sides of the pillar at the cultists and takes cover beside Sev. Grihm detonates both of the explosives, obliterating the oncoming attackers.

There was a sudden change in gunfire sounds: the shots were short controlled bursts. Smoke grenades littered the hall, billowing gray smog. The smoke grenades in addition to the raging fire made the cathedral unbearable. Jin moved from behind the pillars toward the strange device under the cover of the smoke. The device was no longer being powered: The lights were no longer flickering and the swirling abyss had dissipated. Jin raises his sword to strike and brings it down, cutting through the device. He wrenches Hermes to pry it open, revealing the coveted prize: The astral crystal. It was especially large for an AP stone. The amount of energy required to power this device had to have been massive Jin thought. The crystal would be difficult to carry while fighting. He'd have to make his way out of the cathedral immediately.

A voice calls out to Jin from the smoke.

Suave gentleman: "I hope you don't think you're going to walk away with that?"

Spoke a middle-aged man. He had a black devil's lock, thick sideburns, a black suit, with a pauldron and gauntlet on his left arm. He was the personification of refinement amid the chaos all around. Jin glimpses a group of soldiers moving through the smog before losing them again. Jin makes the assumption that they were the ones who shot the smoke and are likely with this man.

Jin: "I hope you don't think you're going to stop me."

The gentleman steps out of the smoke. In his other hand he held a straight sword with a guarded hilt.

Suave gentleman: "You've had your fun playing soldier, but it's time you and your friends depart…We'll take care of the astral crystal for you."

Jin waits for a cloud of smog to wave between them before making his move. He had no intention of exchanging words with the gentlemen. Talking would only give the gentlemen a chance to gain an advantage. Smog drifts lazily by and in a flash Jin rushes low into the miasma. He reappears almost underneath the gentlemen with a rising slash. The gentleman easily blocks but Jin's awkward attack angle didn't present opportunity for a counter attack. Jin recovers and the two swordsman square off. He attempts to bait the gentlemen into attacking first this time.

Jin: "Now that I've seen someone else do it, I see how ridiculous I look only carrying a sword around."

Suave gentleman: "It's only ridiculous to people who don't know how to use them. So you're Damien's newest? It's nice to see him trying something different for a change."

The gentleman didn't go for the taunt. He was far too calm for Jin's liking.

Jin: "Who the hell are you?"

The gentleman answered with a stab of his blade that sent a sharp distortion hissing at Jin; he was another AP caster. The attack surged directly at Jin's core. The timing and speed of the attack barely left Jin with a chance to evade. The distortion scrapes Jin's stomach as he narrowly steps to the side. The gentleman rears his sword arm back for another distortion blade, but Jin was prepared. The gentleman thrusts his sword again and Jin steps toward the attack with his free hand before him. An ethereal barrier materializes in front of Jin. The barrier waved like a ghostly fabric. The gentleman's distortion blade stabs hard into the barrier, shooting mystical sparks as it crashed. The barrier bevels inward under the pressure of the attack, but holds. Seeing his attack fail against Jin's barrier, the gentleman moves in close to meet blades with Jin. The gentleman was quick, but Jin was stronger. The gentleman favored stabbing over slashing; while Jin was almost exclusively a slasher. Their two styles contrasted each other down to the basics of technique; even their use of AP was opposite. The gentleman made effective use of his shielded arm, enticing Jin with a potential hit, but angling his arm so the attack slides away. It creates a brief opening, but Jin allows himself to fall to the floor and roll back to his feet, gaining some distance in the process. Jin didn't want to create too much of a gap since the gentleman has the advantage at a distance. Jin springs back toward the gentleman to deny him the chance to think about his next attack. Jin's blade was noticeably heavier, but the gentleman's quick and precise movements never gave Jin anything to exploit. Jin struggled to keep the pressure on the gentleman, who hadn't broken a sweat; Jin sought to fix that. The gentleman turns following another parry and awaits Jin's counter-attack. He angles his shoulder to protect his body from Jin's strike. In mid-swing, Jin alters his attack from aiming at the torso to be deflected, to attacking the shield arm itself. He brings his second arm into the attack to add power. Jin's strike had more heft behind it than the gentleman had anticipated. Nor did he anticipate Jin attacking his shield arm directly. The gauntlet cracks under the weight of Jin's blade, lodging itself in the armor. With Hermes wedged in the gentleman's armor, Jin was unable to follow through with a killing blow, but the gentleman still had his sword free and was in ideal positioning for a strike to Jin's ribs. Jin cuts his losses and kicks away, bringing Hermes with him.

Damien began to feel the exhaustion of being chased by Hellcrow. Hellcrow was relentless, tireless, and unforgiving. Damien took a few serious cuts and it was only a matter of time before he would be unable to fight. He scored a number of solid hits on Hellcrow but it was either unaffected or didn't show it. The environment in the cathedral had deteriorated enough to need to abort the mission. It was time for a tactical evacuation. Damien briefly opens COMMs.

Damien: "Disperse!"

The only word Damien could spare.

Trigger: "All the doors are locked D. Second floor has plenty of windows and less smoke."

Everyone but Damien and Jin acknowledge. Damien hears the clashing of steel a few feet behind him and heads in that direction with a gun in hand. In a clearing in the smoke, Damien sees Jin fighting the gentleman. Not in the mood for questions, Damien fires a gray shot at the gentleman. The gentleman parries Jin and whips his shielded arm at Damien's shot, repelling it back toward Damien, albeit slightly off course. Damien was no longer there to receive the reflected shot. Hellcrow emerges from the smoke in Damien's wake in time to catch the loose shot. The impact detonates the shell and sends Hellcrow staggering. It struggles to regain its footing as it stumbles into the smoke. The burst of energy from the shell creates a small clearing in the smoky cathedral. With Hellcrow stunned, Damien finally had a moment of reprieve from his pursuer but seeing the astral crystal encouraged him to push on. He switches to his other gun. He opens fire on the gentleman. The gentleman may have been able to deflect a large shell, but a hail of small shots at short range would prove more of a challenge for him. The gentleman slides behind the strange device, taking cover. Damien begins to swing around wide to get him back into sights. Jin walks around to the other side. There's a hissing sound as a broad distortion blade curves from around the device. Damien ducks the distortion slash and it continues around until Jin presents it to his ethereal barrier, scattering the energy. Before Damien and Jin have a chance to refocus on the gentleman, two soldiers step out of the smoke and open fire at them. Jin's barrier defends him from the gunfire as he moves closer to cover Damien as well. Damien had no clue as to how Jin was creating the barrier, but didn't care to think about it at the moment. Damien leans out from the barrier and with a few well-placed shots, takes out each soldier. They quickly turn their attention back toward the gentleman, only able to catch a glimpse of his silhouette disappear into the smoke.

Suave gentleman: "Don't get too attached to it Damien. We'll take that from you along with everything else."

Damien: "Jin, grab the crystal. I'll hold off Hellcrow."

Jin: "Not a chance. You've already done your part. It's my turn to hold him off."

Damien hated the idea of anyone else facing Hellcrow, but he knew that he was in no condition to continue fighting. He rips the astral crystal from the device. It was warm to the touch and of a black so dark it didn't reflect any light. He could only see the edges of its outside contours.

Damien: "Fine, if it comes to that. Let's go."

     Damien and Jin stumble low through the smoke and fire and located the stairs to the second floor. They hear the menacing laughter of Hellcrow bellow from the cloud, echoing throughout the cathedral. There was a broken window with a repelling rope leading outside and a carpet of bodies littered around it. They take the rope down and Damien COMMs the team.

Damien: "Grihm, we're out. Det..."

Damien's words are cut off by the sounds of explosions. To Grihm's amazement, more of the cathedral collapsed than she anticipated. The ceiling had completely caved in, taking much of the walls down with it. Only a few pillars and some parts of the wall managed to remain somewhat intact. An impressive feat considering how few explosives she had set. The rubble continued to burn and the smoke billowed from the remains like the final breath of an ancient beast. Damien and Jin headed to meet with the rest of DL. Jin had a few cuts from his fight with the gentleman, but Damien was far worse for wear. Saber is the first to get to Damien to help. She still had blood on her face. Jin wondered why no one had bothered to tell her that.

Saber: "Baby, are you okay? What the hell was that thing?"

She checked over Damien's considerable wounds and with a few small medical items she had on hand, began addressing his more urgent injuries.

Damien: "I don't know but I really hope it's dead. Let's get out of here before anyone else shows up."

After Saber's quick patch-up, Damien was able to catch his second wind. He wasn't much better, but at least he could limp on his own. Damien COMMs Styner to pick them up and return home. Now no longer under the guise of stealth, Styner could bring the truck closer to the cathedral.

Jin: "I take it missions aren't always this interesting."

Damien: "Not even close."

A familiar sound rumbled from the debris and crawled into their ears: the laughing. At first, it was so low and subtle; everyone thought they were only remembering the sound. The laughter grew until it became audible. From the remains of the cathedral emerged the boney silhouette of Hellcrow. Its laughter grew more hysterical as it sprinted down the hill. Damien, Trigger, and Sev open fire without hesitation. The collective efforts of firing balked Hellcrow. Its sprint slowed to a walk and it covered its face. Their weapons were overheating and needed to vent. Whenever the firing subdued, Hellcrow increased its advance. Grihm slowed him down with a fistful of anti-personnel bomblets. Hellcrow covers its face as they detonate, recovering in time to catch sight of a truck crashing into it with enough speed to push it back several feet. Hellcrow dug its sharp feet into the ground, rooting itself deep enough to stop the truck. The front grill bent around Hellcrow's sharp frame. Styner grabs the large shotgun he keeps in the cabin of the truck. He tries to reverse the truck but Hellcrow wraps his arms around the truck and clenches it in place. Styner presses the accelerator to the floor, slips his shotgun out of the window and fires. The first few shots didn't have much effect on Hellcrow. Eventually, the shots begin to wear away Hellcrow's glossy skin. It was a difficult angle to shoot Hellcrow without damaging the truck. Styner was only able to hit the arm and shoulder safely. Hellcrow cocks his head back as it digs its claws deeper into the truck, giving Styner a clear head-shot. Hellcrow's head kicks back and its claws dislodge from the truck. Hellcrow falls from the grill of the truck and under the tires. Styner waits for the bumps under the truck before kicking open his door, Shotgun in hand. He finds a mangled, pile of bones and skin that once resembled Hellcrow and shoots it until his gun overheats. It writhes and convulses before curling into a pile of limbs wrapped in skin. Styner returns to the truck, smoking gun in hand. He backs up over Hellcrow's corpse one last time before pulling out of the Cathedral grounds.

Everyone waited for Styner to say something, but he never did. He just whistled the entire ride back to DLC.

08– THE DOCTOR IS OUT

-Please tell me everything that's on your mind. I'm here to help.-

At the DLC war room, the severity of Damien's injuries had begun to take weight but he refused to be taken to medical before debrief. He felt there was a lot that needed to be covered before he could truly consider the mission over. Everyone took a seat at the table, and for the first time Jin had seen, all the seats were filled. Despite his injuries, Damien leaned over the table. He removed his shades (another first for Jin) and rubbed his eyes to help them adjust to the light before addressing the team. His eyes were vibrant amber.

Damien: "DL... Salena, Everett, Oska, Bianca, Amon, Sayaires, Jin. For a moment, let's just take off the military titles, pretenses, and professionalism, and just look at each other as people. Before we go any further, I want you all to know that I couldn't be more proud of you. Everyone performed their jobs, without incident and pulled out an even greater success than I ever could have imagined. We were hit with everything, and still managed to pull out a best-case scenario. Damn fine work team."

The room was stunned. Damien was known for being hard and direct. He never lost his bearing under any circumstance. No one knew how to respond; no one except Grihm.

Grihm: "New guy joins the team and suddenly Damien's full of compliments."

Trigger: "Crack jokes if you want Grihm but he's right. I don't think we coulda done any better."

Grihm: "Thanks boss. It means a lot to hear you say that."

Damien: "Speaking of Jin, allow me to properly introduce the newest DL member. I steamrolled over it before, but he's definitely proven he deserves better than that. So on behalf of everyone here, welcome to Dread Locked Jin."

There was a round of applause from everyone. The team felt a mutual appreciation for the addition. And for the first time in as long as he could remember, Jin felt the love of family. Damien plopped back into his seat, and placed his shades back on. It was time for business again.

Damien: "With that out of the way, let's get started. To say the least, things got out of hand. I think our approach to the situation was too lax. Then again, it's hard to be prepared for so many outliers. But it's shown us that our Intel collection on factions can be lacking. We had no information on the Black Tempest Cult. They were packing a small militia in there and we knew nothing about it; even less about what they were doing. But with their leader fleeing and the entire cult killed, it'll be some time before Turchess can muster up another gathering like that."

Oska: "I'll take responsibility for that. They never seemed as important compared to the other gangs and factions. When they *became* noteworthy, I couldn't find out what they were up to. Once I have a chance to go over the data you've collected, I might be able to provide more info on what he was up to."

Jin: "If you don't mind, I can throw in my two cents."

Damien: "We don't."

The attention of the room shifted to Jin.

Jin: "There was a lot going on in there and I'm not sure if you're aware of what those things were. Between the astral crystal, the AP casting, and what happened with Hellcrow, it's a lot to take in. These are all things that were once sort of commonplace. But almost no one has passed this knowledge on in… ages."

Trigger: "Slow down there. You already lost me."

Jin: "I'm sure I'm going to lose you a few times; it gets weird… weirder. I'll start off easy. Remember what Turchess did when he set the cathedral on fire? That's called *AP casting*."

The room was filled with confused looks.

Jin: "That didn't take long. See, we're all used to AP being used by machines to provide our modern conveniences. But a long time ago people used to be able to manipulate the same forces without any machinery; there were even schools dedicated to it. But over the years it went the way of technology and people forgot how to do it without machines. Eventually it became a lost art, so I have no idea how Turchess learned it."

Damien: "Is that what you were doing with the shield?"

Jin: "Yes."

Trigger: "You mean to tell me I can shoot lighting and you knew how this whole time? You been holdin' out on me?"

Jin: "It's not that easy. I trained for years before I could do what little I know. And I had a mentor. I don't know who taught Turchess, but it's not something you can just pick up on a whim. And even if I knew enough to teach anyone, it could still take years to learn."

Grihm: "If there are people who can manipulate elements, how do you fight that?"

Jin: "Just because someone can breathe fire, doesn't mean they can't be stabbed. But I don't think we have to worry about too many people doing it."

Damien: "There was another AP caster in there."

Jin hadn't forgotten about the gentleman swordsman. In fact he was next on Jin's list of things to discuss. He was very interested in finding out more about the swordsman.

Jin: "Yeah, the guy with the sword was one."

Damien: "We've seen him before but didn't know he was anyone special. He's the bodyguard of Revco's CEO. Whenever he makes a public appearance, you can usually find the bodyguard nearby. But now we know he's a caster who doubles as an operative."

Jin: "He was also interested in the astral crystal, which would make a lot of sense. An AP crystal *that* large is priceless. The things you could do with it are unimaginable."

Damien: "Then it's a damn good thing we got it."

Oska: "I could only get so much from the sensors other than energy spikes. What happened?"

Damien: "There was a device that opened a portal to an abyss and something came out of it."

Jin: "From what I know about astral element, the cult performed a ritual that summoned Hellcrow. There was a legend that people did these to bind their souls with akasheans to gain power. But I don't think this one worked because Hellcrow tried to kill everyone. I can't imagine the ritual catching on if this is the end result."

Styner: "Wherever it came from, it's done now. I made sure of that."

Damien wasn't convinced. Hellcrow was resilient. It didn't react to pain and took a collective effort from nearly everyone in the cathedral to wear it down. Damien considered a follow-up investigation.

Damien: "I think the big take-away from all of this is that we need to improve our Intel collection efforts and that we have a lot of new things to add to our records. It's a back burner project, but I'm going to be on the lookout for people who study and know things about AP. If nothing else it may start us on a path that leads to Turchess. As for the astral crystal, we'll hold it in R&D until we figure out how to use it. Anybody got anything else?"

There were no additions.

Damien: "Dismissed. Now if you'll excuse me, I'm going to go to medical before I die."

*   *   *

Despite his previously grievous injuries, Damien was beginning to feel better by the time he got to medical. His wounds however told a different story. He had a number of gashes and contusions but claimed they didn't hurt as bad as they looked. Damien pushed his body far beyond the limit during the mission and the medical staff was convinced he was alive through sheer willpower. Saber sat beside his bed reading a cosplay magazine. It was stark contrast to her regular work and one of her favorite hobbies. There was a gentle tap at the door. Saber told the visitor to enter. It was Dr. Malerius.

Malerius: "Hello Damien. Salena. Do you have a moment?"

Saber: "Sure. What do you need?"

Malerius: "I understand that you've recently had a rather… unusual mission. I just wanted to speak to the team and see how everyone was holding up."

Saber: "I think we'll manage, although Damien's down for the count right now."

Damien: "I can talk. I'm not tired anyway."

Malerius: "Salena, would you mind if I spoke to him alone?"

Saber: "Go for it. I'll get us something to eat. See you in a bit babe."

Saber caressed Damien's forehead before leaving Damien and Dr. Malerius alone.

Damien: "So you want to get into my head?"

Malerius: "Just checking in since no one on the team will ever come see me on their own. I figured I'd hunt you down instead."

Damien: "I can't go anywhere. Okay, let's do it."

Malerius: "Not one for mincing words. I like that about you. I understand that the mission was eventful. It looks like you had your hands full. I've never known you to come back with any injuries; let alone enough to be incapacitated. What happened?"

Damien: "Everything. There were more of them than expected, they were better equipped, and more prepared than we ever could have anticipated among other things."

Malerius: "Other things? Damien, as a medical professional I'm sworn to keep everything about my patients confidential. You don't have to hide anything from me."

Damien: "All you need to know is that we were unprepared. Knowing who did this won't do you any good."

Malerius: "Actually, any detail helps me. By knowing what happened, I can better understand what you're going through."

Dr. Malerius' logic rang true. Damien didn't have an immediate answer other than the truth; or at least part of it.

Damien: "In that case: We went in blind and shot from the hip. I didn't make the best call, but I'm the only one who's paying for it. So I think we made the best out of an ugly situation. And that's all I have for you. You know the way out."

Malerius gave Damien a nod and left without another word. He saw Saber approaching with a bag of food for Damien.

Malerius: "Perfect timing. Can you spare a moment?"

Saber took a swig of her soda as she continued around the Doctor.

Saber: "Sure. Let me just drop this off."

Saber gave the bag to Damien and they spoke for a moment. Malerius watched them interact; Saber was more upbeat than he was used to seeing her. She smiled more around Damien. At least when she thought no one was paying attention. After sharing a kiss, Saber returned, closing the door behind her.

Saber: "What do you want to know about the mission?"

Malerius: "I just wanted to see how you're dealing with the stress. You guys do a lot of missions. Violent missions. Not everyone can deal with that on their conscious."

Saber: "You get used to it."

Malerius: "That's not necessarily a good thing. Can I be honest with you for a second?"

Saber: "I thought that was the point of this conversation."

Malerius: "Hearing you say that worries me. Because that's exactly what Damien would say. I don't mean to say anything negative about him, but he's not known for his empathy. I don't want to risk you picking up some of his negative philosophies.

It's okay to have some aversion to being a soldier. It would be *normal* of you."

Saber: "Damien may not seem as empathetic as most people because of what he does. But the reasons he does them are what defines him. I also understand how you could miss that even though you're a doctor. Damien isn't the easiest person to get to know. You don't have to worry about us; we'll keep each other in-check. I promise."

Malerius: "I see. Thank you. I don't want to keep you from your food. I suppose I'll see you around."

Malerius: *"I expected Damien to be closed-off, but not Saber. I suppose I should have; couples tend to work in tandem. Saber's picking up more of Damien's traits, which will make it nearly impossible to get anything out of her soon. Perhaps the rest of DL will be more inclined to talk."*

The next person on Dr. Malerius' list was Grihm. As he approached her dormitory, the smell of food being cooked wafted from the door. He rang the bell and heard a slew of curses before Grihm opened the door. She was in casual clothing, clearly not expecting anyone to stop by; shorts and a tank-top. She had a few bandages from minor cuts and scrapes that were still red. Grihm looked irritated at Malerius' poor timing. She returned to the stove to tend to her food, leaving the door open for Malerius to enter.

Malerius: "I can come back at a better time."

Grihm: "No you're fine. What's up?"

Malerius: "I just thought I'd check in with everyone. Seeing how you're holding up with Damien being injured. He'll likely be out of commission for a while."

Grihm: "Only if we force him. He's not going to stay down for long."

Malerius: "You don't seem worried."

Grihm: "Should I be? That guy's too tough for his own good; mentally *and* physically. Unless he dies on the spot, he's probably fine. And even then he might come back as a ghost to kill whoever killed him."

Grihm began plating the food. It looked even better than it smelled. Grihm took great pride in her cooking as well as presentation of her food. Dr. Malerius secretly hoped she would offer him a plate.

Malerius: "You're very talented."

Grihm: "Thanks. It's a passion of mine."

She made another plate for Malerius, emptying the pan. Malerius thanked her and dug in. He kept his manners about him. He had never enjoyed a meal quite like this one.

Grihm: "I'm sure you had more questions for me. What's up?"

Malerius: "I'm sorry, I was distracted. Thank you. Honestly, I just wanted to gauge how everyone was doing after the mission. Since the team never comes to speak to me, I thought I'd try seeking you out. So far it hasn't been going too well, but this meal has made it worth it."

Grihm: "You've got to understand Doc; we aren't normal soldiers. We don't deal with stress the way most people would. It's one of the requirements of being on the team. It takes a lot to shake us. Don't be offended if we don't come to talk to you about our problems because we've learned to deal with them on our own."

Malerius: "I'm starting to understand that now. It seems Damien has had a lot of influence over the team then."

Grihm: "Don't… I'm not like that. When I say on our own, I mean within the team. We help each other."

Malerius: "You don't trust a medical professional? It seems odd that Damien would hire me just to ignore me. I want to do more. To justify the money he's paying me. But you're making it difficult."

Grihm: "That's something you should speak to Damien about."

Malerius: "He was even less willing to share than you. Just barely though."

Grihm: "(Sigh) Fine. If you have to know *something*, I'm really on edge. We pretty much uncovered a corpse stinger's nest. Turns out there're a lot of things going on that we had no idea existed and I'm sure Damien's going to stick our hands right inside."

Malerius: "Corpse stinger?"

Grihm: "Oh. They're these big-ass bugs that sting things and lays eggs inside the victim. Then the eggs hatch a few days later out of the already or soon-to-be corpse."

Malerius: "I wish I hadn't asked. But what did you uncover that's so bad?"

Grihm: "Questions."

Malerius: "Questions?"

Grihm: "Just questions."

Malerius: "I see. If you see a problem in Damien's mission direction, why don't you speak up?"

Grihm: "We don't make moves off gut feelings unless we have to. I don't have a concrete reason to back it up. So unless something comes up or he gives me a reason to, I can't and won't."

Malerius: "Thank you Bianca for taking the time to speak to me. You've done wonders. And thank you for the food as well. But I have to finish my rounds. And good luck standing up to Damien. I think you're the only one who will."

Dr. Malerius cleaned his plate and placed it in the sink. He thanked her one last time before he left.

Malerius: *"That went better than expected. If I can stay on her good side, she might be more inclined to speak to me about her thoughts; which are insightful. It's interesting to see that she's more open about her reservations to Damien. I don't think she can speak of her feelings on the matter with anyone else in the team. If that's the case, she may be my primary source of insight. But more importantly; what an amazing cook."*

Dr. Malerius wasn't sure where to begin looking for the remaining five members of DL. He considered paging them to his office but was sure the requests would be ignored as always; especially by Oska. She would be the most difficult to pin down for even a moment. He remembered that she would most likely be her in her office, but it would be difficult to get her to stop working. The upper office was quiet. Damien and Saber were still at medical and Styner was nowhere to be seen. Oska was the only one working, slaving away at her battle station. Oska worked too fast for Dr. Malerius to make out any details of what she was doing.

Malerius: "Have a minute?"

Oska: "Nope."

Malerius: "I won't take up too much of your time."

Oska: "Too late."

Malerius: "How was the mission?"

Oska: "Classified."

Malerius: "Are you working on it now?"

Oska: "Classified"

Malerius: "Have you taken a break since the last mission?"

Oska: "No."

Malerius: "Don't you think you should?"

Oska: "No."

Malerius: "Do you think Damien works you too hard?"

There was a brief pause in her computing.

Oska: ".... Yes."

Malerius: "Then why don't you take a break?"

She stopped completely and turned to face Dr. Malerius.

Oska: "Because I can't. I thought about what you said before. And I *did* take it easy for a while. And as soon as I did, there were holes all over the mission. I missed so many things. Things that could've gotten one of us killed. I know Damien demands a lot from us but seeing him come back after that mission shows that he's willing to take a heavy burden himself. And if I take a step back, he's going to take another step forward. The difference being that I don't have to put myself in danger to work harder. He does."

Malerius: "Danger isn't always apparent Oska. Sometimes it comes from within."

Without another word, he departed.

Malerius: "She was becoming hostile. Best to take a step back for now. She seems hell-bent on redeeming herself for a perceived mission failure. This new attitude will likely affect her future work ethic, which I don't think she'll be able to maintain for much longer."

Dr. Malerius looked over the open hangar floor as he exited the upper office. It was a lively sight; operations here never seemed to stop. There was always something that needed to be repaired or built, someone who needed training, deliveries and moving of equipment. He wondered how quickly everyone could shift from one operation to the next; how much time did they need to rally or scramble. Dr. Malerius caught a glimpse of Trigger and Sev in the crowd. They were walking away from the hangar toward the common areas. He lost sight of them by the time he reached the lower level, but managed to find them again in one of the side lounges. They were watching a movie. There were three men in a desert having a stand-off. They all drew their pistols; a man in a poncho shoots the man to his right, while the other failed to fire his weapon. Trigger was excited by the scene. Sev however was less than impressed.

Trigger: "How cool was that?"

Sev: "Iunno. Cool I guess."

Trigger: "Okay, I'm gonna need you to at least *pretend* to appreciate cinema greatness."

Sev: "I'm sure it is great, but it's old. They make better movies now."

Trigger: "So we just give up on great art because it ain't got the bells and whistles?"

Sev: "It's not like that, I just... Oh hey Malerius!"

Trigger: "Doc, please tell this kid he's missing out."

Malerius: "To be honest Amon, art eventually only becomes appreciated by those that wish to study the art form. Not everyone is going to see it the same way. But he's right Sayaires, it's a great movie."

Trigger: "That's all I needed to hear. So what can I do for you Doc? You don't normally come around unless... well, I don't know what you go looking for."

Malerius: "Turns out part of my job involves looking for people."

Sev: "I'm guessing you were looking for us?"

Malerius: "I was. Just checking in. But it looks like you two are pretty relaxed after the mission."

Trigger: "Yeah. Sometimes the best thing you can do is wind down after a mission. Helps you cope with all the craziness."

Malerius: "I get the impression things *did* get hectic out there. I've never seen Damien come back in that condition."

Sev: "I didn't see what happened to him, but I saw…"

Trigger nudged Sev and he paused briefly. It was subtle, but Dr. Malerius caught it.

Sev: "The aftermath. It's good to know he's okay."

Malerius: "I spoke to him not too long ago. He'll probably be back on his feet in no time. I'm also glad to see you two are winding down just fine. Would you happen to know where Jin is by any chance?"

Trigger: "Check the training area. He said he needed to figure some things out before he could take a break."

Malerius: "Thank you. Gentlemen…"

With a nod Malerius departed.

Malerius: *"I suppose I should have spoken to them individually. I think it's safe to say I'd only hear the same thing from the remaining team members, but I must do my job no matter how tedious. Sev is more likely to let his tongue slip than Trigger. The disadvantages of inexperience."*

Just as he was told, Jin was in one of the private training rooms. He looked like he'd been training for a few hours. He had removed his shirt and shoes and was at it long enough to be glistening with sweat. Jin stopped when he heard Malerius enter.

Malerius: "You sure are dedicated to your craft."

Jin: "It's how you get better than those who aren't."

Malerius: "Indeed. But don't let me stop you."

Jin turned to continue running through a series of katas. They looked improvised and more practical than a typical kata. Jin's movements were loose and relaxed, with quick, precise footwork and bursts of aggressive motions. Dr. Malerius couldn't figure out the origin of his fighting style.

Jin: "I know you didn't come here to watch me train."

Malerius: "Just checking in. Seeing how the team's doing. You know, the whole doctor bit."

Jin: "I've been told about you, but never had a chance to meet you. Sorry I never made time to come to your office, but you're never in there. Eventually I just forgot."

Malerius: "That's fair. I think I'd rather catch everyone in a more relaxed atmosphere anyway. Well… more familiar atmosphere."

Jin: "If you want to know where my head is? It's still in the mission. I learned a few things out there. I just want to commit them to memory before I relax."

Malerius: "Oh? What'd you learn?"

Jin: "Just combat stuff. Holes in my fighting style and what-not. Nothing you'd be interested in."

Malerius: "You have no idea what I'm interested in. I might even surprise you."

Dr. Malerius grabbed two wooden swords from the wall and tossed one to Jin. He caught it and smiled before setting Hermes aside. Jin respected Dr. Malerius' gesture and made mental note that this would be a lesson, not a sparring match. Dr. Malerius took a formal stance; it showed he had some training. The stance was rigid and high; uncomfortable to maintain, and impractical. Jin stepped back into an unfamiliar stance; he imitated the gentleman from the cathedral. Dr. Malerius curiously tilted his head. Jin waited patiently for Dr. Malerius to make the first move; a rising attack. It was slow and easy to read. Jin simply moved his front leg out of the way, allowing the rest of the attack to drift by harmlessly. He took note of his opponent's vulnerabilities and how he could counter from this stance. Jin jabbed forward gently at Dr. Malerius' ribs.

Jin: "Kill."

They reset positions and tried again. Jin waited again for Malerius to make the first attack. This time, Malerius stepped forward and stabbed high. It was much faster and more aggressive, yet still easy to counter from Jin's stance. He simply stepped back and thrusted his weapon.

Jin: "Kill."

It suddenly dawned on Jin. The gentlemen's style was built specifically for countering aggressive opponents. He only had to wait for Jin to do anything before simply stepping back and stabbing. And when Jin tried to create a gap, he had his distortion blade. The gentleman had dictated the flow of the duel. Malerius noticed Jin's distracted state and attempted to score a strike. Jin stepped forward, dropping his wooden sword, catching Malerius' in one hand and placed his off hand on Malerius' chest, stopping the attack.

Jin: "I think that's enough for now."

Maleirus: "Sorry, I got carried away."

Jin: "It's fine. You've actually helped me out a lot."

Malerius: "Actually, so have you. I'll leave you to your thoughts then. Take a break, you've earned it."

Malerius: *"People don't realize how much they say with their bodies. Jin must've been unable to solve all of his problems with his sword during the mission. He's going through the same issues Oska is right now; working harder now to make sure the same mistakes don't happen again. Maybe he was unable to help Damien. It's hard to say. I think that's enough research for now. Time to file the report."*

Malerius returned to his office, leaving the clinic sign dim.

09– GRAVE GHOST

-The ritual is sacred. It should never be fabricated or manufactured, for those it attracts are not the ones who belong on this plane of existence.-

-Excerpt from the Celestilium

Against the advice of his staff, Damien checked himself out of medical the following cycle. He claimed that he was no longer in any pain and didn't need anyone to care for him. He did however, promise to limit himself to administrative and overseer duties. Until he recovered, he would assist Oska more with coordinating and gathering intelligence. He called a meeting in the war room for Oska and Saber. Through his protest Saber helped Damien to his seat. He gave in, accepting her aid.

Damien: "I don't want us to be idle for too long. I want to keep this momentum going. Our next objective is to fill in our Intel gaps."

Oska slumped in her seat.

Damien: "It's not your fault Oska."

Oska: "Feels like it."

Damien: "We're not going to play take the blame here. It happens. We're just going to do better in the future."

Oska nodded and picked herself back up. It wasn't much, but it made her feel better.

Damien: "The biggest gaps are that we didn't know anything about the Black Tempest Cult, and that Revco is also invested in this."

Saber: "I can put my ear to the ground but I don't think I'll be able to find out any more about the cult now that they're all gone."

Damien: "Their leader is still out there, so our best bet may be to pull strings with his name on them. Maybe you can find an associate or teacher."

Oska: "I started working on that after debrief. I put together an association matrix and started researching members."

Oska accessed the many projectors in the room through her sidearm. The projectors above the table created a hologram of a large web of names, portraits, and dots. There were too many to make sense of at a glance. Impressed, the others waited for Oska to explain.

Oska: "Unfortunately most of these people are probably dead cult members. A few of them are suppliers: weapons, food, equipment parts, and anything else they needed."

Damien: "Did they buy the astral machine? Where'd they get so much money from?"

Oska: "They bought the parts and built it on site. No idea where the money came from though. Someone would've noticed if it came in large amounts. I'm thinking they've been funneling it in tiny portions from all over."

Saber: "Turchess probably convinced all of their members to give up their worldly possessions and money to him. Took the money, repurposed what he could, and sold the junk. You do that for over a hundred people and that would at least cover supplies."

Damien: "That would only cover them for a short time though. He probably never intended on keeping them around for long."

Oska: "Ugh. He *planned* on taking advantage of those people?"

Saber: "I almost feel bad for them."

Oska: "Almost?"

Saber: "They *did* try to kill us. And Damien didn't fire the first shots this time. We can honestly say they attacked us first."

Oska: "I still feel like they're also victims in all this too. So many people brainwashed into dying for someone else's belief. I just think they should at least be buried instead of just left in a smoldering crater."

The battle at the cathedral was the largest battle either district had seen in decades and the largest DL had ever fought. Damien agreed with Oska, they were also victims.

Damien: "Not to sound cold…"

Oska: "Here we go."

Damien: "…but it'd be unrealistic to expect to identify all of those bodies and send them to their families if any. The best option is a mass grave at the site. Eventually, we'll build them some kind of monument."

Oska was surprised at Damien's solution. It was an obtainable compromise that both fit his need to always move forward yet wasn't as cold as he was often made out to be.

Oska: "I think that's more than fair."

Saber: "Speaking of corpses: Hellcrow."

Damien: "I was thinking about that too. Styner seemed pretty confident it was dead. If it was even alive in the first place. I was planning on sending 4A Squad out to survey the aftermath as well as check on Hellcrow."

Oska: "You never told me what happened with Hellcrow. It must be pretty bad to if it's got *you* spooked."

Damien: "Hellcrow made everything about that mission more difficult than it should've been. I don't want that thing walking around."

Oska: "I'll send 4A Squad as soon as the brief's over."

Damien: "Good. What I'll need from you two is to start chasing down leads on Turchess."

Oska: "Gladly. Maybe Shina can pick out something from the wreckage to get us started."

Saber: "Now that he's used up his cult, he may be in the market to start a new one. He said he was trying to summon his god which apparently needs a lot of sacrifices. He'll be recruiting again. I can go undercover and try to join his new cult."

Damien: "That may be our best bet at this point. Hopefully we'll get some answers before he tries anything this big again. If that's it, dismissed."

*　　　*　　　*

Shina had never been to Grave Town before. She didn't like the abandoned sector of the city; it was the eerie silence that made her uncomfortable. It was easy to hear someone approaching, for better or for worse. She wanted to complete the mission as soon as possible. As her squad approached the battle site, they heard a group of scavengers rummaging through the ruins and checking the pockets of the deceased. The scavengers were young; likely no older than mid-teens. They were too busy scavenging to notice 4A Squad's approach.

Shina: "Alright listen up! I want everyone here to line up in front of me now!"

The scavengers perked up and gave each other a series of confused looks before staring blankly back at Shina. Shina commanded one of her robots to fire its rifle into the air; the gunshots echoed into the distance and the scavengers scattered in all directions. Shina let them leave. Two of the scavengers remained behind crouched in the rubble. After a few seconds, they timidly climbed down the rubble, holding hands, and stood in front of Shina. They were young and scrawny, a boy and a girl. Shina approached them and crouched to meet their eyes.

Shina: "Sorry about that. I didn't see you in there. Don't be afraid, we're here to help. What're your names?"

Boy: "Kid."

Girl: "Other kid."

Boy: "That's what everyone else called us."

Shina: "That's not going to work anymore. Let's give you some real names. How's that sound?"

The kid's eyes lit up. An enthusiasm washed over them as if names were the only thing missing from their lives. Shina looked at the girl and thought for a moment. She had dark frizzy hair that had been slightly sun colored and dark brown eyes. She cracked an adorable smile in anticipation of Shina's next words.

Shina: "How about Leila?"

She squealed and gave Shina a firm hug. She adored the name. Leila's enthusiasm was contagious and had infected the boy who had been as patient as his child body could manage. He had a different look than he did a moment ago. It was a combination of newfound excitement and determination; as if being nameless was the only thing holding him back from a lifetime of adventure.

Shina: "And for you, Quirin."

Quirin: "That's so cool. Thank you!"

The children jabbered back and forward to one another using each other's names in as many different ways as they could.

Shina: "You two don't have homes do you?"

Quirin: "Nope. We never stay in one place."

Leila: "It sucks. Can we come with you?"

Living space at Eratech HQ was becoming limited as the noon season was coming to an end. Most of the military personnel lived there, but other employees move in during the evening season to avoid having to brave the increasingly harsh weather. In addition, children were rarely taken in since most of them are runaways that had a home to return. But Leila and Quirin were just abandoned by what little family they had; a family that didn't even bother to give them names. Shina felt that it was up to her to take care of Leila and Quirin. She wondered how her girlfriend would react when she brought home two children.

Shina: "Absolutely. You can stay with me."

Shina was overcome with a feeling of unease. A quiet laughter rolled into the back of her mind. Although the moment was a happy one, the type of laughter was not one of pleasure, but of malice. Her support robots displayed her apprehension. Leila and Quirin were terrified.

Leila: "It's the Grave Ghost. We gotta go."

Shina: "What's a Grave Ghost?"

Quirin: "I don't know but it killed everyone here and doesn't like people on its land."

Haunting voice: "The kids are right; I *did* kill these people."

The voice came to them in echoes. It was difficult to tell where it was coming from. It seemed to come from below them, but the voice also surrounded them. The sound came through clearly as if the voice was inside their heads.

Haunting voice: "They're also right to be fearful."

Shina: "If you killed these people, then that would make you Hellcrow."

The voice screeched. This time the sound came from one direction; from atop a hill in the distance.

Hellcrow: "You've met him, the one without eyes. I've seen through him and he's seen through me. He can't escape me. I'm closer... than... he knows..."

Hellcrow's words trailed off followed by an insidious chuckle.

Shina: "What the hell are you talking about? What are you?"

Hellcrow: "I made sure I'm always close. Tell eyeless I wish him good health..."

The voice trailed off again into a fading laughter. The feelings of unease and fear also faded, leaving the familiar silence. Shina now found the silence comforting when compared to speaking to Hellcrow. She had more than enough evidence for Damien to complete her mission.

*　　*　　*

Shina COMMed Damien to request to delay the debriefing until next cycle which he granted without question to her surprise. She made her way back to her dormitory with Quirin and Leila following closely behind. They looked on in awe at their busy surroundings, having never been around so many people or activity. Shina opened the door and was immediately greeted by her girlfriend, Cel'yst, who drifted to Shina and shrouded her within her arms. Cel'yst was akashean: akasheans are rare within the city, most of which lived in an area to the north called Little Akasha. Cel'yst was æthean shaped, but carried with her ghostly properties. She was always enveloped in a spectral aura and hovered weightlessly above the ground. Her touch was gentle and to be embraced in her aura was to physically feel her emotions. The room was blanketed with relief and love. Quirin and Leila's initial reaction to Cel'yst was caution, but her aura quickly put them at ease.

Cel'yst: "Once again my stalwart warrior returns home to the embrace of her lovers arms. Welcome back dear heart."

Cel'yst hugged Shina tightly and kissed her deeply. As she pulled back to take in the sight of Shina once more, she saw Quirin and Leila staring back at her; trying to figure her out.

Cel'yst: "Why do you have tiny ætheans with you?"

Shina: "This is Quirin and Leila. I kind of adopted them."

Shina spoke timidly in anticipation of Cel'yst's disapproval. Unable to completely hide her emotions, Cel'yst's aura became a combination of frustration and disappointment before softening into a reluctant joy.

Cel'yst: "We'll talk about this."

Cel'yst drifted down to meet the eyes of Quirin and Leila, presenting them with a beautiful motherly smile.

Cel'yst: "You two look like you've come a long way. What do you say we get you cleaned up? And afterwards there may be sweets for you... maybe."

Cel'yst wafted down the hall with the children enthusiastically following behind. They weren't bothered by her ghostly presence. They were quickly taken in by her inviting motherly charm. Shina took the time to get cleaned up as well and find herself a snack. In the hours that followed, Shina and Cel'yst familiarized themselves with the children through games. Quirin enjoyed playing with toys related to working machines like cars; which Shina found boyish of him, and Leila enjoyed talking and being the center of attention. The two of them were a handful but the couple managed. Hours passed and the children grew weary, falling fast asleep on the floor. Neither Shina nor Cel'yst dared wake them out of fear that they would never fall asleep again. Cel'yst covered them with blankets and let them lie where they were before joining Shina in bed. Cel'yst's ghostly condition made sleeping under blankets unique, but not difficult. The bed was always warm sleeping next to Cel'yst, even if she entered the bed last. Shina pulled Cel'yst close, worried that she may hold some animosity toward her for her rash decision. Cel'yst was quiet, but her aura spoke volumes.

Shina: "I know you're not happy with me. You can't hide anything."

Cel'yst: "It's not that I'm unhappy with you, it's that I had no say in this."

Shina: "I know, but it wasn't something that I could just think about. They were there, they didn't have anyone else. The only family they had just abandoned them. I couldn't leave them to fend for themselves."

Cel'yst: "I know. You did the right thing. But it's not just that. It's other things."

Shina: "Like what?"

Cel'yst: "The 4A Squad. You're on call at all hours to do who knows what and every time you leave this bed, I wonder if you're going to come back. I wonder if my last sight of you is going to be you walking away to your doom."

Shina: "It's not always a life or death mission. It hardly ever is. When I'm called for support missions, I only need to do just that: support. There's almost never any real danger."

Cel'yst: "Like what you did in Grave Town?"

Shina: "That was an exception. And I was careful."

Cel'yst: "What about when you went into the Grove?"

Shina: "Sure that didn't go as planned but it doesn't mean I was in any danger. We could go back and forth with his until we turn blue in the face. Just driving a car I could be in danger."

Cel'yst's aura burned orange and became uncomfortably warm for a moment.

Cel'yst: "Don't pull that. This is serious. I worry about you when you're called out on a mission. And I have nothing to do around here except think about you."

Shina: "Well now you have Quirin and Leila."

The orange quickly cooled into a soft red as a smile crept onto her face.

Cel'yst: "I do. They're adorable."

Shina: "I thought you'd be angrier about me bringing them home. You always said you weren't ready for kids."

Cel'yst: "Well, no one is ever ready for kids. But you just find a way to make it work. I think they'll keep me busy when you're gone."

Shina: "You don't know how much I love hearing you say that."

Cel'yst: "Just promise me this: That you'll be extra careful the next time you're on call. I don't want to raise kids on my own."

Shina: "I'll do better than that."

Shina kissed Cel'yst sweetly and held her. They fall asleep in each other's arms. Cel'yst's aura slowly shifted to a deep blue-violet as she slept. It wasn't the most comfortable position, but they worked through it for each other; they always did.

10– THE PROPHET CALLS...

-From beyond the grave he called, promising power, knowledge. He calls us his children. All he wants in return is everything.-

Oska's preliminary research only gave Saber a vague direction in which to start her half of the investigation. The only lead Oska had found was the name of one of the suppliers, who was a bulk merchant. Saber's search for more leads, led her to a better, albeit expensive, source of information: Vangard.

Saber arrived at *Cyclebreak* during corporate business hours; the club was still closed from the night Damien visited. Vangard had begun construction. There were construction workers hard at work all throughout the building. With Damien covering the bill, Vangard would likely spare no expense in overhauling the club. The work inside was even louder than the work going on at the entrance. She located the foreman and asked for Vangard. He directed her to the back offices, where he and Scratch wrapped up their conversation as they saw Saber enter; both surprised. Vangard was, as always, wearing a tailored suit. This suit was a deep navy blue with a black shirt and a red tie. Scratch had let her hair down and her dress was more casual and shorter than Saber had ever seen her wear although it was still black with plenty of lace.

Vangard: "Never in a million years would I have thought you'd come to see me without Damien."

Scratch: "Something must be wrong at home if *you're* here alone."

Scratch's tone came off as snide, although it wasn't her intention. Saber took it as a slight at Damien being out of commission; something Vangard and Scratch would have undoubtedly heard about.

Saber: "That's none of your business Scratch."

Vangard: "I'll not have you two arguing in my office when there's business to be had. Scratch, show some manners. Drinks!"

Scratch rolled her eyes and began pouring for three. She showed her protest by doing so noisily.

Saber: "I don't think that'll be necessary."

Vangard: "Nonsense. I conclude all of my transactions with my favorite clients with a drink. That *is* why you're here right? For business?"

Saber: "I guess I'll have a drink then."

Vangard: "Excellent. So how's Damien doing? I hear he's in rough shape after the cathedral fiasco."

Saber: "He's fine. He'll be back here giving you a hard time soon enough."

Vangard: "Oh I don't know about that, I think I've grown on him. Last time he was here we made a breakthrough. Helping you may earn me even more favor points. But for a fee of course."

Saber: "I wouldn't expect anything for free from you."

Vangard: "To business then. I have to admit though; I don't need much right now."

Saber: "What to offer the man who thinks he has everything?

Vangard: "I'll tell you what: Tell me what you need, and I'll tell you what it's worth."

Saber: "I need to know about the Black Tempest Cult?"

Vangard: "Ooh. Fresh intel is expensive."

Saber: "What if I convinced Damien to look the other way for some of your shadier transactions?"

Vangard: "That would be tempting if it were coming from him. But second-hand promises are unreliable at best. Besides, I'm trying to be legit. Don't tempt me."

Saber: "How about I do a job for you. One operation."

Scratch dropped a glass.

Vangard: "That sounds like a winner. What are your conditions?"

Saber: "Nothing against the Citadel's interest. DLC always come first."

Vangard: "That seems fair. And if my chosen task takes you away for an extended period of time?"

Saber: "How long are we talking?"

Vangard: "Who knows? I'm just speculating. I have two conditions of my own: you don't tell anyone else about our deal, and I'll need some sort of collateral."

Saber: "That's not fair. You didn't make Damien give you any collateral."

Vangard: "That's because Damien is incapable of lying. You on the other hand can don an outfit and pretend to be someone else if the job calls for it. No offense, I'm just covering my ass."

Saber thought for a time. She only had one thing of any value on her at the time; something of considerable value to others but priceless to her. She reached back to undo the clasp of a necklace she had tucked into her blouse. It was an opalescent crystal wrapped in a net weaving on a silver chain. The crystal was of a rare ore called Fisenite that was always cool to the touch. Fisenite exists in two forms: as a minable ore, or grown organically in some akasheans as natural armor in the form of scales or horns. The necklace was of the former. The necklace was given to her by Damien early in their relationship to symbolize his appreciation for her shortly after she started working for him. She didn't immediately realize how difficult it must have been for him to show honest affection until she truly got to know him better throughout their relationship. Damien had one of the engineers at the Citadel break off a small piece of the Fisenite chunk Eratech had recently mined for personal purposes. He claimed that he personally shaped the crystal himself which was believable as there were many imperfections in the carving, but made it all the more charming. She took a long look at it before holding it out for Vangard to examine

Saber: "This is one of the last fragments of Fisenite on the peninsula. It's priceless for a number of reasons."

Vangard's eyes glinted with desire.

Vangard: "I've never seen Fisenite before. It's even more beautiful than I've read. I'm going to have a hard time giving this back when the time comes. It's a deal then."

Vangard extended his hand for a shake. Saber suddenly felt unsure about the deal. Giving up the first gift ever given to her by Damien to someone she barely trusted was rash, even if the reason was to help Damien in the long run. If she thought of it more she would back out. She complied and gripped his hand hard. She handed over the necklace and Vangard gazed into it one last time before handing it gently to Scratch who also peered into it before putting it into a tiny chest on a shelf behind her. Scratch then passed out three whisky glasses and everyone took the shots together. It was an extremely potent drink that burned all the way down to the stomach. Saber was barely able to choke the drink down before coughing. It felt like she breathed fire as she exhaled.

Scratch: "C'mon. A veast should be able to hold her moonshine better than that."

Saber: "I don't drink much."

Vangard: "I wish you would have said that before. You might have a hard time walking for a few hours."

Saber: "What the hell was that?"

Vangard: "Scratch's been working on a signature drink for the new club. We're calling it *Dayglow*. It sounds friendlier than it really is. We may want to get to business before it kicks in."

Saber: "Yeah, let's."

Vangard gestured for Saber to take a seat as he sat behind his desk. As Saber plopped down into the soft cushion, she felt the first wave of drunkenness set upon her.

Vangard: "Black Tempest Cult: a loosely organized cult of suicidal outcast and misfits collected by a master manipulator. Nearly all members are dead from either suicide or accidental death from using… equipment which resulted in the destruction of their base of operations in Grave Town."

Saber: "Everyone knows that. It's on the news."

Vangard: "But they don't know that the leader, Turchess, has already moved onto his next operation. They also don't know that he has followers in reserves. Those people at the cathedral were only a portion of them. And with talk of his exploits on all district news channels, his flock continues to grow. But now it's not just crazies; it's people who want power. Apparently he's showing off his *talents* and it's a much better recruiting slogan than "die for the glory of my master."''

Saber: "Where's he holed up this time?"

Vangard: "A pretty unusual spot. His new clubhouse is in Little Akasha."

Saber: "How? I thought they didn't like æatheans. At least not enough to let us live there."

Vangard: "I'm guessing it's his little secret that's gotten him through. But that'll only get him so far. If his plan is to amass his forces again, they're not going to let him invite a horde of æatheans on their land. He'll be set up near the border."

Saber: "Thanks. Anything else?"

Vangard: "That's all I have. Are you going to go shoot up the place now?"

Saber: "No. That's a Damien thing. This calls for a deft touch."

Scratch: "Don't drive anything."

Saber had barely made it outside when the alcohol set in. As a veast, her body is able process toxins faster than an æthean, but *Dayglow* was created for the purpose of getting veasts drunk quickly, and it was effective. She stepped into a quiet street to COMMs Oska before she got any worse.

Saber: "Oska, I uh got some stuff for you."

Oska: "Sweet. I'm so sick of chasing down dead ends."

Saber: "Turchess is in Lil' Akasha. He's teaching magic …and he still has an army."

Oska: "Magic? Army? What're you talking about?"

Saber: "He's teaching people secret stuff and he has all these followers now. Well, he never ran out of followers."

Oska: "Are you okay? You're barely making sense."

Saber: "I'm great. I just wanted to update you. I'll be home… in a few I guess."

Oska: "You're worrying me right now."

Saber: "It's all good. I just waved over a cab and I'm giving him money now."

Oska: "You don't pay the driver before you go anywhere. Are you drunk?"

Saber: "Bye!"

Saber didn't count the wad of bills she handed to the driver. She told him to stop by a fast food drive-through before heading to an apartment near the Eratech office building. The driver handed her some of the bills back. He didn't feel right being paid an absurd amount of money for such a short drive. After sitting down and eating some food, Saber began to sober up. She would at least be able to explain in detail what she learned. Using Damien's apartment entrance, Saber returned to the Citadel and made her way to the overseer's office. There sat Oska slaving away as usual.

Saber: "Sorry about that call earlier. Are you hungry?"

Oska: "Holy hell yes. You're a lifesaver."

Oska dropped her work at her battle station and immediately dove into a burger.

Oska: "Maybe I should get someone to bring me food all the time."

Saber: "Or maybe you should get away from this room and feed yourself. We appreciate the work you do, but we'd rather not have you die."

Oska: "I know. But there's been too much to do lately. Speaking of which, I began looking into that little bit of information you gave me earlier. I found a few strings to pull and they lead to Little Akasha. So I started a message board on the subject, and people started flocking. Turchess' got something that is drawing in even more followers than before."

Oska displayed several web pages of the online forums discussing Turchess. Most of the messages were from anonymous posters expressing their desire to join the cult. There were also long arguments against the cult. One of the discussion boards talked about how people formed groups to travel out to Little Akasha and the perils they may see along the way. The longest thread warned female travelers about the dangers of predatory male travel companions who sought to take advantage of them once they were out of the city.

Saber: "Damn, you did all of that from one drunken clue?"

Oska: "Yeah. Turns out we were searching all around the answer; we just needed a tiny nudge. I haven't had a chance to brief Damien yet."

Saber: "Don't. Not yet anyway. He'll try to make this a larger operation than it needs to be. And this is still our mission."

Oska: "Okay, what've you got in mind?"

Saber: "Turchess is taking in anyone it seems. I'll join his cult as another follower. Once I figure out what the big deal is, I'll get the hell out of there."

Oska: "I don't know, that sounds iffy. You don't want to take Grihm with you?"

Saber: "We don't want to send both covert specialists on the same mission."

Oska: "Its missions like this that keep me glued to my console. You never know when something's wrong and by the time you learn it could be too late."

Saber: "I know you'll keep me safe out there. That's why I'm not worried. That's why we never worry."

Oska swelled with pride. Despite what she tells herself, her indirect contributions to the team are what made each operation so successful.

11– ... AND THE LOST ONES ANSWER

-Everything is a small price to pay when the reward transcends comprehension.-

Saber set off the following cycle after preparing some final details for her trip; she would be gone for a few cycles. She dressed for travel with a light pair of jeans and a thin jacket for the windier parts of the journey. In a backpack she brought some dehydrated snacks, bottled water, a sleeping roll, two logs of synthetic kindle, and of course, her blade Beyonder. From DLC, she headed to the train station on foot. There was no point in bringing a car and having to pay parking fees. Of the two commercial short line trains, Saber took the northern train. The east train traveled toward the council super-structure. If one wanted to continue on toward Revco, they would transfer there. The northern train headed to the edge of Eratech, stopping at a suburb known as Gateway Village. Saber fell asleep shortly after departure. She awakened as the train was leaving the inner city, passing over the beltway. The urban skyline gave way to a more suburban one that housed domestic rows of trees that blocked the train's view of much of the streets below. In the quick glimpses of the neighborhoods, Saber could see verdant green lawns separating houses, candy colored cars parked in driveways instead of the sides of the roads, and quaint little village shops. Gateway Village had a small population of those who worked in either district of the city but wanted a slower lifestyle. The area they settled was nestled between the city and the barrens to the north. The barrens, as implied by the name, is largely uninhabited. With the expansion of the city and the frequent hazard spouts in the area, many of the creatures that once lived in the area were forced to migrate north. There, strange and bizarre creatures are said to exist. Some even moreso than those in the grove.

Among the citizens of Gateway Village was a belief that the Little Akasheans were hostile toward them; a fear born of ignorance. But the belief was rooted deep enough that they simply kept to themselves. Although a few akasheans lived in the city, not all of them had lived in Little Akasha. In fact, despite being neighbors, little is known about akasheans. When asked how they came to be on Æther, many of them claim to have been born there.

The train had filled since their original departure. There was a group of teens sitting a few rows ahead of Saber. There were four of them: two boys, and two girls. None of them were talking to one another; each lost in their own minds. The train made its final stop at the Gateway Village train station and all passengers departed. The station was as scenic as the rest of the village. The community manages to provide for itself entirely even though it officially resides in Eratech; Eratech had not been able to support the village financially in years due to other obligations. The villagers have a strong sense of civic duty and work hard to keep it as beatific as possible. Most of the passengers were picked up at the train station or jumped in their own vehicles to return to their homes. The four teens from Saber's train car however, began walking north out of the city limits. Saber hoisted her backpack over her shoulder and headed toward them.

Saber: "Headed north? Mind if I join you?"

One of the boys quickly spoke up. He had an athletic build but neglected to work out his lower body as much. He wore simple clothing: shorts, t-shit, and a plain cap. The boy looked completely unremarkable.

Basic teen: "Sure, I don't mind."

Saber: "It's nice to meet you. I'm Saber."

The other boy and one of the girls stepped up. The boy was soft spoken compared to the other but not unconfident and came off as genuine. He wore glasses, medium, shaggy brown hair, and was trying to grow his first beard. His eyes were a bright, veastial gold. He would be wonderfully handsome in a few years Saber thought.

Handsome teen: "Saber's a really cool nick-name. We were trying to think of some on the train but couldn't decide on anything."

Saber: "Let's just do the real ones for now."

Handsome teen: "Right. I'm Duke, and this is my girlfriend Chamila."

Chamila was a thin but cute girl who also wore glasses. She wore an assortment of styles and accessories: Mixed match striped stockings, buckled sleeves, a band shirt, a large jacket with a fur collar, boots, and a skirt. She was not dressed for a journey into the barrens. Saber wondered if she even had a full grasp on what she was getting herself into. Chamila smiled and waved at Saber.

Duke: "The big guy is Randal and the other girl goes by Malia."

Malia stood away from the group, looking toward the barrens to the north. She didn't seem to be paying attention to the conversation.

Randal: "Don't mind her. She's kind of weird but she knows more about this than anyone else so she's actually leading the way."

Chamila: "She's not weird. She's just quiet."

Hearing her name, Malia turned back and looked at Saber. As she joined the group Saber got a better look at her. She wore an old Citadel military jacket which still had the service patches and a dusty pair of jeans. She had a sepia skin with freckles lightly speckled across her nose and black curly hair with four colored locks: purple, teal, white, and orange.

Malia: "We've got a long trip ahead of us. Might as well get started now."

Malia briefly greeted Saber before making her way to the front of the pack. The barrens between the city and Little Akasha were rugged and craggy with no road or path to follow. They only had the knowledge that traveling north would get them there and had to hope that they wouldn't miss it. Chamila was having a difficult time traversing the terrain in her street attire. Duke helped her along, carrying both his and her backpacks and even carried her through some parts. He was a sweet kid and Chamila loved him for it. Saber stayed in the rear to keep an eye on them all. Randal, as Saber expected, had no trouble and enjoyed it as a mere treacherous hike. What surprised Saber the most was Malia's athleticism. She consistently outperformed Randal at every obstacle: She climbed faster, jumped further, and was in better shape. In fact, he couldn't keep up with her and this annoyed him greatly. The hours of hiking and climbing had begun to take its toll on the teens: Chamila tried to keep her whimpering down but it was still heard by the others, Duke was having a hard time carrying both his and her weight, and Randal was becoming clumsy in his movements as well (although he tried to hide it). Malia seemed tireless and didn't notice the others lagging behind. Saber decided it was time to set up camp. They happened upon a spacious nook near the summit of a crag. There was slight incline that wrapped around the outside of the nook and to the summit. The view was astonishing. None of them had seen the city like this before. The crag sat high above much of the city. They could see the difference in scale and development between Eratech and Revco. Revco's super structures made the district massive in comparison; having built outward as well as upward to develop their district. A faint glow emanated from the city that shone even against the light of late noon sun. It hadn't begun to cool yet, but the dusk season would be upon Æther soon. To the north, the view was of the barrens and Little Akasha. A small rural village nestled at the base of a small mountain.

Atop the crag it was windy but the nook shielded them from the worst of it so they set up camp inside. Duke and Chamila were relieved to rest. Saber grabbed the kindling out of her bag and started a campfire to the delight of the others; bringing their own kindling had not occurred to them. None of them did the proper research on the environment they would be in. The kindling was synthetic and designed to easily burn for hours. As the fire burned, everyone gathered around. Duke cuddled around Chamila to help keep her warm. Malia set up a cooking spit to make a stew. It was a small pot and wouldn't be able to fill everyone up, but would hold off their hunger for the cycle. Saber broke the silence.

Saber: "You seem like a nice bunch of kids. What makes you want to join a suicide cult?"

Chamila: "It's not a suicide cult. It's a gathering for people who feel that there's something else in this world."

Saber: "That's a vague description. Do you mean more to daily life?"

Duke: "Sort of. More like there's something else to *us*. A hidden potential that we'd otherwise never learn in our mundane lives."

Randal: "He said there's a power that lies deep within all of us that comes from the planets themselves. And he's the only person who knows how to tap into it."

Saber: "He's not going to teach you and just let you go home."

Randal: "What do you mean?"

Saber: "He's recruited others to do the same thing. He's not going to let you learn and go home. You're going to become his soldiers."

Randal: "That's pretty cool."

Saber: "No dummy, it's not. Soldiers are expected to fight. Usually until they die."

Saber snapped, becoming more frustrated with their lack of reasoning. Randal flinched at Saber's sudden outburst.

Duke: "He said you don't have to be a soldier. You can study and do other things for the cult. Chamila and I will learn the craft and teach others. One day we'll return to the city as prophets ourselves and show our peers the way."

Saber: "The way? What *way*? You don't even know what you're learning."

Chamila: "Whatever it is, we're willing to learn. We don't have a choice."

Saber: "How do you not have a choice? You're choosing now."

Randal: "I don't want to go back home. My dad was an all-star athlete his entire life. As his only child, I have to follow in his footsteps so he can relive the best years of his life and parade me around. This hat; I hate it. I'm just so use to wearing it I don't even think about it anymore."

Randal removed his hat and apathetically threw it over the cliff without a second thought.

Randal: "Do you know what I *do* like? I don't. I'm a shadow of my father. So if there's a chance for me to start my own life away from everything related to him, I'll take it."

Randal went silent as he stared into the fire.

Chamila: "We left because our families didn't approve of us. Duke's a veast. His parents are pretty harsh and don't approve of him dating "meat". When *my* parents found out he was a veast, they told me that if I left the house with him to never come back. So I did. The only things I own are what I left at Duke's place. Duke could always go back home, but he decided to stay with me."

Chamila looked up at Duke with a heartfelt affection in her eyes and kissed him. He hugged her tightly. Saber looked to Malia, anticipating another story of teenage angst. Malia continued tending to the stew without looking up. She knew that all eyes were on her, but hoped they would realize her disinterest in sharing. They did not.

Malia: "I'd rather not."

Chamila: "Aw c'mon. We all just poured our hearts out. Talking about it might make you feel better."

Malia: "All you need to know about me is that I have questions only Turchess can answer. And as soon as I get those answered, I'm out of there."

Saber: "We just went over this. What makes you think he'll let that happen?"

Malia: "Because once I get what I want, he won't have a say in the matter."

Saber: "And what if the answers you get don't answer the questions you're asking? Will he still not have a say in the matter?"

Malia: "I... hadn't thought about that. It doesn't matter; this is the best lead I've ever had. I need this."

Saber was slowly getting a better understanding of Turchess' target demographic; vulnerable, troubled youth. Feeling abandoned by their families, hoping to fill holes in their lives from empty promises. They looked to each other to make a new family and to the cult for a home.

Duke: "What's your story? If you don't want us to, why're you going?"

Saber hadn't created her character beforehand. She wanted her persona to closely relate to the situation at hand; blending tidbits of her real life with a fictitious version of herself. Building a lie around the truth made it easier for people to swallow what she had learned from her experiences. Her mind flashed back to her meeting with Vangard; she was indeed excellent at creating new personas on a whim.

Saber: "My boyfriend and I had another fight; it was the last one I could stand. I left everything he ever touched and walked away. I don't have any friends left; ditched them all for him. I was homeless. When I heard rumblings about the cult I didn't hesitate to move on. I am the end result of the decisions you're making now. You're families may not be what you want or what you deserve, but they are still your family and you need to try and fix things between you. If you feel abandoned now, imagine how much worse it's going to be when they really are gone and you didn't even so much as say goodbye."

Malia: "Stew's ready."

Duke, Chamila, and Randal gave Saber's story heavy thought. Malia didn't care much for it, or rather she didn't show any signs of concern. She poured four bowls for the others. For herself, she soaked up the remaining broth with a large piece of bread.

Duke: "Why aren't you eating any?"

Malia: "I don't eat meat."

Randal: "But you made it."

Malia: "I didn't make it for myself. Don't worry about me; I've got other things to snack on."

The stew wasn't the best tasting; made from dehydrated marlo flakes (marlos are a versatile, starchy vegetable that grow underground–, tacrons –a bright colored spear shaped vegetable said to be good for eyesight), and coiler jerky, but was appreciated for being the only substantial food anyone had eaten since leaving the city. Saber used the break in conversation to shift the topic to something positive.

Saber: "Has anyone thought of a new name to take up yet?"

Randal: "I was thinking since this is a fresh start and I don't have anything behind me, that I'd start going as Blank."

Saber: "After the drug? You're not always going to be a blank slate though. Eventually you're going to become something."

Randal: "Shit. Come back to me."

Malia: "You don't *have* to come up with a new name. If you're leaving your identity behind, then Randal can be anyone you want."

Randal: "That's awesome. I like it."

Chamila: "Hearing you say that makes me want to keep mine as well. I don't think we should discard our names. It's not like we need to hide who we are."

Duke: "I'm glad you changed your mind because I really like my name."

Malia: "Saber, did you get your name because of the sword you carry? I saw the handle when you were making the fire."

Saber noticed the handle of Beyonder sticking out of from under her bedroll. She played into her character some more.

Saber: "Yeah. My boyfriend came up with it. I guess I'm still holding onto old names too. It's funny because it's actually not a saber. But Saber is catchier than tanto."

Chamila: "Did your boyfriend have a cool name too?"

Saber: "Eyeless. He was the man with no eyes."

Malia: "That's a little intimidating. I don't think I want to know how he earned that name.

Saber: "My boyfriend… I mean my ex is known for always wearing shades. Hardly anyone's ever seen his eyes so to most people the shades are part of his face. Truth is he just has a mild light sensitivity."

Chamila: "Did you ever have to do anything you didn't want to? Like kill someone?"

Saber: "We were goons for a crime lord. I had to do a lot of things I didn't want to. It's not my proudest work."

Chamila: "Is that why you don't want us to join the cult; so we don't run into the same problems you did?"

Saber: "Yes. The path you're looking at, if you have any doubts, attachments, or holdups about this new life you won't last. And if you can't adjust, they won't let you leave either. I know you don't want to go home but there are other places that can take you in."

Randal: "You mean the Citadel? I thought you didn't want me to become a soldier?"

Saber: "You don't have to be a soldier."

Saber stopped herself when she realized her pitch was going to sound like the Black Tempest Cult's, and for a fleeting moment she wondered if the cult may not be doing a bad thing. The thought was swiftly defeated by flashes of her battle at the cathedral followed by glimpses of Saber stabbing Randal as the bodies of Duke and Chamila lied on the ground in a pool of blood, still holding hands.

Saber: "Just promise me that no matter what, you won't become soldiers."

Everyone felt Saber's sincerity and they collectively promised not to become soldiers. The conversation ended there. Everyone but Malia retired for the cycle. Malia stated that she wasn't tired, and began writing in a small journal as the others took to their sleeping bags.

12– THE CITY OF CITIES

-Tens of thousands of people living in one massive structure, never seeing the natural light of Morveilus. The open sky is a concept of fiction in their minds.-

Damien called Oska to the war room to discuss her findings on Turchess and Revco. Damien had made a seemingly supernatural recovery in the three cycles that had passed since the cathedral and no longer needed help to get around. He was eager to resume running operations.

Damien: "I've been out of the loop longer than I would've liked. Just give me the highlights for now."

Oska: "Sure. In regards to Turchess and the cult, we found out that he still has a lot of followers. He's setting up his new camp in Little Akasha and luring recruits with promises of power. Saber went in undercover to investigate. She's going dark for this mission so we won't hear from her until she returns."

Damien: "That would explain why I haven't seen her in a while. It'd be nice if she let me know. What's the plan once she gets in?"

Oska: "She's only there to gather Intel. We assess Turchess is promising to teach AP casting, but we're trying to uncover how he learned. Hopefully it's something we can replicate. After that, she's coming home."

Damien: "Sounds good to me. What's next?"

Oska: "As for Revco, there isn't a short version of this and there's a lot of misinformation. They started off as a small construction company in the eastern city decades before the corporate districts were established. Over the years the company bought out more and more land for developments until they were large enough to purchase a military license, making them the Council's original military. Eratech was established and made a fortune making weapons and equipment for them. When Revco tried to annex Eratech, we fought back."

Damien: "I know our history of The Mag City divide. What're you getting at?"

Oska: "Throughout the back half of this period, they went through changes in management. They conveniently have inconsistent records for that time. After that, everyone was accounted for under the new CEO: Joseph Bradley."

Damien: "How long ago was that?"

Oska: "That's the weird part. He's been listed as CEO since the end of the divide."

Damien: "That would make him older than Styner. There's no way. He barely looks thirty."

Oska: "That's what I said. But there are over thirty years of videos and pictures of him as the CEO. He doesn't look a day older."

Damien: "I think we're going to have to keep looking into this."

Oska: "Way ahead of you. Although Joe Bradley seems timeless, his staff is not."

Oska presented a photo of a studious woman with blonde hair and glasses. There was another man in the photo; the sword fighting gentleman from the cathedral.

Oska: "Her name is Ezra Martel and she's Joe Bradley's personal assistant. We could find out a lot from her."

Damien: "Did you find out the bodyguard's name?"

Oska: "Emil Estoque. But that's the only useful information on him. His background's as barren as Jin's."

Damien: "That's more than enough. Get Jin and Grihm in here."

Jin and Grihm arrived in the war room after receiving Oska's page. Grihm was her usual energetic self, while Jin who had just woken up from a nap, was still gathering his senses.

Grihm: "Damien, you're looking better."

Damien: "I'm still not at one-hundred percent but thanks."

Jin: "What's up boss?"

Damien: "We have a potential new lead on getting some inside info on Revco. The target is Ezra Martel: Joseph Bradley's personal assistant. We need you to spy on her and get as much information out of her as you can."

Grihm: "You want us to go rough her up?"

Damien: "No. She might recognize Jin. She's associated with Bradley's bodyguard Emil; the swordsman from the cathedral."

Jin: "Finally he has a name."

Damien: "He's definitely got you marked, so you need to avoid him at all cost. The point of the mission is information gathering."

Oska: "I went ahead and found an apartment down the street from hers. You'll be staying there for a few weeks. Jin, here's your district passport and new ID. Get familiar with it. Questions?"

Oska presented Jin and Grihm with hard copy dossiers on the mission. Jin's folder had less in it than Grihm's. He scanned through his district passport to find his alias.

Jin: "Yeah, who came up with the name Oronoko Landown? You couldn't ask me what I wanted?"

Damien: "If there are no serious questions, dismissed. Good luck out there. Come back home."

*   *   *

After they finished gearing up and brushing up on mission details, Jin and Grihm met back in the hangar. To their surprise, Oska was there talking with Trigger and Sev.

Oska: "…I only won the award because the girl who actually won went missing."

Sev: "Have you tried looking through her Eranet profiles?"

Oska: "Other than her student accounts she doesn't have anything."

Trigger: "A lot of young people have gone missing lately. Makes you wonder how many of them were at the cathedral. I'm getting sick just thinking about it."

It was a somber possibility. No one in DL had even bothered to look upon the faces of the many cultists slain at that battle. If they had, they would have seen an ugly truth. That not every fighter made an ideal villain, and that not every soldier understood their cause. The conversation hovered on that dark note for a moment. Jin and Grihm had nothing to contribute, and so they walked on, trying to put the thoughts out of their minds.

Jin and Grihm headed to the train station to catch the eastern train. Since they wouldn't be coming back for some time, it would be best that they walked. They also only had one small bag of items from home with them. The apartment was supposedly furnished and had the essentials. They would buy anything else they needed when the time came.

Grihm: "For this mission, I'm supposed to teach you about spying and being a ninja or whatever. But to be honest, I don't really have anything to teach you. As long as you're not an idiot it's easy to watch someone who doesn't know you're there. So it's really just going to be a two week stake out."

Jin: "My packet didn't say that. Just to follow your orders."

Grihm: "Don't worry, it'll be great. We'll eat junk food, play video games, and stay up late. You'll love it."

Jin: "Shouldn't we be keeping an eye on Ezra?"

Grihm: "She's got to sleep sometime. And we won't be able to see her the entire time. At least not until we set up surveillance."

Jin: "This seems like Saber kind of work. Why'd he choose me for this mission?"

Grihm was slightly annoyed at Jin's lack of enthusiasm.

Grihm: "Saber's out on another mission. And besides, what else do you have to do? You're going to be living out in town again with nothing but time and money. It's a vacation."

They reached the train station and hopped on the east train to Council. Once there, they had to go through district customs before transferring to the Revco train. Their passports were checked without incident and they were on their way in moments. Jin had never been to Revco before and was curious to see it up close. The train emerged from the dark tunnel and into the glow of the district. The skyscrapers pierced the clouds, towering far above everything outside of Revco's walls and seemed as if it were looking down on the rest of the city. A person could easily live their entire life in one superstructure and never need to step on the street below; bizarre concept Jin thought. You could see many of the largest structures from anywhere in the city, but seeing them up close gave a true sense of scale. Jin had trouble containing his disbelief, but managed. The other riders on the train must have been desensitized to the majesty of the view because most of them didn't bother looking up. Grihm looked on with a contained awe. After a few stops, Jin and Grihm departed. The area was well-to-do and they looked out of place, especially Jin. His studded brow and poorly tucked blade made him stand out. Grihm on the other hand was comfortably dressed in light summery clothing: capris, loose blouse, flats, oval sunglasses, and a sun hat. They both agreed to get to the apartment sooner rather than later.

Jin: "How do we own an apartment here?"

Grihm: "It's an open market. It's not like we're on some corporate alert list. Not to mention Oska can find a way around anything."

An energetic old man interrupted the conversation.

Old man: "Still working' for shades?"

It was an uncomfortably accurate question from a random stranger. Simultaneously they realized it was the old man from the cathedral.

Jin: "Who the hell are you old man?"

Jin put his hand on his sword although he had no intention of using it; it was a natural reflex. The old man laughed. Grihm put her hand over Jin's sword hand and stepped between the two. Grihm's gesture reminded him of where he was. Eratech district wasn't as nice as Revco's and was almost entirely unpoliced; Revco was also likely to have security in the area. He loosened his grip.

Old man: "I'm just a crazy old man. Take it easy."

Grihm: "Sorry, my friend's a little jumpy. Maybe we got off on the wrong foot. What's your name?"

Grihm was calm yet playful, which seemed to relax the old man. He returned a friendly, bearded smile.

Old man: "People down here call me old man Faux. Now that I think about it, everybody calls me that. I'm Faux."

Grihm: "Pleasure to meet you Mister old man Faux. I'm Bianca and this is my friend, Oronoko. What brings you around these parts? You seem to get around pretty well."

Faux: "I'm waiting again."

Grihm: "What're you waiting for around here? There can't be anything as exciting as what happened in Grave Town."

Faux: "That's what I'm trying to figure out."

Jin: "You're waiting to figure out what you're waiting for?"

Faux: "No stupid. I'm waiting to figure out how much longer we need to wait. You'd understand if you were older."

Jin was sure Faux had long since run out of his medication and shouldn't be allowed to be alone.

Grihm: "We? Do you mean your twinkling friend?"

The old man laughed giddily.

Faux: "Ya know Bianca; you got a good head on your shoulders. Yeah, he's how I keep finding you!"

Faux positioned himself between the two of them and pointed up at Akasha. It was an agonizingly long moment. Faux held perfectly still, his smile chiseled onto his face. Right as Jin opened his mouth to speak, he was immediately shushed. The light Faux had pointed out to them outside of the Cathedral glinted into view. It shined brightly and stopped suddenly. For a fleeting second, Grihm almost believed Faux truly did have a friend on Akasha watching them. Jin on the other hand was convinced that Faux was addled.

Faux: "Welp, I've taken enough of your time. Best let you get back to your job for Shades."

And with that, he was gone. Jin fought the urge to question the old man further, but reasoned that he was only full of nonsense.

Jin: "At least we have a name for him now."

Out of habit, Jin checked all of his pockets to see if Faux had stolen anything, a common pickpocket tactic. He found in his back pocket a business card. On one side of the card was the word "Faux", and the other side was written in akashean.

Grihm: "I'll have Oska look into it when we get to the apartment."

The rest of the walk to the apartment was uneventful. Jin felt uncomfortable casually strolling around Revco, but Grihm took advantage of her disguise as a tourist. She had forgotten entirely that they were in a rush to get to the apartment and dragged Jin into a number of shops along the way: a video game store, a department store (to check their cookware), and lastly an ice cream cart. Grihm went for the twist-grapes flavor, while Jin settled for hornberry crunch since they didn't have any mega melon. After a series of detours, they arrived at the apartment. It was a fully furnished studio with a grand window facing the streets. The décor was modern with a light industrial touch. It certainly looked expensive and considering its prime location near the Revco Central superstructure and close proximity to the shopping district and parks, it likely was. Once inside the apartment, having a seat revealed how tired they were from traveling and walking. They decided to discuss details and a plan early the next cycle. Grihm took the master bedroom and Jin agreed to sleep in the guest room.

13– THE BRIDGE BETWEEN WORLDS

-One of the greatest mysteries of our worlds is how so many akasheans have come to live on Æther. Every akashean keeps their secret to themselves. The Truth is, many of them are as native to Æther as any ætherling.-

Saber awakened to the sound of Malia rustling about. She had laid out a towel and was chopping fruits: kaleidopears, hornberries (small berries with tiny cones on the skin that give them a crunch), and malcy malcs (a palm sized fruit with a skin covered in a fabulous fiber). There were also a few pieces of bread. Malia woke the others for breakfast, informing them that it was the last of the food.

Malia: "How'd everyone sleep?"

Chamila: "It was hard to stay asleep. I guess I'm a little anxious. Did you sleep at all Malia?"

Malia: "I couldn't sleep either."

From atop the crag, Saber looked down at their destination. There was still a long walk ahead of them. She thought she'd try one last time to deter them.

Saber: "If you're thinking about turning around, now's the time to do it."

There were solid looks all around. They all had made up their minds and were going to see it through. After breakfast, they set off down the crag. The descent was easier than the climb up and eventually became a brisk stroll by the halfway point to Chamila's relief. They arrived in town after nearly three hours; although the collection of buildings before them barely qualified as a town. It was more of a village with a handful of large buildings scattered throughout. They wondered if they even had power and running water. What amazed the travelers most were the villagers themselves. The sheer diversity of life was like nothing in the city. It was as if there were no two of the same race or species: people walking on six limbs, a giant arachnid with were icy and jagged limbs, and a person who was living metal to name a few. Some of the denizens took notice of the five of them as they stared on, but none spared more than that. A man wearing a hooded robe approached them from behind. Underneath his hood was a plague mask that covered his face. He spoke dramatically with a flair of theatrics.

Robed gentlemen: "Greetings travelers. I take it your journey from the city was… arduous. You must be weary and eager for rest. Perhaps a rest and a meal at my inn?"

Saber: "That would be lovely. Please after you, mister…"

Robed gentlemen: "Eridanus, Draxis Eridanus. Please, follow me dear heart."

Draxis bowed as he introduced himself before leading them to a nearby building; one of the larger buildings in the village. A sign on the outside was written in what everyone assumed to be akashean. The painting on the sign was of a bridge connecting to circles. One of the circles resembled planet Akasha. Draxis opened the doors for his guests, letting them enter first.

Draxis: "Welcome to the *Bridge between Worlds*."

The inside seemed much larger than it did on the outside. There was a crackling fireplace with a large malice cat pelt on the floor, a long bar and several tables each with a diverse cast of akasheans sitting at them. The inn continued on around a corner and had a second floor which they didn't explore. Draxis showed them to a booth before tending to his other customers. There were a stack of menus at the end of the table. They were pleasantly surprised at the familiarity of customs in Little Akasha. The menu was also written in akashean, but every item had a photo-realistic drawing of the dish. Malia perked up when she saw that there was a vegetarian section labeled "herbivores." Draxis returned almost instinctively with glasses of water after everyone had decided. Malia ordered first; nettle pasta with sprig mushrooms. The others point to the pictures of what they thought they wanted to order. Draxis realized his mistake.

Draxis: "I beg a thousand pardons. I thought this table had the æthean menus."

Chamila: "It's fine. I'm sure anything you make will be delicious."

Draxis: "You're too kind. But just so you're aware, you've ordered: Barren glider breast in akashean plains sauce, Mag stag bisque, Dusk hunter's salad, and scaler turnovers."

Randal: "You just said a bunch of amazing words."

Draxis: "I hope you enjoy your time here before you go off to meet the scorched prophet. It will probably be the last time we see each other."

Duke: "How'd you know we were here to see the prophet?"

Draxis: "It's the main reason ætheans come here. Before the prophet came, we might've see one or two here and there, but now you all flock here in droves."

Randal: "You're not an æthean? You don't look…"

Draxis: "As different as the others? There's no limit to what an akashean can be. Some of us look exactly like ætheans. There's probably quite a few of them living in the city and you'd never even know it."

Saber: "I know some but their species is far from a secret."

Randal: "So is that a mask or your face?"

There was a collective grunt of discomfort. Draxis however, was amused.

Chamila: "I'm sorry he asked that. We're just not use to all of this and he…"

Draxis: "It's fine. Most ætheans don't ask outright, but it is a mask. It's to protect everyone from what I've become. You see, I'm both æthean *and* akashean; A being called a pact-maker. A child of both worlds."

Malia's eyes lit up at Draxis' words. She leaned forward onto the table to get a better view of him.

Chamila: "You shouldn't feel the need to hide who you are. I'm sure your face is fine."

Draxis: "That's where you are mistaken dear heart. My face is… well, you're going to be eating soon. Best keep the conversation on more tasteful topics. Perhaps I can regale you with a different tale."

Malia: "You said that you became a pact-maker. How did that happen?"

Draxis: "A smidgen of chance and a lifetime of mistakes. Maybe it was fate that we found each other if you believe in that sort of thing. Ages ago I was a somewhat wealthy noble. Through inheritance mind you. I didn't know a thing about work or hardship at the time. But I had a way with words and was irresistibly handsome. I used people to get what I wanted, which was everything. After years of gallivanting, I grew bored with society and became a socialite that wanted to be alone. One night during my occasional lonely stroll, I heard someone stalking me. I challenged him to step into the open and he warned me that I would regret it. I readied my cutlass and prepared for combat. Luckily for me, he wasn't looking for a fight because it was a monstrous akashean and I would have stood no chance against him. He had heard of me and came to humble me; A challenge not of combat, but of will. Being a man of arrogance and bravado, I accepted without hesitation. He and I became as one; his strength became mine and mine his. His challenge made me stronger in more ways than I ever could have hoped. My handsomeness became a thing of the past and ultimately what was holding me back. He took that away from me and now the content of my character is the merit of my existence, not my vanity. Apologies. A bit of a tangent that. I hope it answered your question."

Malia: "It did. Are pacts always so dramatic?"

Draxis: "Usually more-so. Mine was relatively mild compared to others. Akasheans are not always subtle when it comes to pact-making."

Malia: "Did you have to do anything? How do pacts work?"

Draxis: "The fine details are a blur. Asag, my akashean half, did most of the work. The ritual or process however is more of an academic question. A friend of mine can answer your question on the matter. He wrote the book on the subject. I'll call for him once I have the chance, although I'm not sure how long before he arrives."

Malia: "That would be amazing. Thank you."

Draxis: "My pleasure. It's good to see a young æthean eager to learn such things."

Draxis left to place their orders and check on his other patrons. The table wasn't sure of what to make of the story they had heard or of akasheans in general. Malia was far more interested in the subject than the others. She hung on Draxis' every word like an exuberant student in her favorite class. She leaned back in her seat and looked pensive; as if she had come to a major realization.

Duke: "Is everything okay? You completely changed moods on us."

Malia: "I may not join you at the cult right away. There may be more to what I'm looking for than I thought. I don't want to join the cult and miss out other opportunities."

Randal: "Just like that? You came all this way to change your mind?"

Malia: "I thought I knew exactly what I needed to know. It turns out that I have a few more things to figure out."

Chamila: "What are you trying to learn? Why are you keeping it secret? Just tell us."

Malia started to speak but changed her mind before any words come out. She shut herself off again.

Malia: "I need answers. That's all."

Chamila: "You're traveling with four runaways about to join a cult surrounded by akasheans. What are you so afraid of?"

Chamila's words weighed heavily on Malia. She never thought of herself as afraid and so she didn't realize that she truly was. But *why* she was afraid was beyond her. She thought of how strong she had to be to make it to this moment and her fear of letting people know her seemed trivial. Chamila was right: she should not have to hide who she is. If she thought on the matter any longer, she would shut herself off again.

Malia: "A year ago I started having dreams of complete darkness where a voice would whisper to me in another language. I'd wake up the next cycle exhausted. Then the voice started to multiply. There was so much noise in my head that I couldn't sleep; but the voices persisted. One cycle, I collapsed into a coma. This time, I could see ghostly silhouettes leering toward me, screaming. But something else was there that terrified the ghost. I only got a glimpse of it as it chased the others away, but it was long and serpentine. I then felt it wrap around me slowly and I woke up. I've been awake ever since. At first I was looking for any answer. But after listening to Draxis, I'm not sure what to think anymore."

Saber: "It sounds more like you might be a pact-maker."

Malia: "Draxis said that you'd know it if you made a pact. I don't think it's something I'd sleep through."

Saber: "You didn't. In fact, you haven't slept *since* then."

Malia: "But those were just dreams. How can I make a pact with something I've never met?"

Duke: "Draxis didn't really remember how his worked either."

Had Malia told them this last cycle on the crag, they may have reacted with confusion, concern, and even suspicion. After having just met a particularly unique akashean, the impact of this development was subdued. They didn't see it as an issue at all. Malia was touched by everyone's support.

Draxis returned to the table with a tray of food almost as if he had been called. He distributes the dishes and wished them a good meal.

Malia: "Draxis, is it possible to be an akashean or pact-maker and not know it?"

Draxis laughed. He was difficult to read with the mask on, which made the physical projection of emotions a necessity for him. This time, his laughter was audible and required no gesture.

Draxis: "That's not something an akashean would be confused about. Due to the nature of our existence, it is impossible for an akashean to *not* know what we are. You see, akasheans aren't born; we awaken into existence. All akasheans pre-exist in single collective consciousness we call Veloryx'cthn-forlah—there is no æthean translation for the word but roughly it means, *"the us(me) that existed before we(I)."* Sporadically, a fragment of consciousness will break off from the whole and begin to discover its own identity. When it has fully awakened, through sheer force of will, it manifests itself into the physical realm. We know everything there is to know about ourselves when we awaken. And while I'd love to enlighten you more on the subject of our existence, I would much rather have you enjoy your meals before they cool. Enjoy."

The food was beyond excellent: filled with exotic flavors and styles unheard of in the city. The table was almost completely silent as everyone ate until Randal sparked up a conversation about how he had no idea of what a barren glider looked like and hoped they weren't adorable. The group exchanged myths and rumors they used to believe about Little Akasha. It was a more lighthearted conversation than what they've had recently and was long overdue. After the meal, cocktails followed. The others convinced Malia to have a drink as well; her first. They ordered her a drink called *supreme team*: A potent spirit consisting of solar spice vodka, aurora liqueur, mirage whiskey, and boople juice. The juice mixed with the alcohol, but the alcohol always separated from each other after it settled; no matter how much it was shaken or stirred. The flavors melded together as it was sipped. The drink helped Malia open up and relax more, although she had started warming up to everyone before that. It was a pleasant way to spend the rest of the cycle. The teens wondered if they even needed the cult now or just each other. Draxis checked on their table for the last time.

Draxis: "Now I know that you all have big plans after this, but due to the state of your curious friend, I suggest that you rest here and head out next cycle."

Saber: "I think you're right. How much do we owe you?"

Draxis: "You're my special guest. This cycle's hospitality is on the house."

Saber: "We couldn't."

Draxis: "Nonsense. Most ætheans don't even bother stopping for a break. They go straight to the caverns. But you stopped to ask questions and let a bard spin a tale about his life. This is something I will always have unlike currency or objects. For what you have given me, I will be taking care of you as best I can."

The table collectively thanked Draxis for his generosity, even though they still felt he did more for them.

Draxis: "Oh and one last thing; I signaled for my friend the scholar while you were dining. I'll send for you when he arrives."

Draxis led them to the rooms upstairs. Duke and Chamila took a room while Saber roomed with Malia, leaving Randal to his own room much to his disappointment. The rooms were simple, but cozy. Each had their own stove fireplace and fur blankets that lay on beds of down feathers. Everything akasheans did was either simple or completely natural. There was nothing synthetic about their lifestyle.

Saber: "If you don't sleep, that hangover is going to be killer."

Malia sat on her bed with a smile on her face, still beaming from the alcohol.

Malia: "It's not so bad. I enjoyed myself… Thanks for coming with us to Little Akasha. I'm glad to have met you Saber."

Saber: "Call me Salena. And I'm really glad we met too."

14– FAUXETRY

-I am ever high
To someone, somewhere I shine
I ask: What am I?

Jin was an early riser compared to Grihm. It would be a few more hours before she dragged herself out of bed which left Jin to fend for himself for breakfast. Jin decided to surprise Grihm by bringing breakfast back. She expressed excitement the previous cycle at a nearby burrito shop which Jin found odd considering her taste for upscale food and restaurants. Outside, it was still early enough to where the streets were quiet; only a handful of people rushing to their corporate jobs. He stopped in the burrito shop and bought two breakfast burritos: one with coiler sausage and the other with bacon. On his walk back he noticed a woman leaving her apartment; it was Ezra and she was heading toward Revco Central. More commonly known simply as Central, it is the corporate head of the district and was almost a small city in itself. It was the superstructure that towered over nearly everything else in Mag city. Jin carried on with his walk. There was nothing for him to do in the situation except risk compromising the entire mission.

Grihm was still asleep when he returned. She didn't respond to his first knock, but sprung to life at the word "burrito". Barely dressed, Grihm joined Jin in the common room and chose the bacon burrito. She scarfed it down as she laid out a dossier on the table.

Grihm: "Okay, here's what we already know about Miss Martel: Perpetually single, lives alone, both parents are well and live in the same town. Oska couldn't find any friends and her online presence is barren."

Jin: "She has absolutely no social life and is dedicated to her job. Tracking her should be easy. By the way, I saw her leaving her apartment when I went out for breakfast. Don't worry, I didn't go anywhere near her."

Grihm: "Good. I'd like to keep our interactions with her to a minimum for now."

Jin: "Are we supposed to bug her room or anything like that?"

Grihm: "That comes later. For now we just have to figure out when would be a good time to sneak over there. We know she doesn't have a social life, so it'll have to be while she's at work. But we have to make sure she doesn't come home in the middle of the day for lunch."

Jin: "I don't think anyone would walk all the way from Central corporate to come home for lunch. I say we go over there now. She just left for work and won't be back for at least 9 hours."

Grihm pondered on Jin's proposal. They had at least a few hours to do what they needed to before Ezra returned. If they acted now, they could begin their surveillance proper even sooner than anticipated.

Grihm: "I think you're right. I'll grab the stuff."

Grihm grabbed a backpack and arbitrarily tossed in surveillance equipment: microphones, micro-cameras, and a transmitter.

After a quick clean-up, she was dressed and they headed out. Ezra's apartment was only a brisk walk away from theirs. The front door of the building was locked and required a number code. Grihm told Jin to keep an eye out as she placed a decoder over the number pad. The display on the screen rapidly cycled through numbers as it interacted with the key pad until it identified the combination, which it then displayed to the user. The code worked and they were inside in moments. The inside of the building was small and a little underwhelming; it was undecorated, plain, and a little dejected. To their immediate left was a door that led to the stairwell; directly ahead were the elevators.

The silence of the elevator ride gave Jin time to dwell on his thoughts. Even though he knew he should focus on the mission at hand, his mind drifted back to breakfast.

Jin: "You know a lot about food, what's bacon?"

Grihm: "What do you mean?"

Jin: "I mean what animal does it come from? There're things like coiler sausage, crest avian, and glider steaks. But then we have just bacon."

Grihm: "Bacon is bacon. Why would you bother questioning anything as delicious as bacon?"

Jin: "Have you ever *seen* a bacon animal?"

Grihm thought for a moment. In all her life this is the first time she'd ever considered the origin of bacon. The elevator doors opened, breaking her train of thought.

Grihm: "We can look it up later. C'mon, let's go."

Jin wasn't finished with the topic, but would eventually go on to forget to research the matter; leaving the mystery of bacon for another time.

As they stepped out of the elevator, an elderly lady walking her pet ulor greeted them as she passed. Grihm never understood people's interests in ulors; their floating, gelatinous form made her skin crawl. The elderly lady took the elevator down leaving the hallway empty again. The doors to each apartment used a keycard for access, which was also bypassable with the decoder. This time it took but a second. Ezra's apartment was an efficient use of space. There was only room for the essentials: a bed, a desk with a laptop, a kitchenette with a small breakfast nook, and a bathroom. The room looked as if a hotel crew had recently cleaned it in preparation for the next tenant. They were surprised at the state someone as significant to the company as Ezra was living in; especially this close to central. It wasn't poor, but it was unimpressive. Jin immediately got to work looking for inconspicuous locations for the microphones and camera, being careful not to make a mess while Grihm opened the laptop. It was unlocked.

Grihm: "I guess when you live alone and don't have any company, there's no need to lock your computer."

Jin: "Must be nice to not have to worry about anything like people breaking into your room and stealing anything."

Grihm: "Okay, time to get Oska on here."

Grihm used open MagWeb to contact Oska on the laptop. The MagWeb is the open city-wide inter-district computer network used for communications between other interconnected networks. Each district also houses their own district based network: Eranet for Eratech and Revnet for Revco. Once connected, Oska COMMed Grihm.

Oska: "Damn you guys are fast. I wasn't expecting you to start this soon."

Grihm: "Turns out that the target is a little workaholic so we're just going to knock out step two right away."

Oska: "Sounds like a plan. I'm just going to open some back doors and run some software to monitor keystrokes. She's got some commercial security on this thing, which shouldn't be a problem so I'll erase all traces…"

Grihm: "Just let us know when you're done."

Grihm's curiosity got the better of her and she began browsing through Ezra's files to see if there was anything mission related. It only took a few minutes for her to stray from the path and into Ezra's personal files. Grihm skimmed through her music library which was a collection of jazz, bossa nova, easy listening, and R&B. Her taste in movies was nearly the opposite; which consisted entirely of action and martial arts movies. Grihm then found a hidden folder that was unlabeled. She opened it and immediately closed it once she realized what it was.

Oska: "And done. Good work. Let me know when you make it back."

Grihm: "Got it. Thanks again. Oh! Could you look into something else for us?"

Oska: "What is it?"

Grihm: "We got a strange business card from someone today but we don't recognize the language. Do you think you could figure it out?"

Oska: "I'll try. Hold it up in front of the camera and I'll take a snapshot of it."

Grihm did so, showing both sides of the card.

Oska: "From what I've seen on the net it looks like it could be akashean. I'll ask if Cel'yst can translate it for us."

Grihm: "Thanks. We'll wrap things up here."

Jin finished hiding the equipment: a microphone in a cabinet in the kichenette, a microphone tucked away behind the desk, and a camera just above the window on the outside looking inward toward the computer. After tidying up, they left the apartment and passed by the ulor lady again as they stepped outside. They both breathed a sigh of relief once on the street again. The transmitter needed to be placed somewhere in between the two locations; Jin suggested the inside roof of a trash bin.

Once back at the apartment, they ran a systems check. Grihm opened a laptop and COMMed Oska again. Oska checked communications between the three computers and determined that everything was running smoothly.

Oska: "I'm having no problems on my end and it looks like you are receiving everything loud and clear as well. Perfect."

Grihm: "I was worried I was going to mess that up."

Oska: "No, you did great. We don't want too many people accessing her computer at once, so I'll connect to yours only. Leave this computer on from now on."

Grihm: "Got it."

Oska: "Before I go; I talked to Cel'yst and she was more than happy to translate. It's a poem."

Removed from the flame

Tempered in the cold of life

Not a sword, a shield

While the words were lost on Jin, the poem itself reminded him of his old mentor who used to use cryptic poetry in the same short precise syllabic form. As Jin pondered on the poem and Faux, he began to see similarities the old man had with his mentor. Both were jovial yet wise, cryptic yet instructional. But the old man looked at least a hundred years older. At the time of their separation, Jin's mentor may have been a few years older than Jin is now. Jin concluded that the old man was connected to his mentor in some way and that he would find out somehow. Jin kept his many thoughts on the matter to himself; he didn't want to draw attention to a personal mystery.

Grihm: "More gibberish from the old man. At least he's consistent. Oh well. Thanks Oska."

Grihm leaned back on the couch. While being somewhat handy and an explosives expert, she didn't have the patience to work with computers on a professional level. She checked on Jin, remembering his hand in the mission.

Grihm: "You were awfully quiet. You okay?"

Jin: "There's a lot to this I need to figure out."

Grihm: "You don't have too much to figure out. You did great."

Jin realized she was talking about the mission. His head was still on the poem.

Jin: "Thanks. I'm just glad we're done."

Grihm: "You're telling me. But now's the fun part. We get to do whatever the hell we want while occasionally checking up on her."

Jin: "We still have a lot of time before she gets off work."

Grihm: "Got anything in mind?"

Jin: "We need to get some food in here."

Grihm: "Oh. I'll get cleaned up and we can go shopping."

Having skipped her shower earlier, Grihm took a luxurious amount of time to bathe. She finally emerged billowed in steam, towel wrapped high around her chest and looking radiant. Jin was only able to catch a glimpse before she stole away to her room. It would be over an hour before she came out again.

Everything they needed in the neighborhood was within walking distance. They made the mistake of grocery shopping on empty stomachs and their end haul was loaded with impulse purchases and quick snacks. Since Grihm was a practiced chef, she picked out nearly everything. Jin caught on quickly that he could only suggest or ask why one item was better than the other. The cost was irrelevant to them as the Citadel was paying all of their expenses. With their treasures in hand, they returned to the apartment. Jin started on putting away the food and Grihm fired up the stove. Her meal: horned-avian paella. There was enough remaining to have leftovers for the rest of the cycle and into the next as well. They stayed in the common room to keep a close eye on the laptop. They turned on the television but when they realized there was nothing on but programming for hyperactive teenagers and reality TV, decided to use *webfilms*. Jin put on a stand-up comedian, which Grihm opposed initially, but ended up enjoying it immensely. Hours passed and there was still no sign of Ezra. In the dwindling hours of the cycle, when nearly everyone else who had returned to their homes were readying for sleep, Ezra was still hard at work. At the latest hour of the cycle, there was a rustling in Ezra's apartment; she had finally returned from work. Based on when Jin saw her leaving, she would only give herself about seven hours to sleep before departing for work, and that was if she only stayed awake for another hour; meaning the other twenty-two hours of the cycle are dedicated to her job. Jin and Grihm watched carefully to learn Ezra's post-work routine, but it was over in seconds: she dropped her bag, barely removed her work clothes, and slithered under the sheets from the bottom of the bed.

Jin: "Looks like she had a long day at work."

Grihm: "Poor thing."

Jin: "Now that I think about it, how does Oska deal with it?"

Grihm: "She doesn't always work that hard. It's only been recently that she's been worked like that. Not sure what they put

Ezra through up there, but assisting someone who runs a massive corporation like Revco's got to be rough."

Jin: "At least we have her work week schedule, which apparently is nonstop."

Grihm: "We might have to wait for the weekend to get anything."

Jin: "I don't think personal assistants get weekends off."

Grihm: "It's not like we have a choice either way."

*   *   *

Ezra's work schedule throughout the rest of the work week was just as demanding. She spent little to no time to herself. When she would wake up, her routine was a quick shower followed by a small breakfast. She would then eat at her laptop as she briefly browsed the internet which only showcased her personal taste in music, clothing, and happenings around town. It seemed she at least had aspirations of a life outside of work.

Grihm and Jin took turns sleeping early and waking early as they kept watch over Ezra who only needed six hours of sleep a cycle. With Ezra giving them so little information, by the end of the week, they were running out of small talk and things to watch on webfilms. During the sleeping hours of the cycle, it had begun to rain; one of only ten rainy days that noon season. It was also the longest storm of the season and served as a reminder of the encroaching dusk season.

Grihm: "I'm curious: tell me about your last girlfriend."

Jin: "Where'd that come from?"

Grihm: "You've never talked about any relationships before and I need to talk about something."

Jin: "Exs are never a good topic for anyone."

Grihm: "It's a dreary day out and we're stuck inside waiting for something to happen. It fits the mood."

Jin: "It's just a regular story of a relationship that didn't work out."

Grihm: "Jin there's nothing regular about you. C'mon."

Jin: "Fine. We had known each other for a while but neither of us thought to be together right away. She was smart, really smart. She must've thought I was the funniest person in the city. Things moved fast for us. We went through the entire relationship cycle before I even knew it. I thought it was going well but I guess she didn't see it the same way. It got complicated for her when someone else showed up and that was pretty much it for us. In the end I realized that if she could just call it off so casually, then we didn't have what I thought we did. I haven't really thought much about dating since then."

Grihm: "I'm sorry. She doesn't know what she lost."

Jin: "Thanks. You know what I hate the most about it? I don't think she knows either. She's going to carry on happily with her life."

Grihm: "Don't let her hold you back; she doesn't deserve that."

Jin appreciated Grihm's sympathy but he had long since severed that limb and left it in the past. His new life of distance from others was part of that result. Jin was curious how other people dealt with loss. Surely there were better methods than starting a new life.

Jin: "I know. What about you? Any bad breakups?"

Grihm: "Sure, when I was a teen but those don't count. My last boyfriend was trapped in the past. Even before we started dating I knew that he still had a soft spot for his ex but I never thought that it was such a persistent thing. I must've reminded him of her in all the right ways, because even though they hadn't spoken in years he went back to her in the end. It hurt, but I know now that it would never work out between us with his mind on her all the time. I was mad at him for a while but I've moved on. But I will say this; I hope that I can find someone who cares about me as much as he cares about her."

Jin: "Don't we all? But then again, considering our lifestyle it's probably for the best that we haven't."

Grihm didn't like the sting of Jin's words but agreed: it would often force them to choose between love and duty. And if the situation ever presented itself, she wasn't sure if she could ever choose duty.

15– THE WINTER STAR

-Every year, a beam of light blazes across the sky trailed by gray clouds that bring the first snowfall; this marks the start of winter. It is precise, it is calculable, and it is a complete mystery.-

Saber was awakened by the sound of the room door closing. Malia was returning from the tavern on the first floor. The alcohol had worn off and she was now dealing with the aftermath. She held up well but it was obvious that she was miserable. After gathering the others, they intended to have a quick breakfast before setting off but Draxis refused to let them leave without another full meal. He made a palette of various foods for the table that included: Coiler egg quiche, waffles with whipped cream and mixed fruit, marlo hash, coffee, and juice. After breakfast, Draxis saw them to the door.

Draxis: "It saddens me to see you all leave. I hope you enjoyed your time with us. Should you ever find yourself in Little Akasha again, please come see me."

Saber: "We can't thank you enough for taking care of us."

Draxis: "It's been an absolute pleasure having you. I wish you safe journeys."

Saber stayed behind for a moment to speak with Draxis.

Saber: "I know you've done a lot for us but I need to ask you for one more favor."

Draxis: "Please, helping you gives my life purpose."

Saber: "Could you hold onto this for me?"

She handed Draxis her bag with her personal belongings to include Beyonder. Draxis promised to keep it close to him.

The location of the entrance to the cult was a long walk outside of the village toward the mountain. The entrance was a cavern at the base that led deep underground. The light from outside only illuminated the way until the first bend which after a small patch of complete darkness, was lit by several wall torches and opened into a natural room. There was a robed individual standing before a narrow passageway. Saber noticed that these robes were of a higher quality than the burlap robes worn by the cathedral cultists, but the cavern was dimly lit and she couldn't make out the finer details. The robed individual was already aware of their arrival; he challenged the group as they approached.

Robed guard: "Greetings. Have you come to join the ranks of the exalted?"

Saber: "We have. We've heard the call of the prophet and seek his wisdom."

Robed guard: "Very well. Come with me."

He led them through another narrow passageway that descended further into the depths. The passage expanded into a vast ceremonial chamber decorated with tapestries along the walls with several other tunnels that sprawled further into the darkness. At the head of the chamber was an altar upon a stage. The guard told them to wait near the stage while he went to find the prophet. Saber took in her surroundings making a mental map of the caverns in the meantime. After a few minutes the guard arrived with the prophet and returned to his post. Saber never had the chance to see him at the cathedral. He was a grave, elderly man with a bald head and a weathered face. His eyes burned the color of fiery ochre. He wore an extravagant black robe stitched with a mountain exploding from being struck by lightning.

Turchess: "My children, although we have never met, I have missed you. You've traveled far and have no doubt overcome the adversity that has led you here. Whatever it was that caused you to seek us out, it is irrelevant. You are home now."

Saber: "Thank you father. You honor us."

Turchess: "No, the honor of bestowing divine blessing upon the children of Æther is mine. There is much to your indoctrination process. Are you truly ready to join the exalted ranks of the Black Tempest?"

They all agreed without words.

Turchess: "Excellent. The first step is easy; for you at least. I must read your auras to determine how you fit into our cause. Please hold still."

He stood them in a line on the stage a few feet apart from one another. Saber noticed a grate beneath their feet filled with ash. Turchess began with Saber, bringing her attention back to the matter at hand. He reached into his robe and pulled out a colorless AP crystal. The crystal was as clear as glass; a sign of AP purity. She was familiar with AP crystal being used to power everyday appliances and militarily in equipment and weapons, but never had she seen them used without the aid of a machine. He held it up to Saber and stared deeply into it, reading it like some sort of crystal ball. It hummed with a melodious energy.

Turchess: "Interesting. There is a well of untapped affinity that lies deep within you. And a veast as well. You undoubtedly are exalted material."

Saber: "What exactly is an exalted?"

Turchess: "The exalted are the elites of our fold with the potential for power beyond anything you've ever seen. But that's all in due time. There is a bright future for my exalted."

He moved down the line to Randal and used the stone again but was far less impressed with the reading.

Turchess: "Your affinity levels are pathetically low. Unfortunately you are not able to become exalted."

Randal remembered his promise to Saber and was a little relieved that he would be able to keep it without having to make waves. Duke was next in line.

Turchess: "You're a veast as well? This bodes well for you, because your affinities are also low. Not as low as his though. But with some extra work, you will be able to keep up just fine."

As he scanned Chamila, his face soured.

Turchess: "You may have the lowest affinities I've seen yet. The path of the exalted would be a mistake for you dear child."

Chamila: "Does that mean Duke and I won't be together?"

Turchess: "No. You and Duke *can't* be together. The trials of the exalted are demanding, calling for things you don't seem to be capable of. I'm sorry but you and your other friend are not cut out for this."

Duke: "Please father. She's a smart and dedicated girl. She'll rise to any challenge you throw at her."

Turchess: "You don't seem to understand, she is *unable*. It's not about wanting to become exalted."

Duke: "Then I don't want to become exalted either."

Turchess' face soured again.

Turchess: "What I need are exalted. If you don't fit the criteria, you have considerably fewer options with us."

Duke: "I understand. I don't think I had the heart to be exalted anyway."

Turchess looked at Duke with disappointment in his eyes.

Turchess: "Very well. I will keep the three of you together.

He turned his attention at last to Malia. His disappointment with the others was quickly whisked away. The AP crystal radiated violently, shimmering a rainbow of colors. Turchess pulled it away from her, afraid the stone would shatter.

Turchess: "I've never seen a reaction this powerful. Your affinities are even greater than mine."

Malia: "I take it I'm exalted material then?"

Turchess: "Exalted? You have something I've never seen before. I must return to my quarters to meditate on the matter. In the meantime, I will have the rest of you prepare for the indoctrination ceremony."

Turchess called for several exalted to help the others prepare. The robes of the cult were thrown over their clothes: Saber's and Malia's robes bared the colors and design of the cult similar to Turchess' but less extravagant while Randal, Duke, and Chamila were given burlap robes. Being exalted was an honor above the alternative it seemed. Everything happened so quickly that none of them had time to consider that after the ceremony they may not see each other again for some time. A cultist in the main chamber began to ring a large bell which rallied others from throughout the caverns. Quickly pouring into the ceremonial chamber, they gathered in front of the altar. Saber noticed that everyone wore the robes of the exalted, but what was even stranger was that there were only forty or-so. From what Oska told her about the online traffic and interest, there should have been hundreds of people. Saber, Malia, Randal, Duke, and Chamila were again directed toward the stage as Turchess returned from his study wearing the hood of his robe up so that it covered his face entirely. He took his position behind the altar looking down at everyone in the chamber. As he raised his arms, the chamber fell to a dead silence.

Turchess: "My children, fellow exalted. This cycle we welcome two new sisters into our fold. They came to us as many of you had: lost and looking for direction. They sought power and enlightenment. And here they will find it. Step forth and be honored sisters."

The cultists collectively bowed in silence. Saber and Malia were then directed to the back of the stage near Turchess as Randal, Duke, and Chamila were led forward.

Turchess: "Though we are welcoming two unique individuals into the ranks of exalted, others who are unable or *unwilling* to bend to the absolute will of our lord are only able to serve in one way: as inspiration. They will show us what we've come from, and the difference between the exalted, and those who have not awakened. They will serve to show us what we are capable of in time. Behold your potential!"

Turchess' hands become encased in a shroud of red energy. He throws both of his hands skyward and there is an explosive flash on stage. When everyone's eyes are able to focus again, they see a massive pillar of flame where Randal, Duke, and Chamila once stood. There is a brief scream of anguish before the fires burn the oxygen and choke the sound from their lungs. In seconds, the flesh is burned away. In a few more, their bones become brittle and erode into ash. The ash billows into the grate on stage leaving nothing but the horrid smell of their incinerated flesh. The cultists bow deep in silence.

Saber and Malia are mortified and left stunned, unable to move or react. In a few brief seconds, their companions; who had in only a short time, shared aspirations, sorrows, laughs, and a possible future together, were reduced to a pile of ash and a fading memory without so much as a goodbye or even a chance to protest. Malia breaks the silence with a shriek that echoes throughout the caverns and forever in Saber's mind. Her scream breaks Saber out of her daze of disbelief and back into the ceremonial chamber of atrocity. Her heart was seething with a rage of which she never believed she was capable. Without another thought, she rushes toward Turchess with a ceremonial dagger in hand, having no idea when or where she picked it up. Her arm surges forward, propelled with hatred and sadness. Turchess, now the one in disbelief, turns to defend himself but is vastly slower than Saber. Her blade finds its mark: in his chest between his ribs and narrowly reaching his heart. Before she has a chance to tear her blade out, Turchess' hands erupt with a jet of flames, causing Saber to leave the dagger and evade. Turchess staggers back with a hand on his wound. The exalted charge the stage; half toward Saber and the others tend to Turchess. Turchess agonizingly yanks the blade out of his wound and with his mastery of fire, cauterizes his wound shut. Although in incredible pain he rises to challenge his attacker.

As Saber steps away from her many attackers, she has a much needed moment of clarity. She weighs her limited options: Attempt to avenge her companions and risk getting killed herself, or escape and accept the fact that she failed her mission. She wanted nothing more than to kill Turchess at this moment, but self preservation had taken over. She hated herself for it, but decided that revenge will have to wait. She cuts one last look at Malia who was still distraught at the loss of her new friends.

Saber wanted to take Malia with her but knew it would be impossible.

The positioning of the Stage put the exalted between Saber and the exit and Turchess to her back. Saber wasted too much time considering her options and would have to pay for her inaction. A gout of flame jets out at her from Turchess, burning her sword arm. A few of the exalted ahead of her were attempting to cast AP but the castings fizzled without taking form. Having met teens who just as easily could have been exalted, she does not want to hurt them. Then a thought enters her mind: she remembers why she was here in the first place, what she came here to do. She was a spy and assassin. She knew that there would be times when her job caused her emotional pain of her own. She accepts the hatred she will inevitably feel for herself, but would have to overcome. Saber charges into the crowd of exalted, directing the anger she feels for herself toward them. With her burned arm she punches the first of the exalted, following through and smashing his face into the cavern floor. A fist meets her face, but before it could be pulled back Saber grabs the arm and with her veastial jaw strength, violently chomps through the limb in a few bites. She uses the severed forearm to beat another exalted to the ground. Her gory display horrified the others. They were not as indoctrinated as those from the cathedral. Turchess didn't want to cast more fire at Saber out of fear of hitting his exalted, but after seeing how they fared against her; decided that it was worth the risk. He charges his hands and fires a thinner, more direct jet of flame at Saber. She heard his gathering of energy and grabs an exalted, placing him in front of the attack. The jet pierces through the exalted and again sears Saber's sword arm, this time on the shoulder.

Her arm grievously wounded, it only served as a painful reminder of her diminishing odds of winning this fight. With no weapon, no help, and nearly surrounded, she had no idea of how she would escape. Another eruption of flames came barreling toward her. She attempts to dive out of the way only to find herself heading toward another exalted. She closes her eyes, and braces for the impact and her engulfing of flame. A sensation wells up within her that washes over her body as she hits the exalted. Her mind scatters for only the shortest of moments; one that passes by so quickly, she wonders if how she even took notice of it at all. She feels her body hit the hard cavern floor and instinctively rolls to her feet, sliding out of a puddle, her body drenched with water. Looking back, she sees a charred exalted fall to the floor. Turchess looks on in awe as do the exalted. Saber wastes no more time making her dash for the exit.

The exalted guard at the entrance was still at his post, unaware of what had occurred and that Saber was approaching; he would die having no idea that she had broken his neck on her way out. Cradling her wound, she made haste to the Bridge between Worlds to retrieve her pack, disrobing and wiping the blood from her face before entering. Draxis immediately tended to her.

Draxis: "What the hell happened?"

Saber: "It doesn't matter. Do you have my bag?"

Draxis: "I believe it *does* matter. What did they do to you down there?"

Saber: "I just need to get out of here as soon as possible. Please."

Draxis gave Saber a long, stern look of disapproval. She couldn't see it visually but she could feel it. Countless thoughts ran through the old bard's mind.

Draxis: "Fine. I'll do as you ask even though I don't like this at all. If I need to…"

Saber: "Draxis, you are the sweetest person I've ever met but this isn't a fight I want you or anyone else to have. In time, I'll solve this on my own. Just let me have that. Don't look into this, please."

Draxis returned her bag as he had truly kept it close to him. He grabbed her unburned arm, preventing her from leaving.

Draxis: "I won't fight or pursue, but I *will* help."

He slowly slid his hand gently down her burned arm. His hand illuminated with a soft green energy. As his hand passed, the burning pains were soothed, healing nearly all of the burn wounds. Only a slight lingering sensation remained.

Draxis: "It'll get better in time. Now go."

Saber hugged Draxis, thanking him for all he'd done for her. And without another word, she was on her way back to the city.

*   *   *

Turchess called back his exalted, ordering them to clean the ceremonial chamber instead.

Turchess: "Let her go. She's just more garbage from the city. No one important."

He looked to Malia who had begun to gather herself, still shaken from the ceremony and the ensuing battle. Turchess was elated that she was still there.

Turchess: "I must admit I was expecting you to attack me as well."

Malia: "Why? They were people. They wanted to join you. How could you just kill them like that?"

Turchess: "Not long ago, I took in everyone who was interested in my cause. The problem was that it was unsustainable. I didn't have the resources to provide for all of them. But in a miraculously unfortunate turn of events, they were killed. I was then forced to start from the bottom. I needed a new plan, a new agenda, and new followers. I decided on personally training a few with what I've learned. Although I realized now that I need to scrutinize initiates more."

Malia: "Is that what you've been doing with all of the people who don't have the right affinities? You just burn them?"

Turchess looked down on Malia wearing a face of unrepentance; as if any other choice was foolish.

Turchess: "Yes. I only need exalted: those who have the potential to become awakened. All others are… ash at my feet. Unfit for my purposes, and unfit to serve our lord. But you are the most capable I have ever seen. I want to train you personally."

Malia was lost in a torrent of emotions. She felt the same anger inside of her that Saber felt. She also had the opportunity to find the answers that brought her here in the first place. If she was patient, she could feign loyalty long enough to unlock her own potential and eventually avenge her friends. Malia wiped her eyes and steadied her heart.

Malia: "Teach me everything."

Turchess smiled as he extended his hand.

Turchess: "Come with me. There's much to learn."

Turchess took her down a long passageway and into his personal study. It was a small room with bookshelves, a wall lined with a chalkboard, and a desk. On the desk sat a large ancient tome, its pages were yellowed, tattered, and brimming with energy. There was something mystical about the book, Malia felt it. She was drawn to it. She looked back at Turchess who encouraged her to explore the tome. The cover was black hardened leather speckled with a dust that shimmered like the winter night sky and was clasped closed with leather straps. Malia opened the tome; it was frigid against her hands. The inside cover bared a title and an inscription.

Turchess: "This tome is the secret to my awakening. It contains…"

Malia: "*The Celestillium: A look at our worlds, from above and within.*"

Turchess was stunned.

Turchess: "You can read that?"

Malia: "Yeah why?"

Turchess: "It's written in akashean. Tell me, how can you make this language out? I've studied this for years before I came to the conclusion that it's indecipherable. There's no consistency in the characters."

Malia: "I don't know. It just makes sense to me."

Turchess: "Nonsense. You read it like you've been doing so for you entire life."

Malia: "Why didn't you ask an akashean to translate it for you? You live right next them."

Turchess: "No one must know that I have this book. Not until I've copied it. The akasheans would probably try to reclaim it for themselves. The knowledge on these pages is priceless. But with you here, you can teach me."

Malia: "I don't think it's something that you can learn, I sure as hell didn't. For starters, there's no alphabet. Every character is just an expression of will; what they want the reader to feel. Sometimes they overlap. You have to be able to feel what the writer wanted. Not only that, any person can create a word to express a specific meaning or idea that any akashean who hears or reads it will naturally understand. *Celestillium* is one of those words."

Turchess stared dumbfounded once again, resenting the fact that he had wasted years on a fruitless endeavor. Malia continued to lecture him. She flipped to a page with a scientific sketch of an æthean and what Malia assumed to be an akashean on either side of the page, connected to one another via a hole in their chests. She read the words of the section aloud.

Malia: *"Pact-makers: The souls of beings from different origins bound together to become greater than the sum of their individual halves."*

Turchess: "You must be a pact-maker! You hold within you the soul of an akashean. That's why the AP crystal reacted that way to you."

Malia: "You're the second person to say that. I'm starting to believe it myself."

Turchess: "We have to learn more. Keep reading."

The subject intrigued Malia as well. She never would have imagined that she would find the answers she sought in a book. She began reading as Turchess wrote down the words.

Malia: *"Pact-making is quite possibly the most elusive and inconsistent mystery of our worlds. Every theory I've developed was destroyed upon meeting another pact-maker. The only conclusion that I can safely draw is that a pact can be made between sentient creatures of separate origins…"*

The chapter continued on with examples the writer claims to have seen of pacts being made between creatures on different planets throughout the universe. He then with great reluctance due to an event called the *pact-hunts*, gave an extensive list of known pact-makers of significance: There was an angelic avian, a fiery old man, and a being of light shrouded in steel to name a few. There was an entry on Draxis but the face had been scribbled over. The final bio in the section was of a creature called *Blackhorn;* A heavy draconic beast with gray scales studded with black horns and plates, solid black tusks and a single curved ebon horn that protruded from the top of his head. There were pages upon pages of information on him: his exploits, affinities, and personality. What Malia found unusual was that while most of the other pact-makers looked æthean or at least had æthean traits, Blackhorn was his own being entirely and shared no æthean traits. Turchess swelled in admiration of the beast.

Turchess: "That my dear, is our lord. The Black Tempest."

Malia: "The author says some pretty sordid things about him."

Turchess: "He is a fool and a blasphemer."

Malia: "Fools don't write encyclopedias."

Turchess: "Just keep reading."

Malia: *"Blackhorn is a pact-maker of seemingly limitless potential. His origins are largely a mystery to me as he never spoke of them and I dared not pry. Ultimately it is quite fortunate that he prefers to keep to himself. While he never thought highly of ætheans. Even after thousands of years of æthean cultural maturity, he still looks at them as a planetary cancer."*

Malia: "Thousands of years?"

Turchess: "Akasheans don't seem to age. Perhaps that's a trait they share when they form a pact.

Malia: "The next chapter is pact rituals."

The cover page of this section was of several intricate glyphs that were difficult to comprehend but some of them had recognizable shapes. One resembled a pair of wings shrouding an eye.

"I once again foolishly thought that I could explain the process, but as I began my research, I was quickly reminded that there are countless examples, inconsistencies, and close to no order to pact-making. I should know by now that explaining the occult of the universe will never be a straight-forward or simple endeavor. Usually however, the more powerful of the beings will contact the lesser and

occasionally more desperate being through a means that is unique to their existence. For example, when I was contacted, I noticed a light flickering on Akasha one night. I had never seen it before, so I watched it for a time. As I gazed into it longer, I felt myself enthralled, unable to turn away. My sight was filled with white, and the silhouette of the Avalerion stood before me. She had been watching me from her roost on Akasha. She enjoyed watching my journeys and found my soul to be virtuous yet naïve; that I could not see the world as it truly was. She offered to open my eyes to the path ahead of me. I accepted and so my ordeal began.

This is one of the strangest parts of the ritual: The initiator will become a weaker being after forming the pact at first. But over the years, they will grow into something far superior to their original halves."

Malia turns the page to find a loose sheet slid arbitrarily in between the others. On the page was a sketch of a figure holding a sphere of energy. The figure's eyes were covered with a bandage with rays of light radiating from underneath. In the background were countless eyes surrounding the figure and staring back at him. One of the eyes was drawn in a way that it appeared to follow the reader no matter what angle they viewed the page. There was only a single word angrily scratched beneath the sketch; the handwriting looked like it was written at a much earlier time than the rest of the pages she had seen so far. The state of the paper itself supported this thought. Malia looked at the word with intense focus. Turchess sat in total silence in anticipation.

Malia: "Do you want the long version or the short one?"

Turchess: "The literal version."

Malia: *"I see. Or rather I saw the truth. I could see everything. The universe unveiled itself to me. I bore witness to the unfathomable concepts of reality. I gazed out and saw within. Then I looked beyond reality; beyond the truth. I saw beyond the lies of my failed senses and into the Infinity Stream. To say it was beautiful beyond comparison is to do it great injustice, for its beauty exists outside our understanding of it, so no words could ever appropriately describe the indescribable. Every word drags it closer to existence, and further from what it is. The stream took from me my old perception. I will never see again. Not as I did before."*

Turchess: "How can one word say all of that?"

Malia: "Think of it less as a word and more as a story. If I had to condense it into one term, it'd be *My Ordeal.*"

Turchess: "How do you say the real word?"

Malia attempted to read the word aloud. Her voice transcended what should be capable of coming out of an æthean mouth. It had an angelic euphony to it that was as pleasant to hear as it was to say. When she concluded the word, she felt a complex series of emotions. First, images of darkness and snarling rows of teeth. She then questioned why such an image would suddenly occur to her. She settled that she did not understand as an undeserved sense of entitlement came to her; feeling it beneath her to work for someone less capable than her. Quickly, she realized that while she is able to descipher the tome, Turchess was still her surperior in that he was able to learn so much by comprehending images alone. The next emotion that washed over her was of the unbearable pressure of all of her past and future mistakes crushing her from all sides. The suddenness of them all made her briefly desire death as a release. To shake off the longing for death, she thought about how the future could only be better because nothing she will ever experience in her life will feel as bad as she did in that moment. That final realization left her in a moment of bliss before that too fluttered away and finally gave her back to her own emotions. All of this occurred in a matter of seconds. Turchess had no idea of the mental journey Malia had taken.

Turchess: "Bah! Useless. I don't need ancient epiphanies. I want to know how to become a pact maker. Move onto the next part."

Turchess looked down at his notes to realize that everything he had written was in akashean. Despite having written it, he couldn't read anything on the page. He incinerated his pen in rage.

Malia: "It looks like you can't just copy this down after all."

Turchess: "Then why would he bother writing an encyclopedia? He already knows everything in the book."

Malia: "I guess I'll be the one teaching you."

Turchess' face twisted with a combination of jealousy and pure hatred. He attempted to control himself but failed. Flames erupted from his eyes and mouth as he howled in anger. He blazed out of the study without a word, leaving the smell of burning metal lingering behind him and Malia alone with the Celestillium. Malia felt compelled to continue reading on her own to study in peace, even if for only a few minutes. She knew that she would have plenty of time to study the tome if she stole it and made her escape but she would have to be fast. Without another thought, she closed the tome and stuffed it uncomfortably under her robe. It didn't hide well, but in the darkness wouldn't be noticed at a distance. She exited the study quickly and cautiously. The smell of burning metal wafted away from the back caverns toward the exit. There were exalted still cleaning and repairing the stage and altar from the skirmish that had only recently occurred. One of them noticed her and shouted.

Exalted drone: "Father said you're to remain in his study. Get back in there now!"

Malia was not about to follow the orders of Turchess or any of his exalted for that matter. She tightened her grip on the Celestillium and made a dash for the exit. She made it to the passageway well before the exalted. The light of the approaching surface was a strain on her eyes as well as a welcome sight. Silhouettes blocked the light and her eyes adjusted to see two more exalted guarding the exit. With the other exalted rapidly approaching behind her, she knew that she had no time to wrestle with exalted ahead of her. As the first exalted leaped forward to grab her, she jumped to the side and into the hands of another. As the exalted grabbed her arm, she rushed in and smashed her nose with a head-butt, laying the exalted flat on her back. As Malia stepped over the down body, she lost her footing. The remaining exalted descended upon her. To escape his grip Malia slithered out of her robe, leaving him with a fistful of fabric. Malia sprinted on toward *The Bridge between Worlds* to seek Draxis' help. She burst through the door and the entire tavern turned their attention to her. Draxis wrapped up a conversation with a guest and rushed to greet Malia.

Draxis: "You and your friend have a habit of barging in here. What happened *this* time?"

Malia: "They killed them and they're trying to kill me."

Draxis: "They killed who? Your friends?"

Malia gave Draxis a tearful nod.

Draxis: "I've heard enough about this cult."

The exalted rushed into the tavern, winded and stumbling. They attempted to make their way toward Malia, but were balked by Draxis. They gazed fearfully into his haunting mask. One of them belted out a sentence.

Exalted: "This doesn't concern you. We're here for her and nothing else."

Draxis: "Let's talk about this outside please?"

The exalted held their ground. Anxious to avenge his new friends, Draxis slowly removed his mask and lowered his hood, revealing a foul, putrid visage dripping with nightmares. As Draxis uncovered his face, the tavern patrons all looked away; the exalted did not. Their reaction was a combination of instant insanity, nausea, and terror. They dropped to the floor, convulsing and spasming hard enough to break and dislocate their own bones. Their screams of pain, fear, and sickness became gurgles of blood from screaming their throats out. The sounds subsided as they died in absolute agony. Draxis covered up again before returning to Malia.

Draxis: "And that's why my face makes terrible table talk."

Draxis gestured for someone to clean the bodies and a pair of possibly young akasheans came to help. One looked entirely æathean other than a second face on her back while the other had a crystalline skin that cracked with every movement. Slowly, the patrons return to their own business.

Malia: "There are more of them coming. And the prophet can shoot fire."

Draxis: "When they get here, we'll make them pay for what they did to our friends."

Malia: "Did Saber make it out?"

Draxis: "She did. Her arm was badly burned. I did what I could for her but she was tight of lip and made me promise not to get involved. She swore revenge and didn't want me to take that from her. I'm having a hard time keeping that promise now."

Malia was relieved to find out that Saber had made it out alive. She barely remembered the fight.

Draxis: "Ah. I have *some* good news for you. My scholar friend was free and came here to see you. Malia, meet Doctor Ava Grand."

Doctor Grand was a tall, slim gentleman with an afro that crested back like a mane of feathers. His eyes were the most striking thing about him. They were gentle and pleasing to look at, yet had a distant and cold quality to them and shimmered like an aurora. The longer she looked at them, the more she saw, even though she had no idea what it was she was seeing. He wore a traveler's cloak that draped down to his shins, covering his entire body save for a slot on the side for his arm.

Dr. Grand: "Draxis tells me you had some questions about the occult."

A large bladed-spider akashean entered the tavern.

Blade spider: "That prophet asshole is here and he's got like thirty dudes with him. I think you better take this one outside."

Dr. Grand: "We'll continue once this prophet mess is over with. Draxis, I'll take care of this one. I owe you. You, come with me."

Malia nodded compliantly.

Outside, Turchess and the exalted approached the open market outside of the tavern. The tavern patrons barreled out onto the village's main road (the only road) to witness the confrontation. Dr. Grand stood in the middle of the street with Malia close to his side. Turchess and his cult stopped far enough away from him that they needed to shout to one another, taking caution of a man who dared stand before a mob.

Turchess: "I don't know what lies this girl has undoubtedly told you and it is of no consequence. Return her to me at once and I'll be on my way."

Dr. Grand: "She only told us that you were coming after her and that you killed her friends. What is so important about this girl that you would bring your cult here after her?"

Turchess: "I've killed no one. She is a student of mine. She is not well and must be cared for."

Dr. Grand: "Then she will be cared for here or in the city. Not in your caverns."

Turchess: "Please. She has stolen something of great value to our cause. It must be returned."

Dr. Grand: "And what would that be?"

Turchess: "Return the girl."

Dr. Grand leaned down and spoke softly to Malia.

Dr. Grand: "What's he talking about? What did you steal?"

Malia: "A book. It's how he taught himself to breathe fire, but he can only read the pictures. So he needs me to read the rest."

Malia showed Dr. Grand the Celestillium. His eyes flashed. A gust of frigid air surrounded them and raised skyward, clearing the sky of clouds over the village and subsided. Dr. Grand's attention shifted back to Turchess who still hadn't moved.

Dr. Grand: "I thank you for finding this, but you will not be leaving with the girl or the book. This discussion is over."

Turchess: "The book and the girl are mine!"

Turchess' eyes and mouth erupt with white hot flames. He hurls a blaze at Dr. Grand that expanded as it traveled. By the time it reached Dr. Grand, its flames reached three-times his height. Dr. Grand flaps his cloak at the blaze and it chills harmlessly into a glimmering snow drift. The snow wafts skyward as the winds begin to blow. The clouds above reformed into a dark ominous cluster. The heat of the summer was replaced by the arctic bite of winter. A swirl of ice and wind surrounds Dr. Grand and dissipates. Where once stood a man, now stands the angelic avian Malia saw in the Celestillium; his broad wings stretching out from his back. The top half of his face was that of an avian, with a large, sharp, black beak and the lower half was that of an æthean. The crest of feathers lay back as his hair did before and bore the colors of an aurora dancing in the sky on a winter night.

With a single furious flap of his wings a gale is conjured, whirling itself into a cyclone as it whips toward Turchess; engulfing him. Scattering the exalted as it climbs skyward, melding with the clouds. Dr. Grand fires a shimmering ray of light from his finger at the top of the cyclone that explodes in a bright flash, blowing away the clouds and leaving a radiant aurora in the sky. The chilling wind subsides, and the warmth of summer returns as the aurora dissipates. Dr. Grand drapes himself in his wings and addresses the battered exalted before him.

Dr. Grand. "The false herald of Blackhorn is no more. Cease your worship of destruction or perish with him."

The exalted rose to their feet only to bow down to their knees in exchange. They began worshipping Dr. Grand.

Exalted: "No. You have shown us the power he promised. It is real and it was you we were meant to follow."

Dr. Grand: "You are not meant to follow anyone. You are your own people. In time I will return to undo the damage the false herald has done to your minds. But for now return to your homes or make a new one here."

Many of the exalted, returned to the cavern, others headed into the village. Dr. Grand did not clearly explain his intentions to them. Were they to wait here for his return or should they return to their own homes and wait for him to find them they wondered. No clarity was given. Dr. Grand turned his gaze unto Malia.

Dr. Grand: "As for you; you have done me wonders by returning my book to me and I owe you a great deal."

Malia: "You wrote this? Then you're the one who made the pact with Avalerion. I have so many questions. I don't even know where to start."

Dr. Grand: "It pleases me to see such enthusiasm in my work. Let's start with your name."

Malia: "Malia."

Dr. Grand: "Malia, it's a pleasure to meet you. Now, you said that the prophet needed you to read the Celestillium. You can read akashean then?"

Malia: "Yes. It's one of the things I wanted to ask you, but after reading some of the book I think that I may be a pact-maker."

Dr. Grand: "Let's find out then."

Dr. Grand got as close to Malia's face as he could without having his beak touch her and peered deeply into her eyes. Malia stared back into his; behind the aurora was a sea of black littered with countless stars twinkling against the cosmos. She could feel him combing the essence of her being with his eyes. He plucked something within her that caused a stirring in her soul.

Dr. Grand: "There is indeed a pact-being in there. But he's asleep."

Malia: "How can you see that?"

Dr. Grand: "I can see anything as long as I know what to look for. I can help you communicate with him… among other things."

Malia: "You can?"

Dr. Grand: "Absolutely. As a matter of fact, I'd like to make you my personal student."

Malia: "First Turchess, now you. Why does everyone want to make me their student?"

Dr. Grand: "You clearly don't seem to understand how unique you are. Without guidance, you'd live an interesting life trying to figure it all out. But there's no need for that if you can learn from those who've traveled that path before. Why rediscover something that others have refined into a science?"

Malia: "I'd love to become your student. It'd be a dream come true."

Dr. Grand whisked her in his arms, taking flight with his powerful wings. The air above was cold, she wasn't sure if it was of his doing or not but the view from the sky was more than worth bearing the chill. Malia imagined having the ability to chase this view at any time; to be able to travel anywhere in the city and beyond in minutes. She began to wonder about all of the things she would learn under Dr. Grand's tutelage.

16– A GRIHM REALIZATION

-Perspective adds a world of insight.-

The first cycle of the weekend had finally arrived. Not soon enough for Jin and Grihm who had grown tired of watching an empty apartment. They found a distraction one cycle by combing the magweb to try and figure out what happened in the sky north of the city. In the end, they learned that the rest of the city was just as confused. Ezra's weekend began differently than her work week. She slept in to catch up on all of the sleep she missed during the week. She finally awoke at mid-cycle and cleaned up. Ezra took her time: making herself a coiler eggs and toast breakfast. She played some coffee shop R&B while picking out her outfit. Jin always found something else to do while Ezra was changing; he felt perverted otherwise. She decided on a short floral sundress with leggings and boots. On her way out the door, she grabbed her purse and headed toward the markets. Jin and Grihm set out as well, making sure to keep a considerable distance.

At the markets, Ezra perused the stalls, joking and conversing with many of the vendors. She bought handcrafted candles and soaps at one stall, but took special interest in a knife and leather vendor. She tried on many of the knife sheathes and tested the ease and comfort of quick drawing a sample wooden knife. Jin noticed that she had practiced hands and was familiar around knives.

Jin: "Maybe I'm crazy, but what does following her around have to do with learning about her job?"

Grihm: "Being that she's Bradley's personal assistant, the plan was to find out more about him through her. But she doesn't take any work home so we might need to go to where she works in Central."

Jin: "I hope not. Let's check in and see what they got in mind back at base first."

Grihm: "Good call."

Grihm stepped to the side and called Oska with her phone while Jin kept an eye on Ezra.

Oska: "What's up?"

Grihm: "Jin and I were talking and realized that we're not going to get anything out of the target this way. She's pretty normal and leaves her work at work. Unless you guys have something else, I think the only way to get anything out of her would be to get into her desk at Central."

Oska: "We've noticed and we're on the same page. Damien wants you to keep an eye on her for a little longer. Finish out the cycle and we'll have a new plan for you."

Grihm: "Got it. I'll pass that along."

Jin: "What's the word?"

Grihm: "We're going to keep at it until we get new orders next cycle."

Ezra wrapped up her conversation with the knife vendor. In the end she didn't buy anything from him.

Having finished at the markets, Ezra headed further into town. She went to the movie theatre and purchased a ticket to see *Negative Zero*. Jin and Grihm followed suit and took a seat in the back. The movie was an excessively complicated plot about a group of assassins trying to kill competing assassins. They go on to find out they were hunting each other, with the protagonists learning in the end that he was hunting himself, only to be betrayed by the person who hired them all. They rushed out of the theater as the credits began to roll and waited inconspicuously for Ezra to emerge. Ezra's next destination was toward the town center for lunch upscale lunch at Petal Gust Park. Petal Gust housed dozens of wonder blossom trees which are famous for their periwinkle leaves that gave the park a pastel hue. The café was hosting a jazz band for the lunch period, which drew in a small gathering of people sitting and relaxing in the grass. Grihm wanted a seat at the restaurant but didn't want to get too close to Ezra, so she and Jin relaxed in the grass while Ezra ate. Jin spotted the ulor lady walking her pet yet again. She waved to Jin and Grihm as she passed.

Grihm: "Why does she walk that thing? It doesn't have legs."

Jin: "Maybe she's going for a walk herself and just wants to take her pet with her."

The old lady saw Ezra at the restaurant and stopped for a quick chat with her neighbor before continuing her walk. Ezra made a phone call shortly after. She stood up and scanned the area as if she were looking for someone. Grihm and Jin turned their heads away as she looked in their direction. After finishing her phone call, Ezra ate the last bite of her meal and sat back to enjoy the atmosphere.

Grihm: "I've been thinking. You don't talk much about where you're from. I think being from outside of the city is pretty cool."

Jin: "That's because there isn't really a lot to talk about. But shouldn't we be focused on Ezra?"

Grihm: "Just look around you. It's hard to be serious with this kind of ambiance."

With those words, Jin looked back at her with a different filter. Among a vibrancy of the blue petals billowing gently alongside the whispers of the trees carried by a gentle breeze, the pillow-soft bed of grass beneath them, the rhythm of the band in tune with the beating of hearts, and rays of sunshine speckling her face, Jin saw her for the first time, not as a teammate or fellow soldier, but for the beautiful woman that she was throughout. Her eyes spoke in a way that only a woman is capable. He had finally seen her as she had seen him.

Jin: "Sorry. I guess I'm still trying not to get ahead of myself. I'm just trying to integrate."

Grihm: "Relax. You've proven yourself plenty already. You don't have to impress anyone anymore; especially me. While it *is* serious, we all know when to turn it on and off. Well, except maybe Damien."

Jin: "Thanks. Damien *does* seem pretty wound up though."

Grihm: "Don't get me wrong; I respect the guy and his drive to accomplish whatever he sets his eyes to, but it's the same determination that I'm afraid will lead him or all of us into some shit. Salena keeps him grounded. She's probably the best thing that's ever happened to him."

Jin: "Damien's really standoffish. It's hard to imagine him being open with anyone."

Grihm: "No, they're good together. They both used to be out there. But they have this weird dynamic now where they *tame* each other. To be honest I'm little jealous."

Jin: "About the taming or the relationship?"

Grihm: "Don't get cute."

Grihm said jokingly as she returned a cute smile of her own.

Grihm: "I meant finding someone who balances you out. That perfect yin/yang relationship."

Jin: "How long have you been looking?"

Grihm: "Just long enough."

The band ended their set to take a lunchbreak. Ezra was joined by a suited-gentleman carrying a briefcase and Jin recognized him the instant he laid eyes on him: Emil Estoque. Grihm and Jin's conversation would have to wait for another time.

Jin: "Looks like this mission isn't a bust afterall."

Ezra and Emil exchanged pleasantries and Emil ordered himself a small dish to snack on and a glass of red wine. In the meantime, Ezra sat the briefcase in her lap and opened it, examining its contents. The briefcase was opened away from Jin and Grihm, blocking their view as Ezra constructed something inside. Grihm attempted to COMMs Oska to alert her of the recent turn of events, but the transmission was weak and failed. Jin attempted as well with the same results. Grihm was forced to make a call using her phone. The call went through, but was quickly dropped before anyone could say a word. Emil looked down at a tablet screen and smiled. A heavy feeling of danger washed over Grihm. Jin was putting the pieces together just as quickly.

Grihm: "Something's wrong. They're onto us."

Jin: "How?"

Grihm: "I don't know. We'll figure it out later."

Jin: "I don't think they know where we are though. Not yet."

Grihm: "I'll make us some cover. If we get separated, try to get away from the park and COMMs me."

Grihm reached into her jacket to grab a handful of bomblets. She covertly flicked them in different directions. She tossed one more at the restaurant toward Ezra and Emil. Grihm took one last look at Jin deep in his eyes; her eyes said more than the words that followed.

Grihm: "Be safe."

Grihm detonates the bomblets, filling the area with dense clouds of white smoke. The crowd screams in panic between the fits of coughing. Jin and Grihm make an immediate dash for the streets. They clear the last cloud of smoke revealing the streets ahead behind trees a line of trees. In the distance, police vehicles were arriving with their sirens blaring.

Jin: "How the hell are they responding this fast?"

Grihm: "They were already on their way. This is bad. The whole district could be looking for us."

Gunshots are fired into the air, causing the crowd to instinctively drop to the ground and take cover.

Emil: "The smoke didn't help you last time either Jin."

Emil shouts out from the smoke cloud; he was fairly close. If there was any doubt that Emil knew that they were here, it was gone now. The crowd slowly begins to rise again to continue escaping. Now more determined to escape, the gunshots didn't slow them down. Standing on a stony park wall, Ezra spots Grihm and Jin and points them out to Emil. Emil closes the distance, blade drawn. Unable to hide among the crowd, Jin faces Emil and readies for combat. Ezra hops down and rushes into the fray wielding a pair of bladed semi-auto pistols. She reaches Jin first and begins the battle proper. As she raises her pistols, Jin raises his barrier and plows into her. Jin redirects his attention to Emil just in time to defend himself, locking blades with his rival. Grihm moves to engage Ezra.

Emil breaks sword-lock with Jin and follows with a lunging strike from an extremely close distance. Although quick, Emil barely gave himself time to line up the attack. He misses the blade, but follows with a spin elbow to Jin's face before bringing his sword around for another stab. Emil was far more aggressive than Jin had prepared himself for but Jin was determined to not let him dictate the flow of the fight again. Jin allows himself to fall to the ground, letting the stab whiz by above him. On his way down Jin kicks Emil's knee, causing him to buckle and lose his stance. Jin bounces back to his feet, swinging wildly as he does. Emil blindly blocks the strike behind his back, putting himself in an awkward position. Jin retorts with a swift kick to the face.

Ezra sweeps at Grihm's legs, narrowly missing but recovers to her feet. She fires both pistols at Grihm; Grihm dips low to dodge the shots. Grihm was close enough to grab one of Ezra's arms to pull her in closer as she rises for a head-butt to Ezra's nose. In an impressive display of flexibility, Ezra raises her leg over Grihm's shoulder and wraps it around her neck, using her weight to take Grihm down; although dropping one of her pistols in the process. Grihm knocks the dropped pistol away and grabs Ezra's arm as she attempts to slice or shoot Grihm: both were options that Grihm had no intentions in exploring. Grihm was considerably stronger than Ezra and could at least hold her off with one arm. Grihm uses her free hand to punch Ezra in the face. The pistol fires off a burst, narrowly missing Grihm's head. The jab was enough to give Grihm a chance to turn over.

Both Emil and Ezra stumble back toward one another. Now back-to-back, they crisscross opponents: Emil striking at Grihm, while Ezra fires several bursts at Jin. Emil powers up his distortion blade and slices wildly at Grihm; the attack was almost lazily obvious. Grihm ducks low, letting the attack sail at Jin who had defended himself from Ezra's gunfire with his barrier. As the distortion blade collides with Jin's barrier, it shatters, sending shards of ethereal energy whipping toward Grihm. The ethereal shards superficially cut her before dissipating. The wounds were not lethal, but debilitating. Ezra jumps at Jin's barrier and springs herself skyward toward Grihm, lining up a clear shot. Grihm hurls a hail of concussive bomblets that knock Ezra from the air. Jin, distraught that his barrier was used to his opponents advantage, retaliates with a foolishly desperate surprise attack: he whips Hermes at Emil. Emil shows Jin that if he is capable of deflecting a large shell fired from a gun, he is certainly capable of deflecting a thrown sword. Emil backhands Hermes into the air with his shield arm and prepares for a finishing lunge. Jin charges Emil with his barrier and Emil thrusts his distortion blade into the center of Jin's barrier; it bevels inward. Jin struggles to maintain the spell. Emil's distortion blade, only sustainable for quick and direct strikes, dissipates as does Jin's barrier. The dissipation of Jin's barrier sends Emil's arm recoiling back. Jin continues his forward motion, catching Hermes from the air as well as catching Emil unprepared. Jin brings Hermes down hard, but is still only able to graze Emil's shoulder as he slips out of range. He staggers back, holding his wound.

Emil: "You're going to regret that."

In the momentary break in combat, Grihm realizes the situation: they are only being toyed with while backup forces move in to surround them. Jin and Grihm would have to flee as soon as possible if they were to have any hopes of escaping. Grihm hurls the last of her bomblets at Ezra to distract her opponent. Ezra reacts quickly, shooting them out of the air; they were small burst anti-personnel bomblets, which were most effective at close range due to their low explosive yield. One of which was a flash bang that blinded Ezra for a moment. By the time Ezra was able to focus again, Grihm had already dashed away and was making her way toward Jin.

Grihm: "Jin, they're stalling! Let's go."

Her words fall on deaf ears. Jin was far too engaged with his rival to focus on anything else. Ezra aims her pistols again at Grihm, forcing her to take cover behind a nearby stone wall. Ezra however, did not pursue, standing to guard Emil and Jin from Grihm. The approaching police forces were entering the park. Time had run out for the two of them. Grihm didn't want to think about what would happen if they failed to escape. Unable to pry Jin away from Emil, and held at bay by Ezra, Grihm moves to buy some time by taking out the first responding police officers. Grihm blazes at them like a furious beast. By the time the first officer had seen her approach, she was already airborne with a flying knee that connected with his face; finishing him off by slamming his head into the police car. The second officer caught a swift back kick to the chin. He falls flat on the ground and was rendered unconscious by a series of rapid face punches.

The break in combat gave Jin a chance to assess the situation: Grihm was nowhere to be seen. His ears tune into the sound of sirens in the distance. He remembers that the plan was to escape before he got tied up with Emil. He hears Grihm call out to him.

Grihm: "Jin, you idiot. Let's go!"

Ezra was standing idly, with no concern for Grihm.

Ezra: "Do you want me to hunt her down?"

Emil: "No. Let's focus on what he have now. No use risking both."

Jin: "Grihm, I think you're going to have to put this one in the loss column."

Grihm: "Stop being ridiculous."

Grihm shouts out from behind the police vehicle. She only pokes her head out to speak.

Jin: "Either you get out of here, or we both go down."

Grihm: "Then we're both going down."

Jin: "Grihm, you don't have time for this."

Ezra: "I do. I've been waiting all week for this."

Jin slashes at Ezra, who evades with a slight back step. The first move is made and the fighting resumes: Jin now, sandwiched between Emil and Ezra. Jin is forced to divide his attacks between the two opponents, who now fight conservatively to wear him down slowly. Ezra never let Jin focus on Emil for more than a few seconds, disrupting his flow of battle with an attack of her own or distracting with gunfire that she never aimed directly at him.

Grihm steps out from her cover to rejoin the fight. She picks up the pistols of the downed officers and carefully takes aim at Ezra, waiting for her to back far enough away from Jin. Ezra takes a step back after Jin deflects one of her attacks, giving Grihm a clear shot. Grihm fires freely, hitting Ezra in the arm, leg, and torso. Grihm, in her haste, overheats the weapon and discards it for the other. She moves closer to the battle with her pistol aimed and ready. Ezra falls to one knee holding her side, the most critical of her wounds. Without a second thought she fires a burst of shots into Jin's back, bringing the fight to an abrupt end. Grihm, enraged, unloads another hail of gunfire at Ezra. At a closer distance, she misses less than she did before. In her angered state, didn't aim or see where she hit Ezra, who collapses to the ground. Grihm aims the pistol at Emil and pulls the trigger only to hear the hissing of an overheated weapon venting. Emil ignites his distortion blade and takes aim at Grihm. Fighting through the pain, Jin attempts to pick Hermes up off the ground to fight on. Emil steps on the sword and redirects his aim at Jin, plunging it deep into him.

Emil: "That's quite enough out of you two. Toss the gun and lie down or I splatter Jin's blood all over this park. Five seconds."

Jin: "Don't you dare Grihm."

Jin sputters. The distortion of the blade had dissipated, leaving only the wound.

Emil: "Either you both come with me or Jin doesn't come at all."

Emil prepares to stab again but halts when Grihm throws the gun aside.

Jin: "Get out of here. I messed up, we can't both go down."

Grihm: "We both messed up. I won't let you take the full weight of our mistakes."

Jin: "You don't have time for this."

Jin's voice was fading from the stab wound in his shoulder. With the last of his strength, Jin attempts to rise and strike Emil with his fist. Emil instinctively skewers Jin through his shoulder again. Jin's world immediately goes black as he collapses. Emil was both confused and frustrated with the turn of events. Having lost his leverage, he looks unto Grihm with scorn. Conscious of the passing of time, he turns to tend to Ezra, who like Jin, was also losing blood. Unlike Jin however, she was still awake; fighting to rise to her feet. Emil eases her back down as he calls for assistance.

Witnessing Jin fall lifelessly to the ground hurt as if she herself had been stabbed. What hurt even more was knowing that the only option left was to leave him behind. She tapped back into her soldiers instincts to break free of her emotional paralysis. Grihm escaped by cutting through the far side of the park to avoid the police arriving directly to the scene. There was a crowd building around the edge of the park; people wanting to see what was going on, but not wanting to get too close. Upon seeing Grihm's wounds, they asked if she saw what happened or if she was involved. She ignored them. Her phone began to vibrate, alerting her of all the calls and messages she'd missed now that it was no longer being blocked: all from Oska. Grihm returned the call.

Grihm: "Mission's a bust."

Oska: "Are you okay? What happened?"

Grihm: "Our cover was compromised and I need a way out."

Oska: "I? What about Jin?"

Grihm: "… Jin is down."

The words hurt to say. There was a pause on the other end.

Oska: "Got it. Are you hurt and do you need assistance?"

Grihm: "No. Just a way out of here."

Oska: "Revco used a series of tunnels when they were developing the city. It's mostly used to move heavy construction vehicles and equipment around the city without creating traffic. That's your best bet right now."

Grihm: "Just point me in the right direction."

Oska: "You're going to have to go underground so I'll need to COMMs you."

Grihm: "We were being denied service earlier. It should be fine now."

Oska: "Take the nearest manhole down and I'll lead you from there."

The first few manholes were in the middle of busy streets. Grihm searched a few blocks over for one that had fewer eyes on it. She finds a crowbar in one of the alleys and used it as a makeshift manhole key. She lifted the manhole cover; albeit through great effort and hopped into the depths. The tunnels were dimly lit by a series of emergency lights that functioned continuously even when the tunnels were not in use. Oska directed Grihm to a maintenance door that, after Grihm broke the lock with her crowbar, allowed her to descend further below. The passageway opened into a massive vehicle tunnel. This tunnel's lighting was lower than the previous. Grihm's phone would have to provide the rest of the light. Oska's signal began to break up as Grihm descended.

Oska: "You've got a long … ahead of you now. When you reach the end of the tunnel … under the council transfer station."

Grihm: "Why didn't we take these tunnels *into* Revco?"

Oska: "… wasn't a need … patrolled … take longer."

Grihm: "You're breaking up. I'll COMMs you when I get there."

Traversing the tunnel took several hours, during which her phone died, leaving her almost completely in the dark. This turned out to be beneficial when a roving patrol vehicle headed toward her. She spotted their headlights in the distance and took cover against the wall.

Grihm: "Help! Please someone help me!"

Grihm screamed out in her best panicked voice; which didn't require much effort in her current state. The vehicle immediately slowed down and used its lights to scan the area. It spotted Grihm leaning against the wall cradling her wounds and smeared with dirt. The vehicle stopped and two people stepped out: a man and a woman. They approached her cautiously with soft voices.

Male guard: "I don't know what you're doing down here, but relax. It's going to be okay. We're going to get you some help."

Female guard: "Are you hurt, can you walk?"

Grihm curled into a ball and shied away from their aid. The woman attempted to calm her by caressing her head and shushing her, repeating "It's going to be okay." When the male guard kneeled down next to her as well, Grihm struck him in the face and knocked him flat on his back. She kicked the female guard away, grabbing her gun as she did. Grihm also picked up a flashlight and pointed both at the two patrollers.

Grihm: "You, drop your gun and slowly rise to your feet. Keep your hands up."

Male and Female guard: "What the hell?"

Grihm: "I don't want to leave you stranded in this place without a car. So I'm going to let you drive me to the council transit exit. Get in the car."

The guards complied. Grihm sat in the back with the gun at the ready.

Female guard: "Can I ask what you were doing down here?"

Grihm: "No. As a matter of fact, if you ask me anything else, I'll kill both of you."

Male guard: "Bullshit. How're you…

Grihm fired the gun next to his ear. Not hitting anyone or thing, but deafening him.

Grihm: "I don't need you for anything. This is just convenient for everyone."

The rest of the drive was silent save for the running of the engine. The drive took another twenty minutes, which on foot could have taken Grihm hours. The road led to a large solid wall. On the right side was the door that would lead Grihm to the transfer station. She commanded the guards to drive off back into the tunnels and continue their patrol. She shot the lock to bypass the door and climbed back up to the maintenance tunnels. Grihm COMMed Oska once the signal returned.

Grihm: "I'm back."

Oska: "That was fast. How'd everything go?"

Grihm: "It was quiet. Where exactly in the station am I going to come out? I don't want to come up under a train."

Oska: "It'll be a maintenance closet. You should be able to unlock it from the inside. But you'll probably run into to maintenance crew. They're council citizens so you don't have to worry about them trying to report you to Revco or anything. But *do* try to be cordial if you can. We don't want any issues with the council."

Grihm: "I'm all out of cordial right now Oska."

After a long ladder climb, she opened a hatch into a storage room. The door was open and she could see through into the station. Even though Grihm had little patience left for anyone at this point, she had even less fight left in her. She rummaged through the storage room and found a mechanic's jumpsuit which she donned to avoid drawing extra attention. It was too small, but was another detail that Grihm would ignore. The jumpsuit allowed her to walk out of the station without anyone taking a second glance at her. Once she crossed over into the Eratech section of the station, a feeling of comfort washed over her. She never imagined she would enjoy the idea of simply being in Eratech so much. Outside, the sun beamed onto her skin, another feeling she missed greatly after the time she spent in the chilling darkness. She spotted Saber waiting for her standing beside Damien's car. Seeing her best friend was the best thing she could have asked for. If another strong emotion washed over her again anytime soon, she wasn't sure if she'd be able to keep herself from crying. They hugged, each happy the other had returned from their mission in one piece. Grihm noticed Saber's burns creeping up from her shoulder and onto her neck. Saber noticed Grihm's jumpsuit in addition to her generally battered state.

Saber: "You look like you've been through hell. Are you okay?"

Grihm: "These are nothing. What happened to you?"

Saber: "The short version: I blew my cover and paid for it. Don't worry; it actually doesn't even hurt anymore."

Grihm: "It looks gnarly."

Saber: "It still hurts when you say things like that about it though."

Saber adjusted her collar to hide the scar.

Grihm: "Sorry. I'm not thinking right. It's been… rough. I lost Jin."

Saber: "I heard. Is he..."

Grihm: "No! I don't know. When I last saw him he…"

Grihm's voice trailed off. She took a moment to regain her composure; fighting hard to hold down her emotions.

Grihm: "Please tell me Damien's planning something."

Saber: "Yes. Damien has something in the works right now. The sooner we get back, the sooner we can get started."

Hope washed over Grihm, reinforcing the hope she never lost. They hopped into the car and drove off. Grihm was still feeling agitated and imagined she'd feel this way until Jin was no longer in harm's way. Saber noticed Grihm's restless tapping.

Saber: "Do you want to talk about it?"

Grihm: "Yes! I know I should be worried about what happened to you, and I am. But I can see you. You're safe and out of danger. I hate that something happened to you and if there's anything I can do for you, I will. But Jin's not safe. When I last saw him, he was bleeding on the ground and I had to leave him behind. We've never had anyone from the team go down in combat. And having to leave them behind like that… I feel like shit. I failed the mission, the team, and Jin."

Saber: "Take it easy. It's not your fault. I don't know the details, but I'm sure you did everything you could to help Jin. Guilt-tripping yourself isn't going to fix anything."

Grihm: "I know. I just hate the fact that nothing I did helped. I've never lost anyone close to me before and the idea that I could lose Jin…"

Grihm went silent as she stared out the window; still tapping nervously. Saber attempted to ease Grihm's mind by relating.

Saber: "My mission had me going undercover up north to infiltrate the BTC. On the way there I met up with a group of people; teens actually. Probably not even in college. Good kids. I traveled with them because we were all going to the same place. We talked and I learned a lot about them during the trip. Malia was the shy type, but has an adventurous girl inside of her she desperately wants to unleash. A vegetarian, and had never drank before. Chamila was a girl driven by her love for her boyfriend, Duke. Together, they were ready to face the world if necessary. Randal, came off as a meathead but showed that there was a person inside that wanted to be free. I even told them about myself. I felt *that* comfortable around them."

Grihm: "Why are you telling me this?"

Saber continued with her story without stopping.

Saber: "Inside the cult, Turchess separated us based on our "potential." Duke, Chamila, and Randal were placed in front of us and burned alive for no reason other than he thought they were weak. Three lives looking to start a new life were taken away without a second thought. I won't forget the sounds of their screams. The smell they left behind. Who they were."

Grihm: "I'm sorry. I don't know what to say to that."

Saber: "For the first time in as long as I can remember, I lost it. Seeing them killed like that made me forget the mission, disregard my own well-being, and filled me with rage. Without even thinking I was fighting Turchess and his cult all by myself. Punching and biting my way out. But do you know what the worst part was?"

Grihm hung eagerly on Saber's story. She shook her head to move the tale along.

Saber: "The fact that I left Malia behind. I wanted to grab her and escape, but there was no way. I wanted to stay back there and fight. But in my most desperate moment, I remembered why I was there. It was my moment of clarity that made me realize that fighting to my death wasn't going to solve anything. Our friends were lost, but falling with them wouldn't avenge their souls. That would have to be done in time, but I can't do that if I'm dead. I know it seems like we've abandoned our friends, but that's the most important thing about being soldiers: making hard choices and living with them. I hate it too, but this is the situation we're in and we all have to find a way to make it work."

Grihm remained silent, mulling over Saber's story she saw merit in Saber's words, but not comfort. Saber spoke of death in the past tense but Grihm wanted empathy and action. Grihm couldn't deny Saber's perspective however; it was her sense of duty that pulled her out of that park. Grihm had found a new truth about herself. To her shame, she would not choose love over duty.

17– LOCKDOWN

-Access denied. All systems are currently offline. If you have any questions, please submit them to Overseer Oska and they will be answered in the order that they are received. Thank you for your patience.-

With Grihm having returned from the mission, Damien immediately called for a meeting in the war room; not giving her a moment of reprieve. The rest of DL was already seated (save for Jin's empty chair) and awaiting Saber and Grihm's return.

Damien: "First off, I'm glad you made it back Grihm. I hear things didn't go as planned."

Grihm: "Thanks. I don't know how they knew, but they were waiting for us. Ezra even called me by my real name."

Damien: "I was afraid of that. With what happened at the cathedral and now this, I think it's safe to say someone's been tipping Revco off."

It took a moment for Grihm to take in Damien's words. Once she shook off the immediate reaction of disbelief, she snapped back.

Grihm: "You were *afraid*? You mean you knew about this and you sent Jin and me out there anyway?"

Damien: "That's why the mission was only surveillance. You weren't supposed to do anything to draw attention to yourselves. And if anything suspicious *did* happen, we would know they were being fed information on us."

Grihm: "You mean *you* would know. I can't believe this. Why wouldn't you tell the two people going into harm's way what was really going on?"

Damien: "The only other person who knew about your mission was Oska and it still got leaked. Limiting who knew helped me trust the whole team."

Grihm: "I wish I could say the same thing about trusting you."

Damien: "You've made your point. But that's why we needed you to update us on anything suspicious. So we could get you out of there."

Grihm: "A lot of good *that* did. Jin's still out there. You got a plan for that?"

Damien: "I do. But no part of my original plan involved Jin getting captured. Fixing that is going to take more time."

Grihm: "We don't have time. Jin doesn't have time. I bet if it were Salena over there, you'd be on the first thing smoking to get her back."

The tension in the room spiked as a wave of discomfort washed over the team. Saber glanced briefly at Damien to gauge his reaction before cutting her eyes angrily back at Grihm. Damien remained stoic, hands clasped in front of his face. He breathed deep.

Damien: "It's not about what I want, or what any of us want right now. It's about what's possible, and what's practical for the team, the company and the district as a whole. Rushing in to retrieve Jin isn't good for any of those things right now. But before that even comes into play, let's talk about the fact that there's a spy on the loose in the citadel that has direct and undetected contact with Revco, who knows DL personnel by name and is able to identify when we move and where we're moving to. So even if rescuing someone was at the top of my list right now, I couldn't do that without getting the forces sent to do it, killed in the process. What the hell makes you think that we can just go grab Jin and come home?"

Trigger: "Okay you two. Let's take a step back. This isn't going to do anything to help either of our problems. Let's just take this one problem at a time. What do we know about this spy?"

Damien eased back, visibly relaxing his posture.

Damien: "Close to nothing. Whoever it is keeps a close eye on our movements but isn't directly involved with missions."

Grihm: "Great. So now we've narrowed it down to about a third of the personnel down here. Making progress."

Styner: "The attitude's not helping at all Grihm."

Grihm: "Neither is this meeting. Am I the only person here who cares about Jin right now?"

Oska: "We all care about Jin, but Damien's right: our hands are tied right now. We have to address the problem at home before we can move forward."

Damien: "If you're done… As I said earlier, we don't have much to go on. So in order to try and stir something up, I had Oska place the entire base on complete lockdown: No one enters or leaves, no outside communication, and limited internal communications. We'll be the only one's capable of direct COMMs outside of Oska's office. I'm also putting the base on

MILCON 0. The spy is surely going to try something if they think we're about to mobilize."

Trigger: "How long are we going to be under?"

Damien: "As long as it takes."

Grihm bit her tongue. Convinced another outburst would not help her case. She tapped impatiently on the table.

Sev: "Where do we start looking?"

Damien: "Our spy's going to be the one trying to get out or reestablish communications. Look for the person who's the most out of place. Other than that, I trust you to use your best judgement. If you find anything I'll be in the overseer's office. Dismissed."

Grihm was of course the first out of her seat but was stopped by Damien on her way to the door.

Damien: "Grihm, stay back, we need to talk."

She took her usual seat on the opposite side of the table.

Grihm: "If you're going to give me a lecture about mouthing off in the meetings, let me tell you *that* would be a waste of time."

Damien: "I want you to understand: I'm not disregarding Jin or leaving him out to dry but our current situation would make an immediate operation an absolute failure."

One on one, Grihm's tone softened as Damien's reasoning began to set in. She was still full of residual energy from her mission however and her body had not completely settled.

Grihm: "There's got to be *something* we can do about it. If the entire base is on lockdown, then the rest of the team could mobilize and the spy wouldn't be able to alert Revco."

Damien: "That would leave Oska and maybe Styner to solve the problem."

Grihm: "And the thousands of personnel we have working here."

Damien: "Who don't know that there's a spy. There's also the issue of the mobilized team getting into Revco with no support from base, no information on where Jin's located, and how to get in and out safely. Trust me, I *have* thought this through."

Grihm: "There's that word again."

Damien: "You can snap at me if you want but it doesn't make you any less wrong."

Grihm: "Are we done here?"

Damien: "I can see how much Jin means to you and whether you believe me or not doesn't change the fact that I'm working on helping him. Look, if you find this spy, I will personally lead the charge into Revco. Hell, I'll let you take charge. But I don't know how else to say it to you: We can't do anything as long as this problem persists..."

Damien paused. He removed his sunglasses and rubbed his eyes before looking back at Grihm. His sensitive eyes adjusted quickly to the soft lighting of the war room, although the lights were harsh to him.

Damien: "Never mind. Don't worry about the spy right now. Just get to medical and take some time to gather yourself. You've been through a lot."

It was quite rare for Damien to be kind or sentimental toward anyone other than Saber, especially in an official capacity. While she was sure his claim to lead a raid was just a boast, his sudden concern for her well-being surprised her. Grihm left without another word. Damien remained seated, contemplating his situation. Grihm's unrelenting argument to save Jin urged him to reconsider all possible options. He also thought more about Jin's predicament. In one season, Jin had proven himself to be a valuable asset to the Citadel and DL; he was a skilled fighter, versatile in changing situations, and everyone seemed to like him. He had even grown on Damien. Looking back, Damien began to better understand where Grihm was coming from.

*   *   *

Outside of the war room, Trigger, Sev, and Oska were waiting by the door to listen in but were unable to hear anything. If there were any doors in the base that were soundproof, it would be the door to the war room.

Trigger: "How bad was it?"

Grihm: "It was… unexpected. He told me to take some time off away from the spy task."

Oska: "Really? You didn't get an ass-chewing?"

Grihm: "He started to but he stopped and told me I needed a break. He even took off his sunglasses."

Sev: "He's only done that… twice maybe."

Trigger: "Sorry it seemed like we didn't care about Jin in there."

Oska: "We all feel the same way you do. We want to help, it's just… Damien's got a point."

Grihm: "You don't have to apologize. I get it. It's not something we can rush into. I was being unfair to Damien and the team. I'm just still fired up from the mission. It's hard to relax when you know your partner is still out there."

Trigger: "I know. That's why we're gonna figure this out and get on our way as soon as possible."

Sev: "Too bad we can't go after Jin ourselves and lock the base back down behind us."

Oska: "That's because it's psychotic."

The idea struck Grihm like a club. Her mind swirled around possibilities of a covert defection.

Grihm: "Actually, it's not. In fact, it's a great idea. Since we can only trust each other, the four of us could slip out and that would still leave Damien, Styner, and Saber to find the spy."

Trigger: "Maybe you're forgetting the lockdown part in your little scheme. We'd have no equipment and no way of getting out."

Grihm: "What are you talking about? We have all access right here."

Grihm turned to Oska mischievously. Oska was slow to catch what Grihm was implying.

Oska: "No. I will not help you mutiny."

Grihm: "Too late. Unless you stop me or report it, you're an accomplice."

Oska: "I can't. Damien would kill us if he found out. *When* he found out."

Grihm: "He'd kill *us*, but he'd only get mad at *you*. But that doesn't even matter because we'll have Jin back. He won't even remember that he's pissed off."

Sev: "I don't think Damien can forget about being pissed."

Trigger: "No one's agreed to anything Grihm. You can't force Oska into this."

Grihm: "Of all the possible ways to go about this situation, sending a small group of DLC's finest to retrieve Jin is the best option. And if Oska's with us, she'll be able to provide Intel faster and more accurately than she could here at base."

Trigger: "Bring Oska *with* us? Now you're officially talking crazy."

Oska considered Grihm's proposal in her head. The notion had never occurred to her and her mind was flooded with many new ideas and possibilities. Her internal thoughts became audible enough for the others to hear.

Oska: "…But if I go with them I'll be able to crack into and steal nearly everything from Revco's network. If I were able to get into one of the companies terminals…"

Grihm: "Boom."

Trigger: "That doesn't change the fact that it's dangerous. And what if *she* got captured?"

Grihm: "We're not hiding in plain sight like before. It took them a week to find us last time and they knew we were coming."

Trigger: "Everyone's got a plan until they get punched in the face Bianca. What about when things get out of hand?"

Grihm: "That's what we need you and Sev for. C'mon, you got nothing on me. Are you really going to back out on me again?"

Trigger shook his head in concession. It was a low blow for Grihm to use their past relationship against him, but he felt it was not as low as him backing out on her in the first place.

Trigger: "Fine, but we do it as quietly as possible. No unnecessary risks."

Grihm: "They won't even know we were there. Hell, Damien won't even know we left."

Trigger: "Let's get this over with before I realize how much of a mistake this is."

Oska: "First, we should find someplace quiet. Even though communication inside the base is down, we still want to steer clear of any would be spy."

As they head out to find an isolated location, they notice Dr. Malerius turning the corner looking confused and full of questions.

Malerius: "Oska, what's going on? Phones, Eranet, and even network messaging and intercoms are down. Did we get hacked?"

Oska: "I'm not sure what happened but we're going to look into that right now. Just sit tight; I'll have an answer for you in no time."

Malerius: "Please do hurry. I have a lot of work to do."

Grihm: "No you don't. Your job is to sit around and talk to people. You can still do your job if communications are down."

Malerius: "That shows how much you don't know. Either way, I'll let you get back to it. If you need me…"

Grihm: "Nope. Bye!"

The group hastily escaped Dr. Malerius' conversation. He watched them until they were out of sight before following with caution. Having overheard them say the word "spy" made him suspicious of what they were up to. He quickened his pace to catch them before they made another turn, keeping a healthy distance and waiting a few extra moments before turning a corner or entering a door. He followed them to the server room but stopped just outside. The server room had only one way in. They were unlikely to find a way out without his knowing.

Malerius: *"So she's fixing the servers after all. But why would she bother bringing half the team with her? Where's Jin for that matter?"*

Inside the server room pillars of machinery were stacked to the ceiling, row by row. All of them buzzed with a collective white noise; tiny lights flickered frantically. The noise was loud enough that Grihm, Trigger, Sev, and Oska would have to yell to speak to one another.

Sev: "I don't know what I hate more: the cold or the noise in here."

Oska: "The servers need to be kept cold and the noise is so no one will overhear us."

Grihm: "See, she's already making this mission better."

Oska: "Here's what I've got so far: We need to check in with Damien and give him a bogus update of our search; that'll buy us some extra time before he needs to talk to us again. After that we're on the clock, so we'll have to quickly and inconspicuously get to the armory and grab as much of your gear as you can before we jet to the hidden exit."

Sev: "People are going to catch onto us if they see us dashing all over base together. Shouldn't we split up?"

Oska: "The only person we have to worry about seeing us is Damien. But he'll be in his office overseeing everything."

Grihm: "Sounds good to me. Let's get moving."

*   *   *

Looking back, Styner didn't like how the meeting ended. Having discord within the team could lead to hesitation and issues during a mission. Although they weren't out conducting a typical mission, the task at hand was still dire and required the full attention of everyone involved, free from personal distractions. His concern was for Grihm most of all. Styner hoped that a conversation with Dr. Malerius and himself would ease her mind but more importantly keep her from doing anything rash. Styner made his way to the doctor's office.

The sign was dim and the lights were off. Styner took a moment to COMM Grihm.

Styner: "Grihm, where are you? We need to talk."

Grihm: "I'm doing some running around. I'll come to you."

Styner: "I'm at Malerius' office. See you soon."

Styner sat down outside of the office to wait for Grihm. Thirty minutes passed with no sign from her. He COMMed her again but received no answer. After several attempts with the same results, he COMMed Damien.

Styner: "Damien, have you heard from Grihm lately? She's not responding to my COMMs."

Damien: "No. I told her to take some time off. I'm assuming she's resting or at medical. Why?"

Styner: "It's nothing. I just wanted to make sure she was okay."

Damien: "We had a talk after the meeting and I think we're on the same page now. She'll be fine. How's the hunt going?"

Styner: "I wish I knew that before. I've been wasting time looking for Grihm."

Damien: "It's fine. This isn't going to come to a quick conclusion anyway. No one else has any leads either. Just keep your eyes open, I'm going to move onto the next step."

Styner: "Got it."

Damien closed COMMs without letting Styner get in another word.

With no leads, his side project derailed, and the commencing of the next part of the plan, Styner moved to begin his search at the main hangar floor. He was to serve as an extra set of eyes on the hangar floor; closer and faster to respond if anything happened. He posted on a walkway overlooking the activity. Being that Styner was in charge of logistics and inventory, he was not out of place monitoring the hangar floor. Operations continued as normal under his watch. Styner soon got caught up overlooking operations, nearly forgetting that he was to be looking for suspicious activity, until he caught a glimpse of Dr. Malerius skulking away from the hangar floor. Dr. Malerius had little-to-no business on the hangar floor, even if was just cutting through. Styner moved to follow. He regained sight of Dr. Malerius walking down a long corridor near the armory. Malerius seemed to be moving more slowly than he had been before and stopped before turning the corner. Styner approached without making a sound. He was close enough to hear Malerius muttering inaudibly to himself.

Styner: "Is this why you're never in your office?"

Startled, Malerius turned to face Styner. He gathered his composure quickly.

Malerius: "I'm the senior-most psychological professional and I have to look after hundreds of people. My hours and location are sporadic."

Styner: "I can't imagine a psychologist needing to creep around a military base. What were you doing in the hangar?"

Malerius: "My job can call for such behavior. I sometimes have to see people in casual situations. I usually have permission to use the camera feeds to see where people are but all the systems are down."

Styner: "Then who're you looking for?"

Malerius: "Doctor patient confidentiality."

Styner impatiently brushed Malerius aside and peered around the corner, catching only a glimpse of someone walking into the armory.

Styner: "Who are you following and why? Last time I'm going to ask."

Malerius: "You can't force me to disclose private information about my activities with patients."

Styner: "You are part of a military operation which inherently holds controlled information Doctor. Your jurisdiction is restricted to direct personnel interaction. It does not extend to the hangar floor, the armory, or any other military asset we have down here."

Dr. Malerius picked up on Styner's increasingly aggressive tone. Styner's posture changed to one ready for physical contact and Dr. Malerius braced himself. Styner grabbed him by his lapel and pulled him close. Styner's normally friendly, sunken, blue eyes told the tale of someone who'd seen a lifetime of violence. Dr. Malerius concluded that it would be best for his well-being to tell Styner what he wanted. However, before he had a chance to speak, both he and Styner heard several familiar voices approaching. In a blink, Styner's reverted back to the friendly veteran and released the Doctor.

Styner: "Just get back to your office. Protocol dictates that non-combatant personnel remain on their respective levels unless you are given permission or orders to be elsewhere. Whatever you're doing on this level can wait."

Malerius: "Thank you for understanding."

As Dr. Malerius departed, the group of four turned the corner: Grihm, Oska, Trigger, and Sev; clearly armed and moving fast. Grihm glanced over and made eye contact with Styner, stopping her in her tracks.

Styner: "Couldn't sleep?"

Grihm: "What're you doing here?"

Styner: "My job. You?"

Grihm: "Looking for the spy."

Styner: "If *I* were a spy, I would definitely avoid anyone dressed for war."

Grihm: "Well if *I* were a spy I would follow them because they look like they're heading out on a mission."

Styner: "That's… not a bad idea. What made you change your mind? You were against the idea at first."

Grihm: "I hate to admit it but Damien was right; the sooner we take care of this, the sooner we can get Jin. But don't tell him I said that though."

Styner: "I'll be sure to leave that part out. But you should update him on your plan; he thinks you're still sleeping. Glad you came around Grihm."

Styner left them to return to his post overlooking the hangar floor.

Trigger: "Bianca, I gotta say: that was damn smooth."

Grihm: "The more I have to lie and skulk around my own home, the worse I feel. Let's just hurry up."

Oska: "We still have to call Damien to throw him off but our story needs to change a little. At least we won't need to make four different calls."

They continued on with Oska leading the way. She COMMed Damien who responded immediately.

Damien: "You're just the person I wanted to talk to. Mission update."

Oska: "I'm coordinating efforts with Trigger, Sev, and Grihm. The plan is to overtly prepare for a mission in hopes of drawing the spy's attention to us. If he thinks we're moving out then he might try to follow us."

Damien: "Grihm too? I'm glad to see she's come around. Make another pass over the walkways above the hangar to catch his attention."

Oska: "Already done. If he was anywhere near the hangar he would've seen us."

Damien: "He might back off if he catches on that you're not going anywhere. I want to keep his attention near the hangar, and if he's still there after this then we might have our guy. We're going to MILCON 0. Get back to the hangar."

From Damien's office overlooking the hangar floor, he could monitor most of the Citadel's facilities. The only other console with this much access (more access in fact) was Oska's battle station. He looked down on the hangar floor, watching his personnel. There was still some lingering confusion and some frustration due to the sudden lockdown. Many people's plans would have to be cancelled. But as unhappy as general personnel was, Damien was far more upset knowing that his entire operation was being hindered from within by a single unknown threat. This was an issue he wanted solved by cycle's end. He took a moment before activating the announcement speakers. His voice boomed throughout the entire base; personnel in every room and corridor stopped what they were doing and listened.

Damien: "Attention all Eratech personnel: We are now entering maximum military readiness. MILCON 0 has been activated. All combat personnel are to assume battle ready status and await further orders. All security personnel will arm and prepare for defense. Non-military personnel are restricted to the dormitories. This is *not* a drill."

There was a brief moment of disbelief before even the swiftest minds transitioned into operation mode. When the warning lights began flashing, all others sprang into action. After a few minutes of scrambling, the confusion refined itself into a hive minded machine. Personnel throughout the base scrambled to get to their stations. Engineers directed vehicles mere inches away from columns of soldiers falling into formations. Weapon lines flowed armaments across the facility as fast as they could be brought out. Like a proud father, Damien took in the sight of his training, investments, and organization. A smile almost crept onto his bearded face. Saber entered the office. Damien didn't turn away from his window; he continued to watch steadfastly.

Saber: "I hope you're right about this."

Damien: "It's only a slim chance, but I think our spy is or was in the hangar. Once everything is in position, I'm going to check with hangar crews to see who was hanging around who wasn't supposed to be there."

Saber: "I'll take a post in the hangar as well. Let me know if you see something I don't."

Just as silent as quick, she was gone. It took Damien a few seconds to realize she had left. Damien watched diligently as the final preparations for MILCON 0 fell into place. As the troops finished arming and falling into formation, the fire alarms blared. Most believed it to be part of the normal commotion and continued with their own tasks, being that it wasn't their job to address it even if it were real. Damien dashed to the console to find out where the alarm was activated: the second floor behind the hangar; near the Armory. The armory housed tons of flammable munitions and seeker crystals for weaponry. A fire there could quickly get out of hand, requiring the area to be sealed and the base evacuated. Damien promptly ordered the fire team to the location and opened COMMs in that wing.

Damien: "Saber, I need you to get to the armory as fast as you can."

Saber: "I'm already moving there with the fire team. I'll get back to you when it's clear."

Damien marched his way to the hangar floor. With all other immediate crises contained, the hangar continued organizing. The entire hangar snapped to attention as Damien approached. He ordered them to carry on. A synthetic, luminous voice called for Damien's attention. Heiretsu was running to catch Damien.

Heiretsu: "Hey man it's about time you got down here."

Damien: "If you call me man one more time, this conversation is going to end in a bad way for you."

Heiretsu stepped back.

Heiretsu: "Okay fine. But more important than that, do you know what your employees are doing?"

Damien: "Not all of them, but if I find the one who's not where they're supposed to be…"

Heiretsu: "Good; we're on the same page."

Damien: "What did you see?"

Heiretsu: "I'ma be real with you: I think I know what's going on here but doing my part barely gave me a chance to help."

Heiretsu let his words linger for a moment, staring back at Damien through his tinted helmet. Damien picked up Heiretsu's meaning.

Damien: "Tell me everything."

Heiretsu: "Aight cool. So recently, Oska and I worked out a new deal to stop buying prefabulated amulite base-plates and Turbo-encabulators from…"

Damien: "Tell me everything relevant."

Heiretsu: "My bad. Not long after systems went down, I saw some of DL cut through here. Then after *that*, I saw Malerius. But he wasn't just trying to pass through; he took a weird indirect route across the hangar. Now I trust Oska and them, but Malerius hardly comes here and he was acting weird. I didn't follow him 'cause I was doing my real job, but I last saw him heading down that corridor."

Heiretsu pointed to the corridor leading to the armory where the fire had started. Damien remembered to check in on their status.

Damien: "How's the fire team doing Saber. I need an update."

Saber: "Nothing to worry about here. They took care of the fire before it even got close to the armory. We're looking into the cause now."

Damien: "I just got another lead pointing to your location. I'll be over there soon."

As Damien stormed through the corridors toward the armory, he COMMed Styner and told him to meet him there. Saber was standing in front of the armory doors with a face that warned of troubling news.

Saber: "I took another look around the armory while I was waiting for you."

Damien: "And?"

Saber: "There's some equipment missing."

Damien: "Of course there is; we just prepped for MILCON 0."

Saber: "I mean special equipment that people like Trigger, Sev, and Grihm would use."

Damien: "I talked to Oska not long ago. They grabbed their equipment to help draw the attention of our spy."

Styner: "Where are they?

Damien thought back and didn't recall seeing them in the hangar where they said they'd be. He stepped aside to COMMs Oska; no response. He tried for Grihm, then Trigger, and Sev but received no answer from any of them. All at once, the pieces of the puzzle began to fall into place; so quickly and apparent that he could only stand dumbfounded for a moment, Saber's words whizzing past him. His face turned dour as the information settled. He stroked his beard in irritation as he began to regain his focus. Saber's words became clear again.

Saber: "I know that look. You're spacing out. Something's wrong."

Damien: "I don't want to jump to any conclusions. I just need to talk to Styner."

Styner arrived in time to hear his name.

Styner: "Right here. Make it fast because our spy could be…"

Damien: "Long gone by now. Let's go."

Both Saber and Styner looked at Damien in confusion, but held their questions for Damien to explain on his own. He led them around the corner to a dead-end corridor. As they got closer, they noticed that the back wall was pushed back a few feet creating an opening about four feet wide. The opening was difficult to see from more than a few feet out and being a dead-end, no one had any reason to walk in that direction. Damien muttered a slew of curses under his breath.

Styner: "I always wondered why this hallway led nowhere."

Saber: "Damien, what the hell is this?"

Damien: "It was… is an emergency exit tunnel but it was a little difficult for most people to use so it was going to be a DL exit. Oska and I were going to give access to the team but the idea got back-burnered. Eventually it wasn't important anymore."

Saber: "Did you tell anyone other than Oska about this?"

Damien: "No. The plan didn't go very far."

Damien entered the dark passageway. There were no lights and Damien couldn't recall the layout. He kicked something heavy that caused him to lose his footing. Styner and Saber heard him tumble and entered to help. While Styner was as blind as Damien, Saber's veastial eyesight gave her a better view of her surroundings; her red eyes glowed like an animals amid the darkness. As she reached down to help Damien, something caught her eye and she stopped. Damien flicked open his lighter to illuminate the area. It wasn't much, but was better than nothing. He shined the lighter over object on the ground: a corpse. It was Dr. Malerius Jackson and it appeared as though he had been stabbed repeatedly. Damien realized he was sitting in a pool of not-quite-cold blood. Styner gave Damien a hand standing up. The three of them stared down at the body.

Styner: "I almost had this whole thing figured out. Now I got nothing. That would explain his following Grihm a while ago. I guess their little decoy plan worked."

Damien: "Looks like he tried to follow them right outside the base."

Saber: "Who did this?"

Saber inspected the body. The stab wounds pierced through both sides of the body and the holes were rounded. She looked around for any makeshift weapon that could have made the wounds but found nothing.

Saber: "He wasn't killed with a knife. This doesn't look like anything our guys would do."

Damien: "It couldn't have been them. If Grihm had killed him, she would have just told me about it. There's a chance he was killed by another spy."

Styner: "I was hoping this would be the end of all this spy business."

Damien: "Whoever this other spy may be, I don't think they work for Revco. Grihm being the hot-head that she is, probably rallied the others to go get Jin under the guise of drawing the attention of the spy. I think that's around when Heiretsu saw him. Sometime after that, he got stabbed to death."

Saber: "No. Grihm wouldn't just up and leave like that in the middle of a crisis. She…

Damien and Styner looked at Saber sternly, silently; waiting for her to accept reality.

Saber: "Godammit, she did."

Damien: "And if she took Oska with her inside of Revco, it's not going to be good for anyone involved.

Styner: "Grihm might be rash but she's not an idiot. Let's just focus on this new spy problem. If Heiretsu was the last person to see Malerius alive we need to find him."

A thought Damien and Saber agreed with. They exited the passageway and Damien sealed the exit before they headed back to the hangar.

Styner: "Are you really going to leave that body in there?

Damien: "One thing at a time. We'll clean that up later."

Saber: "Babe, I know you're pissed at Grihm right now, but if it weren't for her we may not have been able to find the spy."

Damien: "That may be the only thing keeping me from choking the life out of her when I see her."

The three of them returned to the hangar floor looking for Heiretsu. They asked some of the other mechanics and soldiers near where they spoke to Heiretsu. No one seemed to know where he disappeared to. In fact, they informed them that Heiretsu was known to leave without anyone noticing for extended periods of time. Everyone assumed it was an illuminaught habit.

With their last lead inconveniently coming up short, they returned to the war room to finish discussing their next course of action.

Saber: "Maybe we shouldn't go with our first conclusion. This could be more complicated than we realize."

Styner: "We're only going with Malerius being the spy…"

Saber: "*One* of the spies."

Styner: "The only spy because that's all we have. You could overanalyze this if you want to but based on personal experience, he's the Revco spy. Everything else is just speculation until we get more information."

Saber: "Maybe Malerius saw Heiretsu following Grihm so he followed them. And when Heiretsu tried to escape, Malerius challenged him and was killed in the process."

Styner: "Damien talked to Heiretsu right before heading to the armory corridor, where you were already waiting and I was overlooking the hangar floor. Unless he can teleport, there's no way he could have made it there and back without you, Damien, or myself seeing him. And besides, I don't think he would have challenged someone on his own."

Saber: "But there's still the possibility that one or both spies left. Malerius could have been killed to throw us off."

Styner: "We have to gather what we can and come to the most likely conclusion. But until we get better and more information, we move forward with what we have."

Saber: "I just don't want us moving forward in the wrong direction. There's just as likely a chance that Malerius is a fall guy and you're taking the obvious bait."

Styner: "If that is a red herring and the Revco spy is free, then based on the fact that the spy left thinking we're mobilizing for war with a special ops team deployed, we can reasonably assume that Revco might be scrambling around to prepare their defenses just to be on the safe side. Right?"

Saber: "Then we check Revco message traffic and activity to see if they're reacting."

Styner: "If not, Malerius was probably the spy."

Both Styner and Saber began to leave the table to check their idea when they noticed that Damien hadn't moved an inch since he sat down, nor had he uttered a word. His shades rested on the table, his hands clasped in front of his face. He remained out of the discussion. At Damien's terminal, Styner and Saber shifted through all incoming messages related to Revco. Through intercepted message traffic, the information they received was hardly ever anything pertinent or secretive, but would occasionally give background information on major business dealings that weren't public but not secret either. An influx of messages however, secret or not, usually indicated that they were reacting to something in the business world. But they found nothing; only routine messages trickling in. Relieved, they returned to the table. Damien still hadn't moved.

Styner: "All quiet on the eastern front. Not a peep. I think our spy problem's been taken care of."

Damien: "I don't know how much of this Grihm planned, but things are falling conveniently in her favor."

They both waited for Damien to clarify.

Damien: "After Grihm's debrief, I told her that if she found the spy I would charge in to help get Jin. I even told her I'd let her lead. And despite this, she chose to take it upon herself to lead a team to do it without any help. But through sheer luck, she kept up her end of the deal. The way I see it, her good is nullified by the bad and I would just let her twist in the wind. But she has Oska with her and she's taken half the team into Revco central to get back one person. If Oska were captured by the enemy, it would be the end of DLC. Not just for the information she would give up, but the fact that she maintains nearly 60% of what we do. Oska *is* DLC. There's no way we can afford to risk her getting captured or killed at Revco and Grihm knows this. With Oska with her, I *have* to be a part of her mission."

Saber: "That's not at all what I expected to hear from you."

Damien: "I'm working hard to contain my anger right now."

Styner: "So what's our next move then?"

Damien: "The new plan is to make sure Grihm's Defector Squad stays undiscovered. I'll continue trying to get in touch with Oska to let her know the change in tactics. Once they've begun their approach on central, we move to draw attention toward us."

Styner: "Is this really happening?"

Damien: "It is. Lift the lockdown and gear up: DLC's going to battle."

18– A WISP IN THE DEPTHS

-A tiny light flickering in the darkness.-

Oska traveling with Grihm's Defector Squad made escaping the Citadel a simple act of deception and distraction. The forgotten DL escape tunnel had finally seen use, although not the way Damien intended. Grihm found the dense city air more refreshing than usual after being cooped up in the Citadel. Even though she'd spent more consecutive cycles inside the citadel on other occasions, being *forced* to stay for even one cycle made it unbearable. Grihm had fully committed to her actions and was now beyond the point of turning back. Her eyes were focused ahead on the mission at hand as well as the consequences to follow.

Grihm: "Okay everyone, we have to get out of here fast. We only have so much time before Damien realizes we're gone and I don't want to be in the district when he does."

Oska: "Our best bet is going back through the council maintenance and service tunnels into Revco."

Grihm: "We're going to need to borrow a car first. Can anyone hotwire a car?"

Oska: "More like remote activation but yeah, I can do that."

Grihm: "We'll take one of Damien's cars."

Trigger: "Are you trying to give Damien as many reasons to kill you as you can?"

Grihm: "Not the hot rod, we'd never fit in that thing. I'm talking about one of the regular cars. And besides; I'm pretty sure corporate treason and kidnapping are at the top of the list of offenses. If he's going to kill me for anything it'd be for one of those."

Trigger: "I guess if you're gonna be wrong, go all the way. Let's do it."

The escape tunnel let them out onto the streets a few blocks away from the apartment entrance. Defector Squad made their way back to the garage where Oska punched a few rapid key strokes to open the door. There were three vehicles inside, Damien's hotrod, a pickup truck, and a third car that was being worked on that was completely inoperable. They went with the truck and drove off being that it was the only realistic option. Trigger and Sev carried their normal equipment: Trigger; a pistol and a long rifle, Sev had a high impact assault rifle, and Grihm grabbed a tactical grenade launcher in addition to her normal payload of anti-personnel bomblets as well as an escape kit. The truck would only alleviate some of the journey; most of their traveling would be done after they entered the tunnels.

Trigger: "What's the plan to get into the council tunnels without starting a scene? They're not going to let a bunch of heavily armed people walk in."

Grihm hadn't made it to that part of the plan. She didn't want to shake everyone's confidence in her so she tried to come up with something on the fly. She recalled what Oska told her about the underground systems and what she learned on her way back from Revco.

Grihm: "Unfortunately we have to go through the council to cross. The train tunnels are our best chance to get through unnoticed."

Oska nodded and began looking at maps of the transit systems to figure out the most efficient way to cross through the district. Grihm exhaled in relief. Oska feverishly scanned through screens and holograms of maps, spreadsheets, and schedules and after a few moments, she shared with the team.

Oska: "We can get into the council connection tunnels from here if we access this maintenance tunnel on our side. The catch is that the tunnel we want is a good distance from the nearest station. We'll have to drive off road to get as close as we can and ditch the truck. It's a good thing we didn't take Damien's car."

Trigger used a dirt road that branched off from the street. It took them to a switching station that overlooked a section of the train tracks. The area was out of sight from the nearest station leaving no witnesses to look out for. They climbed a chain link fence and ran down the hill onto the track and into the tunnel. Oska didn't need as much help climbing as everyone assumed she would. All of the training from Damien that she resented at the time was finally being put to use.

Oska checked her sidearm to compare their location to that of the next oncoming train. As she opened her mouth to alert the others, the train horn blew and lights veered from around the corner. The train would reach them before they could get to the maintenance door. Fortunately, there were tracks for trains going both ways. They simply crossed the tunnel and let the train blaze past. Grihm, Trigger, and Sev thought nothing of it. Oska found being on the tracks near a speeding train unnerving but the relaxed demeanor of the others helped her stay collected herself. With no other trains coming for some time, the rest of the trek to the maintenance tunnel was quiet.

The door was locked. There was an analog combination panel. With no digital or electronic parts, Oska's sidearm couldn't hack into it. Trigger cautioned everyone to stand back and cover their ears. He brandished his long rifle: The Nighthawk. He fired a shot into the lock, blasting a large hole where it used to be. The boom from the shot pounded at their chests as the echo rippiled through the tunnels. They navigated their way through the service tunnels until they found a trapdoor that led further down into the pitch black vehicle tunnels of Revco.

Grihm: "I hoped I wouldn't be back here so soon."

Grihm muttered nervously to herself. Traveling in absolute darkness was one of the more unpleasant experiences in recent memory, Grihm made sure to bring a light source with her this time. Not knowing how long they would be in the tunnels, they staggered the use of their lights beginning with Grihm.

Grihm: "Keep an ear out everyone; they have vehicle patrols down here. We're going to have to steal one of their cars to get through here."

Oska: "No worries. I can pick up on all the transmissions between the patrols down here. Oh! I can also see what they're sending back to Central."

Grihm: "Oska, you are making this so much easier than it would've been without you."

Oska blushed and thanked Grihm. She continued.

Oska: "We're on patrol squad 054's route but they won't be headed this way for another hour. I'll fix that."

Oska channeled into the patrols COMMs systems and spoke into her sidearm.

Oska: "Patrol squadron 054, we're picking up what appears to be a short circuit along the lighting system's wiring, please investigate. We're sending the location to your car now. Over."

054: "Copy. On our way now. Over."

Before anyone had time to congratulate Oska on her cunning plan, she intercepted a confusing series of follow-up messages.

054: "Squad 46, requesting support. A patrol was accosted by an unknown individual recently in that area. Over."

46: "Copy. Making our way to your location with armed support. Squadron HQ, requesting activation of all lights along tunnel N1128. Over."

Squadron HQ: "Copy. Patrol 46 why are you requesting lights along 054's route? Over."

054: "This is 054. We were just asked to investigate a possible problem in the lighting. We requested support from 46 to provide support. Over."

Squadron HQ: "Copy. We have no such readings on our end. Are you sure you didn't overhear another message? Over."

Oska frantically typed into her sidearm while swearing to herself. When she finished, she looked up and waited.

Squadron HQ: "Wait one… Okay now we're reading the problem along that line. Testing all lights along that tunnel. Standby."

From the depths rolled the sounds of rows of lights buzzing to life from the darkness. All of the lights within fifty meters on either side of the team failed to activate, leaving them in a bubble of darkness.

Squadron HQ: "We are tracking a major outage in that area 054. You are authorized to investigate. Patrol 46 will provide support. Once the area has been cleared we'll send in electricians to fix the problem. Over."

Grihm: "Looks like they aren't taking any chances after what I pulled last time."

Trigger: "What's the plan Grihm?"

Grihm: "Oska, can you hack into the patrol cars?"

Oska: "Easy. When they're close, I'll block their COMMs too."

Grihm: "Oska, I wish we could bring you on every mission."

Oska enjoyed the idea of being a specialist more and more. Providing support from base was helpful, but her ability to support the team in the field was superior. She considered requesting to become a field specialist and a true member of DL; provided Damien let her do anything after her defection.

In the distance they heard the sound of engines approaching. They crouched in the darkness near the walls and waited. Trigger looked down the tunnel through the Nighthawk scope.

Trigger: "How do you wanna do this?"

Grihm: "Let's wait until they're close enough for Oska to bring the cars into the shadows. Plain and simple. Sev you ready?"

Sev didn't respond. It dawned on everyone that he hadn't said a word since leaving base. Grihm pushed him to get his attention. He removed his ear buds.

Sev: "Sorry, are we doing stuff?"

Grihm: "Just follow my lead."

The two cars rolled into view from the depths, stopping a few meters away from the darkness. Oska faced away from the guards to smother some of the light emitted from her sidearm as she began hacking their equipment. She first manipulated their communication equipment; closing all channels except for hers to theirs. She spoke into their COMMs equipment.

Oska: "Hold! Step outside of the vehicles and drop your weapons or you *will* be shot. Five seconds."

There was confusion between the guards. Oska began counting down from five. Picking up on Oska's queue, Trigger and Sev stressed her point further by cocking their guns. When Oska reached one, the guards disembarked and disarmed, tossing their weapons away. Oska took remote control of the two vehicles with her sidearm and brought them into the darkness; the Defector Squad piled into them two-by-two. Oska had a moment of concern for the abandoned guards.

Oska: "Should we really just leave them here in the dark?"

Trigger: "Another patrol will come along when they don't report back."

Grihm: "I've been down here in the dark for hours before. They'll be fine."

After a long drive, they arrived at yet another maintenance entrance, this one leading into Revco central: The heart of the district. They disembarked the vehicles and headed for the exit.

Oska: "This is it. This maintenance shaft should lead us out of the transit tunnels into the lowest level town in Rev Central."

Trigger: "You'd think being this close to Central, they'd have more security. At least some cameras."

Oska: "Rev's a pretty big place. They can't cover every hole."

Grihm: "But this is the capital superstructure. Something's gotta be up. Keep your eyes open everyone."

Deep inside the shaft they found a ladder, which Grihm began ascending first. The ladderwell was unlit and made it difficult to determine how far they had climbed. There was a tiny beam of light that shone from above, directly into Grihm's eyes. She pushed aside the manhole cover blocking her way (to everyone's amazement) and was blinded by the torrent of lights. After climbing out, she helped the others out of the shaft and they all took in their new surroundings. The manhole opened up under the sidewalk. It never occurred to them that it might have been under the street; Grihm, more than the others just wanted to get away from dark enclosed tunnels. As her eyes adjusted, Grihm was shocked to see that the area in which they had arrived was an industrial slum; a far cry from the beautiful district she had seen on the surface. Many of the buildings looked as if they had not been renovated or touched up in decades. Constructed with outdated piping and ventilation standards that billowed clouds of AP smog which drifted down to the streets, creating a dense waist high fog. The industrious buildings rose as high as they could and into the ceiling of the underground deck, possibly even going through to the next deck. Eratech's worst slums were in better condition than what they were witnessing. It appeared even Revco and all their money and glory, still had slums of their own.

Trigger: "That explains why there's no security around here. This place is a pisshole."

Grihm: "Okay Oska, How do we get to where Jin is?"

Oska: "First I have to figure out *where* Jin is before I can figure out how to get there. There are plenty of maps of Revco decks and towns, but there's nothing about a deck this low."

Grihm: "I bet. These are not humane living conditions. I wouldn't tell anyone they had people living down here either. We should probably get off of the streets. Too much AP smog will probably give you cancer."

Trigger: "I told you a thousand times: AP smog is a natural side effect of AP crystal expiration. They're just planet particles."

Grihm: "We're not having this debate again. Let's go."

They moved into the second level of what was most likely an abandoned blank-addict house. Oska used the time to figure out the rest of her plan.

Oska: "I can't find a map of this deck, but I *do* see a mass cargo elevator."

Trigger: "What're we waiting for then?"

Oska: "I want to map this deck out. I want as much information about Revco as I can get while I'm out here. I need to find a terminal or system computer so I can leech data from it. The problem is that I'm not picking up anything digital near us."

Grihm: "Is that really necessary right now?"

Oska: "It'll help more in the long run. If nothing else, it can help us plan our escape."

Trigger: "The cargo elevator probably has something being the only thing connected to this deck and the rest of the superstructure."

Oska was a little frustrated that she didn't think of it, but was glad all the same that someone did. The team quickly departed from the blank house to trudge through the smoggy streets. People were scarce. The Defector Squad would occasionally see a silhouette in the distance, but the figure would scurry away before they were close enough to determine any distinguishing features. The team approached corners cautiously and wide. No one approached the team, but the sound of doors opening and closing, skittering footsteps, panting, and whispers followed them across the deck.

They arrived at the street which opened up into a broad major highway leading to a monstrous freight door that stood over forty feet high. Oska's sidearm picked up digital signatures as she approached. The first of which was a security camera resting above the freight door. She accessed it and put the footage on a loop. Beside the massive door was a normal sized door. Oska accessed it as well and lead the team into the Freight dock. The elevator shaft was a long, slanted chamber filled with the scent of industrial chemicals and construction equipment. Far above them, they could see the bottom of the elevator platform. Just under their platform was yet another ladder that led to the base of the elevator platform. Not wanting to risk drawing attention to themselves by activating the elevator, the team begrudgingly began climbing. The climb was long and exhausting, but the slope made it easier. Grihm, who was in the lead, opened a trapdoor onto the elevator platform. It was littered with towers of shipping containers. Oska scanned the area and found a shipping terminal. She physically connected her sidearm to the terminal and began bypassing its security measures. She was in within seconds. The data acquired was mostly manifestos and schedules, but through fragmented data of delivery locations and repair history, she was able to compile a crude map of the lowest deck.

Oska: "Apparently, we're on the construction deck where they keep all of their major construction equipment for the superstructure. But what we're looking for is the delivery elevator, which can take us to any level except for the one we just came from."

Grihm: "Did you find anything about that deck?"

Oska: "Yeah but I can't make sense of it now. I'll have to sit down and spend some time with it later."

Trigger: "Which level are we going to then?"

Oska: "It looks like there's an entire prison deck nestled in between some of the residential decks. My money's on that."

Grihm: "Oska, if it weren't for you there's no way we would've made it this far. Thank you."

Trigger: "Yeah Oska. Not to mention DLC probably would've been swallowed up by Revco years ago. Before you came along, the Citadel was a much harsher place to work."

Oska: "I can imagine. I almost didn't even know where to start when Damien hired me. He was running everything on full pistons. He was going to run everything into the ground."

Grihm: "He's tough on all of us, but sometimes it feels like he's too hard on people; like he's trying to push people past their breaking points. But as frustrating as he can be, I have a lot of respect for the man. He keeps his word, never backpedals and as hard as he is on everyone else, he can be even harder on himself. He reminded me of that at the cathedral when he took on Hellcrow to get him off me without even a second thought. And here I am doing the one thing he asked me *not* to do even though he said he would help when he could."

The intense emotion of the conclusion of her previous mission had abated and she was able to think of things other than fixing her mistake. The dreadful weight of doubt began to set in until Trigger disrupted her thoughts.

Trigger: "I'll have no more of that talk. You can beat yourself up when we get Jin back home. But we need that headstrong determined Bianca with us now. The time for regret is later or not at all. We're all too committed to have doubts now."

Grihm didn't openly respond but took his words to heart. She did after all convince them to be there and any doubts at this point would be dangerous.

Oska was preoccupied with her sidearm and didn't hear their conversation, swiping manically through messages. Trigger again played big brother and brought her back to the mission.

Trigger: "You look worried. And if you're worried, I'm worried."

Oska: "There's a lot of commotion at the surface. There's been an explosion at the district gates. This might make it easier for us to get around. I'll keep an ear on this. Let's go."

The team used an access tunnel to the superstructure elevator. Oska tapped into the terminal and sent them skyward toward the prison district and one step closer to Jin.

19– A NEW TOY IN THE CHEST

-Meticulously kept in his own twisted vision of order.-

Jin awakened. His eyes flickered open slowly, adjusting to the dim lighting. His senses returned one at a time. Pain was the first sensation; his body still aching from the fight. The scene played back in Jin's mind action-by-action; one swing of the sword to the next. As he recalled the final blow, a surge of pain rushed back to him. The stab wound was on his left side just below his collarbone and exited under his shoulder blade. He was amazed to have survived. The wound was dressed and was likely the only reason he was still alive. Whatever reason Emil had to keep him alive would no doubt be bad for Jin. Jin attempted to touch his wound but his arm was held back by something wrapped around his wrist that clanked and jangled. Despite being wounded and unconscious, his captors took no chances and kept him bound uncomfortably to the wall. His bindings didn't allow him to sit, or even kneel fully; forcing him to stand or "relax" into a half-kneel position, suspended by his wrist. The position was a constant pain on his wound. His eyes acclimated at last: to his dismay Jin found himself in a dark prison cell shackled to a wall.

Jin noticed a security camera in the far corner of the room watching him; its tiny red light flicked in the shadowy corner. After a few moments, the door opened and a small man entered the cell. As he approached, Jin thought of him less of a man and more of a teen. His height didn't make it any easier to figure out; Jin guessed that he may have been about Saber's height, perhaps even shorter. The teen had baby-smooth skin, glassy eyes that gave him the appearance of a porcelain doll and a bald head with three budding horns above the forehead. He walked to Jin and stood a foot away, staring eerily into his eyes and wearing an unnaturally forced half-smile.

Jin: "I hope I don't say anything stupid to make this awkward."

Jin's voice was hoarse, being the first words he'd spoken since he was in the park, however long ago that was.

Teen: "Prisoners always have lots to say when they arrive here… until I break them. Put them all into neat little compliant rows. But for you? That's only the first step. It only gets worse from there."

The teen's breath was lifeless and dry. His voice was wispy and wasn't intimidating in the least but his eyes, in their emptiness, spoke the words of a man with no conscious, empathy, or remorse. Jin's hair began to stand on end as the teen raised a single finger. He poked Jin's wound and a jolt of pain surged across Jin's body. The teen gave Jin a tiny smile as he turned to leave the cell. Jin was thankful to be away from him.

With the strange teen gone, Jin immediately began thinking of ways to escape. He looked around the room to see what his options were. He had an isolated cell, no bars; only four concrete walls and a door. Jin hadn't the slightest idea of where he was. He was left in isolation, bound to the wall for what seemed like cycles, but may have only been a few hours. He had no way of telling time other than the turning over of guards outside of his cell. It was difficult to tell from inside his cell, and if he dozed off he would have no idea if a change had occurred or when the next one would happen.

His cell door opened and the teen strode into the cell wearing a wider smile than before.

Teen: "It just occurred to me; I never introduced myself. I'm the warden of this prison. My employees call me Warden, but all my prisoners just call me Master. For you, I'll respond to both."

Jin: "Being that I don't work for you or respect you, I'll just call you whatever I want."

Warden pointed his hand at Jin and arcs of orange electricity jumped from his fingertips and surged through Jin's body.

Warden: "I'm a patient man; I can play this game with you anytime I want from now on. I actually came here to talk."

Jin: "So let's talk."

Warden: "Cooperation is good. Maybe I won't have to break you in after all. You see Jin, you work for Revco now. Whether you want to or not you're going to help us. Or at least you're not going to get in our way."

Jin: "I think we're done talking."

Warden: "You don't have a say in this. From now on, I decide what you do: If I don't like it, I'll stop you. I decide where you can go: If I don't want you there, you won't go. And if I want you dead; you better believe you will be a charred corpse at my feet. I own you."

Jin: "Please tell me we're not going to do the whole dungeon dominance thing. I'm not into the gimp suit"

Warden: "I'm glad you have a steadfast sense of humor. You're going to need it. Sleep tight."

Jin was left alone once again in his cell lit only by a dirty beam of light. Jin wasn't in a favorable position and an opportunity to attempt an escape wasn't likely to present itself anytime soon, and Jin didn't want to waste it when it did. He swallowed hard and prepared himself for a long stay.

*   *   *

Oska was increasingly distracted with her sidearm throughout the elevator ride; becoming less and less attentive to the team. Flicking frantically through the interface screens, the others wondered how she was even able to take in any information. She was completely entranced, her surroundings irrelevant to her. Grihm stirred her back to reality by shaking her shoulder.

Grihm: "Anything in there we should know about?"

Oska: "Sorry. There's a lot going on. I'm trying to sift through the garbage but it seems real."

Trigger perked up to listen in. Sev took notice of everyone's shift in attention and removed his ear buds to listen as well.

Oska: "All kinds of reports are coming in of some sort of terrorist attack at the border. Some crazy asshole bombed the wall. From there, it gets fuzzy. There's talk of trucks driving through, hordes of Eratech citizens plowing into Revco, council occupation; I don't know what's real. But there has been an explosion at the gate. That much is certain. I'll keep an eye on it."

Grihm: "Nope. We need you one-hundred percent with us. Whatever's going on at the gate is secondary to us not getting shot."

Oska acquiesced. As significant as the gate incident was, Grihm was right; she needed to guide the team in and out as quickly and efficiently as possible. However, she felt ignoring it altogether would be irresponsible.

Oska: "Right. We're almost there. Ready your weapons. Security all over the district is responding to the gate occurrence, including prison district personnel. ETA: two minutes!"

The elevator reached their floor. A mechanical rustling echoed through the shaft. Grihm and the team took cover behind crates and equipment. The elevator shaft doors opened and there was silence. No one had showed up to inspect the arrival of the elevator. With haste, they sprinted off the platform and into the depths of the prison district.

Grihm took the lead, with Sev and Trigger following close behind her. Oska was ordered to keep far to the rear and wait for the "Clear" command. Oska directed them deeper into the prison by leading from behind. They reached a large freight door for bringing in supplies and equipment. There were no other doors and nothing other than a small head-level window with an intercom nearby.

Oska: "Dammit. It's analog. I can't do anything with it. Give me a second, I'll see if there's anything else around I can use."

She located a security camera and looped the feed, but was unable to find anything else. Sev tapped the button on the intercom and released it quickly. He waited a moment before pressing the button again, remaining silent. A voice responded back from the other side.

Intercom: "Hello?"

The team stayed silent. Sev paused before pressing the button again, this time scratching slowly and irregularly against the intercom. He repeated the pattern for several minutes. He pressed the button one last time, this time punching the intercom hard. A loud crash rippled into the intercom as its last transmission. The intercom crushed inward under Sev's heavy fist and sparked weakly as it died. As the freight door started to open, the team scattered for cover and watched as an overweight guard waddled out to investigate the scene. He inspected the broken intercom curiously. While he was distracted, the team scurried past him through the freight door without making a noise. Saber would have been impressed.

Being that there were no scheduled deliveries, the facility was virtually abandoned. Defector Squad continued on unchallenged until they reached a T-intersection just outside of the warehouse when they finally saw prison guards. In the distance, the guards seemed to be scrambling chaotically. They checked with Oska for direction.

Oska: "I'm just now getting into systems on this level. I think Jin's somewhere in the eastern side of the prison in special holding. They may be trying to move him soon because of what's going on at the gate. I'll let you know in a minute."

Sev: "You may want to get back, guards coming this way."

A pair of armed prison guards was making their way toward the intersection. The team waited for them to approach. As they turned the corner, Trigger and Sev snatched the guards out of sight, covering their mouths as they did. After a brief struggle, the guards succumbed to sleep. The team checked the pockets for IDs, and keycards. Oska learned that she wasn't comfortable going through people's pockets and asked Sev to retrieve the head piece from one of the guards. The guards didn't carry any cards and the IDs weren't used for access according to Oska. Oska reluctantly attached the earpiece after wiping it off.

Sev: "Shouldn't you take out your other earpiece?"

Oska: "Why? I wouldn't be able to hear everything if I did that."

Sev: "How can you make sense of two different things going on in your ears?"

Oska: "Three if you keep asking questions."

Oska snapped, shushing him as she did with her finger.

Oska: "Central is really messed up right now. The guards have no idea what's going on in this sector because their leadership is focused on the gate. They're trying to muster their military forces, but they're scattered all over the city for standard duty. In the prison, sub-commanders are trying to contact the warden to get orders but no one seems to know where he is."

Trigger: "Why would they need to pull prison guards to go to the gate?"

Oska: "I don't think Revco has nearly as large of a military as we thought."

Trigger: "Anything new about the gate?"

She stopped abruptly. A look of guilt washed over her. She looked at Grihm, then shied away and began typing feverishly. She continued the pattern of listening and then typing, all the while, avoiding eye contact with Grihm.

Oska: "Uh… That thing at the gate? It's here. Rev Central is under attack. We have to find Jin and get out of Central now."

Trigger: "Who the hell would attack central?

Oska dodged the question to the annoyance of the others.

Oska: "I've got it. I know exactly where Jin is. This way!"

20– CONVERGENCE

-And all at once the fragments became whole, yet the fractures remained.-

Jin had run countless scenarios in his head of what he might encounter during an attempted escape: The number of guards, what they would use against him, security measures, and what he would do if he managed to get outside. His planning was interrupted by a commotion outside of his cell. There was a lot of pointing and yelling. Before Jin had time to make a guess to the cause, the door opened and three guards entered. They were lightly armed with batons and tasers. Considering his expertise in melee combat and ability to cast AP, Jin found it odd (and a little insulting) that this was all that was sent to deal with him. A single guard approached Jin and clubbed Jin across the head; it stung, but was nowhere near enough to knock him out. Jin feigned unconsciousness. The guard began releasing Jin's fetters. As the guard released the last latch, Jin sprang back to life. Jin delivered a swift head-butt to the guard undoing his chains, knocking him flat on his back and grabbed his baton from his waist as he fell. Without losing momentum, Jin charged forward to the next guard and unleashed a flurry of quick strikes to his head. Jin turned to address the remaining guard who had just readied his baton in one hand and taser in the other. Jin slung his baton at the guard, crushing the guard's nose. He followed up with a front kick to the guard, knocking him out as he slid across the cell.

The fight was so quick and silent that no one outside of the cell heard anything. Jin pulled the bodies out of view and stripped one of the guards of his uniform. He didn't think the plan would take him far, but he would make it further than he would without a plan. Jin hoisted the battered guard who was now wearing his prison overalls over his shoulder and stepped outside of the cell. There was only one guard in the area and he was at the end of the hall. Jin headed toward the guard.

Jin: "Where do I take this asshole?"

Jin made sure to seem as hurried as possible to appear unavailable for conversation. The guard seemed equally uninterested.

Guard: "No idea. We haven't been given a realistic order in the last hour. Whatever's going on at the gate's got leadership all in a spin. I'm just waiting for my shift to end."

Jin: "I'm trying to get out of here too. They told me to move this prisoner to a different wing. And of course they're making me move him *and* his belongings by myself but they didn't tell me where to go. Can you help me out?"

Guard: "Take him to prisoner processing. They can tell you where he's supposed to go from there."

Jin: "This is my first shift and I haven't even been given a tour. This place is huge and confusing. Where's processing?"

The guard looked irritated but had already admitted that he was waiting for his shift to end and wasn't doing anything.

Guard: "It's a bad time to start. Processing is behind me and to the left. Follow the signs for the tram then get off at the next stop. I'll go with you."

Jin: "I think I can handle it if it's only one stop away."

Guard: "Suit yourself."

The guard gave a nod and Jin headed past him and to the left. Once out of view, Jin quickly shoved the unconscious body into a bathroom stall. He continued onward to processing to reacquire his partner Hermes.

As he traversed the labyrinth of the prison he realized that it was mostly divided into breaks of corridors and cell blocks. Just as the guard had instructed, the signs directed him to the tram. At the tram area was a map overview of the tram systems. The map read "Central Prison Deck". The layout of the prison deck was a complex series of corridors so inefficient that its only purpose must've been to confuse any would-be escapee. Jin made a mental note of the path he would have to take from the tram to in-processing and hopped on the tram to the first stop.

In-processing was a large open room with space for queuing. No one here seemed concerned about the commotion that was escalating in the district. Most of the inmates were too focused on starting their new lives outside. Jin had no doubt his disguise would allow him to skip the queues. He approached one of the men behind the counter. The counter was protected by glass, which was no doubt resistant to gunfire.

Jin: "Uh… Hey. I just started here and I'm still trying to figure things out. I need to pick up some items for a prisoner named Oronoko Landown. Should I come back there to get his stuff so I don't hold up your line?"

Clerk: "I can't let you back here until your clearances are finished. But I'll see if I can get it for you. Are they moving him?"

The man searched the computers for Jin's request. Before joining DLC, Jin would've felt wildly uncomfortable working undercover, but his recent mission with Grihm familiarized him with the aspect enough to where he could resist glaring over his shoulder and looking suspicious himself.

Jin: "Yeah. Whatever's going on outside has the bosses wanting to put him in a more secure area. They just sent me to get his stuff."

Clerk: "Why would they send a new guy?"

Jin: "I guess to help me learn my way around. Show my face."

The clerk shrugged his shoulders.

Clerk: "I guess that makes sense. Hmm… I don't see anyone under that name in this wing."

Jin: "Try J-I-N."

The man at the counter typed it in found it within seconds. He ordered one of the assistants to grab the items and he returned a moment later.

Clerk: "Okay, that's one phone, wallet with no cash, and one antique sword with sheath and belt."

The clerk at the counter slid the items through the slot. A commotion at the entrance of in-processing erupted.

Shouting Guard: "All personnel: there may be an escaped prisoner somewhere in this block dressed as a guard. He is extremely dangerous. Be on the lookout for a man with deep red hair, pale skin, green eyes and stone studs over his left eye. If you see him, sound the alarms and wait for backup."

Jin turned back to the man at the counter who scanned Jin's face, which matched the profile. Jin snatched his items just before the man was able to lock down the window. He wasn't able to grab his phone, but retrieved Hermes and his wallet. The man at the counter set off the alarms and closed all of the windows.

Clerk: "He's here! The prisoner's here at window twenty-seven!"

The available guards descended upon Jin's position. Jin whipped his belt on and unsheathed Hermes in one fluid, extravagant movement. He took a battle stance and the guard's resolve faltered. Jin dared them to make the first move. His bold gesture made even the guards with guns hesitate. Jin would have to make the first move if he didn't want to be surrounded. He created his barrier in front of him. The startled guards immediately begin firing futilely into it. They soon realized they were making no progress and held their fire. Jin saw their change in tactics and made his move. He took a large step to his right and swiped his sword horizontally across the shield. It folded and draped over Jin's sword, leaving a trail of dissipation in its wake. He clenched his fist as a physical gesture to help him focus on maintaining the barrier in this concentrated form. Jin sprinted at the guard and slashed wide, cleaving through the guard and effortlessly followed through to cut open the counter window. The energy from the barrier now saturating the counter; Jin unclenched his fist to release the energy violently. The counter exploded, creating an opening wide enough for Jin to slip through. Such a casting was as draining mentally as it was physically for Jin and a wave dizziness washed over him. Jin considered using it as an opener against Emil since it would be to slow and easy to read during any other point in the duel; should they ever meet again. Behind the counter were a number of frightened employees.

Jin: "Where do you keep the confiscated weapons?!"

The employees collectively indicated around the corner. Jin grabbed one of the employees and headed to the back. The room opened up to a caged area with scores of weapons, armor, and other items taken from the inmates during the time of their incarceration or from raids. Jin ordered the employee to open the cage. He didn't have time to consider his options and snagged the largest, most dangerous looking weapon he could carry. Jin had no idea what it was or what it did, but he was confident it was what he needed. It was a shoulder-mounted launcher of some sort with several warning symbols on the side. He powered up the weapon and waited for the guards to turn the corner. As soon as he saw the first one, he pulled the trigger. There was a chest pounding boom as a bizarre static-like distortion fired from the barrel. The shot engulfed the first guard and exploded in a flash of static and arcing energy. Everything the static touched disintegrated. To Jin's horror, not every guard was fortunate enough to be completely dissolved. Those on the fringe of the blast radius only had limbs and portions of their torso destroyed. Jin quickly refocused his mind on escaping. The blast had completely dissolved the wall leading back to the main lobby of out-processing. Jin hurried through with the launcher in hand.

The launcher needed to finish venting before it could be fired again. Jin hoped he would not need to use the weapon again, it scared him. The confusion Jin had seen earlier, spread into the out-processing lobby. The queues had dispersed and everyone was trying to escape, or take cover. There were only a few guards in the lobby and they were busy trying (and failing) to maintain order. Jin sprinted through the lobby uncontested. The launcher finished venting and gave a weak chime. It was ready to fire again, but it sounded as if it were almost burned out. Jin didn't expect to get a third shot.

Following Jin's skirmish, the inmates at in-processing capitalized on the situation. Cautiously at first. But once they saw how few guards were in the room, more of them made their way toward the exits. A number of inmates rushed the counters to grab confiscated weapons from the lockers. In-processing was quickly under inmate control. The inmates were grateful for Jin's intervention. Even though they were already being freed, many of them sought revenge on the guards that harassed them during their incarceration. An opportunity they would have had to pass on had Jin not orchestrated his own escape. Jin grabbed the attention of one of the inmates and handed over the near-empty launcher. The inmate accepted with enthusiasm. The inmate was a heavy-set, olive skinned fellow with slightly balding black hair. His hands were large enough to palm Jin's entire head.

Jin: "Don't hurt yourself with that thing."

Inmate: "Someone's getting hurt but it won't be me. What's your name guy?"

Jin: "Jin."

Inmate: "Well Jin, if you ever find yourself in Eratech stop by Vincent's place in Prism Ray just outside of Old Light and tell 'em Marl sent you."

Jin: "I'll remember that. Good luck."

Jin was glad to be rid of the burden of its weight, and its power.

As the riot began to spread, the prison was locked down to prevent any further escapes, allowing time for more guards to enter and reclaim order. The exit at in-processing was one of the first exits locked. Jin would have to seek his exit elsewhere. He headed in the opposite direction of the inmates. By cutting through the cell blocks, Jin found out that that the less occupied throughways provided less resistance and guards.

Jin turned down a long empty corridor. As he approached the center, he realized how vulnerable he would be if he were attacked from both sides. One direction he could handle, but not even his barrier could save him from being sandwiched. He made haste.

Half of his fears are realized when he sees someone step out from the end of the corridor and fire a volley of grenades at him. Instinctively, Jin defends with his barrier. The grenades crash hard and explode even harder. The force slows Jin's advance, buckling his arm. The explosions kept coming one after the other: Four, five, six. It was an excessive amount of force to kill one person. Jin's will began to wane. Not knowing what he would encounter during his escape, he opts to reserve as much energy as possible. The repeated blasts destroy the walls of the corridor, creating nooks on either side large enough for Jin to hide in. There is a long silence as Jin waits for his attacker to move-in to confirm their kill. He hears their orders: "Moving. Covering. Clear." Jin counts three sets of footsteps. As he prepares to blitz them, he hears a fourth set lagging far behind the others. With the enemy spread out, he decides to lead again with his barrier.

The leader stops a few meters away from Jin's nook. Jin listens as they shuffle their positioning before going silent again. They were onto him. As Jin anticipated, another grenade was fired; this time at an angle to detonate in Jin's hiding spot. His barrier defends him again. Outnumbered and outgunned, Jin's best hope was a surprise charge. No normal person would be able to withstand seven explosions, which gave him the element of surprise. As he rushes in he raises his barrier, flexing his ability to expand it large enough to block off the narrow corridor. The added effort in addition to his already spent energy required the use of both hands to uphold the barrier. Jin holds Hermes underhanded, using his fist rather than his palm as the focal point of the other half of the barrier. The spread of power over a wider area would mean he would not be able to defend against a direct attack like Emil's distortion blade, or another volley of grenades, but at this distance, they would not have the chance to do either.

A hail of gunfire pummels uselessly against the shimmering blockade. Jin hears the sound of another grenade fire from the rear of the attackers. He drops the barrier and sidesteps, allowing the shot to whiz past. Jin whips Hermes underhanded at the grenadier and reconstructs his barrier in between the gunfire. For the split second Jin dropped the barrier, he scanned the area and attackers. Their positioning was staggered: the primary gunner was more heavily armed and was firing from a crouched position in front, the second gunner was dressed more lightly firing a pistol, and the grenadier was in the rear also wearing light combat armor. The grenadier sacrifices her grenade launcher by using it to block Hermes. She recognizes the blade.

Grenadier: "Break-fire! Friendly-fire!"

The gunfire stopped in unison. The rippling in Jin's barrier subsided, giving him a better view. The grenadier was running toward him, weaponless. It was Grihm. He recognized Sev and Trigger as the two gunners and he dropped the barrier. Grihm hugged Jin violently squeezing him tightly enough to crack his back.

Grihm: "I don't even know what to say to you right now. I'm glad you're okay, but I'm pissed that we came all this way and you're already free. I…I'm just really glad you're okay."

Grihm was more emotional than Jin had seen her before. She was always cool and quick to joke. But she was short of words here, or at least did not care for them at the moment.

Jin: "Well I'm glad I didn't get blown up."

Jin joked. He noticed Grihm was still holding him burying her head into his shoulder. He grabbed hold of the situation and Grihm.

Jin: "I'm really glad to see you too. I can't believe you came here to rescue me. I don't know what to say either."

Grihm let Jin go and took a step back.

Grihm: "I couldn't just leave you on your own. Especially since I was supposed to be your partner."

Jin: "It wasn't anyone's fault. They were ahead of us and we didn't realize it. We'll get them back."

Trigger and Sev approached Jin. Trigger leaned in and gave a brotherly hug. Sev offered up a simple nod of respect. Sev looked back and called the clear command. Oska turned the corner, first tactically then curiously as she wondered why the others were so friendly with a prison guard. Before she could form the question, she recognized Jin's face.

Jin: "Why is Oska here? This is the *last* place she should be!"

Grihm: "That's complicated."

Oska: "Why am I here? I'm helping you. How'd you get out?"

Jin: "It's complicated.

Trigger: "Jin, it's great to see you but we gotta move ya'll. All those explosions've gotten somebodies attention for sure. We'll celebrate once we're out of here."

Oska: "Bad news: They've locked the prison down due to the riots and they're sending in troops from all over central to regain control."

Sev: "Why can't you do what you did on the way in?"

Oska: "I think they're onto me. They've started using countermeasures and I don't want to risk losing any of the data I've already stolen, or worse; they steal data from me."

Sev: "The data's not going to be any good if we get killed over it."

Oska: "Don't worry. I've got us another way out."

Oska began typing into her sidearm and swiped the hologram to transmit. She spoke into her headset.

Oska: "Did you get our location? ... Good…. We'll move there now. Okay, I just got us a way out but we have to move."

Grihm: "Oska what's going on?"

Oska: "You know that explosion at the gate? Damien brought back up."

21– A CLASSIC CASE OF TRANSFERENCE

-What is reality but the interpretations of our own erroneous senses? Are you sure you are what you think you are? How do you know you're not just a part of my reality?-

Damien stepped out of the transport truck, dressed in all black battle garb; pistols and combat knives at the ready. He marched toward Revco's Central Corporate entrance used by corporate executives as a direct means of travel to the upper levels. Saber walked at his side, just as prepared for combat as he. By comparison, she was considerably shorter than Damien, but was arguably the more dangerous of the two. Damien continued his COMMs with Oska.

Damien: "Coordinates received. What's your situation look like. I'll do whatever you need to get you guys out."

Oska: "The team is fine and now we have Jin as well. There's a riot going on and the prison's been locked down so escaping just got more complicated."

Damien: "Based on the maps you sent, we can get you out from the cafeteria. That should put you right overtop of us."

Oska: "We'll get there now."

Damien: "I'll send 4A Squad to extract you from that location. When you get back to ground level, Styner will be waiting for you as the battle coordinator since Saber and I will be headed inside. All COMMs are open."

Shina joined the COMMs conversation, having been listening in for her instructions.

Shina: "I'm tracking on all of that Damien. Oska I'll meet you inside. Keep us updated on your every move."

DLC's surprise attack on Revco allowed them to dominate the area. Damien's truck had arrived ahead of the main force. As the other transport trucks arrived, they positioned themselves in a broad "U" to establish a perimeter and prevent any Revco forces from getting close to Central Corporate's main entrance. High caliber turrets mounted and manned on each transport truck further emphasized their dominance of the surrounding area. The Revco Central personal stationed at ground level were chased off by the turrets during the approach. DLC's military completely outclassed Revco's standard police forces, forcing them back to maintain civil order and protect civilians from entering the area.

The time it took Damien's forces to reach Central Corporate from the gate gave Revco enough time to rally their first response forces or FRF. The FRF used highly mobile teams of three to approach from different angles and obfuscate the enemy and prevent focused fire. They were successful in preventing DLC forces from completely disembarking the trucks. However, The FRF were unsuccessful in killing or even hurting any DLC troops.

The first casualty of the battle went to a young DLC gunner by the name of Corvana Lang; who fired her truck's turret at the ground to create a trench along the FRF's circular route. This forced the first of the FRF who encountered it to slow down just enough to receive a burst of turret-fire. Corvana's tactic forced the FRF to use a more complex and irregular route, but the FRF had delayed DLC forces long enough for the next wave of Revco forces to arrive from the district. Revco forces began making their own perimeter far outside of DLC's turret range, trapping them between Central and a soon-to-be-reinforced defensive barrier. The two forces had placed themselves at a stalemate; only able to fire suppressive shots to prevent the other from getting too bold.

Damien and Saber had made their way into Central Corporate's entrance level. The massive elevator station was only defended by security personnel who upon seeing the approach of Damien, Saber, and 4A Squad surrendered without a fight. There was a private express elevator Mr. Bradley uses to go directly to his office floor. The elevator was tucked away in a small nook around the corner facing away from the entrance behind automatic glass doors. The doors opened but demanded a code to use. Damien COMMed Oska.

Damien: "Oska. I need you to find and open the security door for the express elevator."

Oska: "The code to his office is 111. It's less of a password and more of an address. 222 takes you to the morgue, 333 brings you to the prison, 444 goes to corporate offices, and 555 leads to an underground construction site."

Damien: "If the elevator can go straight to your deck, then getting you out shouldn't be a problem."

Oska: "With the lockdown, only high level corporate heads and specific personnel can access anything on this level. Anything I try to access gets blocked and I think they're counter-syphoning data from me when I do. Once the door closes on this level it can't be opened again from this side."

Damien: "Got it. Shina will get there as soon as possible. Saber and I will continue onto Mr. Bradley's office."

Oska: "Why would you go there?"

Damien: "Business. Stay safe up there. We'll have you home soon."

Damien, Saber, Shina and her robots crammed into the elevator and Damien typed in the first code: 333. The elevator shook and began to rise. The express elevator was fast and violently efficient and not built for comfort as its decor would imply. It arrived quickly at the prison level. 4A Squad exited to find Defector Squad while Damien and Saber remained in the elevator.

Damien: "You're here to get Defector Squad out as fast as possible. This is the most important thing anyone is doing right now. We're counting on you."

Damien ordered as the doors closed. Shina turned and COMMed Oska.

Shina: "Oska, this is Shina. We've arrived on your deck and are en route your position. Please respond."

Oska: "Got it Shina. You're near our location but there's heavy resistance between us, or at least a prison riot."

Shina: "If you're not in it, then the riot's not a concern. But your well-being is. Remain at your current location. We'll rendezvous with you and continue on to the extraction zone. Ten minutes."

Shina closed COMMs as she and her robots moved out. They kept a moderate pace as they ran through the long labyrinthine corridors. If it weren't for her added mental capacity of her robots, she would not have been able to keep her bearings through the maze. As she turned a corner, Shina was hit with a wall of noise from the riot. The entire squad fired their rifles into the air to scare the crowd away but only added to the chaos of the noise. The next option would be to fire through them all or find another way around. She opted for the latter. Shina COMMed Oska to update her on the change in the situation.

*　　　*　　　*

Grihm: "How much longer?"

Oska: "She didn't say."

Grihm: "I don't like the idea of waiting. Why don't we just meet her at the extraction zone?"

Oska: "We'd still have to wait. She has all of the equipment to get out."

Jin: "Grihm, this spot actually isn't that bad. There's nothing but corridors behind us. If the riot does come this way, we can hold it off easily."

Oska received an urgent incoming COMM from Shina.

Shina: "Come in Oska. Be aware: There is an individual rioters are calling "The Warden" said to be headed in your direction. Recommend taking defensive positioning while you have time. I'll get there as soon as I can."

Oska: "Got it. Thanks for the heads up."

Trigger noticed someone marching furiously down the corridor toward them and alerted the others.

Trigger: "Hold on guys. We got company comin'."

Jin instantly recognized the doll-face youth as the Warden and his skin began to crawl. The rest of the team looked on as he approached. The Warden stopped and stared at the team silently, his hands clasped behind his back.

Jin: "If you could just give us another ten minutes, we'd appreciate it."

Warden: "There's that sense of humor again."

Grihm: "Jin, I take it that's the Warden? He doesn't look that bad."

Warden: "As a close friend of Salena, I think you of all people would know not to underestimate small people."

Grihm: "How do you know Salena?"

Warden: "We have a mutual friend."

Grihm considered that the "mutual friend" could be the spy Damien was looking for. It also dawned on her that if Damien had lifted the lock down to assist her, than the spy must have been dealt with.

Warden: "But enough about that. You've stalled long enough."

A sinister energy that made everyone's hair stand on end filled the area. There was a distinct cracking of electricity discharging. With a thunderous boom, the Warden began dashing toward them.

Jin: "What are you waiting for? Shoot him!"

No one questions the command. Having lost her grenade launcher in the scuffle with Jin, she only had a handful of anti-personnel bomblets to use, which she hurls at the oncoming Warden. The Warden's hands begin sparking with electricity. He points a hand at the bomblets and electricity juts out in a web-like arc, detonating them all in the air. The Warden continues sprinting toward them without breaking Stride. Sev and Trigger step forward and begin firing their weapons at the Warden. The Warden uses bursts of electricity to jump himself around the corridor, leaping from wall to wall and ceiling. In between bursts, he notices Oska in the back not firing weapons and takes aim. He springs into a ceiling corner to line up his next charge. His entire body becomes shrouded with electricity, making everyone's hair stand on end. In a flash of light, a bolt of energy surges at Oska. Jin steps in the way, manifesting his ethereal barrier. The energy slithers over the surface of the barrier. As it reaches the edge, the energy scatters in all directions, shocking everyone but Jin and Oska. Having discharged the energy, The Warden reappears with his fist against the barrier. There was a look of surprise on his face as he gazed through it. The Warden kicks away, landing a fair distance away; crouched and preparing for another arc-charge.

Grihm was without any more weapons and shifts her focus to defending Oska. The Warden electrifies both hands and dashes forward again. He throws an orb of electricity at the team and they scatter for cover. With his remaining charge, the Warden connects the two charges with a bolt of electricity and pulls himself toward the team; directly over Oska and Grihm. Sev isn't daunted by the Warden's attack and takes aim. The remaining charge in the Warden's hand zaps Sev's gunfire inert rather than strike at Oska. Jin's barrier further dissuaded his attempt at an attack. As the Warden's remaining charge was used to defend against Sev, he drifted slowly back down to the floor. Jin took the opportunity to charge, using his barrier to coat his blade and clenching his other fist as he swung. The Warden was the type of opponent Jin couldn't afford to hold back against and was worth the extra effort. The Warden glowers venomously at Jin and an intense shock jolts through him emanating from the wound given to him by Emil. The shock is enough to bring Jin to his knees, giving the Warden enough time to charge his other hand and defend against both Sev and Trigger's gunfire, but little else. Jin's fist loosens, losing the energy but keeping the exhaustion that came with it.

Oska had always overseen missions through communications and text. She had never witnessed the intensity or danger of combat before. The shock of being a part of it and further still being targeted was becoming more than she could handle. Her heart beat harder than she had ever felt before. Her body was frozen. She wanted to run, but her muscles didn't respond. She couldn't even scream in terror. Fear had consumed her. Grihm's hand clasping hers was her sanctuary among the chaos. Grihm's hand felt warm as her own was frigid. Grihm led her further away from the Warden. Oska's legs followed instinctively.

Grihm: "Don't worry, Oska, we won't let anything happen to you."

Grihm's words seemed distant but made their way to Oska's core and soothed her heart. Seeing Grihm stand ready to fight the Warden without a weapon was the personification of bravery to Oska. She wanted to help but knew there was nothing she could do against such an opponent. Oska offered the only assistance she could: she unsheathed a knife from the underside of her sidearm. Damien had encouraged her to keep one on her and at this time, is the best advice she's ever received from him. Oska hand's Grihm the knife, handle first.

Grihm: "You're just full of surprises Oska."

A female voice shouts from the far end of the corridor where the Warden emerged.

Voice: "Focus Fire!"

A hail of gunfire fills the corridor; it was 4A Squad; firing in an endless rotation that allowed one of them to vent while the other three continued firing. Defector Squad dips to the sides of the corridor to avoid getting shot. The Warden's electricity arcs from his body in all directions as his body buckles from the surprise attack. The Warden was quickly enveloped in a dome of dancing electricity, defending himself from the gunfire.

Shina: "Quit standing around. C'mon!"

The corridor was barely wide enough for the team to slide narrowly by the sparking Warden. Tiny bolts of electricity snap at their faces as they shimmy past, making their hair stand tall. The Warden was too focused on the continuous gunfire to divert even the slightest bit of attention away; his eyes followed however. The Defector Squad dashes toward Shina once past the Warden, still careful not to step into the line of fire.

Shina: "You should have the location of the exit point. Get there, we'll hold him off and make our way there soon."

Shina shouts during her venting opportunity, never taking her eyes off of the Warden. Grihm acknowledges the command and places a thankful hand on Shina's shoulder as she starts toward the extraction zone with Oska in hand. The other's follow close behind, although with some reluctance.

Trigger: "We're not gonna leave her here are we?"

Grihm: "I don't like it either but she's better equipped and in better condition to handle that than we are. And now getting Oska out safely is our top priority."

Jin: "To hell with that. Backing you up Shina!"

Shina: "Negative! Extraction is our mission; we can't complete our mission until you leave. Now stop distracting me and move!"

The Warden had acclimated to their gunfire and began a slow advance toward them; matching the overlapping gunfire with equal defense. As he stepped closer, his shield began jolting and snapping at them. A bolt juts out and strikes through the chest of one of Shina's robots. It tenses up and convulses as it falls to the ground lifelessly. A pain sears through Shina's augments. It passes quickly, but leaves her feeling lighter; as if she could keep a finer focus on the remaining two. Shina commands a robot forward to wrestle the Warden. It grapples and tears its way through the Warden's electricity (to his surprise) and clutches him violently. The electricity dissipates. Shina hated having to sacrifice a robot, but was glad it wasn't a person. She and the remaining robot open fire, shooting both the robot and the Warden. The heavy robot fell to its knees, dragging the Warden down as well. He was still alive, struggling against the weight pulling him down and the pain of being shot. As Shina fires a final volley to finish him off, electricity sparks up and the shot is redirected away. The Warden frees his hand and grabs the back of the robot. With a surge of electricity, he pries its chest from the rest of the body. The limbs drop to the floor as did Shina's burden of controlling it. The Warden still had fight left and it showed in his eyes now filled with a murderous intent. Shina wisely decides to meet up with the others.

Shina darts around the corner, leaving behind her last robot to combat the Warden. With more focus than she's ever had during a mission, she is able to have a greater deal of control over the last robot's actions. The Warden lunges forward with his electrified arm, striking straight at the chest of the robot. Shina deflects the attack in her mind and nearly loses her own balance; he images in her mind of her last robot were almost too vivid for her liking. She commands the robot to grab the Warden's attacking hand and lifts him effortlessly over its head. The Warden transfers the charge to his free arm and chops through the robots arm with a knife-handed strike. The robot raises its remaining arm to shoot, but the gun is kicked away by the descending Warden. As his feet hit the floor, he bolts forward with a direct strike of his electrified hand, piercing through the chest of the robot. Shina feels another surge course through her, but her control does not falter; however, the strength of the robot begins to fade. She urges the robot to grab the Warden's arm again as hard as its own body would allow. It grips so tightly that its fingers puncture flesh and crush the bones. The Warden's harrowing scream echoes throughout the entire prison. With it followed a pulse of energy that surged through the bodies of anyone close enough to have heard him. It hit Shina the hardest; disorienting her, twisting her perspective, debilitating the control she had over either body. She no longer had control over her last robot, only able to feel its presence.

Shina had finally caught up with the others in the cafeteria. Her pace increased once she was able to shake-off the disorientation from the Warden's pulse affliction. The cafeteria was the staff and guard dining hall for the cell block, as it was designed to be appealing, rather than the most efficient. The entire back wall was glass, giving a beatific view of the city, looking down over sun-silhouetted Revco and the lands far beyond the city. The cafeteria had become a gathering point for both inmates and employees looking to take no part in the surrounding chaos.

Shina: "The Warden's still out there so we have to hurry."

Shina handed Grihm a device called a sonic breacher: a device that can be planted on a weak structural surface that emits rapid sonic vibrations to create breach in a building. It required time to set and calculate the required tones. Grihm cautioned everyone to stand back as she activated it. It emitted a faint high-pitched chime as it charged, and then blasted thick chunks of glass outward before it fell to the floor. The entire cafeteria was filled with powerful gusts.

Shina: "I only have the one descent kit with me since all of my robots are gone. Only two people can ride in tandem at a time. The rest of us will have to wait for the kit to be sent back up."

Grihm: "Obviously Oska's going first. Jin you ride with her."

Jin: "I'll go last. I can at least hold him off the best with my barrier."

Grihm: "The entire point of us being here was to get you out. I'm not leaving you behind again."

Jin: "You're out of weapons and you've done more than your share. Get out of here and get Oska to Safety. There's no time to argue."

Jin turned away from her and faced the entrance, taking a battle stance and awaited the inevitable arrival of the Warden. He glanced over his shoulder at her and flashed a smile that assured her that he would be right behind her. Grihm had seen enough in Jin and was taken in by everything she saw. Her last memory of Jin was turning her back on him as he fell to the ground. She didn't want to leave him behind again but had faith in promises. She would leave him with something to entice him to come back safely. She grabbed him and kissed him urgently, assuring him that she'd be waiting for him down below.

Grihm fired the top end of the descent kit into the floor: it bored down into the floor and rooted itself. She dropped the bottom anchor out of the window. It hit the ground hard, burrowing deep as it did. Once set, it created a translucent "wire" of energy between the two points. The energy synchronizes with a belt and pair of grips that allow the user to ride between the anchors. Grihm attached the belt around the shaky Oska.

Grihm: "Just hold onto me real hard and keep your eyes closed. We'll be on the ground before you know it."

Grihm jumped out the window without giving Oska a chance to protest or prepare herself mentally. The ride down was fast, but smooth. As they approached the ground, their speed decreased evenly until their feet touched gently on the ground.

Grihm: "See? Painless."

 Oska's hair was frazzled as was her mind. With a simple press of a button, the grips and belt zipped back to the top for the next rider. Trigger stood on the edge watching as it arrived.

Trigger: "Go 'head Sev. You're the youngest."

Shina: "Thank you for understanding the situation."

Trigger: "I hate the idea of leaving a lady behind but orders are orders. Just hurry up."

As Trigger and Sev depart, the Warden lurches around the corner into the cafeteria, clasping his crippled limb and gnashing his teeth. Shina opens fire, only expecting to slow him down. The Warden had been shot at enough and would no longer stand to bide his time; he dashes into the gunfire with his electricity shielding him. Jin steps forward to meet him. As he attempts to raise his barrier, the Warden simply points at Jin and pain jolts through his shoulder again. Jin's distraction created a brief opening in the Warden's defenses, and he takes a superficial shot from Shina.

Without the rest of her robots, Shina is unable to lay down continuous fire to hold the Warden at bay. As her gun nears its venting point, the last of Shina's robot approaches the Warden from behind; tattered, broken, missing both arms, and to Shina's surprise, acting independently. The Warden discharges the energy generated from blocking Shina's gunfire. Bolts of electricity fire out from the Warden in all directions. The robot is struck first and collapses where it stood. A bolt strikes at Jin, but hits his barrier. It arcs off of it, striking Shina instead. The bolt pierces her chest and launches her out of the open window. Her senses scatter: Her last sights are of her looking up from the floor at the Warden where the final robot had fallen. Her last sensation was her body freefalling, and frigid air. Her last thoughts are of Cel'yst, Leila, and Quirin.

Jin reacts without a sensible thought in his head. He dives out of the open window after Shina. Her body was falling close to the building and the descent line. Jin narrows his body profile to fall faster. He grabs Shina's leg and with his free hand, reaches for the approaching descent grip. He snags it and it slams hard into his hand. The grip adjusts to compensate for the sudden change in direction and weight. Jin does his best to bring Shina closer to his body to prevent her from landing on her neck. Their descent was fast but not deadly; their landing painful. The crash knocks the air out of Jin's lungs. Grihm was the first to help.

Grihm: "What the hell happened? Are you okay?"

Jin: "I'm fine. But Shina took a bad hit and fell."

Trigger: "Godammit! I'll carry Shina. We all need to get to our forces. I want to get Shina and Oska out of here."

It was a sentiment felt by all. Shina paid greatly for their escape but none of them wanted their lives paid for with another.

22– PILEBUNKER

-A single driving force with so much weight and power behind it that the only viable option is to not be in its path.-

Defector Squad and Shina had touched down within the perimeter established by DLC forces thanks to the coordinated efforts of Damien and Oska. They moved quickly while staying low to avoid gunfire and not worsen Shina's condition. They crowded into the back of the first truck they saw. It was a fair distance inside the defensive perimeter. Only when they got inside did they realize that it was the medical vehicle. It was unoccupied so they each began to look for any medical supplies that they might have recognized. None of them were properly trained as medics and only knew basic first aid; Shina's wound far exceeded their level of knowledge. The wound was a severe electrical burn that singed both sides of the torso with some minor bleeding. Shina's eyes had dilated almost completely black and were dead to the world around her. Grihm checked for a pulse at Shina's wrist and neck; the hands were twitching spasmodically and made the wrist unreliable. Grihm placed two fingers on Shina's neck and everyone in the truck fell silent. After nearly eight seconds, she felt the first pathetic beat of

Shina's whimpering heart. The next beat was ten seconds later and five following that. Shina was still fighting to hold on; to the relief of everyone.

Grihm: "Why is everyone standing around? Someone find a medic and COMM Styner."

Trigger was the closest to the exit and jumped out to find proper assistance. Other than being the largest and heaviest lifter among them, Sev only took up space. So he left to assist Trigger.

Jin expected Oska to COMM Styner being that she handled all of the communications until he saw that she was fixated on Shina, her eyes just as vacant. Jin's COMMs implant hadn't worked since he was captured which prevented him from hearing any COMMs from anyone even as teammates approached his position.

Jin: "Oska, we need your help. My COMMs piece is busted. Can you get in touch with Styner for us?"

Oska drifted back to respond to Jin. Her words were monotone and her face never changed from the blank stare centered on Shina.

Oska: "Styner come-in. We have personnel down in the medical truck. Requesting emergency medical treatment."

Styner: "Dammit. I'll send someone your way."

There wasn't much Grihm could do for Shina and she felt uncomfortable doing nothing. Her heart was torn between the mentally shaken Oska, the recently rescued Jin, and the critically injured Shina, but Shina's injuries superseded the other two. She wanted desperately to exchange words with Jin, but being that he was sound of mind and body, he was at the bottom of her urgency list.

Not long after Oska's COMM, a woman entered the vehicle wearing a soldier's uniform with a medic patch on her left shoulder. She looked to be in her late twenties. As she entered the vehicle, she removed her cover revealing her wavy dark brown hair that was tied in a bun. Her eyes flashed a vibrant teal as she stepped out of the light and into the shade.

Medic: "Sorry I took so long. I've never been shot at before."

Grihm: "We understand. Please help her. I don't know what to do."

Medic: "I'll see what I can do… Oh my."

As the medic looked over Shina, her confidence visibly waned. Although trained in field medicine, she wasn't mentally prepared for such a critical injury. She had a lot of questions.

Medic: "How did this happen? What is this?"

Jin: "There was a guy who could throw electricity. It's really complicated."

Medic: "Right. Electrical burn. Get her armor off while I get ready to address the wound. What's Oska doing?"

Grihm: "She's a little shell-shocked. I'll get her out of here."

Medic: "No, leave her here. I'll treat her next. Ms. Grihm, are you and Mr. Jin okay?"

Grihm: "I'm fine but Jin might need to be looked at."

Jin: "I'm good too."

The medic caught a glimpse of Jin's undershirt as he was working to prep Shina. His stab wound had opened up from his crash saving Shina. He hid it well from the others, but the fresh blood gave him away.

Medic: "Mr. Jin, have a seat. I'll not have you passing out on me. Ms. Grihm, you're my assistant."

Grihm acknowledged and preferred it this way. She could help the situation rather than pass the problem onto someone else. Jin began to protest, but was eased into a seat by Grihm. Jin's injury made it easier but Grihm was plenty strong in her own right and didn't need a handicap. She helped him remove his shirts. The stab wound was stitched shut but had opened up again and was also showing signs of bruising. She tore some gauze from a roll to place over Jin's wound. She looked into his eyes but was interrupted before she could speak.

Medic: "Ms. Grihm, would you kindly hand me that bottle of salve and come over here? I hope you're not squeamish."

Grihm returned with the bottle and gazed upon the grotesque wound that lay upon Shina's bare chest. The wound was glossy and soft from the incarnadine flesh that was now exposed. The skin at the edge of the burn had been charred black and the skin that remained was pale and yellowed as it was no longer connected to the rest of the body and dead. Glancing at a sight such as this on a battle was one thing to Grihm, but to have to stare tested one's constitution. She forever more would have an even greater respect for medical professionals from this point on. The medic had Grihm help her cut the dead skin followed by a sterilization of the area. The medic then patted the wound dry before gently adding a layer of the salve to the wound. She finished by bandaging the injury. All was done in a matter of minutes and through the sound of gunfire outside of their little haven.

Medic: "That'll take care of the risk of infection. If we don't get blown up, she might stabilize but that's up to her at this point. If she survived that injury, I'm not worried about her willpower."

Grihm: "Thank you Doctor…"

Medic: "It's Esperanza Zhadore. I think I can handle these two on my own. Thanks for the help, you did fine."

Grihm took her words as a hint to make room in the truck. She felt comfortable leaving Jin and Oska in her hands after seeing her handle Shina. Grihm set off to join the others and find Styner.

*   *   *

Revco had bolstered their forces once again and were prodding DLC's defenses to create an opening. The FRF pulled back once the second reinforcements had arrived. The battle still raged as a mid-range firefight leaving the former business park entrance war-torn and ravaged.

Styner coordinated the combat efforts from the first truck that had arrived on scene. It sat further within the perimeter than the others but closer than the medical truck. It replaced its turret with a more sophisticated COMMs suite which would have suited Oska better than Styner had the circumstances been different. He had been so enveloped with overseeing the battle that he hadn't stuck his head outside of the truck since it had arrived on scene. While the battle was still being fought, he thought seeing things with his own eyes would help him conceptualize strategies. He stepped out of the back of the truck and sprinted to the nearest truck to take cover with some of the other soldiers. Two trucks down from his position, he saw Sev and Trigger spotting and sniping targets together. Grihm was taking cover at the next truck over. When she saw Styner she made a quick dash to his position.

Grihm: "How goes the war effort?"

Styner: "It goes. I take it Esperanza sorted you out?

Grihm: "She did."

Styner: "What happened up there?"

Grihm: "Shina took a really bad hit but she's stable for now. We got Jin and everyone else out mostly fine."

Styner: "Glad to hear you're okay. Now we can prepare to puncture their blockade and wait for Damien and Saber to finish."

Grihm: "What're they doing?"

Styner: "They're going straight for the head."

Styner's answer was irritatingly cryptic and he realized it as the words left his mouth. As he was preparing to clarify, he was interrupted by a ground-shaking explosion; the sound of metal shredding ripped across the battlefield. The COMMs truck had been crushed by a massive force that beveled the vehicle inward from above. Styner thanked his decision to scout the area with his own eyes. A hissing sound and AP steam wafted from the crushed truck as a large, stocky man climbed out of the wreckage. The man was completely nude with skin made of stone and every muscle a dark gray. Veins of molten red streaked throughout his body, billowing AP steam. As his body cooled, the steam subsided and the red dulled to black. The stone man jumped from the wreckage, shaking the ground as he landed. With each step a super-heated fissure rippled under his feet as he stomped toward Styner and Grihm.

The attention of DLC forces shift erratically. With the COMMs truck destroyed, Styner would have more difficulty coordinating the effort of DLC forces. Some trucks continue firing against Revco forces assuming that at least one other truck would address the new threat. Most did, barraging the stone man from nearly all directions. The stone man stops and spreads his arms to make himself an even easier target. As each shot hit his chiseled muscles, the red veins began to glow again, hissing AP steam. He dashed directly at Styner and Grihm. They could feel the quakes of his steps even from their distance and scurry to escape the path of the rampaging statue. Corvana Lang picked up on the counter productivity of direct gunfire and tried her trick of breaking the path. She fired a hail of shots at the ground just in front of the stone man, creating several large potholes. Too heavy to jump, he attempted to maneuver awkwardly and stumbled to his knees. As his body made contact with the ground he detonated, launching jagged red-hot stones in all directions. He had been far enough away from all of the trucks to cause mostly superficial damage although the truck Styner and Grihm took cover behind was rocked hard.

The stone man was shrouded in AP steam that hid him from view. Styner stepped out in front and gestured the "break fire" command followed by horizontal wave of the hand that indicated change targets. With more soldiers looking in the same direction and keeping in COMMs with their respective trucks, some unity was regained on the battlefield. In unison, all turrets turned back toward the outer perimeter. Soldiers on foot using small arms remained locked onto the steaming stone man. As the steam subsided, a man of flesh emerged. He held a stance ready for battle, unafraid of his situation and wore a smile that dared them to shoot. The soldiers held their fire being unsure of how fast the man could conjure his stone armor, and how he was able to do it in the first place. For good measure, Styner gave the hold fire command. The stone man's smile faded, but returned as Styner began walking toward him.

Grihm: "Styner, what the hell are you doing?"

Styner: "You saw what happened. We can't shoot him."

Grihm: "So you're going to punch him instead?"

Styner: "Not by myself I won't."

Styner stopped a healthy distance away from the stone man as he waited for Grihm; who was still armed with the knife given to her by Oska.

Grihm: "How're we going to do this?"

Styner didn't have a plan on defeating this opponent. He only sought to keep his attention focused on Grihm and himself so the rest of DLC forces could resume holding the line.

Styner: "Focus on evasion and one-for-one attacks. Nothing risky."

Once he realized Styner and Grihm weren't coming any closer, he climbed out of his self-made crater.

Stone man: "Smart move calling off your guns old man."

The stone man spoke with a gravelly voice that came deep from the gut.

Styner: "I've been around a lot of fighting and this is the first time I've seen anyone do that. There've been a lot of first for me lately."

Stone man: "I don't care. Fight me coward."

Styner: "I need a name first. I can't be bothered to fight no-names anymore."

Stone man: "My brothers call me Shrapnel."

Grihm: "Are we ignoring the fact that he's still naked?"

Styner: "Get over it, we're going."

Styner rushes at Shrapnel with Grihm close behind, he heads to Shrapnel's left as Grihm moves to attack from the other side. Shrapnel covers both of his arms in a sleek black refined stone and opens his arms wide. As they get just out of his reach he slams his hands together, creating an unbearable soundwave of clanging metal screeching across the battlefield. The harsh soundwave stopped Styner and Grihm in their tracks. Shrapnel shifts the stone on one hand to grow coarse, no longer bearing the contours of his forearm, now resembling a large stone brick. Shrapnel strikes the dazed Styner with a hard backhand, sending him sliding away. Grihm regains enough of her wits to see the brick-fist coming her way next. She ducks to let the attack sail overhead and with her knife, cuts across his torso as she scurries out of range of his counter attack. As the knife meets its mark, Shrapnel hardens the area fast enough to stop the knife from cutting more than skin.

Having gained distance from Shrapnel, Grihm peeked to see how Styner faired but kept an eye on her opponent. Grihm expected Shrapnel to charge them unrelentingly but he took a defensive stance and watched them with two brick fists. Styner wiped the blood away from his mouth as he rose to his feet. He used the silhouette of Grihm to help correct his double vision.

Grihm: "Are you okay?"

Styner opened his mouth but only a grunt escaped. He grabbed his jaw and with a sudden jerk and an audible cracking of bones, popped it back into place. He looked around at his soldier's watching the tense fight. They'd lowered their weapons and accepted their use would only be a burden to him and Grihm. They looked on intently as they had never had the opportunity to see Styner in action. His fearlessness and valor made him a legend. And those who knew of Grihm's role in DL also watched her; to see what made her a specialist. More than the tide of battle was being fought here; they were fighting to uphold legends.

Styner: "I'm fine."

Grihm: "Good."

Shrapnel began muttering to himself. He was being COMMed, but the sound of battle muddled the words before they reached Grihm and Styner. He snorts a plume of smog from his nostrils as he begins walking to position himself between the DLC soldiers and Grihm and Styner, never unlocking eyes. Shrapnel clasps both hands and raises them above his head and brings them down hard, smashing them into the ground. A molten fissure rips through the ground at Styner and Grihm and erupts violently, stabbing magma spires in all directions. The spires cool and harden instantly as they reach their peak. Grihm preemptively evaded, sprinting around the attack as soon as she saw Shrapnel's fist impact the ground. Styner, lacking the youth and energy of Grihm, sought to use only the minimal amount of energy required to dodge; He jumps back as the attack explodes and turns his body to elude the molten spears. Grihm continues her sprint around the attack and charges Shrapnel with her knife. Shrapnel had no stone on his body having expended it on his attack, takes a stance in anticipation of Grihm. He springs forward at the last second with a heavy clothesline. Shrapnel's massive limb barreled through the air at Grihm. She blocks the blow with both arms and is lifted off of her feet and knocked to the ground some feet away. Shrapnel follows the attack with another; his strength had returned and he forms a boulder, this time on his foot. He stomps the ground hard creating another racing fissure. Grihm was knocked flat on her back and was unable to scurry away from the attack. Styner sprints by and grabs Grihm as he dives with her in hand out of range of the attack. The fissure continues toward the gun line and erupts under a truck, easily piercing through it. The soldiers in the vicinity of the truck scattered to dodge the attack although those watching the other side of the gun line were not fortunate enough to see the attack coming.

Styner had been waiting for an opportunity to be close to an unarmored Shrapnel. Styner watched his opponent alternate between offense and defense for the use of his stones: one powerful attack or he holds out to counter his opponent, for once he attacks he is vulnerable for a time. Styner rolls to recover and brandishes his shotgun he now keeps on his person after his encounter with Hellcrow (where it also earned the name "Facemelter") and fires at the unsuspecting Shrapnel. The scattered shot pelt Shrapnel's body, rending dozens of tiny wounds. It was difficult to tell if he was immune to the pain or too dense to feel it. His only reaction was as steadfast as Damien. The wounds bled slightly before his body tensed up and turning entirely black with sleek stone. Styner fires again but the shots scatter dangerously in all directions. Styner vents the gun while he has the chance. Shrapnel's body grows in mass, less refined and into a bulkier, rough stone armor. Shrapnel stops to speak into his COMMs; his voice growing more subordinate after each pause.

Shrapnel: "I'm handling mine. Why can't you deal with yours? ... All of your men are gone…? I understand. I'm on my way."

Shrapnel sneered condescendingly at Styner and Grihm. He snorted another plume of smog from his nostrils before he turned away and leapt explosively into the distance. An enormous boom could be heard out of sight. Styner and Grihm looked on unsatisfied with the turn of events, yet relieved at their fortune. The soldiers watching the fight looked unsure as well. They knew victory was not in the future for Grihm and Styner and were disappointed that their first time witnessing them fight ended in their defeat. Styner helped Grihm to her feet as he gave commands to the soldiers to return to the battle which had not slowed down at all.

Grihm: "What the hell was that about?"

Styner: "I don't know but Damien needs to hurry up before this situation deteriorates anymore. We can't handle another hit like that."

A shot ricocheted along the ground in front of them and they wisely moved to the nearest truck. Styner had quickly forgotten about the second truck that Shrapnel destroyed; he COMMed the nearest squad leaders to order the others to tighten the gap between the trucks.

Styner: "Thanks for the assist but I've got everything here. Go check on Esperanza and the others."

Grihm silently agreed and headed that way.

Styner: "We're really lucky Shrapnel decided to attack the COMMs truck and not the medical truck."

Grihm: "I don't even want to think about that right now."

But she did anyway. The fate of Jin and Oska was decided not by her own actions but by a split decision of her enemy. All of her sneaking, lying, betrayals, and fighting to protect and keep them safe could have been for naught despite her efforts and this realization of her powerlessness brought her emotionally to her knees.

23– A BEAST AWAKENS, A BEAST IS SLAIN

-The gift of the pact always comes before the ordeal. The ordeal is not a test or a price, it is a curse and it is eternal.-

The elevator ride to the top of Rev Central was long. As it reached its destination at the top floor, it shut down abruptly and left Damien and Saber in complete darkness. Saber's eyes glowed red and were the only sight amidst the darkness. After a moment, the backup lights activated, covering the space in a red light. Her eyes then reflected green as she moved about.

Saber: "It would've been too convenient any other way."

Damien: "We're lucky it lasted this long. Help me get this door open."

They got a firm grip and pried apart the doors. With the elevator dead, the path back down was now closed and the only way left was forward. The president's office was just down a long hallway. Damien lit a cigarette and shared it with Saber. Both took a minute to prepare themselves for their meeting with Damien's rival. In all their years of competing with one another, not once had Damien met Mr. Bradley in person and for the first time in as long as he could remember, he had no idea what to expect. Since they hadn't run into any resistance, they opened the door cautiously from as close to the walls as possible but nothing came at them but the sound of ambient jazz music.

Suited gentleman: "No tricks or lies in this office. Only business."

A suited-man stood arms clasped, gazing out a massive window; the entire back wall of the office was one solid sheet of glass. The setting sun shone heavily into the office, casting deep elongated shadows that stretched to Damien's and Saber's feet. There were two people in the room: one standing and the other was sitting in a wheelchair; both of them gazing at the setting sun. With neither of them looking in their direction, Saber quietly slipped away to the far left side of the office and out of view.

The suited gentleman turned right to face Damien. The setting sun silhouetted his details, but Damien recognized his shape. The suited gentleman walked around his desk and as he approached, his shadow stretched across the room and climbed the ceiling, towering over the room. He was close enough that the details of his face were no longer hidden. He had black curly hair and a chin-strap beard that contrasted his dark, olive skin. His eyes were as dark as pitch and the bags under them made him look exhausted (which seemed to cast their own shadows as well). The face of Revco: Mr. Joseph Bradley.

Mr. Bradley: "We're a lot alike you and I; we're both tenacious in our endeavors, methodical, unwilling to take a step back, and several steps ahead of our opponents."

Damien: "We both can't be ahead of each other. I think you know as well as I do who's losing here."

Mr. Bradley: "It looks like you are at a glance. But what about the next battle or the one after that? *I* already know how our district competition will end. I can afford to plan ahead. But your battle plan for the long run is predictable and pathetic; survive. As a district, as a business, as a military, and as a person. Let's face it Damien, the Citadel in all regards is a scavenger. And what does a starving scavenger do when presented with a nice juicy steak? They lunge, unaware of the traps that await them."

Damien's face twisted. He hated the idea that Mr. Bradley was not only unperturbed by DLC's assault, but may have allowed it. Mr. Bradley derived great pleasure in knowing that he had snared Damien. Damien however, didn't feel ensnared. In fact, he felt emboldened.

Damien: "I can see that. But there's a reason why scavengers always outlive predators: we've evolved to survive. We adapt to change and only attack what we know we can kill because we're never seen as a threat until we're at your throat."

Mr. Bradley: "You've got an answer for everything don't you? You think we don't know about everything you're up to? Do you know how much information we have been fed on you?"

Damien: "Are you talking about Malerius? He's been dealt with."

Mr. Bradley: "Who cares? He's already done everything we've needed him to do. You and I could go back and forth forever over who's playing who, but neither you nor your soldiers have that sort of time. All it takes is for my brother Swarm over here to give the command and reinforcements will overwhelm the area."

Mr. Bradley leaned back on the desk facing Damien, silhouetted again.

Mr. Bradley: "Starting now, the Citadel will wither away in the shadow of Revco."

His silhouette began to drip to the floor and his shadow expanded in all directions, until the entire office floor was blackened. The black glaze flowed like oil. Damien and Saber could feel it peering back at them, probing their essence. Alarmed, Mr. Bradley jumped to his feet and looked behind him, realizing that he didn't notice Saber creeping her way along the wall toward the window. She was only a few feet away from the man in the chair. The man in the chair was middle-aged with pale hair. His face drooped and drool dribbled off of his agape mouth. Only his left eye was open, peering down at the streets below. A bizarre symbol that was loosely reminenscent of akashean writing wrapped around his iris. He was completely vegetative and unresponsive to the world around him.

Mr. Bradley shouted a repulsive series of words that could only be akashean and the man in the chair twitched violently. The rest of Mr. Bradley's words were in aethean.

Mr. Bradley: "Swarm, kill her!"

Swarm, the man in the chair, cuts his eyes toward Saber as the rest of the body springs to life. He had switched eyes; his right eye had an entirely new symbol, just as alien to Saber as the other.

Mr. Bradley: "You think she'll make a difference?"

From the darkness on the floor whips a wave of tendrils. They roll from Mr. Bradley's feet and wriggle toward Damien. Damien's first move was instinctive: He brandishes both guns; Ragnarok and Cataclysm. He aims one at the tendrils and one at Mr. Bradley, firing two gray shells. The first shot splits the tendril wave down the middle and momentarily creates a part in the blackness. Only slightly distressed, tendrils peel away from each other before racing toward Damien. Damien dashes down the center path between them. The second shot never detonated. Mr. Bradley stood holding the shell in swirling dark energy in front of his face. He clenches his fist, crushing the shell, releasing a flash of complete darkness followed by an expanding force that destroyed the tendrils. Damien and Mr. Bradley are flung away from each other. The discharge of energy shakes the entire room; knocking objects off the walls, desk and cracks the massive window.

The blast knocks Saber to the ground and rolling toward the window. Swarm manages to recover faster than Saber and leaps on top of her, pinning her arms to the floor. He was deceptively strong, or at least stronger than Saber in a disadvantaged position. Swarm's open eye was even more alien than before; the sclera of his eye was now as black as his pupil. The eye began glowing as if gathering energy. With her small frame, Saber was easily able to get her legs under Swarm. She kicks him off, his nails slashing her wrists as his grip slips. His head rocks back and a beam of mysterious blue energy fires out of his eye. The beam cracks as it carved a line along the wall and ceiling before dissipating. Saber takes advantage of the break in combat to assist Damien.

Ears ringing, Damien staggers to his feet. His shades had been knocked away in the blast but fortunately for his eyes, Mr. Bradley's dark shroud made the light level tolerable. Both of his guns were also missing in the shadows on the floor. He couldn't afford to lose those but for the moment he decides to make do without them. He draws his knives and steps toward the recovering Mr. Bradley, who could feel Damien's steps in his shadows. Mr. Bradley waits, counting them, timing his attack. Unexpectedly, Damien throws one of his knives at Mr. Bradley. A shadowy hand rises from the darkness and returns the knife to Damien at twice the speed. Damien considers for an instant, attempting to catch the blade but decides against it. He evades and looks back to see the knife hit the wall and continue through, tearing a large hole along with it. The shadowy hand rushes toward him as a clenched fist; he braces for impact as the fist slams him hard. As Damien rolls backward toward the wall, the darkness in the room begins to lift and take the shape of dozens of jagged black shards, all pointed at Damien. As Mr. Bradley gestures for the shards to attack, Saber attacks from behind by jamming Beyonder between his neck and shoulder. The shards immediately shatter and the office fills with natural light again. Saber twists Beyonder, but is unable to drive it further having already jammed it down to the hilt. Saber feels a rapid building of vile energy around her. She pulls Beyonder but is unable to get away herself. The sinister energy rises around Mr. Bradley, blasting her up and away.

Mr. Bradley staggers, cradling his crippling wound. Darkness pours out of Mr. Bradley like a fountain of tar. It sloshes around the floor and sticks to everything it touches.

Mr. Bradley: "Swarm! What're you doing? Kill her!"

Quickly growing tired of picking himself off the ground, Damien rises to his feet again. He looks around and locates Ragnarok on the floor. Damien makes a dash for the weapon before the oozy ichor could claim it. As he reaches for it, the ichor lunges for Damien's hand. He rears back and watches as Ragnarok is pulled into an oozy demise. The ichor begins to take form as it slithers back toward Mr. Bradley. The ichor was no longer pouring out of his wound, wrapping itself around his body and transmuting into a grotesque limb with a maw on the end. Mr. Bradley pulls his maw back and jabs it at Damien with jaws wide open. Damien cuts to the side, narrowly dodging the attack. Tiny bits of the maw ripple off, splashing Damien as it passed. He felt the ichor pull away from his skin, trying to reconnect to the body. It felt alive.

The maw chomps into the wall behind Damien, taking several bites. It seemed as if it had a mind of its own. With the maw biting the wall and Mr. Bradley's shadow glaze receeding, Damien saw an opportunity to attack; He slung his remaining knife at Mr. Bradley. It lodges itself in his chest, just off center.

Mr. Bradley bellows a series of obscenities. Damien watches as more ichor pours out of the new wound. As he wonders what shape it would take, the maw smashes into him. It drags him around the room, reshaping itself in the process. It grew a new set of tiny teeth against Damien's chest and with a violent twist; the maw gouges Damien before he falls away.

Saber recovered physically, but her vision was impaired. Her sight was several shades darker within the short distance she could still see. She looks around frantically and catches a glimpse of an ominous bead of light, pulsing in the darkness. Saber dives low as the beam of light surges inches away from her head. She sprints toward the source of the beam with Beyonder at the ready. From the darkness emerges a fist, closer and faster than she had anticipated. It hits her face crumpling her to her knees. However, Swarm was now within her reduced field of vision. He raises his leg to kick her face. Saber stabs his leg as it swung, but he doesn't stop; he didn't yelp, he didn't flinch. Saber rolls to her feet from the attack and she feels a frigid breeze and sees the light from the cracked window.

In addition to being weaponless against an AP casting enemy, Damien was also injured now. He could only watch as Mr. Bradley's wound mutates into another bizarre limb. The ichor flows out over Mr. Bradley's remaining arm and becomes another maw. The ichor continues to flow; this time however, it crawls up his entire body.

Mr. Bradley: "Damien, you have no idea what you've unleashed."

Mr. Bradley gurgles his final words as the ichor slithers over his face, covering every trace of him. Tethered to the mound that was once Mr. Bradley, the maws writhe and snap at Damien in frustration. Without warning, four more maws burst out in all directions, one of which rams into Saber, knocking her out of the way of another beam from Swarm that shatters the weakened glass and the room fills with brisk atmospheric air.

The hydra rallies its six maws. They chomp and hiss at each other as if arguing who would attack first. Two maws suddenly bite the floor in front of Damien, and two more charged at him from the sides as the final two roll overhead to dive down. Damien rushes up the necks of the two maws biting the floor. He felt his feet sink as he stepped on the hydra's putrid flesh. The four maws crisscross each other after their narrow miss. The hydra untangles its heads and rolls in an attempt to shake Damien off. He crawls on the hydra and manages to stay on top. Damien catches a glimpse of the knife he threw at Mr. Bradley sticking out of the hydra's flesh. He gets a strong grip and rips it up the body of the hydra. As he cuts, the black ichor splashes out at him. It crawls parasitically up his arm up to his shoulder, to his neck and over his head.

Saber slips several times from the ichor as she tried to make it to her feet. The shadow glaze covering the floor made her movements feel sluggish. Her vision was still impaired but she was still able to make out the shape of the monstrous creature taking up most of the office, albeit with great disbelief. The sound of jaws snapping toward her gave her enough of a warning to dash away from the danger, stumbling over bits of broken desk as she does. One of the heads follows her movements as she runs into a wall. The head lunges, narrowly missing the acrobatic Saber as she runs up the wall and flips off, landing back where she started. She holds still and opens her ears in anticipation of the next attack: she feels strong gusts of ice cold air stiffening the ichor on her body, she hears the hydra thrashing about toward the center of the room, a set of footsteps shuffling clumsily through the ichor that was too flat-footed and careless to be Damien, and the charging of energy she had become familiar with. Based on the timing of the other shots, she evades the beam and rushes toward the point of origin with her hands guarding her face this time and moving erratically as she does. The glint of a sword flashes in the darkness as it stabs at her face; it was Beyonder. A slight tilt of her head is enough for the attack to miss. Saber grabs the arm wielding the blade and kicks away with her weapon back in her possession. A growl from the darkness precedes a maw of the hydra as it lunges between her and Swarm.

Darkness overtakes Damien too quickly for him to resist. He feels the ichor attack his body, pulling him in. It worsens his wound and steals his breath. Damien sinks into a putrid black abyss. It was larger on the inside than the outside; a vast realm of liquid darkness and negativity. Damien feels a mass brush his fingertips; he grabs it. His mind is rushed with emotions and thoughts he knew weren't his own: surprise, frustration, and murderous anger. As Damien yanks the body toward him, he feels something sharp scrape his neck. The object continues on and Damien grabs it. It was an arm; He breaks it. The abyss writhes and shares its anguish with Damien. Damien feels the arm release the sharp object; a knife, *his* knife. Another wave of emotion washes over Damien. This time it was disbelief. And for a fraction of a second, before he jammed the knife into bone and flesh, the abyss felt fear.

Like a balloon filled with tar, the hydra exploded. The ichor splattered over nearly every inch of the office. In the center stood Damien holding a knife jammed into Mr. Bradley's chest. Damien's body shook from the pain and adrenaline, gasping to fill his lungs with air rather than the vile liquid that currently filled them. Mr. Bradley dropped to his knees but Damien kept the knife lodged in the wound. The ichor dripped from of Mr. Bradley's eyes, nose, mouth, and ears as he sputtered his words.

Mr. Bradley: "This changes nothing Damien! You will all be swept away in the black tempest…"

Something welled up within Damien; a lingering sensation from the abyss. The feeling started in his chest and pulsed outward with every pump of his heart. It stung his veins as it coursed throughout. Once it reached his head, the pain had become an intoxicating sensation that made Damien smile wide. He laughed under his breath.

Damien: "I think I *like* what I've unleashed."

Damien clawed his hands into Mr. Bradley's chest and with a single pull, tore the former CEO in half, drenching himself in the last of the black ooze. Saber wasn't sure what was more disconcerting: Damien's lack of poise or his uncharacteristically smiley demeanor.

Saber: "Damien? Are you okay?"

In an instant, everything about Damien shifted. The ichor plummeted from his body, he stood upright, and his smile abated. The sound of her voice brought him back from wherever he had gone.

Saber: "Are you okay? Where's Swarm?"

Saber was more concerned about what had happened to Damien but Swarm was a more urgent threat. Both of their visions were impaired; for Damien, the room was too bright, for Saber, too dark. Saber listened for the threat but only heard the sound of soft sobbing.

Swarm: "I'm sorry brother. The rest of us will make this right."

The sound of footsteps sloshing through the ichor could be heard as they made their way to the only exit in the office. Swarm stopped and turned back to the weary, blind, and injured couple as they held each other up.

Swarm: "You have thirty minutes to get out of our district or we're shooting you in the back. This battle is over, but the war is far from won."

If the door hadn't been destroyed in the battle, Swarm surly would have slammed it on his way out. Damien and Saber stood alone in the ravaged office with only the howl of wind and panting of their own breath. Saber's bearings had returned to her as did eyesight. She looked upon her battle weary love with eyes of relief as well as worry.

Saber: "Are you okay?"

Damien: "I feel… great."

Without concern for his wounds Damien whisked Saber off of her feet and into his arms and headed for the door. Saber was battered from her fight but not so injured to need or even want Damien to carry her but she let him anyway; she ended up enjoying it more than she thought she would. Damien kicked a heavy lump on the floor. A slight blue glow shone through the ichor on the floor that he recognized to be one of his guns: Cataclysm. Holding Saber with one hand, he grabbed the gun and holstered it. Damien was showing no signs of fatigue. He seemed to be better than he had been in some time. As she prepared to inquire about his current state, Damien opened COMMs with Styner.

Damien: "Damien and Saber checking in. We are en route the gun line. Requesting status report."

Styner: "You don't know how good it is to hear that right now. Gun line is holding strong. We were attacked by an AP casting enemy briefly before he departed. His whereabouts are unknown. Since then enemy forces have just begun pulling back. What did you do up there?"

Damien: "We took out their leadership. We have thirty minutes to get the hell out of here before they rally their forces. Prepare ours for immediate departure."

Styner: "Got it. See you groundside."

The elevator they rode on the way up was active again and invited them in with open doors.

Saber: "Damien, what is going on with you? Your shirt is soaked in your own blood. How are you okay?"

Damien looked down his shirt as if he had forgotten about the injury. He rose what was left of his shirt revealing no open wound. Only darkened skin that had already healed.

Damien: "That's new."

Saber: "That's new? That thing that came out of Bradley's body gouged your chest open, you get up like nothing happened and all you have to say about the situation is "that's new?""

Damien: "That would make him an AP caster."

Saber: "No, Jin is an AP caster. Bradley did something entirely different. That was…"

She recalled the conversation she had with Draxis about pact makers; beings of multiple souls. Draxis claimed to be one but seemed more æthean than any of the akasheans she had met, even Cel'yst and Malerius. She had never spoke to Damien about what she'd learned during the mission that wasn't directly related to the information she was sent to gather. It didn't seem relevant. But more so, she scarcely believed it herself.

Damien: "Are you going to finish that thought?"

Saber: "It was dark and there was a lot going on. I don't know *what* I saw. Seeing AP casting is one thing but what we just fought in there is beyond us."

Damien: "All the blood splattered around the office says otherwise."

Saber: "That's not blood. Maybe we can have R&D study it."

Saber looked at her own body that was covered in the black ichor. Damien however, only had on him what rubbed off from her.

Damien: "We're going to need more than R&D."

*   *   *

At ground level Saber stopped Damien before heading into the lobby.

Saber: "Let me down. I don't want everyone thinking you're rescuing me."

Damien gently let her down, and she stretched her legs. She continued.

Saber: "Everyone already fears and respects you. I don't want people to think I can't take care of myself."

They stepped out of the Central entranceway to a roar of cheers. Not just in celebration of their assumed success, but of their immediate departure. Styner waved the two of them over next to the medical truck. He looked them over; first at Damien who was tattered, bruised, and missing weapons, then at Saber who was still smeared with sludge.

Styner: "What the hell happened in there?"

Saber: "We're still trying to figure that out."

Damien: "We'll talk about it once we're out of the district. Are we ready to move yet?"

Styner: "As soon as you hop on a truck we're out of here."

Damien: "Let's do it."

Damien started toward the medical truck but Styner redirected him toward another. While he wanted Damien to see Jin and Oska, Grihm was also on that truck. Styner decided it would be best to at least let the adrenaline die down before letting Damien see her. Saber however volunteered to ride with medical.

24– WAR WOUNDS

-It's not war that changes… it's the people.-

Saber greeted Grihm with a firm hug that left a black imprint on Grihm's body. They were so excited to see each other that neither of them noticed. Saber's elation abated as she looked at the others: Jin's arm was wrapped in a bloody bandage and sling, Oska curled into a ball with her knees to her chest and face hidden from view, Esperanza (whom she had never met before) monitored the Shina's vitals as she lay motionless on a stretcher.

Saber: "Is she…"

Grihm's voice was somber and soft.

Grihm: "She's holding on. We ran into an AP caster on our way out. Shina's the only reason the rest of us were able to get away. Then Styner and I got attacked by another one just before you and Damien came back."

Saber: "Damien and I fought two as well."

The truck was small and didn't have enough room for private conversations. Jin chimed in.

Jin: "That brings the number of AP caster in Revco to five. Not to mention Turchess was also one. So much for it being a lost art."

Saber: "Then Revco only has four because we killed Mr. Bradley."

Grihm: "Shit. You guys did better than we did. Never would've thought Mr. Bradley to be one though."

Saber: "I think he was more than just a caster but we don't know how else to classify him."

With Jin having joined the conversation, Saber changed the subject to check in with her team mates.

Saber: "Jin, how're you holding up?"

Jin: "Just a critical stab wound and a dislocated shoulder. But I'll be fine."

Saber: "And what about…"

Saber pointed to the dejected Oska. The conversation drifted to whispers. Esperanza picked up on the silence and joined the discussion.

Esperanza: "Physically she's unharmed. They did an excellent job of keeping her safe but she's going through the first stages of PTSD. I want to remove her from the environment as soon as possible so we can start moving forward to help prevent the onset of long-term trauma. If you don't mind, I'd like to bring her with me to medical as soon as we return. I know you normally debrief right after a mission but I think this would be for the best."

Saber: "I'll let Damien know."

Grihm: "Speaking of Damien… how dead am I?"

Saber exhaled softly and prepared herself mentally for the conversation.

Saber: "He hasn't said anything about you since we departed the Citadel which means he's saving up for you. But I want to hear your side of it first. I want to know what the hell you were thinking pulling all of this."

Grihm: "I don't know what came over me. I felt that Damien was throwing Jin to the wind. I couldn't just walk away knowing that."

Saber: "You're going to need more than that because if you stand in front of Damien and say that he's going to kill you on the spot."

Grihm: "I don't *have* anything else. What else is there? I was selfish and reckless, I convinced others to go against orders with me, and I put key personnel at risk. I messed up. But I know that if I hadn't done something, Jin might still be in there trying to fight his way out and Damien would be twiddling his thumbs trying to figure out the best course of action."

Saber: "Exactly! He can't just act on emotion like that. There are consequences to what we do as a military. I don't even want to think about the backdraft that's going to come from what we just did."

Grihm: "I'm sure Damien's going to say the same thing so can we skip past this part?"

Saber: "Stop acting like a child. The situation you put us in is a disaster. I want to help you. I want to be on your side but I can't if you don't let me."

Grihm: "What can you possibly say to Damien to stop him from dropping the hammer on me? It doesn't matter why."

Saber: "Bianca."

Grihm: "Stop it. There's nothing left for me to say about this."

Saber: "Bianca."

Grihm: "I…"

Grihm's defenses were broken down by her best friend's patience and sincerity. Grihm buried her face in her hands to hide her overwhelming emotion. Jin didn't like eavesdropping on something clearly not meant for him to hear but it was hard not to in the proximity of the truck. Esperanza tried to block out the conversation by keeping busy with Shina. Oska missed every word.

Grihm: "None of this was supposed to happen. We were supposed to be in and out before anyone even knew what happened. That was the whole point of bringing Oska. I didn't think Damien would start a war over her alone."

Saber: "It wasn't just Oska. If anything had gone wrong in there, and it did, there was no way to get you out safely. Especially if half of DL is captured or worse. He came for *all* of you."

Saber's words cut across Grihm's heart as true to her name, and opened an emotional gash that bled tears. She covered her nose and mouth to suppress the sound of her heart wrenching. Saber was cruel and did not let up.

Saber: "You never gave Damien a chance to help. And what's worse is that you didn't even *talk* to me. You turned your back on us."

Grihm: "I'm sorry I had no idea. I…I thought I could do this while Damien handled the problem at home. And I didn't want to talk to you because I didn't want to make you choose between me and Damien."

Saber: "This wasn't something that needed to divide us. We could have found another way."

Saber grabbed Grihm's hands and clasped them in hers.

Saber: "I'll talk to Damien as soon as I can to get him to clear his head first. We're going make it through this; whatever it brings. I promise."

Grihm: "I don't deserve this, you as a friend."

Jin placed his remaining good hand on Grihm's shoulder to offer his support as well. Grihm had succeeded in her goal of bringing Jin back but she failed in doing so quietly. Shina helped take a considerable load to make this happen and ended up paying the price that Grihm was unwilling to let Jin pay. A debt she will now owe for some time.

Jin: "I'm a little biased but I appreciate everything you've done for me."

Saber: "It's good to have you back Jin. I know Damien and Styner will be glad to see you too even if they don't show it. Both of you."

*   *   *

Damien and Styner rode in a truck with Sev, Trigger, and Corvana Lang, who had not had any interactions with Damien since her basic training two years before. She was still young herself, only older than Oska and Sev by two years. Little about her stood out in her fledgling career with the Citadel but this battle presented the opportunity for her to make a name for herself; an opportunity she did not miss. Styner invited her to ride with Damien (whom she idolized) and himself to thank her personally for her help with Shrapnel as well as causing the first enemy casualty of the battle. Her large, round eyes lit up at the offer and she sat gleefully across from her leadership, waiting respectfully to be addressed.

Styner: "Damn good work out there Lang. You made a hell of an impact in this fight and if Grihm were here she'd want to thank you too."

Lang: "Thank you for your kind words Sir. I'm just trying to follow yours and Colonel Master's example."

Damien: "That sounds like grounds for a field promotion."

Damien gestured to Styner a subtle nod. Styner dug around in his pockets until he found a challenge coin: a medallion often awarded to military service members for a variety of reasons. One given personally from leadership is a gesture of exceptional appreciation. The coin itself was gold with an embossed image of Mag City with the Citadel emblem and the letters *DL* on one side. The reverse side was a creed:

Strength in arms,

Strength in knowledge,

Strength in trust,

Power in all.

Lang held the cherished gift tight and thanked them.

Damien: "You're going to hear some things in this truck. Things that will remain in this truck. Understood?"

Lang nodded in compliance and slid back in her seat.

Damien: "Trigger, Sev, welcome back. Good work bringing the others back safely as well."

Trigger: "D, we're awfully sorry about what we did but we did what we thought was best. We wanted to make sure Grihm and Oska were safe out there."

Sev: "If we didn't go with them there was no way they would have made it without us."

Damien: "Keeping them safe would have been letting me know what she was planning as soon as you found out, not letting her get into danger and then pulling her out."

Trigger: "We understand. It was a bad call on my part. If I can, I'd like to take on whatever punishment you have planned for Sev in addition to my own. He's my trainee and was just following my lead."

Damien: "Noted. With that being said there will be no debrief. You'll submit a full mission report by cycle's end."

Styner: "I'll give you the battle debrief when we get back. For now, where's your head Damien?"

Damien: "We have some research to do. Mr. Bradley turned out to be some sort of monster on top of being an AP caster."

Styner: "Monster? Do you mean like Hellcrow?"

Damien: "Bigger. Big enough for me to claw my way inside and stab my way out."

Styner: "Then why was Saber covered in sludge not you?"

Damien had not noticed that he didn't have any of the ichor on him despite his swimming in it. Looking back, he was having trouble recalling details of the fight.

Damien: "I'm still trying to figure that one out. There was another person in the office that was also a caster and claimed that he was in charge of their reinforcements. After we killed Mr. Bradley, he told us his forces would let us withdraw. By the time I COMMed you, you said they were already pulling back. He didn't use COMMs or gesture anything to control his people."

Styner: "That's a lot different than what Jin said AP casters could do. And a lot worse."

Damien: "We're going to have to pick Jin's brain some more and see if Saber may have left anything out from her mission up north. All of these monsters and casters showing up at the same time can't be a coincidence."

Lang: "Do you think that freak aurora north of the city recently means anything?"

Both Styner and Damien looked at her blankly, upset that they didn't consider the possibility themselves (especially since it occurred the cycle before Saber returned from the area). Lang misread their silence and shrank into her seat and apologized."

Damien: "You've brought up a good point. That phenomenon could be seen from anywhere in the city. But I hope it has nothing to do with what we're dealing with. If there are people who can do that then we might be stumbling into something we can't fight."

*   *   *

Revco had already diverted traffic away from Central due to the battle which made the transit out of the district much easier for the convoy. DLC forces disregarded most traffic laws on their way out. People looked on in disbelief and confusion. Many of them took pictures and recorded videos of the convoy tearing through the streets. The convoy departed through the same gate they arrived, which had been ripped to shreds by the turret fire to create an opening. There was a collective sigh of relief as they passed back into Eratech without further incident, locking the Eratech doors of the gate behind them.

The convoy pulled into the hangar through the deployment tunnel and the ramshackle vehicles parked where they would remain for some time before they were safe for operation again. Personnel disembarked, kissing the ground, sharing hugs, exchanged high fives, and blessed their safe return. There was also a somber atmosphere looming about as not everyone returned and many of those who did would suffer from life-long afflictions or injuries. Some of whom were holding on within an inch of their lives.

Damien headed toward the medical truck that he had been steered away from before when he locked eyes with Grihm as she disembarked. A bolt of dread surged through her heart. Damien seethed with anger as he approached her. Damien had a nearly irresistible urge to punch Grihm in the face, but as his muscles tensed, he felt his hand routing for one of his knives. Thankfully, both were lost in Mr. Bradley's office. As angry as he was, the urge to harm her had never truly crossed his mind. He wasn't sure why his hand reached for his knife. The hesitation encouraged him to form words over action.

Damien: "You're lucky to be back here and able to stand up on your own feet. Not everyone who went out on this mission can do the same. After everything we talked about, you still spit in my face."

The energy in the hangar died down and all attention was directed toward Damien and Grihm. The various members of DL pushed their way to the front of the crowd with the exception of Oska, who along with Shina, was taken to medical by Esperanza.

Grihm: "I know I was wrong and I'm sorry."

Damien: "I don't want an apology! An apology won't bring back the people we lost saving you. An apology won't heal Shina or earn back the funds we just burned or convince the city and Council that our actions were justified. You owe not just me and DL, but the Citadel and the district more than just an apology."

Grihm: "I know I was wrong but it didn't warrant all of this. That was the point. We're... *I'm* not worth this. Why would you waste so much on me?"

Damien: "You are not a waste. You're the second in command of DL and in my absence become standing leader of operations. You're just as vital to the Citadel as Oska, Styner, or myself."

She was stunned at Damien's words. Even in anger he valued her as a person.

Grihm: "You're right. I have a lot to answer for, more than I can say with words. I lost sight of my purpose here and neglected the people who've always had my back who continued looking out for me even after I turned my back on them. I know this won't mean much if anything coming from me right now but I'll make things right. For Shina, the people I've betrayed, and those who fought for me."

Damien: "You're right. Your words don't mean much of anything right now."

Damien took a deep breath before he addressed the crowd.

Damien: "There's a lot of standing around considering we're still at MILCON 0!"

The onlookers scattered to their various post-mission operations. In an instant the hustle of the hangar resumed without error.

Damien: "The rest of you take the rest of this cycle and the next to decompress."

Damien waited for Saber before the two of them departed, leaving the rest of DL on their own. Styner looked at Grihm one last time before turning away to manage the efforts in the hangar. She wasn't sure what to make of the look. It wasn't as fierce as Damien's but spoke many emotions.

Grihm, Trigger, and Sev walked with Jin to medical. Trigger and Sev managed to go the entire mission and battle without sustaining a single injury and were going to offer their support. The scene at medical was chaotic as the expected. The now understaffed medical facility was still trying to find a place to put the injured. Critically wounded personnel took precedence and were already in rooms being helped, Shina included. They had a look around to find Oska among the commotion when Sev spotted her standing alone outside one of the side doors. She was leaning against a wall and seemed more relaxed. There was a half smoked cigarette stomped out at her feet.

Oska: "Did you know that cigarettes are terrible?"

Grihm: "What're you doing smoking?"

Oska: "I heard they take the edge off but all I want now is some gum."

Grihm: "It must have done something because you look like you're doing better. I'm not telling you to pick up smoking though."

Oska: "Esperanza gave me some pills earlier too."

Grihm: "Are you okay then?"

Oska: "I think so. I don't know how you guys can do what you do over and over again. Putting yourself in danger like that. People trying to kill you, having to kill them first, the gunfire, explosions, the screaming. It's terrifying."

Trigger: "It can be tough. It hits some of us harder than others but we've all gone through it at some point. You wouldn't be wrong if you never wanted to do that again."

Oska: "I don't *want* to be in danger again but there's a big difference between what I can provide on the field and what I can do here."

Grihm: "Let's not worry about that right now. I'm just glad you're you again."

Oska: "Thanks. I'm happy to have helped. Welcome home Jin."

Oska gave Jin a long hug, careful not to hurt his injured arm.

Oska: "I'm going to stay here and wait for Esperanza and then I'll get some rest. You guys should do the same."

Oska headed back inside amidst the chaos to help her drown out the thoughts of death trapped in her head. The pills only helped her physically contain herself. Her mind was still a hurricane, unable to hold a thought other than the madness of combat for longer than a moment before it was thrown about wildly into the storm. In her time with the Citadel, she'd never imagined how it felt to be out in the heat of battle. But the thought of dying weighed heavily on her. It was the first time she truly realized her mortality. Watching Shina go from a living, breathing, dreaming mass of life with every intention to see another cycle, to a lifeless corpse haunted her. Shina had become an object to Oska; a pile of bones, blood and flesh with no more of an objection to the events around it than the space it occupied. She struggled to remember Shina as she was, but could only picture her empty body in her place. That hideous corpse could have been anyone. Oska didn't want be become one of those.

*   *   *

The dreadful task of informing personnel that loved ones had been wounded or worse fell upon the shoulders of the medical staff member who worked on the patient. Esperanza made the call to Cel'yst. She had never met the reclusive akashean woman before and didn't know what to expect. The phone didn't finish its first ring before it was answered. There was the sound of children's television programming and young voices in the background.

Cel'yst: "Hello?"

Esperanza: "Mrs. Cel'yst? This is Medic Esperanza Zhadore from medical. Is there any way that you could come down to see me?"

Cel'yst: "Sure. Is something wrong?"

Esperanza: "I'd prefer to discuss this with you in person."

The background noises dampened. There was a silence for a time before Cel'yst answered.

Cel'yst: "I understand. I'll be there soon."

Cel'yst hung up the phone and stood in dread, mentally preparing herself for the worst. Leila picked up on Cel'yst's change of mood. Her aura was much smaller than it had been before, which was her best attempt at keeping her feelings to herself.

Leila: "What's wrong?"

Cel'yst: "I have to step out for a little bit. Leila, you're in charge. Our neighbors across the hall are home if you need anything. You know how to reach me."

After a kiss for both Leila and Quirin, she left. Cel'yst knew in her mind what the call meant, but wouldn't accept it without seeing it with her own eyes. She hurried to medical, holding her aura at bay and her tears back.

When she arrived, all eyes turned to her, but only for a moment. Her ghostly form was both beautiful and ominous, but in her current state more so the latter. Cel'yst approached the staff at the desk. He made a quiet phone call and shortly afterwards Esperanza arrived to escort her. The look on Esperanza's face was somber; she was as afraid to deliver the news as Cel'yst was to receive it. They walked along side one another in uncomfortable silence.

Esperanza opened the door for Cel'yst to enter but remained outside herself. There were two nurses in the room checking on Shina's vitals. Cel'yst wafted slowly to Shina's bedside and placed her hand on her forehead. She looked upon the unresponsive Shina with a wrenched heart that she could no long hold back. Her aura filled the room with a deep, blackened violet. The nurses were burdened with the crushing emotion of death that collapsed to their knees. The aura made them want to feel anything other than what they were experiencing. It was this near animalistic urge to escape that gave them the strength to crawl out of the room and shut the door behind them. They were short of breath and their hearts were racing as Esperanza helped them to their feet. But for Cel'yst there was no reprieve. This was now her reality.

After giving Cel'yst an hour in private, Esperanza entered to speak with her. She was sitting bedside with her hands in her lap. Her aura had withdrawn to arms length, but was still the same soul-crushing black.

Esperanza: "I'm sure this must be difficult for you. If there's anything I can do for you…"

Cel'yst remained silent. The only sound in the room was that of the heart monitor beeping slowly and softly.

Esperanza: "If you have any questions I'll do my best to answer them."

Esperanza continued closer to Cel'yst, who remained motionless.

Esperanza: "I intend on doing everything I can to help Shina. Physically she's fine, but other than her body's natural reflexes, she's unresponsive. It may only be a matter of time but…"

Cel'yst: "There's no one there."

Her voice cracked from not speaking for the entire hour.

Esperanza: "Excuse me?"

Cel'yst: "I can't feel her anymore. There's no one there."

Cel'yst reached her hand out to Esperanza. She looked at the hand shrouded in misery and reluctantly grabbed it. Her mind raced away from her own thoughts. She felt her consciousness travel further and further away from herself, then an abrupt stop. The images around her were warped and misshapen. Structures stretched as high and blocked out the light of the sun, leaving her in cold shadows. Cel'yst retracted her hand and Esperanza was dragged back into the hospital room. The experience left her cold and winded. She could see ice on her breath.

Cel'yst: "The light of my world has gone and I wallow in the mire of emptiness."

Esperanza's warmth returned to her slowly, but the experience remained. She had no idea what to say to Cel'yst, so she left. Cel'yst was only the first loved one of the injured or dead that she spoke to. Esperanza had many more difficult conversations ahead of her.

* * *

Jin had arrived back at his room, his muscles relaxed at the familiarity of it. Everything was exactly as he left it; even his television was still on. Exhaustion soon set in and the weight of his battered body descended upon him. He resisted the urge to sleep long enough to take a much needed shower. Afterwards, he crashed onto his bed and was asleep before he finished bouncing.

No sooner than Jin closed his eyes it seemed, there was a knock at the door. He reluctantly dragged his aching body out of bed and answered the door wearing only a pair of pants he had thrown on in haste. It was Grihm and she looked completely refreshed. She was stunning.

Grihm: "Can I come in?"

Jin: "Sure. You want anything to drink?"

Grihm: "Something strong."

Jin rummaged through his forgotten suitcase filled with alcohol that he procured from Cyclebreak all those weeks ago to accommodate her request. He found a bottle of "His Majesty", a dark whiskey with a distinct sweetness and is sold with a purple felt bag around it. He poured a glass, neat, and she downed it before he finished pouring his own. He topped her off and sat next to her on the bed.

Jin: "I'm sure there's a lot on your mind."

Grihm: "Actually, I was wondering how *you* were holding up. You've been through a lot."

Jin: "We both have. But you went through hell out there for me. I haven't heard what you had to do to get there, but I'm glad you did."

Grihm: "It felt like the right thing to do. It ended up being even more complicated than that, but I don't regret my choice."

Jin: "I owe you everything. So if you need help setting things right or anything for that matter, I'm with you."

Grihm: "Hearing that from you means the world to me right now."

Grihm looked into Jin's eyes with a longing that said more than words could hope to express. She pulled Jin in, guiding him with her hand and they kissed. A chill surged through Grihm, completing a feeling she had been holding onto since they met. She reeled his body to hers and Jin began to feel the weight of her emotions. For a time, there was nothing else; no war or battles to be fought, no lost friends, no injuries. Just the embrace of two lovers.

*   *   *

Grihm stirred awake in the dimly lit room. Her rustling woke Jin. He kissed her again but her attention was drawn elsewhere; to voices across the room. In their passion, they never turned off the television. There was some urgency to the voices.

A banner along the top of the screen alerted "Breaking news." They both listened.

Newscaster: "...Revco's previously announced press conference addressing recent events is beginning. We have been informed that someone other than Mr. Joseph Bradley will be speaking on behalf of the district. We now take you live to the conference."

The man who approached the podium to speak was Emil. He was wearing a black, razor sharp suit with a broad red tie. His signature gauntlet that Jin had come to know him for was missing. He stood with his hair slicked back, even more poised and professional than ever before.

Emil: "Greetings everyone. I thank you all for coming. Many of you have never seen me before. My name is Emil Estoque and for years I worked closely alongside Mr. Bradley, whom I've known as a brother. I am standing in for the late Mr. Joseph Bradley to inform you that he was killed in the recent cowardly attack by Citadel forces. The assault itself was a means to invade Central and assassinate Mr. Bradley. Our forces fought bravely to prevent the enemy from completing any other unknown objectives and once they realized they would get nothing else from us, they retreated back to their hole. It will take more than a few of us to fill the void that now exists, but I believe that we will recover and become stronger than ever before. We will never be caught off guard again. This I can assure you. We have now seen the true face of Eratech's DLC; a militia of terrorist who commit acts of violence throughout the city. From their heartless mass murder of veast gangs within their own district, to the destruction of the ancient cathedral on the outskirts, to their assault on Central, DLC has proven that they are in the business of death. The Citadel's unprovoked attack and occupation of Central was more than an act of terror or hatred, but a declaration of war. To our citizens within Eratech District, you have sixty hours to return home before our gates will be shut to you. To the leader of the DLC: Colonel Masters, you will pay dearly for the lives you've taken. Your brute force tactics have put you against an enemy you cannot hope to defeat. The storm is coming for you and your supporters. Thank you for your time everyone."

Emil stepped away from the podium and departed without answering any questions. The television then returned to the newscaster's undoubtedly biased opinion on the matter. Grihm and Jin looked at one another with mixed emotions. Neither one of them had any idea of what to say. But no matter what the future held for them or Eratech, they knew they would fight for each other.

25– THE AUGUR

*-The avian, unusual changes in weather, the mysterious lights in the
sky; she reads them like pages in a book.-*

The brief period of rest given to DL following the assault
on Central had passed and operations were to resume as normal.
Damien and Styner however, worked through the break to
ensure the others could enjoy their time of recuperation. The two
of them watched as Revco transitioned into a war time society:
from their various forms of corporate funded media becoming
more propagandous, to the rapid shifting of public opinion
against Eratech District –the Citadel in particular. It didn't take
much to convince their generally confused public that Eratech
was the villain in this war, especially since Damien never
released an official statement or explanation for the Citadel's
actions to either district. This in turn brought into question his
intentions within Eratech as well. The city entered a new state of
intensity within only two cycles; the once awkward peace
between the two districts had now burned into a full war as the
world entered cool dusk season.

After an in-depth discussion that transpired from one
cycle to the next, Damien and Styner had come to a conclusion

and were prepared to enact the first major action of this new phase. Grihm was summoned to the war room where Damien and Styner sat awaiting her arrival. Damien, who was not wearing his usual shades, offered Grihm a seat which she declined. She preferred to stand for the tense situation.

Damien: "I'm sure you're aware of the circumstances of this hearing correct?"

Grihm: "I am."

Styner: "Then we'll get straight to it. Bianca Calenite you are currently under scrutiny regarding your recent actions which include but are not limited to: Going AWOL, disobeying direct orders, conspiracy, undirected corporate espionage, reckless endangerment of commanding personnel, commandeering mission equipment for use other than official operations, grand theft auto, and inciting armed conflict. Do you deny any of these claims?"

Grihm: "I do not."

Styner: "Would you like to say anything on your behalf before we proceed?"

Grihm: "I would. I understand the gravity of my actions. I saw a problem and attempted to address it without your approval or knowledge. The consequence of my actions was paid for by allies and friends and I will do whatever I must to correct my actions… and if I may speak off the record."

Damien nodded.

Grihm: "I'm truly sorry for how things turned out. I can't say that enough but I want to make this right. For Shina, for you, for everyone."

Damien: "I know. But this isn't something that can be smoothed over quickly or easily. This is beyond what I can control alone.

This is a situation that is so broken that it can never be fixed. We're all going to have to make the best of what's to come."

Grihm's posture visibly shrank.

Damien: "And while taking Oska with you is one of your key offenses, it was also your saving grace. If it weren't for her passing us updates on your movements we may not have been able to find you to bring you back home."

Styner: "Not to mention the data she stole while she was there is going to help us tremendously now that we're at war."

Damien: "These still don't justify your initial actions. After considerable debate, we've concluded that your status as a DL specialist has been revoked until further notice. You've been reduced to recruit level access and you're activities will be heavily monitored both inside and outside of the Citadel. You will be accompanied by at least one other person whenever you are not in your dormitory."

Styner: "This hurts us because we're losing the full capabilities of our best at a time when we could use you the most."

Damien: "Do you have any questions?"

Grihm: "I do not."

Damien: "For the time being, you'll be reporting to…"

The screens at the war room lit up with an alert message from Oska. Before he could dismiss the interruption, Oska opened COMMs to the room.

Oska: "I know this is a bad time but you're going to want to hear this."

Damien: "I thought I told you to take time off?"

Oska: "I need to do something to keep my mind occupied now more than ever."

Damien: "Fine. What is it?"

Oska: "Someone showed up at your apartment entrance requesting to speak to you."

Damien: "What do they want specifically?"

Oska: "She said that she knows what's going on and has been sent to warn us, you in particular, of what you've gotten into."

Damien: "Where is she?"

Oska: "She's at the door. I'll patch you through."

Oska's face was replaced with the camera feed of the entrance. There was a girl wearing an old Citadel military jacket which still had the service patches and a dusty pair of jeans. She had a sepia skin with freckles lightly speckled across her nose and black curly hair with faded colored locks: purple, teal, white, and orange. She was holding what appeared to be a large tome. Damien's voice boomed out of a speaker hidden to look like a brick. His voice startled her.

Damien: "Who are you and who sent you here?"

Curly haired girl: "Uhh… Hello. I'm Raptor and I've been sent by my mentor to speak with you."

Damien: "Why doesn't he come himself?"

Raptor: "He can't be openly associated with you. If he did, there'd be even more trouble coming your way."

Damien: "Who's your mentor?"

Raptor: "I can't tell you. But I *can* tell you I've been sent to help. We know what you're getting involved in and without our help you're going to get yourselves killed. And we need your help as well."

Damien: "You're asking for a lot and not providing much."

Raptor took a moment to prepare her words. She expected reluctance on Damien's part.

Raptor: "We know what came through when you were at the cathedral, I saw what happened to Turchess, and we know what happened at Central… with Mr. Bradley."

There was the distinct click of a bolt unlocking. Raptor cautiously opened the door into the dark apartment. The door slammed shut behind her and locked itself, leaving her in absolute darkness. She put her hands in front of her chest, palms facing each other and imagined herself holding a sphere. She then imagined if that sphere was alive and had a pulse. She synched the pulse of the ball with her own and gave it life. A sphere of light that illuminated the area around her manifested in her hands and she held the fragile creation delicately. The room was mundane but the floor was littered with an assortment of odds and ends scattered about the loosely furnished room; from dumbbells to fire extinguishers, and unknown machine parts to name a few. She made her way to the back room by following the sound of the elevator doom chime. She stepped inside and descended. When the doors opened she was assaulted with the sounds and lights of the hangar and was greeted by a pair of armed guards headed by Saber. Both their eyes lit up in shock and elation. They hugged each other firmly. Saber took a step back to examine Raptor who was wearing the same outfit she wore when they met at gateway village.

Saber: "Malia, I thought I'd never see you again. What're you doing here? What's this all about?"

Raptor: "A lot happened after you left. I escaped, Turchess was killed, and I've been training under a mentor on… far away from here."

Saber: "Turchess is dead? We're going to need a lot of details. I hope you have time to stay; you and I need to catch up."

Raptor: "I've been given as much time as I need here. So yeah, I'd love that."

Saber gleefully escorted Raptor to the war room with a now more relaxed guard. In the war room, the entirety of DL had been gathered: Damien, Styner, Jin, Grihm, Trigger, Sev, and Oska had arrived since Saber was sent to receive Raptor. Damien considered sending Grihm away but realized it would be a mistake being that she had seen firsthand some of the events that he wanted to discuss. Oska stirred after getting a good look at Raptor's face. She recognized her from the photos and posters she had seen of missing persons.

Saber: "Everyone, this is Malia and she's a good friend of mine. I'll vouch for her credibility."

Oska: "I know you. You're one of the students who went missing a few weeks ago."

Raptor: "I'm sorry. I don't think we've met."

Oska: "We haven't. You were selected for the district's highest honors student award. "

Raptor: "Oh! You're Oska then? I've heard of you. I thought you were just a secretary. Is this what you really do?"

Raptor gestured with her hand indicating the entirety of the Citadel.

Damien: "You know two of my people. That's good. Have a seat, you made some big promises up there."

Raptor: "I'd rather stand, but thank you."

Raptor laid the large tome on the table, it thudded as dust wafted from its yellowed pages.

Raptor: "My name is Raptor. This is the title appointed to me by my mentor. And before you ask, I can only tell you that he needs your help, but you need his more."

Damien: "What kind of help is he offering?"

Raptor: "For now, just me."

Saber: "Where have you been since I last saw you? What happened with Turchess?"

Damien: "Tell us the full story."

Raptor took a deep breath and exhaled as she prepared.

Raptor: "I was one of many people who heard the call of Turchess to come find enlightenment or become "exalted" as he called it. On my journey north to Little Akasha I met Salena who helped me realize that I needed to rethink my joining of the Exalted. Things got out of hand at the induction ceremony and a fight broke out. Salena fought her way out but I couldn't do what she did. I froze."

Saber: "I didn't want to leave you there but I couldn't…"

Raptor: "I know. I would have gotten you killed. But you did something amazing to get away. You did what Turchess had promised to teach."

Saber: "I'm sorry you had to see me bite that guys arm off."

Raptor: "I forgot about that. I meant you casted AP to get away from that fireball. Don't you remember?"

Saber: "I did what?"

Raptor: "As the flare barreled toward you, your body washed away into water and reformed itself after the fire burned away."

Saber attempted to replay the events in her mind but everything happened so quickly that the details were a blur. She remembered diving toward the exalted behind her and bracing for impact. She remembered how tense her muscles were in anticipation of the engulfing flame. Then there was the split moment where she felt the euphoria of nothingness before coming back to reality that was the cavern. Saber looked up from her thoughts to all of DL waiting for her to explain. She had no answer.

Saber: "I don't remember clearly what happened but that can't be possible. I don't know how to cast AP."

Raptor: "Your body does, as did mine when I learned to stop holding myself back."

Damien: "You know how to cast AP?"

Raptor: "I know a lot of things thought to be mystical and lost. That's why I'm here, to teach you."

Jin: "You said your mentor taught you. Would he happen to be a really laid back guy with bright red hair, a beard, glasses, and a taste for open shirts and wooden sandals?"

Raptor looked at Jin sorrowfully.

Raptor: "No. And even if he were I could not tell you. If I may continue, I'll answer most of your initial questions."

Styner: "Please."

Raptor: "After things settled from what happened with Saber I was left with Turchess. He saw great potential in both me and Saber but I didn't try to kill him and escape, so he wanted to make me his prodigy. He showed me how he had learned about AP casting."

Raptor cracked open the tome on the table, revealing to them page after page of handwritten notes, diagrams, and sketches.

Raptor: "This is the *Celestillium*: An ancient book containing the occult history of our worlds; both Æther and Akasha. This book is in part how I learned and how I will teach you as well. But there was a major issue Turchess had with this book."

Raptor turned the book around to let the others examine its akashean text.

Raptor: "He couldn't read it. Only akasheans or those with akashean souls can."

Jin: "I'm guessing you can read akashean then. Could you translate this for me?"

Jin handed her the card given to him by Faux. She read word-for-word what Cel'yst had translated before, proving her claim. She *did* however give her thoughts on what the poem meant; it was a reference to an abandoned project. One that has a different purpose than what it would appear to have.

Raptor: "Once Turchess realized that I would be the one teaching him he left in a fit of rage. That was when I took my chance to steal the book and escape. I didn't make it far before they pursued me. I made it back to the Bridge between Worlds where Draxis introduced me to my mentor. Turchess then attacked my mentor and was killed. You may have seen it: that storm and aurora that appeared over the village? After the fight, he took me under his wing to tutor me. This is my first time back since."

There was a long silence that made Raptor uncomfortable as the center of attention. She spoke out of nervousness.

Raptor: "I know this all seems fantastic but with what you all have seen lately I'm sure this isn't the hardest thing to accept."

Damien: "You're right about that. I'm glad you showed up when you did because you're exactly what we needed."

Raptor: "You'll need more than just me in the end. You've managed to wound the Black Tempest. And now he will respond with disproportionate force."

Damien: "I didn't wound anything other than Mr. Bradley."

Raptor: "And that's the problem. Simply by seeing what Mr. Bradley was, you made yourself a target. But killing him was a declaration of war."

Damien: "We declared war when we invaded their district."

Raptor: "The district war is just a mask. The real war is against Blackhorn. And this new opponent is not fighting the same battle as your rival. The Citadel is now a new player in a very old war."

About the Authors

Kevin Edwards and Joe Swire are two schmucks from Southern Maryland who've seen and read enough creative works and decided to join the ranks of creators.

Kevin Edwards grew up in the suburbs of southern Maryland. After spending nearly 12 years traveling and trying to figure out what he wanted in life, he finally sat down long enough to answer his true calling as a writer. This is his first work. Kevin occasionally post his random mewlings on his tumblr page: https://fisenitewriting.tumblr.com/

Joseph Swire was always interested in art. Pencil to paper was his main outlet but turned to digital art to fulfill his passion. Having worked on DreadLocked since his teens, he's as much a creator as the author. Joe developed his style with the hopes to one day be able to share the project with the world. Joe is available for commission. A small sample of his solo work is available at: https://joeswireart.weebly.com/